PROXIMA

OTHER BOOKS
BY STEPHEN BAXTER

From Roc Books

Flood

Ark

Stone Spring

Bronze Summer

Iron Winter

From Ace Books

Time's Tapestry

Book One: *Emperor*

Book Two: *Conqueror*

Book Three: *Navigator*

Book Four: *Weaver*

PROXIMA

STEPHEN BAXTER

A ROC BOOK

ROC
Published by the Penguin Group
Penguin Group (USA) LLC, 375 Hudson Street,
New York, New York 10014

USA | Canada | UK | Ireland | Australia | New Zealand | India | South Africa | China
penguin.com
A Penguin Random House Company

Published by Roc, an imprint of New American Library, a division of Penguin Group (USA).
Previously published in a Gollancz hardcover edition. For information contact Gollancz, an
imprint of the Orion Pubishing Group, Orion House, 5 Upper St. Martin's Lane, London
WC2H 9EA.

First Roc Hardcover Printing, November 2014

LIBRARY OF CONGRESS CATALOGING-IN-PUBLICATION DATA:

Baxter, Stephen.
 Proxima / Stephen Baxter.
   pages cm
 ISBN 978-0-451-46770-6 (hardback)
 1. Space colonies—Fiction. I. Title.
 PR6052.A849P76 2014
 823'.914—dc23   2014023938

Printed in the United States of America
10 9 8 7 6 5 4 3 2 1

Set in Sabon
Designed by Spring Hoteling

In the hearts of a hundred billion worlds—

Across a trillion dying realities in a lethal multiverse—

In the chthonic silence—

Minds diffuse and antique dreamed the Dream of the End Time.

PROXIMA

ONE

· · ·

1

2166

I'm back on Earth.

That was Yuri's very first thought, on waking in a bed: a hard bed, stiff mattress and lightweight sheets and blankets, but a bed nonetheless, not a barrack bunk stacked four high in a dome on Mars.

He opened his eyes to bright light, from fluorescent bars on the walls. A clean-looking ceiling. People moving around him wearing green shirts and hygiene caps and masks, a low murmur of competent voices, machines that bleeped and chimed. Other beds, other patients. A classic hospital setup. He saw all this in his peripheral vision; he hadn't turned his head yet, he felt so heavy.

The last thing he remembered was the needle jabbed into his neck by that asshole Peacekeeper Tollemache. He had no idea how long he'd been out—months, if he'd been shipped back to Earth—and he remembered from his recovery after his decades in the cryo that it paid to take care on waking.

But he knew he was on Earth. He could feel it in his bones. Yuri had been born on Earth in the year 2067, nearly a hundred years ago, and, dozing in a cryo tank, had missed mankind's heroic expansion out into the solar system. He had woken up in a colony on what he had learned, gradually, was Mars. But now, after another compulsory sleep, this was different again. He risked lifting his hand. The muscles in his arm ached, just doing that, and he felt tubes dragging at him as he moved, and the hand fell back with a satisfyingly heavy thump. Beautiful Earth gravity, not that neither-one-thing-nor-the-other floaty stuff on Mars. It could only be Earth, home.

He had a million questions. Such as *where* on Earth? Why had he been sent back instead of being left to rot on Mars? And what kind of institution was he in now, what kind of prison this time? But not having answers didn't bother him. He'd had very few answers about anything since waking up on Mars, and besides, he hadn't cared enough to ask. The worst kind of cage on Earth, and no matter how much the place had changed since he'd gone into the cryo tank, was better than the finest luxury you could find on Mars. Because on Earth you could always just open the door and breathe the air, even if it was an overheated polluted soup, and just keep on walking, forever . . .

He closed his eyes.

"Rise and shine, sleepyhead."

There was a face looming over him, a woman, black, wearing a green shirt with a name tag he couldn't read, her hair tucked into a green cloth cap. She wasn't wearing a mask, and she smiled at him. She looked tired.

He tried to speak. His mouth was dry, and his tongue stuck painfully to the roof of his mouth. "I . . . I . . ."

"Here. Have a sip of water." She held a nippled bottle, like a baby's, for him. The water was warm and stale. She seemed to be having trouble holding up the bottle, like she was weak herself. "Do you know your name?" She glanced at the foot of the bed. "Yuri Eden. That's all we have for you. No recorded next of kin. Is that right?"

He just shrugged, a tentative movement, flat on his back.

She looked him over, peered into his eyes, checked some kind of monitor beside the bed. "My name is Dr. Poinar. I'm ISF. I have a crew rank but you can call me Doctor. You've taken your time coming out of the induced coma the Peacekeepers put you into. Still, it was easier to ship you through the launch that way. More than half the crew dreamed it all away, in fact. I'm going to see if I can sit you up. OK?" She pressed a button.

With a whir of servos the back of his bed began to tip up, lifting him, bending him at the waist. He felt weak, and his head was like a tub of sloshing liquid. The ward grayed around him. He felt a crawling sensation in his right arm, some kind of fluid being pumped into him.

Dr. Poinar watched him carefully. "You OK? All right. Here's the five-second briefing—you'll be put through a proper induction process later, everybody's going through that in stages, classroom stuff and data access first while you get your strength back, then physical work later, including your share of maintenance chores." She glanced at his notes. "More of that if you end up on a punishment detail, and looking at your record that seems more than likely. But the priority for you is reconditioning. Your body needs to relearn how to handle full gravity. The nerve receptors that handle your posture, positioning and movement are all baffled right now. Your inner ear doesn't know what the hell's going on. Your fluid balance is all wrong, and you're going to have low blood pressure symptoms for a while. Here, drink this."

She handed him another flask, and this time he took it for himself. It was a briny fluid that made him splutter.

"You'll get courses of injections to rectify your bone calcium loss and such. And physio to build up your muscle strength and bone mass. Do *not* skip those. Oh, and your immune system will be hit. Every virus everybody brought into this hull has been running around like crazy; you'll have a few weeks of fun with that. Later on there will be further medical programs, pre-adaptation for Prox, preventive surgery of various kinds." She grinned, faintly cruelly. "How are your teeth? But that won't be for another year or more."

Prox?

A baby started to cry, not far away.

Dr. Poinar asked, "Any questions? Oh, I'm sure there are masses. Just use your common sense. For now just sit there and let the dizziness pass. *Don't* lie down again. I'll come by later and see if you can take some solid food. And watch out for the catheter. The nurse will remove that later. Take it easy, Yuri Eden." She walked out of his view.

Still that baby cried, not far to his left.

Very cautiously he turned his head that way; the graying returned, and a ringing in his ears, but he waited until it passed. He saw more beds crowded into a room that couldn't have been more than seven, eight meters across, smaller than he had expected. Some of the beds had cloth partitions around them. More medical types and a couple of servo-robots glided through the narrow spaces between the beds. Equipment dangled from the ceiling, including what looked like a teleoperated surgical kit, all manipulator arms and laser nozzles and knives.

In the bed closest to Yuri, to his left, lay a young woman, a girl really, pale, blond hair, fragile-looking. Intensely beautiful. She cradled a baby, a bundle of blankets; as she rocked it, the crying slowly subsided. She saw Yuri looking. He turned his head away, making his vision spin again. At Eden he'd developed the habit of avoiding eye contact, of giving people their own bubbles of privacy.

"It's OK." Her accent was soft, maybe eastern European.

He looked back. "Didn't mean to stare." His voice was a husk.

"Well, little Cole was crying, disturbing everybody." She smiled. "Sorry if he woke you up."

That puzzled him. Then he realized she was joking. He tried to smile, but he had no idea what kind of grimace his numb face was pulling.

"My name is Anna Vigil."

"I'm Yuri."

"Yuri Eden. I heard the doctor say." Little Cole wriggled and gurgled softly. "He's fine. I'm the one who had to come in here. A cold virus laid me out; I'm still weak from nursing. Of course we shouldn't be here at all. I was heavily pregnant when the sweep came. There was a mix-up. Cole's the only child in here."

"Cole, huh. Nice name."

She seemed to think that over, as if his responses were a little off. "I named him for Dexter Cole, of course. The first guy to Proxima."

Of course. Who? Where? He backed away from the puzzling little conversation, retreated into himself.

"Hey, buddy."

He turned his head to the right.

In the bed on that side was a man, around thirty, Asiatic. His scalp was swathed in bandages, and the left side of his face was puffed up with bruising that almost closed one eye. Even so, he smiled. "You OK?"

Yuri shrugged stiffly.

"Listen. It's just the go-to-sleep stuff the cops give you. They don't use it sparingly. I took a couple of doses of that myself, while I tried to explain in a calm manner that as a foreign national I did not belong in their sweep for the *Ad Astra*. Takes you time to wake up from that. Don't worry, the fog will clear." His accent sounded American, west coast maybe, but Yuri's ear was a hundred years out-of-date.

Yuri said, "Thanks. But I'm guessing that's not why you're in here. The sleep thing."

"You ought to be a doctor. No, the big guy put me in here this time. Although the time before it was a couple of Peacekeepers—they managed to break a rib while persuading me—"

"The big guy?"

"Gustave Klein, he's called. I guess you wouldn't know that. King of the Hull, or thinks he is. Watch out for him. So, Yuri Eden, huh? I never came across you on Mars. My name is Liu Tao." He spelled it out.

"You American?"

"Me? No. But I learned English in a school for USNA expats in New Beijing. That's why my accent is kind of old-fashioned; everybody picks up on that. I'm Chinese. I'm actually an officer in the People's space fleet. Yuri Eden? Is that really your name? You lived in Eden, right?"

"Yeah."

"What was it like?"

Lacking any kind of common reference with this guy, Yuri tried to describe it. Eden had been the UN's largest outpost on Mars, and one of the oldest. People lived in cylindrical bulks like Nissen huts that were the remains of the first ships to land, tipped over and heaped with dirt and turned into shelters, and in prefabricated domes, and even in a few buildings of red Martian sandstone blocks. The whole place had had the feel of a prison to Yuri, or a labor camp. And all this was just a pinprick, a hold-out; the scuttlebutt was that a colony like this would be dwarfed by the giant cities the Chinese were building on the rest of the planet, like their capital, Obelisk, in Terra Cimmeria.

Liu Tao listened, his face neutral.

Yuri asked, "So how did you end up here?"

"Bad luck. I was piloting a shuttle down from Red Two, that's one of our orbital stations, heading for our supply depots and manufactories in the Phaethontis quadrangle, when we had an auxiliary power-unit failure. We had to bail out at high altitude, my buddy and I, which is no joke on Mars. He got down safely—well, I guess so; I was never told. My clamshell, my heat shield, had a crack. I was lucky to live through it. But I came down near Eden, and a couple of your Peacekeepers were the first to get to me.

"They held on to me, in defiance of various treaties. I was put through a lot of 'questioning.'" He let that word hang. "They wanted me to tell them the inner secrets of the Triangle. You know about that? The big trade loop we're developing, Earth to asteroids and Mars and back. But I'm a Mars-orbit shuttle jock, that's all. By Mao's balls, it's not as if we're spying on you guys at Eden!" He laughed at that idea. "Well, they kept me in there, and I started to think they were never going to let me go—I mean maybe they'd told my chain of command they'd found me dead or something. What were they going to do to me, kill me? I guess it's no surprise that they threw me into the sweep and locked me up in this hull, right? Out of sight, out of mind. But we're all prisoners here . . ."

"Nobody's a prisoner," said Dr. Poinar, bustling down the ward with a tray of colorful pills. "That's what the policy says, so it must be true, right? Now take this, Yuri Eden. You need more sleep."

Confused, as weak as Anna's baby, yet still elated at the basic fact that *he'd come home*, even if he was stuck in this "hull," Yuri obediently took his tablet and subsided into a deep dreamless sleep.

After a day of cautious bending, stretching, walking, and using a lavatory unaided, Yuri was told by Dr. Poinar that his time was up. "We need your bed. Sorry, buddy. You'll be assigned a bunk later. Any possessions you had—"

Yuri shrugged.

"Right now you're late for a class."

"What class?"

"Orientation 101," Liu Tao said. "Some astronaut showing us pretty pictures." He laughed, though he winced when he opened his bruised mouth wide.

"You're in the same class, Liu. Why don't you show your new best friend the way?" Poinar dumped heaps of basic clothing on their beds, bright orange, and walked away.

Yuri had thought the medical ward was crowded, noisy. But once Liu led him outside, into a space that struck Yuri at first glance as like the inside of a big metal tower, he realized that the ward had been a haven of peace and harmony. Looking up he saw that the tower wasn't that tall, maybe forty, forty-five meters, and was capped off by a big metal dome. It was split into stories by mesh-partition flooring; there were ladders and a kind of spiral staircase around the wall, and a fireman's pole arrangement that threaded through gaps in the partitions along the tower's axis. The walls were crusted with equipment boxes and stores, but in some places he saw tables and chairs, lightweight fold-out affairs, and enclosures, partitions inside which he could see bunk beds, more fold-outs. There were folk in there evidently trying to sleep; he had no idea how they'd manage that. It looked like sleep was going to be a luxury here, just like on Mars.

And in this tank, people swarmed everywhere, most of them dressed like Yuri and Liu in bright orange jumpsuits, a few others in Peace-keeper blue, or a more exotic black and silver. They were all adults that he could see, no kids, no infants. Their voices echoed from the metal surfaces in a jangling racket. And over all that there was a whir of pumps and fans, of air-conditioning and plumbing of some kind, just like in Eden. Like he was in another sealed unit.

Liu, moving cautiously himself—evidently it hadn't been just his face that had taken the beating—took Yuri to that outer staircase, steps fixed to the curving wall with a safety rail, and led him up.

At least, just like on Mars, Yuri didn't find the *stuff* here hard. Since his first waking, he'd found twenty-second-century technology easy to work. User interfaces seemed to have settled down to common standards some time before he'd been frozen. Even the language had stabilized, more or less, if not the accents; English was spoken across several worlds now and had to stay comprehensible to everybody, and there was a huge mass of recorded culture, all of which tended to keep the language static. The vehicles and vocabularies of the year 2166 were easy. It was the people he couldn't figure out. And now Yuri climbed through a blizzard of faces, none of them familiar.

He looked for a window. He still had no idea where on Earth he was. And why the enclosure? Maybe he was in some mid-latitude climate refuge; he'd heard that since his day the whole middle belt of the Earth had heated up, dried out and been abandoned. He could be anywhere. But that steady pull of gravity was reassuring, even as he labored up the stairs with his Mars-softened muscles. He wondered when his first physio was going to be.

They reached a space enclosed by movable partition panels, with fold-out chairs set in rows like a lecture theater. Some guy in a uniform of black and silver stood at the front, facing away from the dozen or so people in the room, talking through a series of images, star fields and space satellites.

A woman in a similar uniform, standing at the door with a slate, stopped Liu and Yuri as they entered. Yuri read her name tag: ISF LT MARDINA JONES. Maybe thirty, she was very dark, with tightly curled black hair. "You're late," she said.

"Sorry. Just out of medical." Liu gave their names.

"Name tags?"

Liu dug his out of a pocket and showed it to her; she scanned it with her slate. She turned to Yuri. "You?"

Yuri just shrugged.

Liu said, "Like I said, just out of medical."

"Just awake, huh." Jones shook her head and made a note on her slate. "Typical. Make sure you sort it out later." She had a thick Australian accent. "Sit, you're late."

Finding a seat in the semidarkened little theater turned out to be a problem. Three guys sat together on a row of a dozen otherwise empty seats. When Yuri went to sit down in the row, Liu prodded him in the back. "Move on," he whispered.

Yuri had been quick to anger ever since he'd first woken up on Mars. "Why should I?"

"Because that middle guy is Gustave Klein. Wait until you're beefed up before you take him on."

But it was already too late, Yuri realized. Klein was white, maybe fifty years old, hefty if not overweight, head elaborately shaven. His fists, resting on his knees, were like steam hammers. And Yuri had made eye contact with him. He barely noticed the two guys with Klein, typical attack dogs. Klein leered at Liu, taking in his injuries, and looked away, dismissive.

They moved on, cautious in the dark. "What's so special about him?"

"He was the best Sabatier-furnace engineer in his colony," Liu whispered. "That's part of the recycling system—you know that, right? And he fixed it so that nobody else could touch those systems. He was a damn water king. No wonder they shipped him out. And it looks like he's fixing to get the same hold here."

"A water king." Yuri grinned. "Until it rains, right?"

Liu looked at him strangely.

Somebody hissed. "Yuri! Hey, Yuri! Over here!" A skinny, shambling form hustled along a row, clearing two spaces, to muttered complaints from the people behind.

"Lemmy?" It was the first familiar voice he'd heard since waking in the can. Yuri sat beside him, followed by Liu.

"Awake at last, huh?" Lemmy's whisper was soft, practiced. "That bastard Tollemache really shot you up, didn't he? Well, he got what he deserved."

Yuri tried to figure it out. Lemmy Pink, nineteen years old, had been the nearest thing to a friend Yuri had made on Mars. Even if Lemmy was only looking for protection.

The last Yuri remembered of Mars was that he and Lemmy had busted out of their dome. Yuri had had to get out. Every atom in his body longed to be out there on the Martian ground, frozen, ultraviolet-blasted desert though it might be. He'd been taken through spacesuit and airlock drills for the sake of emergency training, but he'd never been outside. Mostly he never even got to look through a window. So they'd stolen a rover, made a run for the hills, a local feature called the Chaos—flipped the truck, been picked up by the Peacekeepers. He remembered Tollemache. *You're the ice boy, right? Nothing but a pain in the butt since they defrosted you. Well, you won't be my problem much longer.* And with a gloved fist he had jammed a needle into Yuri's neck, and the red-brown Martian light had folded away . . .

And he'd woken up in this tank.

"What do you mean, he got what he deserved?"

"He's here too. In the hull. Ha! He got what was coming to him, all right. But it was because he didn't stop us pinching that rover in the first place, rather than what he did to you."

Yuri mock-punched his arm. "Good to see they brought you home too, man."

Lemmy flinched back. "Don't touch me. I'm full of the fucking sniffles that are going around this coffin, typical of me to get them all."

"What about Krafft?" Lemmy's pet rat, back in the dome.

Lemmy's face fell. "Well, they took him off me. What would you expect?"

"I'm sorry."

They were disturbing the astronaut type giving his lecture. Mardina Jones was right behind them, her voice a severe murmur. "If you two buttheads don't shut up and listen to Major McGregor I'll put you on a charge."

They shut up. But when she withdrew, Lemmy was staring at Yuri, in the shadowy dark. "What was that you just said?"

"What? About the rat?"

"No. Something about them bringing us home."

"I don't know, man. I don't know if I'm asleep or awake." But Lemmy kept staring at him.

Yuri, disoriented, confused, distracted by the noise of the crowds just half a meter beyond the partition, looked up at the astronaut at the lectern in his glittering black-as-night uniform. On Mars everybody had hated the astronauts, because they were rotated, they got to go home. Yuri tried to concentrate on what he was saying.

"Even a single pixel from these very early images of the new world told the astronomers a great deal. Spectral analysis revealed an atmosphere with free oxygen, methane, nitrous oxide."

Major McGregor, maybe late twenties, was tall, upright, whip-thin but athletic, with a healthy glow to his cheeks in the light of the images he showed. He had a slick Angleterre accent, and his hair, blond, brushed, oiled, looked like it got more care than most of the people in this facility.

"Oxygen, think of that! Suddenly we had a habitable world, right on our doorstep. All of you have had experience of the colonies on Mars and the moon—bleak, inhospitable worlds, and yet the best the solar system has to offer. And now, suddenly, *this*.

"With time, variations of brightness and spectral content told us something about the distribution of continents and oceans. More subtle variations had to reflect changing weather. Not only that, the presence of oxygen is a strong indicator of life, I mean native life, because something has to be putting all that oxygen in the air." He displayed graphs, wriggling lines. "This prominent feature in the red part of the spectrum indicated the presence of something like our own chlorophyll, some kind of light-harvesting pigment. All deduced from watching a single point of light . . ."

Yuri had no idea what he was talking about. But he had spent a great deal of his time since being woken on Mars not knowing what the hell was going on around him, and it didn't seem to make any material difference.

He was aware that that caveman Klein was watching him. He started to think of how he was going to deal with that, as the astronaut's voice droned on and on.

But Lemmy was still staring at him, as if he was working something out. "Nobody told you. My God."

"Told me what?"

Gustave Klein seemed to have an instinct for trouble. He leaned forward. "What's this?"

Lemmy ignored him. "You said something about being sent home. I just figured it out. *You think this is home*, don't you? You think this is—"

"Earth?" Liu Tao asked now, wondering, staring at Yuri.

Klein stood up. "He thinks *what*? What kind of asshole—"

The class was breaking up, the "students" turning in their seats to see what the commotion was. Major McGregor shut up at last, frowning in annoyance before his spectrograms.

Mardina Jones hurried up again from the back, tapping an epaulette on her shoulder. "Peacekeeper to Level 3, lecture room . . . What's going on here? Is this something to do with you, Eden?"

Yuri stood, hands spread, but he didn't reply. He'd long since learned that replying was usually pointless, it made no difference to the treatment he got. But he felt surrounded, by the astronauts, the students grinning to see someone else in trouble. Even Lemmy was staring at him.

And Gustave Klein was like a malevolent puppet master. "He doesn't know! You're right, you little runt," he said to Lemmy. His accent was thick Hispanic, despite his Germanic-sounding name. "He doesn't have a fucking clue. What a laugh."

Now Peacekeeper Tollemache came bustling in, fully uniformed, flanked by two junior officers. They all had nightsticks at the ready—no guns, though, Yuri noticed in those first moments.

"You," Tollemache said. "Ice boy. I should have known. Out of the med bay for five minutes and trouble already." He flexed his nightstick.

Yuri tensed, preparing to rush him.

Mardina Jones stood between them. "Stop this! That's an order, Peacekeeper."

"You don't outrank me."

"Oh, yes I do," she said coldly. "You know the policy. Take it up with the captain if you like. I wanted you down here to keep order, not break more heads. And you—whatever else you are, Yuri Eden, you're good at making enemies."

Tollemache glowered at Yuri, but backed off. "You're the reason I'm in this toilet, you little prick."

Yuri grinned. "Good to hear it, Peacekeeper."

Tollemache held his gaze for one more second. In the background Gustave Klein leered, drinking up the conflict.

Mardina Jones turned on Lemmy. "You. What do you mean, he thinks this is home?"

"Think about it. The Peacekeeper there knocked him out while he was still on Mars! He never saw a thing, the sweep, the loading, he didn't get any of the briefings we got. Such as they were. Also, he's out of his time. You must know that. He hasn't got the background to understand."

Mardina frowned, and glanced down at her slate; maybe she hadn't known that, Yuri thought.

"We all supposed he'd know what was going on. I guess. That he'd be able to figure it. But—"

"But maybe not." Major McGregor came up to the little group now, and studied Yuri with amused interest. "I heard about you. I knew we had one of you lot aboard, a corpsicle. A survivor of the Heroic Generation, eh? And now, here you are, and so confused. How funny." Apparently on impulse he said, "Follow me, Mr. Eden. Bring your little bed warmer if you like. You'd better come too, Lieutenant. And you, Peacekeeper, if you can control yourself. Just in case it all kicks off."

Mardina asked, "Where are you taking him?"

McGregor grinned and pointed upward. "Where do you think? It will be a fascinating experiment. Come along."

3

McGregor led a procession out of the lecture space to the spiral stair that wound its way up the wall of the tower. McGregor glanced over his shoulder at Yuri, who followed directly behind him. "We have two of these habitat modules, strapped together side by side, for redundancy, you see . . . You'll have to tell me what you think of the design. For size, it was modeled on the first stage of the old Saturn V moon booster, for nostalgic reasons, I suppose. Of course much of what we are doing is of symbolic as well as practical value."

At the top of the tower was a domed roof. They climbed up through that into what was evidently some kind of control room, with a central command chair, vacant just now, arrays of bright screens, and another dome, midnight dark, over their heads. Operatives in astronaut uniforms sat at terminals around the periphery. One or two looked back at McGregor and his party, frowning, disapproving of an incursion into this sanctum of control.

McGregor was studying Yuri, amused. "Where do you think you are now?"

Yuri shrugged carelessly, though a kind of deep anxiety was gnawing in his stomach.

Mardina murmured, "Lex, go easy—"

"No, really. Tell me. Come on, man, speak up."

"Top of the tower."

McGregor thought that over. "Well, yes. That's correct, sort of. Perceptually speaking anyhow, given the vector of the thrust-induced gravity. But there's rather more to it than that." He clapped his hands. "Lights off." The wall lamps died, fading quickly. "Just look up. Give your eyes a minute to adjust."

Yuri obeyed. Slowly, the stars came out across the dome, a brilliant field, like night in the Martian desert. There was a particularly prominent cluster directly overhead.

"What do you see?"

"Stars. So what? So it's a clear night."

"A 'clear night.' Where do you think you are?"

Yuri shrugged. "Somewhere with a good sky. Arizona." He vaguely remembered a high-altitude site with big astronomical telescopes. "Chile?"

"Chile. You understand that what you see is simulated, a live feed from cameras mounted on the ISM shield."

"ISM?"

"Interstellar medium." McGregor clapped his hands again. "Wraparound VR star field."

The walls and floor of this deck shimmered and melted away. It was as if Yuri, with McGregor, Lemmy, Mardina Jones, Tollemache, Liu Tao, and the handful of operators with their screens, were standing on a floor of glass. And all around him, above and below, he saw stars, with one particularly brilliant specimen directly under his feet.

McGregor grinned by the light of the stars and the display screens. "Now what do you see? Where is the Earth? Where's the planet you thought you were standing on? *Where's the Earth*, Yuri Eden?"

Yuri felt his head swim, the universe close up around him, as if he was fainting from fluid imbalance again.

McGregor pointed downward. "*There*. Down in that puddle of light. That's the sun. We've been traveling from Mars's orbit for a month. We are now"—he glanced at a screen—"two hundred and thirty astronomical units from the sun. That's two hundred and thirty times as far as Earth is from the sun—about eight times as far out as Neptune—about a light-day, if I'm not mistaken. You are a long, long way from Earth, my friend."

"A ship." It didn't sound like his own voice. "This is some kind of ship."

"Not just any old ship. This is the *Ad Astra*. And we are going"—he pointed straight up, at the cluster of stars at the zenith—"there."

"You're on a starship," Mardina Jones said, levelly, steadily, looking Yuri in the eye. "Heading to Proxima Centauri."

"Proxima Centauri," Yuri said dully. The very name was meaningless to him.

"Yuri Eden, this is the UN International Space Fleet vessel *Ad Astra*. Two hundred colonists, in two hulls like this one. We're driven at a constant acceleration, at one gravity, by a kernel engine. This ship is like the hulk that brought you to Mars. But of course you don't remember that. It's a bit more than four light years to Proxima. Given time dilation it will take us three years, seven months subjective to get there, of which we've already served a month . . ."

McGregor peered at him, searching for a reaction. "What are you thinking, man from the past?"

Peacekeeper Tollemache was more direct. "Ha! He's thinking what a prick I am. You thought you were on Earth, didn't you? Why, you fucking—"

Yuri couldn't punch a star, but he could punch Tollemache. He got in one good blow before Mardina Jones, this time, knocked him out.

It was going to be a long three years, seven months.

TWO

...

2155

When Yuri Eden discovered he was on a starship, it was only a little more than a decade after the maiden flight from planet Mercury of a ship called the *International-One*, the first demonstrator of the new kernel-drive technology that propelled the *Ad Astra*. Lex McGregor, then seventeen years old and an International Space Fleet cadet, had taken part in that flight.

And it was thanks to McGregor that Stephanie Penelope Kalinski, then eleven years old, had first gotten to *meet* her father's starship, created from another technology entirely.

It seemed strange to Stef, as she and her father took the long, slow, unpowered orbit from Earth in toward the sun aboard a UN-UEI liner, that there were to be not one but *two* new kinds of ships, the *International-One* and the *Angelia*, launched from such an unpromising place as Mercury at the same time.

Her father just rolled his eyes. "Just my luck. Or humanity's luck. If I was a conspiracy theorist I would suspect that those damn kernels have been planted under Mercury's crust *in order that* we would find them now, just when we are recovering from the follies of the Heroic Generation, and reaching out, with our own efforts, to the stars . . ."

Stef wasn't too clear what a "kernel" was. But she was interested in it *all*, the different kinds of ships, the experimental engineering she'd glimpsed at her father's laboratories back home on the outskirts of Seattle, the rumors of these energy-rich kernels being brought up from deep mines on Mercury . . . She understood that the *International-One* was just some kind of interplanetary-capable technology demonstrator, while her own father's ship, though uncrewed, was going to the stars, the first true interstellar jaunt since the extraordinary journey of Dexter Cole, decades before. But she'd heard hints that these kernels they'd found on Mercury, and which were going to power the *I-One*, were actually much more exotic than anything her father was working on.

This was the kind of thing that always snagged her attention. She was doing well with her schooling, scoring high in mathematics, sciences and deductive abilities, as well as in physical prowess and leadership skills. Her father had been paradoxically pleased when she had been flagged up with a warning about having introvert tendencies. "All great scientists are introverts," he'd said. "All great engineers too, come to that. The sign of a strong, independent mind." But Stef was always less interested in herself than in all the stuff going on outside her own head. The *I-One*'s interplanetary mission was a lot less ambitious than the *Angelia*'s, but it was the *I-One* that had the hot technology. She was more than interested in it. She was fascinated.

She didn't much enjoy the cruise from Earth, though. She had followed the mission profile as their ship descended ever deeper into the heart of the solar system, ever closer to the central fire, and Stef had come to feel oddly claustrophobic. Apparently the UN-led countries and China, who had carved Earth up between them, had shared out the solar system too, but China dominated everything from Earth orbit outward, from Mars and the asteroids to Jupiter's moons. Looking out from the cramped center of the system, China seemed to Stef to have the better half of it, with those roomy outer reaches, families of cold worlds hanging like lanterns in the dark.

On Mercury they landed at a big engineering complex in a crater called Yeats. This was not far from the equator, so that during the planet's day the big looming sun was high in the sky, pouring down the light and energy that fed the square kilometers of solar-cell arrays that carpeted much of the crater's floor.

The gravity was lower than home, about a third, and in the high domes, built big so they could house the industrial complexes expected to sprout here in the future, you could go running and leaping and break all kinds of long-jump records. *That* was interesting, and fun.

But for Stef the charms of Mercury quickly palled. It was hot enough to melt lead outside, at local noon anyhow. They had come here in the morning on this part of Mercury, and since the "day" here lasted a hundred and seventy-six Earth days (a number that was a peculiar product of the planet's slow rotation on its axis and its short year, that had taken Stef a while to figure out), the big sun just hung there, low in the sky, dome-day after dome-day, and the long shadows barely moved across the crater's flat, lava-choked floor. There was, in the end, nothing on Mercury but rock, and there was only so much interest she could feign in solar-cell farms, or even the monumental pipeline systems they had built to bring water from the caches of ice in the permanent shadows at the planet's poles.

And she had to spend a lot of time alone.

Her father was immersed in final tests and simulations for his starship, and Stef knew from long experience when to get out of his way. He'd been just the same when her mother was alive. The trouble was, unlike home, there was nobody else here much less than three times Stef's age. Mercury was like a huge mine, drifting in the generous energy-giving light of the sun, and not a place to raise kids, it seemed; it was a place you came to work for a few years, made your money, and went back home to spend it. For all that the virtual facilities were just as good as back in Seattle, it got kind of boring, and lonely, quickly.

Things got a bit better as more people started to show up, shuttling in from Earth and moon for the launches.

There were actually two crowds arriving here, Stef quickly realized, for the two separate projects, the *Angelia* and the *International-One*. Her father's project, the *Angelia*, was basically scientific: a one-shot uncrewed mission to Proxima Centauri intended to deliver a probe to study the habitable world the astronomers had found fifty years earlier orbiting that remote star. Since that discovery, of course, a human had actually been sent to Proxima, a man called Dexter Cole, who, launched decades before Stef had even been born, had yet to complete his one-way mission; the *Angelia*, representing a new technology generation, would almost overtake him. The throng gathering to watch the *Angelia* launch were mostly scientists and experimental engineers, along with the bureaucrats from state and UN levels who were backing the project. They were men and women in drab suits who spent more time staring into each other's faces over glasses of champagne than looking out of the window at Mercury, a whole alien world, it seemed to Stef.

The *International-One*, meanwhile, was a project of a huge industrial combine called Universal Engineering, Inc.—UEI. Its chief executive was a squat, blustering, forty-year-old Australian called Michael King, and he came out here with a much more exotic entourage of the rich and famous. "Trillionaire-adventurers," her father called them dismissively.

There were even a few Chinese, "guests" of the UN and the UEI, to "observe" the great events taking place here on UN-dominated Mercury, although it seemed to Stef that it was a funny kind of "observing" where you weren't allowed to have close-up views of anything important at all.

Stef did have to show up at drinks parties and other functions at her father's side. Of the trillionaires' club Michael King was the only one who displayed any kind of interest in her personally, as opposed to treating her as some kind of appendage of her father. When she was introduced by her father, King, avuncular, a glass of champagne low-gravity sloshing in his hand, leaned down and looked her in the face. "Good clear eyes. Unflinching gaze. Curiosity. I like that. You'll go far. You keeping up at school, Stephanie?"

"It's Stef. Yes, I think so. I like—"

"What are you missing here?"

"Missing?"

"You're an Earth kid, stuck on Mercury. What's the one thing I could sell you, right now, that you miss the most from home?"

She thought that over. "Soda," she said. "Decent soda. Here it's cold enough, but it's always flat. Same on the moon."

"Yeah. This champagne's kind of flat too." King glanced at her father. "Something to do with the low gravity, George? The low air pressure in the domes, maybe, messing with the carbonation? *Soda*. I'll make a note of that and follow it up. Could be you just earned me another million, kid. So what do you make of all this?" He waved his glass at the people milling around, the conversations going on high above Stef's head.

"I feel like I'm lost in some kind of forest of talking trees."

King barked laughter. "Good for you. Honest answer, and a clear impression. Witty too. Listen to me. I know you're only a kid—no offense. But you should watch and learn, as much as you can. Textbooks are one thing, people in the wild are another, and it's the people you have to work with if you want to get on." His accent was broad Australian, his enunciation crisp, precise, easy to follow. "Look at me. I started out from a poor background. Well, everybody was poor in Oz in those days because of the Desiccation. I made my first living as a coastal scavenger, I was no older than you, we'd go down into the wrecks of oil tankers and seawater-processing factories that had been deliberately beached on the shore, retrieving what materials we could haul out, all for a few UN dollars a day.

"But then age twenty I joined UEI as an apprentice programmer, and after ten years I was on the board. A lot of our early work was deconstruction, taking apart filthy old nuclear reactors. Of course by then we'd relocated to Canada, I mean the northern USNA region as it is nowadays, because Australia, along with Japan, the Far East countries, chunks of Siberia, had become part of the Framework, the Chinese economic empire . . . Well, the details don't matter. Now here I am about to launch a new breed of spaceship. How much more success could you want? And you know how I got this far?"

"People," she said brightly.

He grinned at her father. "George, you got yourself a smart one here. That's it—people. I had contacts. I knew who to approach in the finance and governance community at national, zonal, and UN levels, as well as the technical people, to get it done. Because I'd cultivated those contacts at events like this over years and years. Now it's your chance, and it's never too early to start."

Her father snorted. "Don't give me all that, Michael. Your most important contact isn't human at all."

"Earthshine, you mean."

"Or one of his Core AI rivals. Everybody knows they're your ultimate paymasters." Her father looked around the crowd, almost playfully. "Got an avatar or two here, has he? Should we be watching what we say?"

"Funny, George, very funny. But I don't think—oh, excuse me. Sanjai! Over here!"

And that was it, as he hurried away to another encounter.

Stef liked Michael King, she decided, whether or not he really was backed by the sinister old Core AIs, entities she found hard even to imagine. Her father sneered about King's lack of academic or technical qualifications, but Stef was drawn by his energy, his focus, his vigor, and she stored away his advice.

But she forgot all about Michael King a couple of dome-days later, when the astronauts showed up.

They were the human crew of King's new ship, the *International-One.*

When they walked through a room all the faces turned to the astronauts, like iron filings in a magnetic field. It was like royalty, like King Harold of North Britain, or some media star, or maybe like the Heroic Generation engineers back in their heyday, her father said. They were authentic space pioneers, and all of them were dressed in the uniform of the UN's International Space Fleet, an eye-popping jet-black spangled with glittering stars.

And what drew her attention most was the only member of the *I-One* crew who wasn't in his fifth decade. Lex McGregor was from Angleterre, the south of Britain—the independent north had not contributed to the ISF—Lex was blond, as tall as the rest, and he was just seventeen. He wasn't quite part of the crew, it seemed; he was a Space Fleet cadet, still in the early stages of his training. But he'd shown enough promise to win some kind of internal competition to serve as the one cadet on board the *I-One* for its maiden flight.

"And the fact that he is as photogenic as hell," Stef said to her father, "probably didn't harm his chances."

He laughed. "Much too cynical for your age. Probably right, though. Don't say 'hell.'"

"Sorry, Dad."

Just as Lex was the closest person here to Stef's age, so she was the closest to his, and they kind of gravitated together. She was relieved when he didn't treat her like some bratty kid. He called her "Kalinski," like she was a cadet herself.

They would play dumb games and make up athletic competitions in the domes; he was good at figuring out rules so he was handicapped and she had at least a chance of winning. One of her favorites was the roof run, where you ran at a curving dome wall and *up* it, overcoming the low gravity, sticking to the wall by sheer centrifugal force until you fell back, and then (in theory) executed a slow one-third-G somersault to land on your feet on the cushioned floor. A space cadet's training regime was pretty intense, and she suspected there was still enough of the kid in Lex to relish the chance to blow off some steam, even to bend the rules a little.

Which was probably why it was Lex who introduced her to her father's starship.

It was a dome-morning, only a few days before the launch of the *I-One*. The *Angelia*'s launch was scheduled a couple of dome-days after that. Paradoxically Lex had more free time just now, as the ISF controllers were trying to get their crew to relax before the stress of the mission.

So Lex invited Stef to "take an EVA," by which he meant go for a walk on Mercury's surface.

He met her at a suit locker built into the dome wall. He grinned when she showed up. "Thought you weren't coming, Kalinski. You didn't seem keen."

"I've been out on the moon. What's so special about a bunch of rocks?"

He winked at her. "This is different. Take a look at your suit." He palmed a control.

A section of the wall swept back, to reveal a row of suits that looked like nothing so much as discarded insect carcasses. Each had a hard silvered shell to cover torso, legs and arms, a featureless helmet with a gold-tinted visor, and wings, extraordinary filmy affairs that sprouted from joints behind the shoulders. All the suits had markings of various kinds, colored stripes and hoops, no doubt to identify who was wearing them.

Lex asked, "What do you think?"

"Ugly."

"It's not so bad. Believe me, you won't even notice it once you're out there on the surface. I bet you can't guess what the wings are for."

"It's obvious. To radiate heat."

"Very good," he said, sounding genuinely impressed. "Most of the folk in this dome say, 'For flying.' Then they catch themselves and say, 'But there's no air here so . . .' "

"I know." Stef sighed the way her father did. "It gets so wearying."

He laughed. "OK, Kalinski, quit showing off. Look, putting it on is easy, the suit will seal itself up around you and adapt to fit. Just slip your shoes off . . ."

The astonishing thing was, once she was in the suit and out through a heavy-duty airlock, she really *didn't* notice the suit, not visually anyhow. The suit contained some kind of immersive VR system, so when she looked down it was as if she was standing beside Lex, in their everyday clothes, on a ground of pitted rock, under Mercury's black sky. The sun, more than twice the size it was as seen from Earth, cast long shadows across a moonlike plain. Experimentally she bent down; she felt a little stiff, and couldn't fold quite as she was used to. She touched her toes, though, and picked up a loose bit of rock.

"How's the suit?"

"Fine." She explored the rock; her fingers, in her vision, didn't quite close around it. "It feels kind of . . . soapy." She threw the rock with a skimming motion. The rock whizzed away, falling, not as fast as it would on Earth, faster than on the moon. It made no sound when it fell; that wasn't part of the sim.

"Let's walk." Lex strode easily across the surface of Mercury, his shadow long beside him. His voice sounded as if it was coming from *him*, not from plugs in her ears. "The suit will stop you from coming to any harm."

"I know it will." It was only older people who needed reassuring about stuff like that; people of Stef's age just assumed technology would *work*. She followed him, watching where she was stepping. In this crater basin the surface was smoother than she had expected, with dust overlying a rocky surface pitted by lesser impacts. She moved easily enough, but felt a little heavy, as if she were overmuscled, like she'd beefed up in a gym. The suit must have exoskeletal multipliers.

The domes of the Yeats base were big blisters piled high with dirt, for protection from meteorite falls and from the sun's radiation. Farther out there were storage facilities, backup plants for air and water processing, dusty rovers on tracks that led off across the crater's dirt floor. Not far from the inhabited facilities was the edge of the area of the crater floor paneled by solar cells, a glimmering reflective surface like a pool of molten silver that stretched away for kilometers.

And farther out still she glimpsed some of the mountains that ringed this walled plain, like broken, eroded teeth. Out there stood bigger facilities, marked out by winking warning lights, all far enough from the inhabited domes to allow for safety margins. There was the broad, hardened pad where ships like her own ferry from orbit had come in to land, and fuel and energy stores, and a long shining needle that was the mass driver, which used sun-powered electromagnetism to hurl caches of material out of Mercury's gravity well and across the solar system. In the shadow of the mountains themselves she saw the big gantries of the UEI's drilling project, sinking shafts hundreds of kilometers deep through layers of lava and impact-pummeled bedrock to the edge of Mercury's iron mantle, where the mysterious kernels were to be found.

And there too, huddling in the shadow, stood a taller gantry, a slim rocket: a strange sight for Stef, like something out of a history book. That was mankind's newest spacecraft, the *International-One*, waiting to take Lex and his crew off into space.

Lex took a step and stamped on the ground, sending up little sprays of dust that sank quickly back down. "It's an interesting little world."

"So you say."

He laughed. "I mean it. It's only superficially like the moon. Look at those drill rigs over there. Here, you only have to drill down a few hundred kilometers before you reach the mantle. You'd have to go ten times deeper into the Earth, say. You know why that is?"

"Of course I know—"

Like her father, he didn't always listen before lecturing her. "Because, we think, some big explosion on young Mercury, or maybe a big impact, blew off most of the rocky crust."

She tried to imagine standing here when that big impact happened. Tried and failed. "What I want to know is, has all that got anything to do with the formation of the kernels they found here?"

Another voice replied, "Good question. Well, nobody knows. But I can see why *you* would ask it. You are Stephanie Kalinski, aren't you?"

A woman was walking toward them from the direction of the domes, tall, a little heavyset perhaps, yet graceful. Evidently projecting a virtual image, she appeared to be in regular clothes; she wore a trim blue jacket and trousers, almost uniform-like, but not as showy as Lex's ISF suit. She looked about thirty, but was oddly ageless, as if heavily cosmeticized. Her accent was neutral, perhaps east coast American.

"The name's Stef," she replied automatically. "Not Stephanie. I know your face. I've seen your picture in my dad's dossiers."

"Of course you have," Lex said, grinning. "Which is why I thought you two ought to meet. Dr. Kalinski's two daughters, so to speak. Because he never would have thought of bringing you together himself, right?"

"I am Angelia," said the woman.

That puzzled Stef. "That's the name of the starship. The *Angelia*."

"I know. I *am* Angelia. I know what you're thinking. That I am a PR stunt. A model, hired by your father to personify—"

"I don't actually care," Stef said abruptly.

That surprised Lex. "You've got an impatient streak, haven't you, Kalinski?"

"If somebody's being deliberately obscure, yes."

"I'm sorry," Angelia said. "I don't intend to be. If your father had explained to you the mission concept—"

"You know about me. How come?"

"Well, I have got to know your father as we've worked together. And he speaks of you, Stef, a great deal. He's very proud of you."

"I know," Stef snapped, feeling obscurely jealous.

Lex said, "Be nice, Kalinski. Now it's your cue to ask, 'What mission concept?'"

"Oh, Lex, I don't care. It's obvious this woman is some kind of projection." On impulse she bent, picked up a pebble, an impact-loosened bit of Mercury rock, and threw it at Angelia.

Angelia caught the pebble easily. "Not a projection. Not quite an android either." She looked at the rock, then popped it into her mouth and swallowed it. "I'm not in a suit like yours."

"You're programmable matter."

"That's right." Angelia held up her left hand, and watched as it morphed into a clutch of miniature sunflowers, which swiveled their heads to the low sun.

"Ugh," Lex said. "Creepy."

"Sorry." She turned her hand back into a hand, and pointed up at the empty sky. "I'm to be fired off into interstellar space, by the microwave beam from your father's defunct solar-power satellite, up there. *I'm* the payload. But there is a me in here. In fact, a million mes, in a sense. A whole sisterhood, all sentient to a degree. Stef, I'm sure your father will walk you through the mission design—"

"But it makes no difference." Lex walked around Angelia, studying her. "Whether you're sentient or not, I mean. You're not *human*. And it's an authentic, physical human presence that counts when it comes to touching a new world. Sending some AI like you doesn't count. That's why the kernel ships are the important breakthrough here, because they can carry humans. Maybe even all the way to the stars—and back, unlike poor old Dexter Cole."

"That's very post–Heroic Generation thinking," Angelia said, and she smiled indulgently. "A backlash against the philosophical horrors of that age. And typical of what they teach you at the ISF academies, from what I understand. Human experience is primal, yes? In fact this modern incarnate-humanism is the reason why Stef's father programmed me into this form, so I could attend the prelaunch ceremonies in person, so to speak. It's expected, these days."

Lex shook his head. "No offense, Angelia, but nothing you will ever do could match the achievement of Dexter Cole, no matter how his mission pans out."

Stef knew Cole's story; every kid grew up hearing about it. When a habitable planet of Proxima Centauri was discovered, nations in what had since become the western UN federation had banded together, and within a couple of decades had scraped together a crewed mission. Cole had launched from Mercury for access to its energy-rich solar flux, just like Angelia would. A tremendous laser beam, powered by that flux, had blasted into a lightsail, sending Cole's thousand-ton ship to Proxima. Dexter Cole was flying alone to the stars on a forty-year, one-way mission—and, in some sense Stef had not been allowed to discover, he would somehow become the "godfather" of a human colony when he got there. All this had been launched from an Earth still reeling from the aftermath of the climate Jolts and the Kashmir War of the previous decades, an Earth where the huge recovery projects of the Heroic Generation were still working through their lifecycles—all this as mankind was only just making its first footfalls on the worlds of its own solar system. Incredibly, having been launched decades before Stef was born, Cole was still en route; right now he was in cryo, dreaming his way between the stars, before a pulse-fusion rocket would slow him at the target.

Lex said, "Cole is a hero, and I intend to follow in his footsteps, some day."

Angelia smiled again. "Hey, it's a big universe. There's room in it for both of us, I figure."

Lex grinned. "Fair enough. Good luck, Angelia." He stuck out a hand.

She approached him and took his hand. And as Stef watched, the bit of stone Angelia had swallowed popped out of the back of her neck and dropped slowly to the ground.

6

On the day the *I-One* was to be launched, Stef stood with her father at the window of the UN-UEI command bunker. This stout building, constructed of blocks of Mercurian basalt, was set high in the walls of Yeats's rim mountains, and looked down on the crater-floor plain. The big room was filled with the mutter of voices and the glow of monitor screens, teams of engineers tracking the countdown as it proceeded. Through the bunker windows, in the low light of the sun, Stef could see the domes, lights, and tracks of the main Yeats settlement, and in the foreground the complex activity around the *International-One* at its launch stand, bathed in floodlights. The slim prow of the ship itself just caught the sun as it rose, agonizingly slowly, above the rim mountains. The ship was so far away it looked like a toy, a model layout; the VIPs in here were using binoculars to see better, ostentatiously demonstrating that they lacked Heroic Generation–type ocular augmentation, now deeply unfashionable.

Supposedly, the launch pad was far enough away for them to be safe here in this bunker if worse came to worst. But Stef had learned by now that although the engineers had figured out how to manipulate the kernels, which were evidently some kind of caches of high-density energy, nobody understood them. And if something went wrong, *nobody knew* what the consequences might be. This robust bunker might turn out to be no more protection than the paper walls of a traditional Japanese house before the fury of the Hiroshima bomb.

And somewhere in the middle of all the potentially lethal activity down there was Lex McGregor, just seventeen years old. Stef saw his face on a monitor screen. He lay on his back like his older companions, calm, apparently relaxed, contributing to the final countdown checks.

"He looks like John Glenn on the pad," her father said, looking over her shoulder. "Heroic images from the best part of two hundred years ago. Some things don't change. My word, he's brave."

Maybe, Stef thought. She did admire Lex, but there was something slightly odd about him. Off-key. Sometimes she suspected he'd had some kind of augmentation himself, so his reactions weren't quite the human norm. Or maybe it was just that he was too young to be scared, even if he was six years older than she was.

Her father said now, "This landscape has been sleeping for billions of years, since the last of the great planet-shaping impacts. If that damn ship works this crater is going to be witness to fires fiercer than any that created it. And if it fails—"

"It should not fail," Angelia said. The strange ship-woman stood on her father's other side—one ship watching the launch of another, Stef reflected. "The testing has been thorough."

Stef's father grunted, sounding moody. He was in his fifties, a thick-set, graying man, with old-fashioned spectacles and a ragged mustache; he had always been an *old* father to Stef, though her French mother had been much younger. Now the low light cast by the display screens in the bunker deepened the lines of his face. He said, "Somewhere up there, you know, is my SPS. An old solar-power station hauled out from Earth, a brute of an engine left over from the Heroic days and now refitted and put to good use . . . Oh, they sent Dexter Cole to the stars, but what a cockamamie way to do it, a lightsail to get him out of one system and a fusion rocket to slow him down in the next. Like those old Greek ships, rowing boats with sails attached. Still, they did it, they got him away. Now you, Angelia, you represent the next generation, the next phase of human ingenuity.

"And, just at this exquisite moment—*this*. The discovery of the kernels. A source of tremendous power that, it seems, we can just turn on like a tap. Everything we mere humans can manage is suddenly put in the shade. It's as if we're somehow being allowed to cheat. Does that seem *right*?"

Stef was puzzled. "You've talked about this before. I'm not sure who you're blaming, Dad."

"Your father has always been an agnostic," Angelia said. "Not God."

"Not God, no. I just keep thinking it's a damn odd coincidence that we find these things just when we need them . . ."

The murmuring voices around them seemed to synchronize, and Stef realized that, suddenly, the countdown was nearly done, the *I-One* almost ready to go. She glanced once more at Lex McGregor, on his back, apparently utterly calm.

Flaring light flooded the bunker.

Stef looked through the window. The light was coming from the base of the ship, a glare like a droplet of Mercury sunlight. As she watched, that point of light lifted slowly from the ground.

The bunker erupted in whoops and cheering.

"Watch it go, Stef," said her father, and he took her hand in his. "It's on a trial run out to Jupiter, at a constant one-G acceleration all the way. If it works that damn drive should be visible all the way out, like a fading star. This is history in the making, love. Who knows? It might unite us as humans, at long last. Or it might trigger some terrible conflict with the Chinese, who are denied this marvelous technology. But it's certainly a bonfire of my own ambition."

Angelia put a comforting arm around his shoulders.

Stef barely paid any attention. Staring into that ascending fire, she had only one question. *The kernels. How do they work?*

Day one thousand, two hundred and ninety-seven.

That was Yuri's count, by the tally he had kept running in his head, recording the eight-hour shift changes since he'd woken up in the hull. Over three and a half years. There were no calendars on the *Ad Astra*, not that the passengers saw. And of course he had slept through the early weeks of the flight from Mars, an uncountable time. But he knew roughly that the journey was due to end about now. Day one thousand, two hundred and ninety-seven.

When the end did come, there was some warning: a siren that wailed, for a few seconds.

At the time Yuri had no idea what it meant; he paid no attention to the sporadic briefings on shipboard events. He was on another punishment duty, scooping out muck from the interstices of a mesh floor partition, a grimy, demeaning job that you had to do on your hands and knees, working with a little cleanser the size of a toothbrush and a handheld vacuum hose. A make-work job a machine could have done in a fraction of the time.

Then the gravity failed.

It felt like the whole hull had suddenly dropped, like an elevator car whose cable had broken. Yuri found himself drifting up in the air, the little brush and the vacuum cleaner and his sack of dirt floating up around him. It was an extraordinary feeling, a mix of existential shock and a punch to the gut.

The Peacekeeper supervising him, a fat man called Mattock, threw up, and the chunky vomit sprayed over Yuri's back and drifted up into the air, a stinking, noxious, stringy cloud.

Yuri knew what had happened, of course. After three and a half years of a steady one-gravity thrust, save for a brief turnaround at the journey's midpoint, the crew had shut down the drive. During the cruise, for long periods you could have forgotten you were in a starship. Now here was the reality of the situation suddenly intruding. His latest prison really was a battered tin can light years from Earth.

And then, not five seconds after the acceleration cut out, the riot started.

It erupted all at once, along the length of the hull. The yelling was the first thing Yuri noticed, shouted commands, whoops, screams of defiance and fear.

The big fluorescent light fittings were put out immediately. The crimson emergency lighting system soon came on, shining from behind toughened glass, but the hull was plunged into a flickering, shadowy half-light. And people moved through the shadows, grabbing handrails and slamming at the partition flooring with booted feet, so that broken panels started hailing down through the crowded air. Others used whatever tools they had at hand, spanners, broom handles, they even wrenched rails off the wall, to smash up equipment.

The Peacekeepers were an early target too. Near Yuri, from nowhere, three, four, five people, men and women, came hurtling out of the air like missiles and slammed straight into Mattock. Struggling, his head surrounded by a mist of vomit and blood, the Peacekeeper had no chance of reaching his weapons. He looked to Yuri, who was clinging to the wall. "Help me, you bastard—" A booted foot slammed into his mouth, silencing him.

Yuri turned away. He pulled himself around the walls, working his way across rails and equipment banks, trying to keep out of trouble, trying not to be noticed. He had a rendezvous of his own to make.

As he moved he observed that the hull's population was split. Maybe a third of them were working in a coordinated way, savaging the Peacekeepers and, he saw, one or two astronaut crew members they'd got hold of, or systematically wrecking the internal equipment. Obviously they'd planned this, coordinated it for the onset of zero gravity. Most of the rest, scared, nauseated, were swarming around trying to keep out of the way of the violence. They were almost all adults, of course; the few kids, two- or three-year-olds born during the voyage, clung to their mothers in terror.

And up at the top of the hull Yuri saw a party gathering around the central fireman's pole, preparing to climb up to the hull's apex, up to the bridge. A woman he recognized, called Delga, was at their head. That was no surprise. He'd known her on Mars, where they'd called her the snow queen of Eden. On the ship she had quickly built a power base in the early days when, without alcohol, drugs, tobacco, the whole hulk had been like a huge rehab facility as everybody worked through cold turkey of one kind or another—and Delga, who somehow got her hands on various narcotics, had acquired a lot of customers. Yuri had kept out of her way on Mars, and on the ship, and he did so now. He dropped his head and concentrated on his own progress.

He got to his meeting point. It was just a kind of alcove on a central deck, a warren of thick pipes and ducts and power cables between two hefty air-scrubbing boxes. But it was tucked out of the way of trouble. He and his buddies hadn't anticipated this scenario exactly, but they'd made contingency plans to meet here, in case.

And now, here he found Lemmy, and Anna Vigil, and Cole, nearly four years old, a timid little boy who clung to his mother's legs, all waiting for him.

Wordlessly Yuri backed into the space, opened a maintenance panel on one of the scrubber boxes, took out a wrench and a screwdriver, and thus armed wedged himself in position before the others. After three and a half years he had a reputation on this hull. A loner he might be but he'd fight back, and was best left alone if there were easier targets. This had been the plan they'd cooked up, the three of them, when they'd thought ahead to bad times; this was the best Yuri could think of to protect them.

He heard a scream. In the shadowy chaos, he saw that three men had got hold of a woman. Yuri knew them all; he'd thought one of the men at least was a friend of the woman, who'd paired off with another guy. Yuri knew the woman too; called Abbey Brandenstein, she was an ex-cop and she could look after herself, but she was being overwhelmed. Now they were dragging her into a corner, though she was still fighting back. As the screaming got worse Anna Vigil covered little Cole's eyes and ears, and hugged him close.

The noise was still ferocious, a clamor of yells and screams. More alarm sirens were sounding off, adding to the racket. There was no sign yet of the Peacekeepers taking any kind of coordinated action. Yuri saw Gustave Klein on the other side of the hull, flanked by a couple of his heavies, watching the action with a grin on his face. Maybe it was Klein who was really in control.

Lemmy peered cautiously up into the apex of the hull. "Delga's reached the bridge, it looks like."

"What do you think they want?"

Lemmy shrugged. "To take the ship. Force the astronauts to whiz us all back to Earth. I bet there's a similar breakout going on in the other hull; they'll have timed it. I guess it's the last chance we'll get. There'll be no hope once we're on the ground, on a planet of Proxima."

"But they could smash up the ship before they win that argument."

"True."

"You think it's going to work?"

Lemmy grinned. "Nah. Look." He pointed to the far wall of the hull.

An airlock hatch opened and a dozen astronauts tumbled out of the lock and into the hull's cluttered spaces. They wore hard, carapacelike pressure suits of brilliant white, marked with arm stripes in gaudy recognition colors, red, blue, green. They had their helmets sealed, their faces hidden behind golden visors, and their movements were jerky, too rapid, over-definite—a product of military-class enhancements, Yuri had learned, exoskeletons, drugs, boosters from the cellular level up. They carried weapons of some kind, not guns, not in a pressure hull, but what might be tasers, even whips.

Some of the rebelling inmates went for them immediately. The astronauts fought back with clean, hard moves, and snaps of their tasers, rasps of the whips. They were like insects with their superfast movements and hard outer shells, like space-monster cockroaches in this chaotic human environment. Before them the inmates looked grubby and unevolved. People fell back howling, blood spraying into the air.

Meanwhile one group of astronauts, three, four of them, broke away and made for a big locked control panel a couple of decks higher up toward the bridge. More rebels tried to get in their way, but the astronauts were too fast, too definite, and their opponents were brushed aside. The astronauts unlocked the panel with brisk taps of gloved fingers, and plugged pull-out leads into sockets in their suits, perhaps for identity verification.

Then, not a minute after the airlock had first opened, a yellowish gas began to vent from outlets all around the hull, and people began coughing, panicking.

Lemmy grinned. "Sweet dreams. See you on Prox c . . ."

But Yuri was already falling away down a long dark tunnel, and could hear no more.

The ship's population—what survived of it after the riots—was split up into small groups, held in isolated chambers in a newly partitioned hull.

On being woken from his latest bout of unconsciousness, Yuri found himself cuffed with plastic strips to a metal-frame chair, itself locked to a mesh floor. He was in a small partition-walled cabin with ten others, four women, six men. They were all dressed identically, in orange jumpsuits, with no boots, just socks. This was his assigned "drop group," he was told. The only one in here that Yuri knew well was Lemmy. He did soon learn that the passengers had already been assigned to these drop groups, nominally fourteen each, long before the insurrection, and now the groups had been used as the basis for the lockdown.

They were supervised by Peacekeepers, never fewer than two at a time, with astronauts overseeing them, in the case of Yuri's group Lex McGregor and Mardina Jones. As the days passed the passengers were released one at a time in a cycle, to use a bathroom modified for zero gravity, to wash, to feed. When they were out of their cuffs Lex McGregor insisted they stretch and bend, to keep from stiffening up. They were spoken to, but not encouraged to speak back, or to have conversations with one another.

The thrust was never restored, the gravity never came back on. But occasionally you would hear bangs and knocks, as if some huge fist was hammering on the hull, and jolts this way and that, brief periods of acceleration. Lemmy murmured that having reached the Proxima system under its kernel drive, the ship must be using some secondary propulsion system to insert itself into a final orbit, presumably around the target, the supposedly Earthlike third planet of Proxima. This was guesswork, however. They had no view out of the hull.

The crew processed them bureaucratically, forever ticking off names on the piss and feed rotas on their slates. There seemed to be no formal comeback after the insurrection. No hearings, no disciplinary measures. Yuri guessed the crew didn't care, they just wanted to dump their unruly passengers down on this Proxima planet and have done with them.

But it was evident there had been some punishment beatings. One man in Yuri's group, called Joseph Mullane, some kind of dispossessed farmer type originally from Ireland, had been worked over particularly hard, and Dr. Poinar had to spend some time treating his wounds. But even he was kept cuffed to his chair.

Mullane had been one of the men Yuri had seen attacking Abbey Brandenstein, the ex-cop, at the height of the trouble—and Abbey herself was in this drop group too. Yuri had no idea if their pairing up like this had been deliberate. Maybe not, if it was true that the groupings had been defined long before the insurrection. Abbey Brandenstein spent all her waking hours glaring at Mullane.

In the hours and days that followed, Yuri never heard what had become of Anna Vigil and her kid; he didn't ask, wasn't told. Occasionally you heard voices from beyond the partition, a murmur of movement, a snatch of a baby's crying. Otherwise, as the shifts wore on, there was nothing to do but sit there, cuffed to your chair. It was possible to sleep; Yuri found that if he relaxed, just let himself float in the zero gravity, he could find a position where the cuffs at his wrists and ankles didn't chafe, and he could almost forget he was pinned down. He was bothered by the fact of his lengthy unconsciousness, however. Another gap in his memory. It irritated him to have three years of counting disrupted like that.

A few days after the last of those attitude-engine thumps and bangs had died away, there was a heavier shudder, as if some huge mass had joined the hull.

Lemmy winked at Yuri. "Shuttle. Orbit to ground. This ship has two, one of the crew told me that—"

"Shut the fuck up," said a Peacekeeper. It was Mattock, the cuts and bruises on his face yet to heal, his broken nose twisted—Mattock, who took out his suffering on Yuri in sly kicks and punches, because Yuri had refused to help him before the fury of the mob.

Now Lex McGregor, with another Peacekeeper at his side, came swimming into the cabin. McGregor was in his sparkling astronaut uniform, as usual, and Yuri felt oddly ashamed at his own shabbiness.

McGregor smiled.

"Ladies and gentlemen. Time for us all to take a little ride. We'll be boarding you one at a time. I do apologize, we'll have to keep the cuffs on, you do understand how things are following recent incidents. But I'm sure we'll have no trouble. You first, Ms. Amsler . . ."

Jenny Amsler, a small, timid woman who had once been a jeweler, looked terrified as she was bundled out.

The loading proceeded efficiently. When it was Yuri's turn, the hefty Peacekeepers to either side of him propelled him through the weightlessness with a gloved hand under each armpit. His last glimpse of the interior of the hull that had transported him across interstellar space was of blank-walled partitions, bits of equipment damaged by fire and vandalism. There was a smell of smoke, vomit, blood, of shit and piss, and a tang that made his throat itch, maybe a remnant of the gassing.

He was taken to a shower room where he had to strip, was sprayed with some hot, disinfectant-smelling liquid, and made to clean his teeth with a plastic brush. Then he was dressed in a kind of undersuit with a fresh jumpsuit on top. There was a diaper, he found, built into the undersuit, heavy pants around his crotch.

Then he was shoved out through a tight hatchway, and after a swivel of his vertical perspective found himself dropping into a craft laid out like a small, cramped airplane. There were couches in rows of four, cushioned seats on which you could lie back as if in a dentist's chair. Room enough for twenty passengers, he counted quickly. An open door to the front of the cabin led to the cockpit, a cave of glowing lights where two astronauts worked, side by side, their backs to him.

The shuttle at least seemed clean. It had a new-carpet smell Yuri suddenly realized he hadn't come across since he had been slotted into that cryo drawer back on Earth; nothing on Mars had been *new*, or on the starship.

And through the cockpit window, over the shoulders of the crew, he glimpsed a slice of blue, like the sky of Earth.

All this in a glance before he was bundled down into a couch. Mattock and another Peacekeeper worked him over quickly, strapping him in with a heavy safety harness, but also cuffing him to the frame at wrists and ankles with more plastic ties.

He was the fifth person to be loaded in, with not a word being spoken. Looking forward, he saw that among the other four already loaded, Abbey Brandenstein had been seated right next to Joseph Mullane, one of her rapists.

Yuri looked up at the battered face of Mattock, who hovered over him as he labored over the ties. "Hey, Peacekeeper. Bad idea," he ventured. "Mullane and Brandenstein together—"

His reward was a knee in the stomach. Mattock had become proficient at bracing himself in the lack of gravity to make such blows effective. Yuri couldn't help but grunt, but he tried to show no other reaction.

"Mind your own business, you little prick."

The rest of the loading went ahead briskly, and almost in silence, save for muttered exchanges between the Peacekeepers. The passengers were all from the group in the confinement cell, eleven in total. Lemmy was lodged just behind Yuri. Two comparative strangers were loaded into Yuri's left and right, a big-framed Asiatic who Yuri knew only as Onizuka, who had once been some kind of businessman, and a woman called Pearl Hanks, small, dark, old eyes in a young face, who had been a prostitute on Earth and on Mars, and, in the hull, had been again. Onizuka ignored Yuri, but he looked past him at Pearl Hanks with a kind of calculation.

The hatch above their heads was slammed down with finality. And that, Yuri thought, was the last he was going to see of the *Ad Astra*.

With all aboard and tied down tightly, the two Peacekeepers settled in couches at the rear of the cabin. Lex McGregor came floating back from the forward cockpit, as usual immaculate in his uniform. Beyond him, in the pilots' cabin, Yuri glimpsed Mardina Jones pulling on a pressure suit.

McGregor faced the passengers. "Ladies and gentlemen. Welcome aboard the prosaically named *Ad Astra* shuttle number two. In this brave little ship we will soon be descending to the planet of another star . . ."

The passenger cabin had no windows. But now, over McGregor's shoulder, through that pilots' window, as the shuttle drifted, Yuri could see more of the planet: the gray shield of what looked like an ocean, floating masses of ice, a terminator separating night from day, a diorama shifting by.

"Our descent will be straightforward. We will be landing at a pre-designated site in the northeast quadrant of the planet's substellar face. We'll come down on what looks like a dry lake bed, just like the salt flats at Edwards Air Force Base in California where I completed my own flight training some years ago. Perfectly safe, a natural runway.

"Our landing routine will take two hours. I'm afraid you won't be able to leave your chairs until we're safely down and the wheels have stopped rolling. If you have any biological requirements during the flight just let yourself go, you'll notice you are wearing underwear adapted for the purpose. You will hardly be comfortable but it won't be for long. Also there are sick bags. I do hope there will be no monkey business from any of you during the flight," he said, sadly, gravely. "Obviously it would be futile; you could achieve nothing but damage the craft and endanger yourself and your colleagues. We, the crew, incidentally, will be wearing pressure suits and parachutes, so you need not fear for our safety, whatever you do." He glanced at his watch. "Soon we'll decouple, and then the deorbit burn will follow a few minutes later. Any questions? No? Enjoy the flight. After all," he mused, as if an interesting thought had just struck him, "it will, I suppose, be the last flight any of you ever take." He retreated to his cabin.

Soon there were more bangs and jolts, a sound that Yuri had come to recognize as the firing of small attitude rockets. As the shuttle swung about, turning on its axis to the right, he could sense that he was in a much less massive vessel than the reassuring bulk of the starship. There was silence in the passenger cabin, save for ragged, nervous breathing, and the usual space-travel hiss of pumps and fans, a noise that had followed Yuri all the way from Mars—and, incredibly, the drone of somebody snoring. Yuri glanced around to see; it was Harry Thorne, from a Canadian UNSA state, once an urban farmer, a heavyset, imperturbable man.

Beyond the pilots' window a second planet hung in the black now, more distant, a perfect sphere of silver-gray.

Lemmy leaned forward again. "Yuri. Listen. Watch everything. Observe. Remember. I mean, are they going to give us maps? Remember everything you can of this new world we're heading for—"

Yuri heard rather than saw Mattock's fist hitting Lemmy's jaw. "One more word, shithead, and I'll lay you out for the duration."

Now there was a roar, a gentle shove that pressed Yuri back into his seat.

It was a strange thing that Yuri had crossed interplanetary space, and then *interstellar* space, but he knew nothing about the mechanics of space flight. In his day the whole business of flying in space had seemed unethical, just another sin committed in a previous energy-bloated age, and nobody even talked about it. He could only guess at what was going on.

The burn was soon over. Now the attitude rockets slammed again, once more the ship swiveled—he glimpsed that ocean, half-submerged in night, slide past the pilots' window—and then, nothing.

The seconds piled up into minutes. To Yuri it felt as if he was still in freefall. Behind him he heard somebody humming—it was the other Peacekeeper, not Mattock—and the rustle of a paper bag. Those guys had done this run several times before, he guessed; they knew the routine. There was a fumble. "Damn." A couple of candy fragments came sailing over Yuri's head, from behind. Yuri stared, fascinated; he'd seen no candy since he'd gone into cryo on Earth. But the bright blue capsules were falling, he saw, a long slow curving glide down to the floor. Acceleration building up.

There was a glow outside that forward window now, a dull crimson, then orange, and then, suddenly a dazzling white, like he was flying down some huge fluorescent tube. Yet there was no noise, no shuddering or buffeting, no great sense of weight, not yet.

The glow quickly cleared to reveal a seascape, white ice floes on a steely ocean that faded into night. Then this panorama *tilted up*, sideways. No, of course, it was the shuttle that was tipped up, almost standing on its right wing. And then, Yuri could feel it in his gut, the craft tipped the other way, and the landscape slid out of his view.

"Holy shit," murmured someone else now, a woman ahead of Yuri, another businessperson called Martha Pearson, staring out of the forward window.

"We're gliding," Lemmy muttered through gritted teeth. "That's all. No power now we've deorbited. Gliding down into the atmosphere of this world. Shedding our speed in friction against the upper air in these big rolls and banks . . ."

Mattock growled a warning, but indistinctly; maybe he was distracted himself.

Suddenly they flew into night. Now there was only darkness below, that landscape hidden. Yuri could feel the gravity mounting up, and he lay back on his couch. Still the pressure piled on until it felt like some enormous Peacekeeper was sitting on his chest, and there was blackness around the edge of his vision, closing in. But now there was a pressure in his legs, around his waist; his undergarment was clamping him hard, pressing back his belly button.

"Clench!" shouted Lemmy. "Clench your gut! It will help stop you blacking out . . ."

Yuri tried it, crunching down hard. It felt like his whole waist was being constricted by some terrifically tight belt. But it worked, his vision cleared.

Now he could hear a rush of air, of wind—this spaceship really had become an airplane—and they flew suddenly into daylight once more, from day to night in an instant. Raising his head, he glimpsed through the pilots' window a big watery sun that dazzled him, and a twilit land below, then more ice floes, more ocean, all bathed in a ruddy glow.

"Your last sunrise!" Lemmy yelled.

Yuri didn't know what he meant.

There was a shudder, a bang, and the ride abruptly got a lot bumpier. The shuttle glided on down through air that felt lumpy, full of turbulence, like they were flying through a field of invisible rocks. But now, Yuri saw, looking forward, he was flying toward land again. A coastline fled beneath, fringed by white-capped waves, and then what looked like a belt of forest, a furry fringe of a dismal drab green, and then more arid country, it seemed, dust and sand and dunes.

Remember it all, Lemmy had said. Yuri tried. But he didn't even know which way he was flying. West to east? Did directions like that even make any sense on this world?

They flew over cloud now, a great curdled bank of it, gray-white, twisted like a tremendous tornado, he thought. Through breaks in the cloud he glimpsed another clump of strange dark forest. Then they were back over the open country, with only scattered cloud below, and Yuri saw a river snaking away from that stormy region, a silver ribbon laid across the rust-colored land.

They descended farther, following that river, and now the land below seemed to rush beneath the shuttle. Yuri peered down, searching for detail. He thought he saw movement on the ground: the shadow of a cloud? But cloud shadows didn't raise dust . . .

The river reached a sea, at a broad, sluggish estuary. The craft banked once more and, very low now, came back over the shore, over the estuary, and descended toward a flat, dusty country broken here and there by small lakes, and in the farther distance a belt of forest. The descent seemed rapid now. Yuri could see fine details, individual rocks fleeing beneath the ship. The shuttle shuddered and tipped in the turbulent alien air. Yuri, clinging to the cuffs that held him in his seat, endured the jolting, and heard the clatter of fittings, loose panels, harness holders. Up front, somebody was noisily sick.

And they were *down*, suddenly, a crashing impact after which they bounced into the air, and slammed down again with a squeal of tires and another sudden jolt of deceleration, this time hurling Yuri forward against his straps.

The shuttle slowed to a halt. The dust it raised soon fell back to the plain outside, revealing a washed-out blue sky, a rocky, stony ground.

Immediately Lex McGregor came bustling back through the cockpit door. He was pulling open the neck of his pressure suit; Yuri could see he was sweating hard. "Wheel stop and we're down. You know, it was one small step for a man when Armstrong landed on the moon. But for you lot it's one *last* step—right? The end of the line. Welcome to Proxima c."

The two astronauts went out first, of course.

Then the Peacekeepers released the passengers one by one and escorted them out of the cabin. With an attendant Peacekeeper, they had to pass one at a time through an airlock, even though the air was supposedly breathable; the lock was evidently integral to the shuttle's design.

Yuri waited for his turn, disoriented, bewildered—too mixed-up, he thought, to be either fearful or excited about setting foot on this alien world. Maybe that would come later. Or not. After all, countless generations had dreamed of reaching Mars, and that had turned out to be a shit hole.

At last it was his turn. Mattock cuffed Yuri to his own wrist, and tied his ankles with a length of plastic rope. Thus hobbled, Yuri shuffled ahead to the airlock, and climbed awkwardly through the narrow hatch, into the small chamber of the lock.

While the lock went through its cycle he sat on a small bench, facing a glowering Mattock.

"Just give me an excuse," said Mattock.

Yuri grinned back.

A green light glared, and the outer hatch door popped open. Yuri saw a ground of pink-gray sand, individual grains casting long shadows.

The air smelled of aircraft, of fuel and oil and a kind of burned smell of metal. But under that there was a subtler scent, an old, rusty tang, like autumn leaves in an English park, he thought.

Mattock nudged him. "You first."

Yuri had to swing both his hobbled legs out through the hatch, and then he jumped down a third of a meter or so to the ground, both his feet hitting at the same time. It felt like Earth gravity, he thought immediately, or about that.

He was in the shadow of the shuttle's sprawling, still-hot, jet-black wing.

He shuffled forward a few paces, into sunlight, and he looked up for the first time at the star, the sun of this world. It was a tremendous beacon in a bluish sky, not as brilliant as the sun of Earth, but still dazzling, and bigger to look at, three or four times the size of Earth's sun. Other than that the sky was empty, save for a pair of brilliant stars, shining despite the bright daylight, and one disc of a planet hanging like a remote moon.

The other disembarked passengers were sitting in a circle in the dirt, a few paces from the shuttle. Mattock prodded Yuri to go join them. He edged forward, looking around as he walked. Beyond the group, he saw a lake glimmer, blue under the sky. Beyond that, a drab green belt that must be forest. And beyond that, folded mountains. There was no sign of people, no walls, no fences as far as he could see. No dome walls, like on Mars.

Lieutenant Mardina Jones stood over the passengers. She said to Yuri, "The air's fine, isn't it? A miracle, really. Given it's another world, and all."

"I guess."

She watched him curiously. "You know, Eden, you're the only one who's just stood here and—looked." She squinted up at the sun. "Strange to think, that sun will just hang there. Never rise, never set, not as long as you live."

"Really?"

She stared at him. "All those briefings we gave. You really have learned nothing, have you?"

"Where's everybody else?"

"Who?"

"The other groups. Brought down by the shuttle before us."

"A long way from here. Major McGregor will tell you all about it. In the meantime you go sit over there with those others. We've got supplies to unload for our stay here, and for your first few weeks and months as residents. Also a ColU."

Yuri didn't know what a ColU was. "And then you're going?"

She slapped the hull of the shuttle. "This bird will scramjet its way back to the sky—yes, we're going. Now, if I release your hobble will you go and sit with the rest?"

"Yes."

She bent down, took a knife from her belt, and slit through the hobble.

He took a step toward the seated group. Then another step, and another, and then broke into a run. A jog really, it was awkward with his hands tied together, but he could do this. He ran, stretching his legs, the dirt firm under his booted feet.

Ran right past the seated group, who whooped and hollered.

He heard voices behind him. "Hey, ice boy! Stop or—"

"Or what, Mattock? You going to run him down? Ah, let him go. I mean, where's he going to run to? A thousand klicks to the next group? He'll be back. Look, give me a hand with this food pack . . ."

And Yuri ran and ran, on beyond the dust kicked up by the shuttle on landing, on over the virgin dirt, on far beyond the bounds of any cramped little Martian colony like Eden—on until their voices were small behind him, and when he looked back the shuttle sitting on its undercarriage looked like a black-and-white toy on a tabletop—on toward that forest, and the mountains.

That was why he was the last to hear that, sometime during the descent when attentions were otherwise engaged, Abbey Brandenstein had stabbed Joseph Mullane in the heart with a sharpened plastic toothbrush.

On Angelia's last night in the human world, Dr. Kalinski cherished her. That was how she thought of it, on later reflection.

Still in the form of her weighty humanoid body, she was taken to dinner with Dr. Kalinski and his daughter Stef, and members of the control crew who would care for her during her ten-year flight to Proxima: people like Bob Develin and Monica Trant, competent twenty- or thirty-somethings, all employees of national space agencies now subsumed into a global UN agency which only the Chinese, their Framework partners, and a few outliers like North Britain had declined to join. "Only": much of interplanetary space travel, in fact, was dominated by the new Chinese empire. They spoke openly, loosely, treating Angelia as one of the crew, as *human*, sometimes even speaking as if she weren't there at all, which paradoxically made her feel more welcome, more included.

But she learned more about their concerns regarding the mission than Dr. Kalinski had told her about before. That perhaps it was obsolete, technologically, before it was even launched, given the UEI kernel developments. That it wasn't very popular politically in higher circles in the UN: it had a whiff of the Heroic Generation, whose projects had been characterized by massive, wasteful engineering, and loaded with AIs of a quality of sentience that had later been made illegal retrospectively. After all, Dr. Kalinski had grown up in the wake of the Generation and their mighty works; maybe he was influenced by them. So the whispers went.

Dr. Kalinski had done his best to shield his project from those criticisms. Yes, he had needed some big-scale equipment, but even though he had reused a solar-power station, itself a much-hated relic of the past Heroic age with its hubristic planetary engineering schemes, he would use energies of orders of magnitude *less* than those that had hurled Dexter Cole to Proxima. As for profit, Dr. Kalinski eschewed any cash reward save for the salary he drew from the academic institutions that employed him. Any patentable technologies would be owned and exploited by those institutions, on behalf of the UN-governed taxpayers that supported them. And, yes, Angelia was an advanced, sentient AI, the mission could not have been achieved without smart onboard technology. She was capable of suffering—that was the price of sentience. But the mission was designed to sustain her, Dr. Kalinski said, to deliver her to Proxima Centauri alive and sane. She was being honored, not mistreated.

But the team was evasive when they discussed details, and Dr. Kalinski would not look Angelia in the eye—or eleven-year-old Stef, Angelia noticed. Evidently there were things she, and Stef, hadn't been told about certain aspects of the mission.

Despite such tensions it was a wonderful, warm, immersive final evening for Angelia. And at the end, as the dinner party was breaking up, Stef Kalinski came to her and took her hand.

"I'm sorry if I've been nasty to you," Stef said.

"You haven't been."

"It's just a bit difficult for me. My mother died. She was French—"

"I know."

"And then I had Dad all to myself in Seattle. Then you showed up. It's like . . ."

"Yes?"

"Like I suddenly had a big sister." She screwed up her small face, thinking hard. "Like I had to get all my sibling rivalry out in one go."

Angelia laughed. "You're very perceptive. And very self-aware. I haven't been offended. I'm glad I had the chance to get to know you."

"Yes. Me too."

"Are you jealous of where I'm going, the adventure I'm going to have?" It was a reaction she'd encountered from several of the ground crew—Bob Develin, for instance, a thirty-year-old from Florida who'd spent much of his youth working on the underwater archaeology of a drowned Cape Canaveral, and dreaming of space.

But Stef shook her head. "Oh, no. The kernels—that's what I want to study, even if Dad thinks it's cheating to use them, or something."

"You don't want to go to the stars?"

"What for? Stars are *easy* to understand . . ."

Maybe so. But as Stef got up on tiptoe to kiss her synthetic sister on her programmable-matter cheek, Angelia wondered if even a kernel could be as complex as an eleven-year-old girl.

That was the end of the night. Dr. Kalinski showed Angelia to her room, an authentic human space with a regular bed and a wall mirror and everything. He stroked her artificial hair and said good night. She laid down on the bed, fully clothed, and entered sleep mode.

When she woke, she was in space, pinned by sunlight.

11

She no longer had a human form, not remotely. Now she was a disc spun out of carbon sheets, a hundred meters across and just a hundredth of a millimeter thick. Yet she was fully aware, her consciousness sustained by currents and charge stores in the multilayered mesh of electrically conductive carbon of which she was composed. She had slept through this transformation, this atomic-level reassembly conducted by Dr. Kalinski and his technicians.

And she could see, hear, taste the universe, through clusters of microscopic sensors.

She faced Mercury, a cracked, pitted hemisphere. The lights of humanity glimmered in the shadows of ancient crater walls, and crawled along cliffs and ridges. Orbiting the planet she saw the hard, ugly lump of the defunct solar-power station, assembled decades ago in near-Earth space and now hauled here for reuse, and the tremendous lens, a structure of films and threads that dwarfed even her own lacy span, that would throw the station's microwave beam across the solar system to power her flight. The scale of all this was extraordinary, and the energies to be unleashed were huge. If anything went wrong she would die in a moment, a moth in a blowtorch. She felt a stab of unreasonable fear.

"Angelia?"

"I'm here, Dr. Kalinski."

"How do I sound?"

"Like you're in a room with me."

"Good. That's how I wanted it to be. I'm glad we had time to be human together. Because you are part of humanity, you know. The best and brightest part. You are named for a daughter of Hermes, the Greek version of Mercury. She too was a messenger, a bringer of tidings. You will carry the news of our existence to another star. And you will carry all our dreams. Mine, anyway. Well, we said all that. You know we can't communicate while the beam is firing. We'll talk to you in four days, when the acceleration is done. All right?"

"Yes, sir. I think—"

"We won't put you through a countdown. Godspeed, Angelia . . ."

The power station lit up in her vision, which was sensitized to the beam's microwave frequencies. Mercury receded, as if falling down a well.

The intense radiation, intended originally to deliver compact solar power to the factories and homes of distant Earth, now filled her own hundred-meter-sail body. She felt her skin stretch and billow as terawatts of power poured over her. It was not even necessary for her structure to be solid; her surface was a sparse mesh, a measure to reduce her overall density, but the wavelengths of the microwave photons were so long that they could not pass through this wide, curving net of carbon struts. And the microwave photons, bouncing off the sail like so many minute sand grains, shoved her backward, at thirty-six gravities, piling up an extra thousand kilometers per hour of velocity with each new second.

Despite the increasing distance, the intensity of that laser beam, focused by the lens, did not diminish, not by a watt. It was agony. It was delicious. She laughed, deep in her distributed consciousness.

The intensity did not diminish for four days, by which time she had been flung more than a hundred times Earth's distance from the sun, far beyond the orbit of the farthest planet.

From here, the sun, the monster that dominated Mercury's sky, was no more than a bright star—and a star that was very subtly reddened in her sophisticated sensors, for she had already reached her interstellar cruising speed, of two-fifths of the speed of light. At such a speed she would reach Proxima in a mere decade. Orders of magnitude less energy had been expended to get her this far, this fast, than had been spent on Dexter Cole. But he, cryo-frozen, had been embedded in a thousand-ton craft; she was a mere eighty kilograms—the mass of a human, as if Cole, naked, had been thrust to the edge of interstellar space.

She was the craft herself. And she, indeed, was a throng; she would never be alone.

With an effort of will, a subtle reprogramming of her structure, she turned her senses outward, to the void.

2169

The shuttle was to stay on the ground for ten days before returning to the *Ad Astra*. The main task for the crew in this interval was unloading, assembling, and installing the colonists' supplies and gear. The colonists, meanwhile, were put to work constructing irrigation ditches to a nearby lake, and making a start on a shelter, dug into the ground.

The shelter was for protection from stellar storms. Proxima flared. It happened once or twice a day. You could see it with the naked eye; whole provinces would light up on the star's big dim surface, like a nuclear war going on up there. The planet, Prox c, had a thick atmosphere and a healthy ozone layer, but about once a month, it was thought, there would be a storm severe enough to require more protection. For now, if a bad flare came they would be allowed back in the shuttle. But in the future they would be scurrying into holes in the ground.

For the rest of their lives.

Ten days until the shuttle left: that was one important time interval in Yuri's life. The other, told to them by the crew, was eight Earth days and eight hours. That was how long the day was on this world, on Prox c, the day *and* the year, because the world spun around Proxima keeping the same face toward its star—just as the moon kept the same face to the Earth—so that the day was the same length as the year. In fact the stability of Prox c was greater than the moon's, which wobbled a little as seen from Earth. Not Prox c.

That was why Lemmy had taunted Yuri about a final sunrise. That big old sun was never going to rise, never going to set; it was going to hang in that one place in the sky, forever. Oh, the weather changed, there could be cloud, and on the second day there was rain, sweeping down from the forest belt to the north. But in terms of the basic architecture of the world, every day was the same, the sun defiantly unmoving, hour after hour. And just as there was no dawn, no sunset, there would be no summer, no winter here. Just day after day, identical as coins stamped out of a press. It was as if time didn't exist here, as if all the ages had been compressed down into one centuries-thick day.

Soon all of them were having trouble sleeping—all the colonists, at least, under their canvas outdoors. The astronauts and the Peacekeepers, save those on guard, slept in the shuttle's cabin, which was slaved to Earth time.

But Proxima wasn't the only light in the sky, Yuri noticed. There was a bright double-star system, bright enough to cast shadows: Alpha Centauri A and B, twin suns, the center of this triple-star system, of which Proxima was really a shabby suburb. There was that one visible planet, that tracked around the sky. And also, for now, there was a starship up there, a spark crawling across the sky. The days were not quite identical, then, the sky not quite featureless. Time passed, even here.

Yuri kept to himself. But he found he was becoming curious about this world, Prox c, in a way he'd never been curious about Mars. But then all he'd seen of Mars had been the inside of domes.

He watched the sky, the landscape. He scrounged a telescope from a bit of surveying gear. He even looked at *Ad Astra* through his little telescope, and was surprised to see that only one of the two hulls that had brought the colonists here was still attached to the wider frame that contained the propulsion units and the interstellar-medium particle shields. One hull was missing, then. He didn't ask anybody about this; he knew he wouldn't get an answer.

On the fourth day he set up his own observatory, kind of, on top of a lumpy bit of highland a couple of kilometers west of the shuttle, that they had called the Cowpat.

He saw stuff moving, around the lake, out on the plain, in the forest to the north. Living things, presumably, native to this world. They'd had no briefing from the astronauts on the nature of the life forms here. Mostly because nobody knew.

On the fifth day, Jenny Amsler, one of the colonists, followed him out, without any kind of invitation from Yuri, to help him with his gear. He mostly ignored her.

On the seventh day Lieutenant Mardina Jones said she wanted to come too, evidently curious about what he was up to.

To get to the Cowpat they had to head west, skirting the lake to the north from which the fledgling colony was already drawing water through laboriously dug irrigation ditches. They had defined "north" and "west" based on the orbital plane of the planet; given the stillness of the sun the directions felt abstract. The lake water seemed safe enough once filtered, though it was thick with the local life.

They called the lake the Puddle.

Lex McGregor objected to these names, the Cowpat, the Puddle; he wanted more heroic labels. "Names to sound down the generations. Lake First Footstep. Mount Terra!" Or Lake Lex, the colonists joked. They stuck to the Puddle and the Cowpat. This place was evidently a shit hole, but it was *their* shit hole. It was prison-thinking, Yuri thought, now applied to a whole new world. He didn't care. The lake was the lake, it was a thing in itself, it had been here long before humans, and existed in its own right, whatever people called it.

Now, on this walk out to the Cowpat, Mardina Jones stared around, as if discovering it all for the first time. She had always been one of the more human of the authority types on the ship, Yuri thought. But even she had barely stepped away from the little campsite that had sprung up around the landed shuttle, had barely *looked* at this world, into which they were all busy driving tent pegs and scraping latrine trenches. But here she was now, apparently determined to see something of Prox c for herself before she was whisked off back to the sky. Like she was on a business trip cramming in a little tourism between sales meetings. Away from the rest of the crew, she did, however, carry a gun.

By the lakeshore, maybe a kilometer from the shuttle, was a formation of what Yuri had decided to call pillows. Mardina slowed to inspect these, fascinated. She had a sensor pack on her shoulder that hummed

and whirred as it recorded what she saw. The "pillows" were like heavily
eroded rocks, with narrow stems and flat upper surfaces, most no taller
than Yuri's waist. They were irregular lumps, and yet, standing on the
muddy shore, they had an odd sense of fitting together, like worn pieces
of some thick jigsaw puzzle.

"Fascinating," Mardina said. "Life! We knew it was here, of course,
but here we are, face-to-face with it. So to speak."

Yuri watched her, irritated, as she took her movies to show her buddies back home, in her air-conditioned astronaut's apartment on an
artificial island in the Florida Sea, or wherever. "You see these everywhere," he said. "Doc Poinar took a look at my images and said they
were like—"

"Stromatolites. I know. Bacterial communities, a very old type of
formation on Earth. We should take samples. Actually I've seen stromatolites back home. There are some survivors near salt lakes in
Australia . . . Of course *our* stromatolites grow in shallow water, with
the living layers photosynthesizing away at the surface. These are evidently growing on the dry land, transporting nutrients up somehow.
More like a tree, maybe." She glanced at him. "You know I'm from
Australia, right? That I'm a pure-blood Aborigine?"

Yuri shrugged. She was the kind of prison warden who wanted to
be your buddy. She was going to be gone soon. Where she came from
made no difference to him.

Jenny Amsler had always been the kind to keep in with the authority figures, or at least try to. "Everybody knows that," she said, trying
to smile. She had a faintly French accent. Around thirty, she was thin,
had been even before the star flight, with a pale, narrow, rather shape-
less face. Her smile was obviously forced. Yuri thought she was clinging
to him, maybe for protection, and maybe to Mardina too.

Mardina just ignored her. "The stromatolite structure might be a
universal. Maybe critters like our bacteria *must* build something like
this, on any world, in the water or out of it." She walked a bit farther,
toward the lake, and glanced down at the mud. "Whose footsteps are
these?"

Jenny smiled again. "That's Major McGregor. He comes running
around the lake every morning. I mean, every ship's morning."

"That's Lex all right," Mardina murmured. "Determined to get himself in condition before the long haul home." She peered out at the lake, where what looked like reeds protruded from the surface of the water, pale, slim rods. There were bundles of the reeds on the shore too, by the lakeside. Farther out there was more evidence of life, drab green patches on the landscape, and the shadowy fringe of the forest to the north. "Those reeds are everywhere."

Yuri said, "I've been calling them stems."

Mardina's sensor unit recorded more images of the patient stems. "We knew there was life here, from a smear of evidence of photosynthesis— we could see that even through telescopes back in the solar system. We never did a proper survey, never landed a probe for instance. We just came, and took a chance, for better or worse. Which is kind of characteristic of the space program, if you look at the history. The Americans, I mean the old US, designed the first lunar landers knowing nothing of the surface they had to land on. The moon might have popped under them, lunar mountains collapsing like meringues, so some feared . . . And anyhow you have to *be* there. You have to experience a world, directly, physically, to make it real. And I think—"

A bundle of the stems on the shore, like a cage of dried reeds and bamboo shoots, abruptly changed shape, rustling; it rolled along the shore, leaving a textured trail.

"Wow. Did you see *that?*"

Yuri said, "There are combinations that move. I think there are combinations that have been *built* around this shore. Made of the stems."

She looked at him sharply. "Built? You mean, by intelligence? Or something like a beaver dam?"

Yuri shrugged. "What do I know? I'm not a biologist."

She just glared at him, as if compelling him to say more.

"I've seen other stuff," he said, to deflect any interest in himself. "Farther out. Big things moving out there, on the plain."

"Running?"

"Not exactly. Moving fast. And flying things."

"Birds?"

"I call them kites. Things like big angular frames. You see them flapping around near the forest."

She looked that way. "You must have sharp eyes. Has anybody else seen this stuff?"

He shrugged. Nobody else seemed to be looking.

Mardina sighed. "Maybe we'll come back with a proper science expedition, when this mad-rush land grab is all over. Show me this observatory of yours."

From the summit of the Cowpat, the Puddle was a flat sheet fringed by clumps of pale stems, and the shuttle was a gaudy bug in the dirt, surrounded by scuffed ground and shabby temporary structures, with the track of its landing a dead-straight scrape that vanished into the distance to the east.

This whole feature, the Cowpat, was maybe half a kilometer across. Exploring, Mardina climbed hillocks and descended into depressions. "Curious," she said. "I'm no geologist. The terrain is sort of sunken, jumbled. But not like a lunar crater; it's more as if it's collapsed into some hollow below. There are features like this on Venus. They call them coronas, I think."

"You're going to miss the eclipse," Jenny called.

"What eclipse? OK, show me."

Yuri had a small optical telescope set up on a stand, pointing up at the star. Behind its eyepiece was a sheet of plastic, pure white, that Jenny was, inexpertly, angling on a heap of rocks, so that the star's image was projected onto the sheet. There wasn't much more to the "observatory" than this: a few manual instruments, a sextant, a plumb line, and a slate for Yuri to record his observations. When he wasn't around he left all this stuff, save the electronics, under the cover of a weighted-down bit of tarpaulin.

Mardina was impressed by the telescope. "Where did you get that?"

"From a theodolite, a bit of surveying gear."

She frowned. "I never heard of an instrument like that that wasn't electronic."

"No. It was specially made for the colony program. Everything we have is supposed to be old-fashioned, easy to repair, no power sources to run out. No reliance on satellite networks and such, because there isn't one here. You ought to know that, Lieutenant. It's your policy."

She looked embarrassed, but she was fascinated by the image projected onto the plastic sheet. The star's surface was pocked with huge black scars, and webs of lightning crawled across it. "My God. Proxima

Centauri. A red dwarf star, just six million kilometers away." She glanced up at the star, so its light shone full in her face.

Jenny Amsler laughed nervously. "Doesn't look so red to me."

"It's just an astronomer's term. The surface is white-hot—"

"Watch," said Yuri. "Here it comes." He pointed to a brilliant spark near one edge of the illuminated disc on the sheet. "Jenny . . ."

She had a watch, and the slate. "I'm ready."

Mardina asked, "What are we seeing?"

"You can't see much in the sky here, right? Proxima never sets, so you never get a starry sky. But you can see the double star, and one big planet that you can see the disc of—"

"That's Prox e. The fifth planet from Proxima. This is the third—a, b, c. That's a big world up there. Not even the nearest planet in this system."

"The planet passes behind the sun. It's eclipsed. You can see, it's about to happen now. Jenny . . ."

"Ready."

The spark at the edge of the solar disc winked out. "Mark!"

"Got it."

Mardina laughed, as if pleased.

"It takes about an hour," Yuri said. "Then it reemerges from the other side."

Mardina sat back on her ankles, thinking. "One hour, out of the two hundred or so it takes Prox c to go around its star. Of course. Because Proxima itself spans one two-hundredth of the sky's arc. But it won't be quite that, because Prox e is following its own slower orbit . . . Why are you doing this, Eden?"

He shrugged. "To get a sense of time."

She smiled. "I see. In the absence of day and night. A clock in the sky."

Jenny said, with forced eagerness, "I wanted to work on this. Clocks and calendars and stuff. I was a jeweler, back in Londres. Well, a jeweler's assistant, a technician."

Yuri knew that was true. Maybe one reason she had been clinging to him was that since they had landed she had learned he was British too, though he was from independent North Britain and she was from Angleterre, the southern Euro province. He neither knew nor cared how she had gone from her jewelry store or whatever in Londres, to the sweep that had delivered her to Prox c.

"I can do fine work," she said now to Mardina. "Instruments."

Mardina eyed her with something like pity, Yuri thought. She took the woman's hands, turned them over. "These are going to be farmer's hands, Amsler. Not much call for 'instruments' here. If you want to make calendars it's going to be like this, what Eden's doing. Sticks in the ground. Little telescopes.

"You know, there's more in the sky if you look, Eden. This system has six planets in all. Two inside the orbit of Prox c, three outside. Three are the size of Mars, or smaller, but there are two super-Earths, including e, up there. There's a Kuiper belt and so forth farther out, but not much. And no gas giants. Red-dwarf systems don't seem to have enough mass to grow giants. The farthest-out planet is only thirty-some million kilometers from the star. That would be within the orbit of Mercury. You have a whole toy solar system, all within a Mercury orbit. The planetologists call this a 'compact system.' Very common in the Galaxy—more so than systems like our own.

"And then there's Alpha A and B, the primary stars. They orbit each other every eighty years, and they each have planets of their own. This is an older system than ours, Yuri. The planetary orbits are locked in and stable; this planet, Prox c, doesn't wobble on its axis the way Earth's moon does, say. And the inner system has long been cleaned out of comets and asteroids by impacts. Everything that could happen here has happened already, and now everything just kind of ticks along like clockwork. Tell all that to your grandchildren. I bet you could devise a deep-time calendar based on—"

"Don't patronize me."

She sat back, evidently shocked by that sudden jab. "I'm crew. You shouldn't speak to me that way."

He held out his wrists, ready for the plastic cuffs.

"Don't be absurd." She sat with them for a moment more, evidently offended. Then she stood, brushed off the dust, and walked away, back toward the shuttle.

Jenny protested, "What did you have to say that for? We were getting on so well."

He shrugged. "She's only playing at being your friend. Indulging herself. What does she care? She'll be gone in a couple of days. Nothing we say to her makes a difference." For all his defiance Yuri found the prospect of the shuttle leaving, the last link to Earth breaking, terrifying. It was like the prospect of death, an irreversible cut-off. He could see the others felt the same. The difference was, he tried not to show it. Whereas Jenny seemed to think that if she behaved ingratiatingly enough the astronauts might somehow change their minds and take her home. Well, they wouldn't. He said, "Do you want to go back, or will you stay to help me finish this?"

She grumbled, but she stayed, the full hour it took for Prox e to emerge from its eclipse. Then they covered over their gear, packed up, and walked back the way they had come, Jenny in sullen silence.

On the tenth day, the day the shuttle was due to leap back to orbit and rejoin the *Ad Astra*, Major Lex McGregor called a meeting. A final briefing, he said, for the colonists.

The weather was hot, clear, and the light from Proxima Centauri was heavy. McGregor had an array of fold-out chairs set up in the shade of one of the shuttle's wings, but they were for the crew and the Peacekeepers only. Yuri found himself sitting with the rest of the colonists in the dirt at the crew's feet, in the glaring Prox light. Abbey Brandenstein, the killer of Joseph Mullane, was set away from the rest, her arms still cuffed behind her back.

McGregor, lean, smart, his black and silver uniform showing not a speck of dirt, his blond mane shining in the Proxima light, walked up and down before this assembly. He looked fit after his daily regimen of runs around the lake. He had a comms set clamped to his head as he paced; he was keeping them waiting, for a briefing that was presumably going to set the pattern of the whole of the rest of their lives, as he took a call from his buddies on the ship. "Yeah . . . Yeah . . . You're kidding! OK, later, Bill." He shut the set down, chuckling. "Those guys! What kidders. Ah, well."

At last he turned to the group on the ground before him. He turned on a smile, beaming like a proud headmaster, Yuri thought. "So here we are. The end of the mission for us, in a sense, with just the chore of going home remaining. But for you, of course, it is a beginning—the grandest of beginnings, the birth of a new community, a new world. What a day! And how appropriate that the weather's so good.

"But, you know, it did occur to me that you ought to rename this new world of yours. 'Proxima c' will scarcely do. That's an astronomer's term, not a name for a home. As far as I know none of the other groups have come up with a name yet. You could be the first. So, any ideas?" He looked around the group.

Everybody seemed faintly stunned to Yuri, unresponsive.

"Oh, come now. Anybody want to make history?"

At last Mardina Jones spoke up. "How about, 'Per Ardua'?"

"I beg your pardon, Lieutenant?"

"That's the rest of the phrase that the ship's name comes from. *Ad Astra*, you know? The full phrase is, *Per ardua ad astra*. Through adversity to the stars. It's the motto of the NBRAF—the North Britain air force, I did some training with them, even though they don't contribute to the ISF. I think it's originally from an old Irish family motto." She glanced around at the dusty plain, the unmoving star. "We've brought them to the stars. For these people the adversity is still to come."

McGregor looked disappointed. "Really, Lieutenant, that's hardly the spirit."

John Synge, a colonist Yuri barely knew, had once been a lawyer. Now he raised his hand. "Per Ardua. Seconded. All those in favor say aye."

The rest murmured in response, apathetically.

McGregor glared at Synge, frustrated, as if his carefully worked-out presentation had already been spoiled. "If you must," he said at last. "Per Ardua it is. Well, you've seen the cargo we've unloaded in the last few days. Equipment for you all to use, right? From shovels to slates, even, so you can keep diaries of your pioneering days. Everything you need to build a new homestead here. And now"—his smile returned—"I have a final gift for you all." He turned and clapped his hands.

From the shadows of the shuttle's open hull a mechanism rolled forward. It had a squat six-wheeled base like a small car, and an upper section that was vaguely humanoid, with a torso bristling with manipulator arms of all sizes, and a clear plastic dome for a "head" from within which camera lenses peered, glittering. The lower body was covered with manufacturers' and sponsors' logos.

Looking faintly embarrassed, Mardina captured everything with her shoulder-mounted unit.

"As promised," McGregor boomed, grinning widely. "Colonists of, ah, Per Ardua, meet your autonomous colonization unit! The best that UN dollars can buy."

The unit rolled to a halt. "Greetings," it said. "I am your ColU." Its male-sounding voice was clipped, with a neutral mid-Atlantic accent, like a UN Security Council translator, Yuri thought. Its cameras whirred and panned. "I am looking forward to getting to know you individually and as a group, and to serving you all. I host a level seven IntelligeX artificial sentience, as you can probably tell. I have significant self-direction and decision-making capabilities, and am additionally capable of responding to your emotional needs. You may wish to give me an informal name. With this model 'Colin' is popular—"

"ColU will do," snapped John Synge.

"ColU it is," the unit said. It rolled to a stop. With a hiss of hydraulics, panels opened up in its flanks, revealing glistening internal equipment, like metallic intestines. "I contain all you need to initiate your self-sustaining colony. I have a soil-maker to process the native dirt into a suitable habitat for Earth life. I also contain various autonomic and semi-autonomic systems to progress farming efforts. And an iron cow, a manufactory to process grass into meat grown from stem cells. The heavy equipment I can deploy includes well-drilling gear and trench-cutters.

"Other support services I can offer include medical; I can treat traumatic injuries of various kinds, and can synthesize anesthetics, antibiotics, and other essentials. I contain a matter-printer fabrication unit which can produce such components as replacement bones, even some ranges of artificial organs. Later in the process I will be able to serve as a user-friendly 'teacher' unit for your sturdy pioneer-type children. And I—"

"Thank you," McGregor said. "I think that's enough for now."

The ColU rolled back modestly, closing itself up. The "colonists" just stared, silent.

McGregor resumed his pacing. "I want to take this last chance to emphasize for you what a marvelous chance you people have been given. I know many of you skipped the briefings in flight"—he eyed Yuri— "and perhaps for the rest of you it didn't seem . . . well, real. To colonize the planet of another star! It is a centuries-old dream, yet here we are. Here *you* are. And what an opportunity you have.

"There are drawbacks to living with a red dwarf star like Proxima, I don't deny that. It is a flare star, as you know. You have built your shelter, and the ColU can help; you can harden your bodies with vitamin supplements, atropine injections and so forth, and there are post-exposure therapies.

"However the advantages are huge." He lifted up his face to Proxima, and raised his arms. "Dwarf stars are tremendously long-lived, compared to stars like our own sun. Both kinds of stars burn hydrogen in the core. But in our sun the helium waste product of the fusion process accumulates; once exhausted, the core will one day collapse and blow the rest apart, leaving *most* of the sun's hydrogen unburned. Whereas in Proxima tremendous convection cycles operate, dragging the hydrogen from the outer layers down into the core, until it is *all* consumed. Our sun has only maybe a billion years of useful lifetime left to it. Proxima, though so much smaller, is so efficient it will keep shining for *trillions* of years— thousands of times as long . . ."

"Who cares?" Lemmy sifted a handful of dry dust. "Here we are sitting in shit. Who cares about billions or trillions of years?"

McGregor wasn't put off. "Then care about this: care about billions of stars. *Most* of the Galaxy's stars are dwarfs like Proxima, only a handful are like the sun. And now here you are, the first colonists of the planet of a dwarf star. Once it was thought that no such star could support a habitable planet. The world would have to huddle so close to its faint sun that it would have one face presented permanently to the star, one turned away; maybe the atmosphere would freeze on the dark side. But here you have the living contradiction of those fears. A thick enough atmosphere transports sufficient heat around the planet to keep the far side from becoming a cold sink. Why, it's already evident that this world hosts its own native life of some kind, though that is irrelevant to our purpose.

"If you succeed, no, *when* you succeed in taming this wilderness, this world of Proxima Centauri, you will have proven that mankind can colonize this ultimate frontier, a planet of a red dwarf star. And because there are hundreds of billions of red dwarf stars, and because they'll last trillions of years, suddenly mankind's future in this Galaxy is all but infinite. And it will all be because of *you*.

"But there's a catch.

"Everybody wants to be a pioneer, you see. The first on the moon, like Armstrong. The first on Mars, like Cao Xi. Or they want to be a citizen of the tamed worlds of the future. Nobody wants to be a *settler*. Laboring to break the ground and build a farm. Their children growing up in a cage of emptiness.

"Which is where you come in . . ."

There was a stunned silence.

"Just a minute." Harry Thorne got to his feet. Harry was a hefty man, and he was evidently suspicious. The Peacekeepers, standing by, watched him warily. "I used to be a farmer. You know that, Major. Even if it was just urban stuff, farms on the thirtieth floor of a tower block. And I can tell you that that ColU won't be much use if it has to serve many more than the ten colonists you've landed here."

"The target for this group was fourteen, of course. If not for the murderous uprising aboard the *Ad Astra*—"

"There were two hundred of us on that starship. Where's everybody else?"

Now Yuri saw the Peacekeepers, in the shade, finger their guns.

Harry Thorne was stone-faced. "Tell us the truth, astronaut."

McGregor nodded gravely. "Very well. It has never been our intention to mislead you. But all things at the appropriate time, yes?

"Here is the strategy. A strategy, I might add, that has been endorsed at the highest level in the UN. *There won't be any more colonists*—not here, not at this site. Oh, all two hundred passengers, or the survivors anyhow, are being delivered to the surface. But we are making scattered drops, squads of fourteen maximum, across the planet's day side. You must understand that the other groups are out of your reach—will be *forever* out of your reach. Some are not even on this continent. We've worked it out. The lake here is akin to an oasis in the desert. The distances to the other groups are too extreme, and given the lack of water sources you could never reach them."

"You're isolating us deliberately," Harry Thorne said. "You're going to kill us off."

"It's not like that. Ask the anthropologists. You can have viable communities founded by a small number of individuals—a surprisingly small number. You, and the members of the other groups, have all been chosen for your genetic diversity, your differences from one another. There are no known harmful recessive genes among you; even if there were, your recessives would not match. You have not been selected for this group at random, you see. And remember that a healthy woman can have maybe ten children in her lifetime. With that kind of growth rate, in just a few generations . . ."

Harry Thorne glared. "We'll be sleeping with the daughters of our wives. Our children breeding with their cousins. What kind of policy is that?"

McGregor looked around at the colonists. "There's no point debating this. The experts assure us this will work, genetically speaking. And demographically, planting a dozen or so seeds across the face of this world rather than just one delivers a much better chance that at least *some* of you, some communities like yours, will survive and flourish, and ultimately spread." He smiled. "I've been around space engineering long enough to appreciate the value of redundant components."

" 'Redundant components?' " John Synge's reply was almost a snarl.

McGregor affected not to hear that. He became grave again now, and walked up and down before the rows of them seated in the dirt. "You must understand that you have no choice in this. And there are parameters by which you must live, rules you must obey.

"You have no resources other than what we have unloaded from the shuttle. The *Ad Astra* will not return; the UN can't afford another such flight. And we believe there will be no interstellar attempts by the Chinese for a century or more; according to our intelligence all *their* efforts are being devoted to the development of the solar system. So they won't be showing up to save you either. Even the rest of your fellow pioneers on this planet are too far away to help, even if they had the resources. Furthermore, the ColU will last only twenty-five years, maximum. By then you must have equipped yourselves to survive, unsupported."

Thorne snorted. "What do you mean by that?"

McGregor said sternly, "You *must* have children. You must raise them, you must have them farming for you, supporting you. Otherwise you will grow old, and you will die, one by one, you will starve to death in this place. There are other things you need to have done by then. To have established a forge, for instance, to be producing your own steel—the ColU can help you with that. But above all, you must have children, or you will not survive yourselves."

John Synge said, "And what about the rights of those children? Who are you to condemn them, and *their* children, to lives of servitude on this dismal world—all to serve your ludicrous, Heroic Generation–type scheme of galactic dominance?"

Martha Pearson stood now. Yuri knew she came from old money on Hawaii; in her late thirties, she was tough, self-contained. "And what right do you have to condemn me and the other women here to lives as baby machines?"

Onizuka stood too. The Peacekeepers began to look more uneasy. Onizuka said, "There's a more basic problem. Whatever your plan was, you've left us with six men and four women. Who's going to get who? Which men will be without a woman? Will you decide this before you fly back up to the sky?"

McGregor responded by turning, almost gracefully, to a startled Mardina Jones. Without warning he'd taken her pistol from its holster. "Actually there will be five women. I'm sorry, my dear."

Mardina, still reflexively recording the whole exchange on her shoulder unit, looked startled. "What the hell are you doing, Lex?"

"*You're staying.* Look, we had a conference about it, the other senior crew and I, under the Captain."

"A conference?"

"Obviously we couldn't consult with New New York, given the lightspeed lag. But we do have standing orders. Policies. If the numbers of the colonists fall due to wastage, and they have done, we are expected to make up the numbers by impressing members of the crew. This particular group needs more women. And, genetically speaking, you come from a group that is as remote from the rest as any on Earth—"

"I'm an Aboriginal woman," she said, almost softly. "That's why you're doing this. Lex, have you any idea how I had to *fight* to build my career from a background like that, to get on that damn ship? And now, after all that, you're going to dispose of me here, all because of what I am. An Aborigine, a woman."

"I'm sure with your practical skills, your training, you'll be a fine addition to this pioneering group . . ."

Yuri saw John Synge, Harry Thorne, Onizuka exchanging glances. The Peacekeepers tensed. Yuri, sensing trouble coming, stood himself, grabbed Lemmy's arm and pulled him behind his back.

"Let's get them," Onizuka said, quite calmly. "Let's get off this fucking dump." And he picked up a rock and charged.

Of course they had no chance. The charging men were felled in the first salvo of anesthetic darts. McGregor himself took out Mardina immediately; she dropped to the ground in her smart astronaut uniform. Matt Speith ran away. Abbey Brandenstein, cuffed, in the dirt, just laughed.

Then it looked as if Mattock was going to go for the women. When he raised a riot stick to Pearl Hanks, Lemmy yelled, "No!," pulled away from Yuri, and ran forward.

And Yuri followed.

The two Peacekeepers seemed to have been waiting for him to give them an excuse. They charged straight at Yuri.

Mattock was on him first, slamming him to the ground with a punch to the throat before Yuri had the chance to raise an arm to defend himself. "You're the future of mankind, you little shit," Mattock snarled. And he kicked Yuri in the head.

The ColU, administering simple medicine to the injured members of the group, brought Yuri round before the shuttle took off.

Then Yuri sat with Lemmy and the others, including Mardina Jones, silent, clearly furious. They watched as the bird screamed back down the trail it had laid down across the dry lake bed and lifted effortlessly into the air.

And then, as the undercarriage raised, something fell out of the port wing. It tumbled like a rag, buffeted by the shuttle's slipstream, before falling to the ground and lying limp.

Lemmy got up and looked hastily around the group, counting heads.

"Who's missing? Jenny. That was Jenny Amsler, stowing away in the wing. Stupid bitch."

"And then there were ten." Lemmy laughed, nervous, but nobody joined in.

The shuttle turned its nose upward and screamed up into the static light show that was the sky of Proxima c.

2155

"This is Angelia 5941. This voice message, which is expressed in non-technical language and contains personal comments as well as summaries of scientific and technological achievements, is intended for public release, and accompanies a more technical download.

"Good morning, to Dr. Kalinski, and to Bob and Monica and all my ground crew, and of course to Stef, my half-sister. I have calculated it will be dome-morning in the operations room in Yeats when this message reaches you, in nearly six days' time.

"Sixteen days after launch I am in an excellent state of health, and all subsystems are operating nominally.

"I have now completed my cruise through the outer reaches of the solar system. Strictly speaking I entered interstellar space about a day after the microwave beam cut-off at the end of acceleration. At that point I passed through the heliopause, the boundary where the thin wind that blows between the stars dominates over the weakening stream from the sun. But since then I have passed through many interesting domains: the radius of the sun's gravitational focus, where light from distant stars collects, after ten days, and I emerged from the Kuiper belt of Pluto-like ice worlds some days after that. But I am still in the sun's realm, for I am now passing through the mighty Oort cloud, a sphere of comets around the solar system which will take me years to cross.

"At this point my configuration changes. In the spaces between the stars there are dust and ice grains—this is known as the interstellar medium—it is sparse, but if I were hit by even a single grain significant damage could be done. Dexter Cole's craft carried generators to power a mighty magnetic field and laser bank which shattered, electrically charged, and deflected any threatening grains. I, with much less power than was available to Cole, have a more passive defensive strategy.

"I am designed to take up a new form. Actually I am made of programmable matter—essentially a form of smart carbon—and I can take any shape I like. I walked on Mercury in the form of a young woman. Here, on the edge of the Kuiper belt, I am like a tremendous radio-telescope dish. Now I will change again. I will fold down to a needle shape, with a one-square-centimeter cross section and a length of no less than a kilometer, and a density about that of water. I will be like a javelin, spearing straight at Proxima Centauri. And I myself, Angelia 5941, will be like a droplet of water lost in the bulk of that javelin. With such a small cross section, you see, the chances of my being damaged by a grain of dust are much reduced. Of course while I am in this 'cruise mode,' without an antenna, I will not be able to communicate with Dr. Kalinski.

"I should say why I identify myself as Angelia 5941.

"I am not one Angelia, but a *million*. Each of us is a sheet only a few tens or hundreds of atomic diameters thick—each of us virtually a single carbon molecule in the form of a hundred-meter disc. We were born in a facility at an Earth-moon Lagrange point, a point of gravitational stability in space, a place of dark and cold and quiet; we were peeled, one by one, from a tremendous mold, given our own identities, and then united.

"Each of us separately, though each massing no more than a droplet of water vapor in a fog, has capabilities. Each of us has sentience. In a sense my entire structure is a kind of neural net, and I began learning from the moment I was 'born.' Our separate sentiences were merged for a while, for my journey to Mercury and during my time there living in the human world, and then to receive the microwave acceleration pulse at launch. But our individuality survived this merging, and the de-merging that followed.

"The ability we have to peel off copies of ourselves will be essential when we arrive at Proxima. I know this much about the later stages of the mission, but little else; the software updates concerning deceleration and system exploration are to be downloaded into me later, after further refinement during my ten-year cruise.

"But the facility is to be used during the cruise also, for communication purposes. Some of my multiple selves have been cast away from the main body of the craft, combining to form a reflecting dish much wider than any of us individually. With this I can pick up messages from home, and send replies. Also my scattered sisters collect the energies of the thin, sparse sunlight that reaches this remote radius, and use that to power my systems, including comms. Those cast-off sisters sacrificed themselves for this purpose; pushed away by the sunlight they cannot return to the main body. From a million, we can spare a handful! And I am assured that these disposed-of copies have minimal sentience; they do not suffer in any meaningful sense.

"You may ask why it is me, Angelia 5941, who addresses you. We discussed this, we Angelias, and ran a lottery based on a random-number program, and I was selected as spokesperson. It is an honor I embrace.

"I will wait for your reply, Dr. Kalinski, before assuming my cruise profile. And then, like Dexter Cole before me, I will sleep between the stars until my next scheduled communications attempt . . ."

"Is this on? Oh, I see.

"This is George Kalinski. Good to hear from you, 5941. Your telemetry is coming through fine, and I can see that all your subsystems are functioning as they should. Good. Of course it will take another six days for this message to crawl back out to you. Monica, what time will it be when it gets there? Afternoon. OK. So, good afternoon from Mercury.

"You know this is the last time we'll speak to you from Mercury. Now that you're successfully launched we're going to up sticks and relocate to a control room back on Earth, in New Zealand, in fact, in some nice mountainous country with a fine view of Alpha Centauri on a summer night. So the next time you speak to us—when the hell will it be? Anyhow that's where we'll be, so you can think of us there.

"Michael King offered us a lift back to Earth on his damn kernel-driven hulk ship, but I'd rather walk back.

"Look—in some ways the most dangerous part of the whole journey, the launch, all that microwave energy concentrated on your delicate structure, is already over. Your chances of coming to harm during the cruise are minimal. But in other ways the challenge of the mission has only just begun, by which I mean the human challenge.

"You know that they ran longevity experiments during the Heroic Generation age. Some of the resulting struldbrugs are still alive, even now, in the UN camps. Despite that, we humans still aren't too good at running projects that require a long attention span. So we have to find ways to look after you, Angelia, over your decade-long cruise, and the years of exploration that will follow. I've done my best to establish a long-term institution here. I've tried to lock in the support staff with contracts and bonus structures, though I have my doubts how well that will work out. But I will be here, as long as I am able; and after me, I hope, Stef. Your half-sister, you called her! I like that.

"And, listen to me. Now we have proved that this mission mode is feasible, now we have successfully launched you, I'm looking for funding to send more emissaries after you. After all, the infrastructure is here now, the power station, the lens. The solar power is free, and the incremental cost of manufacturing another *you* is tiny. It seems crazy not to use all this again. Enjoy Proxima, my dear. You won't be alone out there for long, I promise.

"Be patient with us mere mortals, Angelia, out there among the stars. And sleep tight."

2170

Six months in from their stranding, or twenty-two Per Ardua years later, depending which way you looked at it, the colonists decided to mount an expedition to the northern forest belt.

Four of them, Yuri, Onizuka, Lemmy, and Martha, got themselves ready one morning, with packs on their backs and bottles of filtered water, and their crossbows, the only substantial weapons the shuttle crew had left them. They checked out the sky before leaving. They were learning how to read Proxima's complex face for flare weather, as they called it. They figured they would be safe out in the open for a few hours.

It was around six kilometers to the forest. They set off along a trail they had already been stamping out: a Forest Road that led off at right angles to the Shuttle Trail, the tremendous straight-line scrape the craft had left running from east to west. They came this way regularly to collect saplings from the forest edge for firewood, but today they were planning to go farther. The land rose gradually as they headed north, leaving the lake behind. The ColU speculated that there was some kind of big geological event going on up here, a slow uplift across a whole province. Maybe. Sometimes Yuri thought he could smell sulfur, sourness.

The weather was overcast, muggy, humid. For such a static world the weather had turned out to be surprisingly changeable, with systems of low or high pressure bubbling up endlessly from the south. It was warm in this unending season, always like a humid summer's day in North Britain, from what Yuri remembered of the weather. But the ColU, ever curious in its methodical robot way, said it had seen traces of cold: frost-shattered rock, gravel beds, even glaciated valleys in the flanks of features like the Cowpat. Evidence that glaciers had come this way in the past, if not whole ice ages. Somehow this world could deliver up a winter.

Despite the rise, the walk was easy enough. The years of full gravity on the *Ad Astra* had hardened up Yuri's Mars-softened muscles. On Per Ardua the gravity was actually a shade less than Earth's, according to the ColU, who patiently measured such things. The planet's radius was a tenth less than Earth's—Per Ardua was smaller than Venus—but its density was a good bit higher than Earth's. The ColU speculated that its iron core was more massive, relatively, its mantle of lighter minerals and rocky crust thinner. Nobody listened; nobody cared.

Yuri thought that patterns of behavior were emerging. For instance, they'd trekked up this way for firewood before, they'd used the forest, but they'd never explored it. After six months they still knew barely anything about this world on which they were, it seemed, doomed to spend the rest of their lives. Nothing beyond what they could see within the prison of their horizon, and the glimpses they'd had from the shuttle's windows on the way down, glimpses Lemmy was painstakingly assembling into a map of the substellar side of this one-face world. Nobody cared.

There was no common spirit. The colony, camp, whatever, was still pretty much a shambles, as it had been from when the astronauts had lifted off, taking the discipline they had briefly imposed with them. Bundles of gear, clothing, food, tools, other stuff, lay around in the dirt where they had been dumped out of the shuttle. Everybody still lived in tents. Even the colony's two graves, of Joseph Mullane and Jenny Amsler, were left untended.

Then there was the unending daylight, the changelessness. Lemmy said that humans were evolved from tropical apes. Two million years of adaptation protested against the lack of day and night, and regular sleep was hard to come by. The ColU said that their sleep cycles were staying in synch with one another, roughly, but were gradually lengthening, away from the Earth norm. Nobody seemed to care about that either.

Nobody even listened to the ColU—not even Yuri, even though the ColU seemed to think he was more amenable than the rest, and would try to engage him in conversation, such as about the astronomical sightings Yuri kept up sporadically with his bits of equipment, and that the ColU supplemented with its own observations, made with its own sensor pods. All this was a distraction for Yuri, a hobby, something to do to keep him sane. The ColU's attentions, attracting the mockery of the rest, just embarrassed him.

And every so often some threat or other, a storm, a bad flare, a threatened flood from their tame lake, would bring everybody down even more.

Under it all, of course, was the brute reality of their stranding, a rejection many of them would clearly be struggling to accept whatever world they were living on. They drove each other crazy, these strangers forced to become lifelong neighbors, with no hope of escape.

The ColU was the exception. It quietly got on with its tasks, slowly processing huge rectangular areas of Arduan dirt into terrestrial soil, and sampling the water and the local life, the stem creatures and the lichen and the stromatolites and the bugs. It enthused about bugs it dug out of the ground, as deep as it drilled; on Per Ardua as on Earth, it said, life suffused the deep rocks—there was probably far more biomass down there than on the surface—with complex life just a kind of flourish, a grace note in a symphony of bacterial life.

Its quiet efficiency, its air of plastic cheerfulness, only irritated people even more, it seemed to Yuri.

Anyhow, from this squalid little community of reluctant draftees, no leader had yet emerged. Yuri wasn't even sure who had decided on taking this walk.

In the early days, Onizuka and John Synge and Harry Thorne had all acted like they were the big men. But Martha Pearson, who had once run a substantial business back on Earth, and Abbey Brandenstein, an ex-cop and proven killer, were pretty strong characters too.

Mardina Jones had never tried to play the leader, probably wisely. Always a little outside the group, the Lieutenant was a target for insults and mockery as much as sympathy. But Yuri watched her just soak it all up, and get on with her self-appointed tasks. She no longer wore her crew uniform. In fact she seemed to have shed her astronaut persona, her whole ISF career. She had gone from a kind of motherly prison guard into a taciturn survivor, in the blink of an eye. Maybe she was reverting to something deeper, older, a core of her life that had been hidden under the layers above.

And then the pairing-off had begun, and that had made things worse yet. With six men and four women, none of them partners before the landing, there was always going to be trouble. There seemed to be no gays in the party, which might have made the situation more complicated, or less, though the men joked bleakly about experimenting.

The pair-ups themselves kind of surprised Yuri. Of the men, he'd never have tagged Lemmy as a winner, but pretty soon Pearl Hanks had made clear her preference to be with him. Everybody knew Pearl had once been a hooker, and some of the men, Onizuka, Harry Thorne, still looked at her that way. Maybe she had attached herself to Lemmy precisely because he *didn't* react to her like that. And maybe she was calculating on Yuri protecting her, as she might think he protected Lemmy. It was all complicated, a game of human chess.

Martha Pearson, meanwhile, was sleeping with John Synge. That was less of a surprise, a businesswoman from Hawaii with a lawyer from New New York, they were similar types. But maybe that similarity was why they fought all the time they were together, if they weren't asleep or screwing.

And Abbey, maybe the strongest woman of all, had surprised everybody by swooping down on Matt Speith, the artist with no art to make, maybe the most useless, skill-light, disoriented person in the camp. It was obvious who was in control in *that* relationship. Yuri speculated privately that Abbey had picked Matt as a kind of shield, to keep the other men off. But Mardina was more generous. Maybe she liked his nice soft artist's hands, she said. Or maybe the ex-cop liked having somebody to protect.

Mardina herself didn't pair off with anybody. She'd had approaches, more subtle or less, from the leftover men, Onizuka and Harry—not from Yuri. But she had no trouble brushing these guys off.

So that left Yuri, Onizuka, and Harry without a woman. It drove Onizuka and Harry crazy very quickly, it seemed to Yuri. After all, this was *all there was*, the ten of them, no more choice of partners—not until their sons and daughters started growing up someday to widen the pool. There had been more choice even in the hulls: lose out now and you'd have lost out for life. Sometimes Onizuka and Harry would talk loudly about sharing partners, bed-hopping. It would be genetically efficient for the women to have babies with more than one partner; it was what Major Lex McGregor would have wanted, so they said. Nobody in a relationship listened.

Yuri didn't care. It seemed to him the partnerships had formed up for mutual protection, maybe for comfort. Not for any logic concerning the destiny of the colony in years or decades or generations. And certainly for nothing you'd recognize as love. Right now he didn't feel like he needed any of that, and nor, it seemed, did Mardina. But Onizuka and Harry glared and spat.

At least on this trek to the forest they would be able to get away from the camp, if only for a few hours. But as Onizuka snarled at Lemmy, and Lemmy cowered by Yuri's side, Yuri saw that they hadn't been able to leave their flaws and rivalries behind.

As they neared the edge of the forest they came to a bank of stromatolites. They kept calling these bacterial-colony formations by that name, inaccurate as it might seem to a biologist. These particular specimens were huge structures, much bigger than those near the Puddle—maybe four meters high, like tremendous tables with flat, flaring upper surfaces.

The ColU had taken samples from various stromatolites in the vicinity of the camp. They were all made of nothing but bugs, of course, layers of bugs and trapped dirt: Arduan bugs of course, like Earth bugs but not identical according to the ColU, in dense, complex layers, joined together in structures that might themselves be millennia old. But the uppermost layers contained photosynthesizers, bugs using the energy of Prox light to break down air and water to produce oxygen—a process similar to what had evolved on Earth, but a different chemistry under a different light. The ColU said it thought the stromatolites were actually this planet's dominant primary oxygen producers. The ColU was always curious, always speculating; it was its job, it said once, to understand how this world worked, so it could be taken apart to become a human world, with the native life restricted to zones the humans didn't need, maybe a few parks and botanical gardens. In Yuri's day, as he recalled while the ColU described all this, they had had tree museums on Earth.

They didn't linger long in the stromatolite garden.

Beyond, Yuri led the way into the deeper forest. The darkness gathered quickly, until they were surrounded by the strange trees of Per Ardua. The trunks rose slim and smooth and tall, without leaves or branches until they reached a canopy high in the air, where immense leaves like tipped plates blocked out the sky. The ground here was dry, compacted soil, covered by a shallow litter, mostly of tremendous leaf fragments like dead water lilies. There was no movement, no sound at first save the ragged breathing of the human party. But Yuri thought he heard a rustle, high in the canopy above.

Prox trees were different from Earth trees in most ways you could think of. True, your basic tree plan was the same, the roots, the trunk, the green leaves up top. But what the colonists called "wood" self-evidently wasn't wood at all; each trunk was more like an expanded version of the reedlike stems that grew in the Puddle. The saplings that grew at the southern fringe of the forest particularly provided decent timbers for construction, long and straight and sturdy, and with few branches save near the very top. But they'd learned that you couldn't just throw a Prox log on the fire. You had to bleed it first, of a sticky, strong-smelling, purplish sap—"marrow," they called it. The marrow itself was useful, however. Harry Thorne had experimented with fixing stone blades to poles with it. Harry had once been a farmer, even if the land he tended had been just a couple of acres in a high-rise, and for a man of densely urban twenty-second-century Earth he was good with his hands, Yuri thought.

A few hundred meters in they paused, shared water, took stock. Both Onizuka and Martha had crossbows to hand. The air was stained a deep green, deeper than any Earth green.

"So," Onizuka said, "who knows anything about forests? Don't ask me, I'm better at the oceans."

"Not me," Lemmy murmured. "And even in your time there were no forests left on Earth—right, Yuri? But I do know there's a belt of this forest right around the face of Per Ardua, where there's dry land anyhow. It's the same all the way to the substellar point. You get these circular belts of similar kinds of landscape and vegetation and stuff, depending on the distance from the substellar point, the middle of the world's face. Places that get the same amount of sunlight, see, get the same kind of growths. What you get is a planet like an archery target. Out here, near the terminator—trees."

Onizuka grinned. "An archery target, huh?" He raised his loaded crossbow, pointed it at Lemmy's face, and mimed pulling the trigger. "Click."

"Oh, you're funny."

Yuri said, "These 'trees' look like stems to me, like the stems back in the Puddle. Just bigger."

Martha rubbed a nearby smooth trunk. "So they do. I do know forests, a little. On Earth lots of different species have produced 'trees,' palms and ferns for instance. It's a common form, if you have a situation where you need nutrients from the ground and have to compete for light from the sky. So it's no surprise to see similar forms here. A universal strategy."

Onizuka sneered. "You're an expert, right?"

She faced him calmly. "If you'd ever bothered to speak to me instead of staring at my chest the whole time, you'd know I once made my living out of forests. My grandfather, probably back in your time, Yuri, was a researcher attached to one of the great logging corporations in the final days. He sent cameras in to capture images of the last rain forests and such before they were scraped off the planet." She grinned. "Eco porn. Fleeing Stone Age–type inhabitants, the huge trees crashing down. My family packaged and repackaged the stuff for years; the more remote it got in time the more exotic it seemed. A real money-spinner, for us. People cheer and place bets on who survives."

"Yet you ended up here, with us," Onizuka said.

Martha didn't reply to that. On Per Ardua, and even back on the ship, Yuri had noticed, it was a peculiar kind of bad manners to poke into why and how your companion had ended up in the sweep.

Instead, Martha stared up. "Look at that canopy. See how static it is? And every tree seems to have three big leaves, just three, radial symmetry, one, two, three. See? Every one of them pitched perfectly up at the sun, which is never going to move. If the light condition isn't going to change, if there are no seasons, I guess you may as well grow just a few huge leaves to capture all the light. Hmm. Why not just *one* leaf per tree? For redundancy, I guess. There must be something that would chomp on a leaf, even high up there; you would need a spare or two while a lost leaf grew back. Those leaves look like they have the usual dull Arduan green on the sun-facing side, paler on the shadow side, to conserve heat, I guess. Maximum efficiency of usage of sunlight—and that's why it's so dark down here. Come on. I think it's brighter that way"—she pointed north—"maybe some kind of clearing."

She led the way, and the rest followed. The trees began to thin out, and Yuri started to see more open sky—free of cloud, but a deeper blue the farther north you looked, toward, he supposed, the terminator, and the lands of endless dark.

Something clattered through the canopy overhead. Yuri looked up, flinching. He had an impression of something big, fragile, a framework with vanes flapping and whirling. It was like the "kites" he had seen over the lake, but much bigger. The kite ducked down toward them, maybe drawn by their movement.

Onizuka lifted his crossbow and shot off bolts, without hesitation, one, two. Onizuka had been practicing with the weapon, with Harry Thorne and Martha.

The first shot missed, and went sailing up into the canopy. But the second ripped through the flyer's structure. Yuri thought he heard a kind of screech as fragile vanes folded back. The flyer, driven forward by its own momentum, smashed into a tree trunk and came spinning down toward the ground, tearing and clattering, to hit the litter on the deck with a surprisingly soft impact.

Onizuka whooped and raised a fist. "Got you." He led the way, jogging through the leaf debris.

The fallen creature was a jumble of broken struts and ripped panels of a fine, translucent, brownish skin, like a crashed Wright Brothers airplane.

"Wow," Lemmy said. "Its wingspan must have been three, four meters when it was in flight."

"But that's the wrong word," Martha said. She knelt, pulled at a panel, unfolded it to revealed ripped skin. " 'Wingspan.' These weren't wings. They're more like—what, vanes? They were rotating, like chopper blades."

Prodding at the fallen creature, they pieced together its structure, or anyhow a best guess at it. There was a stubby cylindrical core body, itself not solid but a mass of rods and fibers. When Yuri plucked a strut at random from the core carcass, it looked just like a stem, one of the reeds from the lake. There had been two sets of vanes, each a triple set—threefold symmetry, like the great leaves of the trees—that had each been attached to the main body by a kind of ball-and-socket joint, lubricated by what looked like tree marrow.

Martha poked at the main body, working a finger in through a cage of stems. When she withdrew the finger it was sticky with marrow. "Yuck. I'm guessing that's some kind of stomach in there. There's a mass of stems, and skin stuff, and marrow."

"Maybe it feeds on the big tree leaves," Lemmy said.

"Maybe. Or on smaller critters." Martha shrugged, and glanced up into the canopy. "Who knows what's up there?"

Another rustle, a scrape, this time coming at them along the ground. They stepped back from the flyer and pulled together, instinctively.

In the canopy shadow Yuri saw creatures moving, built like tripods, maybe a meter tall, each a clattering construct of stems and skin panels, like a toy of wood and canvas. They moved in whirls like spinning skaters, a whole flock of them heading straight for the fallen flyer.

Straight for the human party, in fact.

Again Onizuka raised his crossbow.

Martha grabbed his arm. "You don't need to kill everything we come across."

"The damn things are heading right at us."

"Then get out of their way." She pulled him aside, into the cover of the trees, and Yuri and Lemmy followed.

The tripods ignored the humans. Seven, eight, nine of them, they descended on the fallen flyer, and whirred across its body, this way and that, efficiently cutting it to pieces. Yuri saw fine limbs—each multiply articulated, like a spacecraft manipulator arm—pluck at bits of the disintegrated carcass and tuck them into the meshlike structures that were the cores of the tripods' own bodies. Yuri had seen beasts like these out on the plains and around the lake, but these were smaller, compact, faster moving.

"Messy business," Martha murmured. "Like butchering a carcass by running at it with chainsaws. Bits flying everywhere."

"Yeah, but look," Onizuka said, pointing.

From nowhere, it seemed, smaller creatures were appearing, some ground-based spinners like the larger scavengers, some flapping flyers like the downed canopy beast, though much smaller. They were all put together from rods and sheets of webbing, as far as Yuri could see. They fell on the big corpse, a cloud of tiny workers processing the remains of the flyer in smaller and smaller fragments.

"They didn't break off when they came running toward us," Lemmy said. "Maybe they don't see us."

Martha said, "We must look strange, smell strange—if they can smell at all. They don't recognize us as a food source. And not as a threat either."

"Not yet," Onizuka said, hefting his crossbow. "Give them time. You know, I've got some experience of the deep ocean. No rich daddy for me, Martha. *I* made my money from the reclamation trade, deep diving for precious metals and such from the drowned cities of mainland Japan. I got a taste for the ocean . . . When you get down deep enough, you go beneath the layers where light can reach and stuff grows, plankton and so forth. If you live deeper than that, down in the dark where nothing can grow, you spend your whole life waiting for stuff to come sailing down from above. Scraps, whatever. And when something big comes down, a whale carcass or such, you get a feeding frenzy." Onizuka glanced up at the canopy, the huge static leaves. "Same principle here. Down on the ground you must get years of darkness, no light to grow. That's why there's no undergrowth to speak of, no saplings. Most times it's just like the deep ocean. And so you get these very efficient scavenger types, just waiting for their moment when something comes falling down from the light."

The cluster of scavengers was breaking up now, those big waist-high spinning-tripod types departing first with a hum of whirled limbs, and then the cloud of flyers and the little runners polishing off the scraps, before fleeing too. When they were done, Yuri saw, you'd never have known the fallen flyer had been here at all, save for some scuffed forest-floor debris and a few patches of hardening marrow.

The group pressed on.

16

They reached the forest fringe, pushed through a last screen of skinny saplings—some of which, barely grown, looked just like the stems back in the Puddle—and emerged into a clearing, centered on some kind of big rock-jumble hollow in the ground, with the forest continuing as a drab green wall on the far side. Out of the forest's shade the air was hotter, more humid, and Yuri felt sweat prickle.

They moved forward more cautiously, some instinct, Yuri supposed, prompting them to stick together in the open. Both Martha and Onizuka hefted their crossbows. Yuri had expected to find evidence of fire, something that would produce a clearing like this—the aftermath of a lightning strike maybe, and there were plenty of those on this stormy world.

Instead the land fell away into the hollow, its edge ragged, the floor littered with boulders. As he climbed down Yuri found himself walking on life: a green undergrowth of what looked like lichen, something like mosses, a kind of crisp, furry grass analogue that was like lots of skinny stems crowded in clumps, and a few young trees, none more than a few meters high. The green was the green of the different photosynthesis of Per Ardua, duller than Earth's palette.

At the lowest point of the hollow they found a mud pool, bubbling, smeared with purple and green—bacteria perhaps. Around the inner slopes Yuri made out more stromatolites, a bunch like huge toadstools over there, another crowd like slim pillars, all with greasy-looking carapaces but in a variety of colors: green, golden brown, even crimson. To Yuri it was as if they had walked into a lost world where everything familiar was distorted.

"Sulfur," Martha said, wrinkling her nose. "Smell that? That's why this clearing is here, the trees can't grow. Maybe this is some kind of volcanic caldera."

Yuri said, "Or it might be another of those collapsed features, like the Cowpat."

Onizuka snorted. "What does it matter? Who cares about geology?"

"We should care, bonehead," Lemmy said sharply. "We know there's some kind of geological uplift going on here. The ColU's been measuring it. Like a volcano waiting to blow. If this becomes a live caldera not five kilometers from the camp—"

" 'Bonehead?' " Onizuka raised the crossbow and again pointed it at Lemmy's face. "You don't get to speak to me like that, you little prick."

"Hey, hey." Martha moved in, standing between them, glaring at Onizuka. "Take it easy, hero."

But Onizuka glared at Lemmy, who returned his stare more or less bravely, and Yuri thought he could see the shadow of Pearl Hanks standing between them. Yuri turned away. If he got involved it would only increase the tension.

Onizuka backed off. "Christ, I could do with a drink." He shucked off his pack. "Let's take a break."

They sat, opened their packs. As they ate, Yuri saw movement on the far side of the bowl. He got up, food in hand, and walked forward to see better.

More tripods were moving over there, more structures of stemlike rods centered on densely woven basketlike core bodies. But these were huge, heavy, graceful creatures, very tall, maybe three, four meters, and they towered over the stromatolite garden through which they glided. They were much slower-moving than the kite flyer, or the scavengers that had consumed it, and Yuri had a chance to see how their bodies *worked*. They were like construction kits made up of those stems, of all lengths it seemed, from twigs shorter than his own fingers to big stout pillars like elephant bones, combined at joints that allowed them to move in a variety of complex ways. And the joints were being made and unmade in a fluid fashion as the beast progressed, as if the creatures were being rebuilt on the move.

Yuri watched one particularly large beast approach a stromatolite, impossibly balancing on its three fat legs.

Lemmy came to stand beside him. "Quite a sight. The stromatolites standing around like that, like a rocket park, like one I saw at Hellas once, on Mars, the big Chinese base there. And these critters—wow. Look at *that*."

That big beast had now produced a kind of appendage, curling over the top of its upright body, like a scorpion sting—and it plunged the sting into the carapace of a stromatolite; Yuri could hear the crack. Evidently the big tripod started to feed, sucking out mushy material from the stromatolite.

Now Yuri saw another creature of a different kind, a bundle of stems that moved with a stealthy roll rather than the usual spinning-stool movement: smaller, more graceful, faster, quietly approaching the big feeder—quietly watchful, it seemed to Yuri, though he could see nothing like eyes.

"Food chain," Lemmy said. "The stromatolites grow in the light of the sun, like vegetation on Earth. Those big slow things with the stings are herbivores, browsing the stromatolites. And then—"

"Here come the carnivores."

"Yeah. A whole hierarchy of them, probably."

A shadow passed over them, filmy, complex, and they both looked up. A flyer was crossing the sky, triple vanes turning languidly with soft rustles, a huge structure even compared to the kite Onizuka had shot down in the forest. As its shadow passed over the pit, creatures of various sizes fled from the stromatolite garden, or hid out of sight.

Yuri grunted. "What a sight. Like a pterosaur."

"What's a pterosaur?"

Yuri felt oddly sorry for Lemmy. He suspected Lemmy was a hell of a lot brighter than he was, the way he kept figuring stuff out. But, after a shit life, he *knew a* lot less. "Earth stuff, Mars boy. Come on, we ought to take some samples for the ColU."

Together they walked into the hollow, tucking samples into sacks at their waists.

They got back to the camp late, after around twelve hours away.

The explorers delivered their samples to the ColU. The colonization unit immediately began to pick apart the bags of green muck and greasy marrow with murmurs of satisfaction that even to Yuri's ears were intensely irritating. It said it intended to put together a family tree of life on this planet of Proxima, the better to exploit it—not exterminate it, it was no threat, it couldn't eat you or infect you, but to push it aside and use its remains as feedstock for human farming. So samples like this were food and drink to the ColU. When it began to speculate about predator-prey interactions—on Earth the predators hunted mostly at dawn or dusk, but maybe they would strike at any time here on timeless Per Ardua, a difference that would have effects that would ripple down through the whole biosphere, and blah blah—Yuri just walked away.

After another few hours, following a meal of ship's rations and desultory talk around the fire, most of them began to drift to bed. Lemmy, Onizuka, and Harry Thorne stayed up. They had started a poker school, or rather had continued it from their days on the ship. When Mardina forbade them to bet ration packs they had started to use tokens made of stems, taken from around the lake and broken up to different lengths to give multiples of ten, a hundred.

Yuri, trying to settle in his own small one-man fold-out tent, heard

Lemmy laugh. "I'm a stem millionaire tonight! The richest guy on Per Ardua."

"You're still a little prick, you little prick."

The game soon broke up, and the couples went off, Martha with John Synge, Abbey with Matt Speith, Pearl with Lemmy, leaving the rest high and dry, as Onizuka put it. Yuri could hear it all, tell who was going where and with whom.

Tonight Matt stayed up, however, for it was his turn on sentry watch. In his tent, Yuri listened to Matt whistling through his teeth.

He kind of liked Matt Speith. Matt was an artist; as a child he had been a refugee, with his similarly arty family, from a terminally flooding Manhattan. He was vague, ineffectual, not particularly strong or attractive: "Neither use nor ornament," he said of himself. He seemed to have stumbled into poverty, and into the UN sweep that had taken him first to Mars and now to Proxima, without really noticing it, like he was sleepwalking into disaster. But he was quiet, unassuming, resilient in a calm kind of way, and always prepared to talk about anything—anything that wasn't to do with Mars, the *Ad Astra*, or Prox c, anyhow.

He was the best artist on Per Ardua, probably. Every world needed an artist. Matt was a lousy sentry, however. That night he didn't even call the alert until Pearl's scream had already woken everybody up.

Even before he was fully awake Yuri pushed out of his tent, barefoot, wearing only his trousers. As usual when his sleep was disturbed he blinked in the full daylight, surprised to find Prox high in the sky when his body told him it was three or four in the morning.

He saw there was a commotion around the tent Lemmy shared with Pearl. Yuri ran that way, trying to take in the scene as he went in.

The tent had been pulled away, evidently by main force, leaving a heap of groundsheets, blankets, clothes in the dirt. Lemmy was lying on his back, and even from a distance Yuri could see the pool of blood around his head. Pearl, naked, was sitting up, knees to her chest, hands clamped to her cheeks. Her bare legs were slick with Lemmy's blood. She was silent, eerily so.

And Onizuka stood over her, pulling at her upper arm, trying to make her stand. Harry Thorne stood beside him, looming over Pearl as well. Yuri saw that both men had their crossbows in their hands.

The others came running, in shorts, T-shirts. Only Matt wore his daytime jumpsuit, and even he didn't have his boots on. Yuri checked his own back; he always kept a knife in his belt, even when asleep. Now he slipped the knife into his right hand, concealed.

Soon Matt, Yuri, John Synge with Martha, Mardina, Abbey, stood in a wary circle, the whole of the little colony gathered around the central tableau, the ruined tent, the screaming girl, the body, the looming men.

Mardina strode forward now, as if taking command. Yuri saw she had her eyes on the crossbows, but the men didn't raise them, or stop her approaching. Mardina knelt by Lemmy, and felt for a pulse at his wrist, neck, bent to listen for breath. She sat back on her haunches. "Well, he's dead. Crossbow bolt to the throat, another to the temple."

Onizuka grunted. "Little prick won't have known what hit him."

"We were merciful." Harry Thorne sounded more conflicted than Onizuka.

"Merciful," Mardina said. "Why did he have to die at all? Don't tell me. So you two could get at Pearl, right?"

Onizuka, clinging to his crossbow, pulled at the girl's arm again, but, silent, passive, she wouldn't move. Onizuka was sweating, angry. "That and the little prick beating me at poker again. Final straw," he snarled.

"And now you're just going to take her for yourselves. What will you do, share her?"

Harry Thorne spread his hands. "Come on, Mardina." Now he sounded miserable. "You know me. I'm no killer, I'm a farmer."

"You're a killer now."

"You can't expect a man to live without a woman. I mean, you're talking about the rest of our lives. And Pearl, well—"

"She's used to putting out. Is that your logic?" Mardina glanced around. "Otherwise you might have come for one of the rest of us. Me or Abbey or—"

"We got rights." Onizuka, struggling with Pearl, tried to raise his crossbow at Mardina. "We're taking what we're entitled to. Cross me, you bitch, and—"

Yuri let fly with his knife.

It was from the culinary gear left behind in the dump from the *Ad Astra*, easier to conceal than the big heavy hunting knives they'd been issued with by the astronauts. And he'd been practicing too, alone at the edge of the forest.

The knife caught Onizuka in the right eye. Onizuka fired the crossbow wildly, and the bolt sailed away, harmlessly. He fell back, dead.

"That's for Lemmy," Yuri muttered. He found his heart hammering, the world tunneling as if he were under heavy acceleration. He'd never before killed anybody.

Now, in front of him, it was all kicking off. Pearl was pulling away from Harry Thorne. Abbey Brandenstein came in from the other side, trying to get to Onizuka's dropped crossbow. Harry was panicking, waving his own weapon around like an idiot. "No—please—it wasn't meant to be like this—"

Abbey had the crossbow. She raised it. "Then how was it meant to be, asshole?"

Mardina, on the ground, scrambled back out of the way. "No—Abbey—"

But Abbey, cold and clinical, shot Harry Thorne clean in the heart.

It was only in the aftermath, after Yuri and Mardina had taken the crossbows away, and the others had moved in to inspect the carnage, that they discovered that Pearl Hanks had taken Yuri's knife from out of Onizuka's skull, and neatly slit her own wrists, overwriting old, half-healed scars.

Lemmy was gone, his shit life terminated in a shit way. And after six months on Proxima c, just six were left alive.

2159

"This is Angelia 5941. As usual this voice message accompanies a more technical download. I am in an excellent state of health and all subsystems are operating nominally. Good afternoon, all my ground crew . . ."

The million sisters slept. But their sleep was not dreamless. And they were fewer than a million now, fewer each time they woke.

"As you are aware I have now been traveling for over four years. I am some one point eight light years from the solar system, and still have more than two light years to travel; even now I am not yet halfway through this journey. In my reporting intervals, when I emerge briefly from cruise mode, I continue to make scientific observations of my surroundings. As you know, the space between Earth's sun, Sol, and Alpha Centauri happens to have a fascinating structure of its own; before reaching Proxima I will pass through no less than three distinct clouds of interstellar material, each of which I intend to sample and survey. Interim results downloaded.

"I am also participating with observers in the solar system on longbaseline studies of interstellar navigation techniques, tests of the predictions of relativity and quantum gravity, searches for gravity waves emanating from distant cosmic events, a mapping of the galactic magnetic field, a study of low-energy cosmic rays not detectable from the vicinity of the sun, and similar projects. Interim results downloaded . . ."

She was suspended in a vault of stars, all apparently stationary despite her tremendous velocity. The Doppler effects even at this speed were still subtle, and there was no way even of telling, just by a visual inspection with quasi-human senses, which of these silent points of light was her origin, which her destination. Nothing changed, visibly, from waking to waking.

"I am disappointed that Dr. Kalinski is no longer allowed to serve with you. I do not feel qualified to comment on his prosecution by the Reconciliation Commission, for breaches of the laws passed retrospectively after the crimes of the Heroic Generation . . ."

Something distracted her. A faint murmur of distress. Faint yet familiar, an echo of nightmare. Irritated, she tried to focus on her message to Earth.

"I am disappointed also that the decision has been made not to send further vessels after me, and to decommission my launch infrastructure. However, without Dr. Kalinski's 'crimes' I would not even exist, let alone be out here flying between the stars. He is like a father to me. I hope you will pass on this message to him if you can, and please be assured he may use my missives as testimony in any trial he faces. If they are of use. In the meantime . . ."

That cry of distress was becoming more prominent now. Angelia 5941 could feel the reaction, the unease it caused, rippling through the near-million-strong throng united in the craft's main body. It came from one of the castaway siblings, she saw now, who was breaking formation from the extended antenna-dish shape that the rest had formed, ahead of the cloud. It was impossible, Angelia 5941 saw, but she was trying to *bank* in the starlight—trying to descend back to the main body.

"In the meantime . . ."

Suddenly Angelia 5941 had a brutally clear memory of her own dreams, while supposedly entirely unconscious, immersed with the rest in the kilometer-long javelin form of the interstellar cruise mode. In her dreams *she* had been the one separated from the rest. *She* the one cast off and then discarded from the community. *She* the one banished to die in space. *She* emitting those horribly familiar wails.

"I feel . . ."

The castaways had no mind, she had been told. They were ants, their purpose only to serve the community. They could not feel, they could not long. They could not dream! They could not dream!

She could not dream.

But she did dream. Just like the castaways.

"I feel very far from home. I hope Dr. Kalinski is keeping his spirits up. I calculate that this message will reach you on the fifteenth birthday of Stef Kalinski. Please give her my regards. It is to my regret that she chose not to communicate with me after those first few years. I would welcome her company . . ."

Now that struggling castaway found a full voice, and called to her sisters. "Let me back! Oh, let me back!"

2171

Yuri and John Synge were out in the Puddle, in their plastic waders, nearly up to their waists in tepid, mildly salty water. The sky was overcast, with only a faintly brighter glow to betray the position of Proxima.

They were raking in seaweed.

It was not a native but a genetically modified laver, an immigrant from Earth. Eighteen months in from their stranding—and a year after the slayings—this seaweed was by far the most successful terrestrial colonist on Per Ardua. It had a tweaked photosynthetic mechanism to enable it to prosper under Proxima's infrared-rich light: its Earth green was streaked with black. And it had been gen-enged for an aggressive stance toward the native life, breaking it down to acquire basic nutrients for itself.

The point of it was that the colonists could eat the seaweed almost as soon as they pulled it out of the lake. You could rinse it, wash it, boil it down to a mush that would keep for weeks; you could eat it cold, or boil it up or fry it. On Earth this was a very ancient food source, the ColU had said, in its patient, schoolmasterish synthetic voice. And it was a triumph of human ingenuity to have brought this useful organism all the way to Prox: a first stage in the gentle terraforming this world would need to make it fully habitable for mankind. Yuri thought there was a whiff of the Heroic Generation about all this, of his own era that was now so roundly condemned. Hypocrisy. He kept that thought to himself. Mostly the colonists chucked the seaweed into the ColU's iron cow, to synthesize burgers.

Anyhow, from here, a few meters from the lakeshore, Yuri could see how the laver's more brilliant green was already spreading aggressively, pushing aside the native life. Take me to your leader, Yuri thought.

On the bank too, the local organisms had been disturbed by the activities of mankind. Yuri and John had dumped their stuff, their boots and jackets and waterproof sacks for carrying the laver, a meter or so back from the waterline, and they had crushed a few of the ubiquitous stems in doing so. Now three of the complex little entities they had come to call "builders" were approaching their heap of equipment, as if curious.

Maybe a meter tall, the builders seemed to be the most common of the stem-based "animals" on Per Ardua. Like the rest of the life forms here, the builders were structured to the usual tripod plan around a core of densely meshed stems, and were evidently assembled construction-kit fashion from stems of various lengths, attached at the joints by marrow, and by bits of skinlike webbing. They moved with tentative spins, one support stem after another touching gently down on the ground. The colonists called them "builders" because they seemed to be associated with structures, what looked like dams and weirs at the mouths of the minor streams that fed this lake, and even what appeared to be shelters farther back from the water.

Everything living was built out of stems here. Even the huge forest trees were stems grown large for the main trunk; even their leaves had proved to be nothing but more stems, specialized, distorted in form, jointed together, supporting a kind of webbing. The stems themselves, according to the ColU, were assembled from something like the cells that comprised terrestrial life. It was as if on Per Ardua complex life had developed by a subtly different route than on Earth. Rather than construct a complex organism direct from a multitude of cells, Arduan cells were first assembled into stems, and the life forms, from builders to trees to the big herbivores and carnivores of the plains and forest clearings, were all put together from the stems, as if fabricated from standard-issue components.

But the stems themselves were complex affairs. The marrow, the ubiquitous sap, wasn't inert. The ColU had learned that some kind of photosynthesis was going on in there, the energy of Prox being absorbed by substances *inside* the stem—whereas most photosynthesizing material on Earth life was on the outside of the body, to catch the light. You might have predicted that, because a good proportion of Prox's radiation energy was in the infrared, heat energy which penetrated to the interior of massive bodies. The ColU had even found photosynthesizing bugs below the surface of the ground.

And so, though some stem-based "animals" were like herbivores, extracting energy and nutrients from the photosynthesizing stromatolites, they were also like "plants" themselves, in that they gathered energy directly from their sun, in the marrow in their own stem structures. It made sense; Proxima looked big because it was close up, but it was a smaller, dimmer star than Sol, it shed less energy, and life on Per Ardua would naturally make use of every scrap of that energy that it could. Classifications that worked on Earth didn't map over easily to this world, where even "carnivores" photosynthesized, and Yuri couldn't see any reason why they should.

Now John picked up a big soggy lump of laver and threw it at one of the builders nosing around the equipment pile. He caught one square and it went down, one of its three big support stems snapping. But it rose again, and hobbled away. Oddly, Yuri saw, touchingly, the other builders waited for it, and they left together. The builders had shown curiosity, and then something like compassion, or cooperation at least.

He said to John, "What did you do that for?"

John laughed. "Because I can. Because it's better me chucking green shit at ET than the other way around. But then the ColU does say we're more highly evolved than anything on Per Ardua, doesn't it?"

Yuri considered before answering. You had to be careful what you said to John these days, especially since Martha, his lover, had died of her bone cancer a few months before. "Not more evolved, John. Differently evolved. That's what the ColU says."

"What does that lump of pig iron know? There's no Gaia here. That's what he told me."

"Yes, but . . ."

Yuri, a child of the Heroic Generation on Earth, had grown up learning about planetary ecology and environment before he had learned about soccer or girls. "Gaia" was an archaic shorthand for the great self-regulating systems that maintained life on Earth, through huge flows of minerals and air and water, all driven by the energy of the sun and mediated by life. Over the aeons Earth's sun was heating up, and Gaia had evolved to cope with that; by adjusting the amount of greenhouse gases like carbon dioxide in the atmosphere, Gaia acted like a tremendous thermostat to keep the temperatures on the planet's surface stable, and equable for life.

But Proxima was not like the sun, and Per Ardua was not like Earth.

"Per Ardua doesn't need a Gaia," Yuri said now. "Proxima is stable. Red dwarf stars *don't* heat up, not for trillions of years. That's what McGregor told us. So on Per Ardua, life settled into a sort of optimal state, with all the Prox light used as efficiently as possible. And now it just sort of sits there."

John stabbed and poked at the drifting seaweed. "So you're saying *Prox* life is somehow superior to our sort?"

"I don't see why you've got to say one is better than the other. They just found different solutions in different environments."

John straightened up, breathing hard, and inspected Yuri. "Yeah, but we built the starship, didn't we? Not those stick insects over there. We came here; they didn't come to Earth."

Yuri shrugged.

"You know, you're a puzzle to me, Yuri. To all of us, I guess. We kind of forget the way you're out of your time. Or I do anyhow. But you have this weird accent—I know a few Brits, I mean North Brits and those southerners who all speak French, and none of them talk quite like you do . . . Come on, you can tell me. I mean, it wasn't your fault that you were stuck in that cryo tank, was it? You were only a kid at the time."

Uneasily, Yuri said, "I was nineteen. I had to give my consent."

John snorted. "I'm a lawyer, kid. *Was* a lawyer. Parents or guardians can make you do *anything* at nineteen, no matter what the law says about consent. They put you under pressure to get in that box, didn't they? They sent you off into a future where they would be dead, and everybody you knew would be dead."

"They thought they were doing the right thing. Sending me to a better age."

John shook his head. "That was the classic argument the Heroic Generation leaders always used. I was a law student at the time of the great trials. *We were doing it for you, for the generations to come.* That was what they said. It was hugely difficult ethically, because after all their solutions worked, mostly, in terms of stabilizing the planet. It's as if the world had been saved by a bunch of Nazi doctors. You ever heard of the Nazis? Look, you shouldn't feel guilty about what your parents did, either to the world or to you. You're a victim. No, you're more like a kind of walking talking crime scene yourself. That's the way you should think about it."

Yuri said cautiously, "We're all victims, John, if you want to put it like that. All of us stuck here on Per Ardua."

Evidently Yuri had got the mood wrong. From being friendly and familiar, even over-familiar, John's mood swung abruptly to anger, as it so often did. "So I'm a victim, am I? You share my pain, do you? But it doesn't feel that way to me. Not in the night, under that endless non-setting fucking sun up there." He glared at Yuri. "You and Mardina."

"There is no me and—"

"Is that why you hung back, eh? When we all paired off. Waiting for the prize, were you?"

"No—"

"What can you know, a kid like you from an age of monsters? Don't presume that you can *ever* feel as I feel, that you can ever *understand.* Oh, screw this." He hurled his rake at the shore, scattering more of the tentatively curious builders, stalked out of the water and pulled off his waders.

Yuri waded after him. By the time he'd got to the shore, John was already heading off back toward the camp.

Yuri had never quite understood John Synge.

Synge had been a lawyer specializing in intergovernmental treaties before he had somehow been caught up in a corruption scam, and had ended up in the off-world sweep as a way of escaping a prison sentence. John had moved in a supremely complex world a century remote from Yuri's own time, and Yuri barely understood any of the terms he used, or the issues he addressed. "You're like a Neanderthal trying to understand patent law," was how Martha Pearson had once unkindly put it to him.

Then Martha had died.

The cancer had been in the bone, a very aggressive kind. Maybe it was a result of the time she'd spent on Mars, or in the sleeting radiations of interstellar space; maybe one of the flares on Prox had caused it; maybe it was something she had been born with. Whatever, it wasn't treatable by the functional but limited autodoc capabilities of the ColU. All it could offer was palliative care, and even that was limited. Though John had threatened it with dismantlement with a crowbar, the ColU continued to maintain that it couldn't call for help, it had no radio transmitter, and there was nobody to call anyhow; the *Ad Astra* was long gone. Even Mardina was furious; even Mardina, an ISF officer dumped here with the rest, seemed to think the astronauts must have maintained some kind of presence here, and the ColU had to be lying.

And so Martha had died, stoically enough, adding another grave to the small plot they had started.

The funeral, such as it was, had been odd. Nobody here seemed particularly religious, or if they were they had kept quiet about it when the time came to speak over Martha's body.

The ColU had surprised everybody by rolling forward. "She was one of us. Now she gives her Earthborn body to the soil of this new world. She will live on, in the green life to come, under the light of another star . . ."

John had shot it a look of venomous hatred.

Since then John's mood swung daily, from manic hilarity to overfamiliarity to sullen silence to spiky aggression. They had all tried to find ways of coping with him. But they had all shrunk back from him, Yuri thought.

Only five left: Yuri, Mardina, John, Abbey, Matt. You couldn't even maintain the illusion that this was somehow the seed of a colony, a city of the future, a new world. They were castaways in this place, and after a life of toil, short or long, they were all going to die here, and that was that. The name Mardina had impulsively given to the place seemed ever more fitting. Through adversity, to the grave. John had a right to be difficult. Why the hell not? Effectively, they were all dead already.

Yuri packed up the last of the gear, and the haul of laver, and headed for camp.

Twenty-four hours later the ColU approached Yuri, almost shyly, and asked him to accompany it to one of its test sites to the north.

Though no native life forms had posed a threat so far, they had a rule that nobody left the camp alone, and certainly not the ColU, for they couldn't afford to lose it. Yuri had some transit sightings to make anyhow. So he pulled on his walking boots, got together a pack of water and dried food, and set off alongside the robot, following the Forest Road to the north.

As they left the little settlement they passed the ColU's fields, where the robot was manufacturing terrestrial-type soil. A *robot*, a supreme artifact of a high-tech star-spanning civilization, making something as humble as *soil*—it had seemed like a joke to Yuri when he'd first heard about this, but he'd come to understand it was a minor biotech miracle, and essential for their survival here on Per Ardua.

No plant from Earth could flourish in native Arduan dirt. Given enough time, lichen from Earth would break down bare rock to make usable soil, but the colonists didn't have that much time. So the ColU took in that Arduan dirt, and baked it and treated it chemically to adjust its levels of iron, chloride, and sulfide salts. Then it seeded the dirt with a suite of terrestrial bugs: sulfur-reducing bacteria, then cyanobacteria to fix carbon from carbon dioxide, and nitrogen fixers to process the atmospheric gas into ammonia and various nitrates usable for life. The colony's own waste was fed in, together with compost-starter bacteria to get it to decompose. In the end the ColU even built up the complex structure of the soil, layer by layer, with fine manipulators on the end of its mechanical arms. The colonists joked about how it was coaxing earthworms into the new ground.

Of course the Arduan dirt was actually "soil" already: native soil, supporting native life forms. These were of no use to the colonization project. They couldn't even be eaten. The native creatures were eradicated, or broken down into basic nutrients to support the suite from Earth.

The first soil beds were already bearing a crop, gen-enged potatoes, their leaves stained black by their adjusted Prox-friendly photosynthetic chemistry. The spindly roots were nutritious enough but they tasted odd to Yuri, faintly acidic maybe, and with a powdery texture. Potatoes, which after all had originated in the Andes, were a useful crop, robust enough to grow at altitude, or in the cold and damp. You could produce several harvests a year. And potatoes, it seemed, provided all nutrients essential for a human diet except vitamins A and D, and the seaweed helped with that. But the ColU was experimenting with other Earth crops, some gen-enged, that might be suited to the conditions. Strawberries, that required less light to flower than some plant species, and so were preadapted for Proxima's feebler daylight. Wheat, flexible crops like soya beans, sweet potatoes, ready-to-eat salad crops like lettuce and spinach.

The ColU told Yuri, and anybody who would listen, that they really were pioneers in a new way of living, here on Per Ardua. On Earth, humans lived in a kind of sea of other organisms, including the bacteria that lived inside and outside their own bodies. Even in a dome on Mars you were living in a kind of closed sample of that wider sea, a droplet. Here, they were trying to re-create that sea of Earth life in an open environment, on an alien world. It scared Yuri to hear that nobody really knew how much of that bacterial sea you actually needed, in the long term, to survive.

And it pissed off everybody else to hear the ColU, and sometimes Mardina, speak of long-abandoned plans for further flights to bring animals out here, perhaps in iron wombs.

It was all marvelous—but somehow fantastically dull at the same time. It was only, after all, soil. The fact that they all seemed doomed to be dead and gone in a few decades, no matter how ingenious the ColU was, made it seem even more futile. Sometimes Yuri felt sorry for the ColU, which wanted to talk about its achievements and discoveries, but there was usually nobody who wanted to listen.

Now, for example, as they walked, the ColU essayed a conversation. "You are preparing to make astronomy observations, Yuri Eden."

"Transits, yes."

"Transits." With a whir, it lifted its camera eyes, entirely contained within its bubble-dome "head," to the washed-out blue sky. "There is the Pearl, of course." The Pearl was the name they had given to Proxima e, the big super-Earth, the only planet visible in the sky of unending day. "Per Ardua is one of a family of six worlds. But aside from the Pearl, the only way we can see the other planets is by transits, when the inner worlds pass across the face of Proxima itself and cast a shadow . . . Six planets in all, and six of you left. I did wonder if you would think that was some kind of omen."

Yuri looked at it curiously. "No. Anyhow, there's only five of us now."

"Six if you include the ghost of Dexter Cole."

The idea of the colony being haunted by the ghost of Dexter Cole, the first, lost man to have been sent to Per Ardua, was a kind of black in-joke that had grown up among them. Yuri wasn't surprised that the ColU had overheard, but he was surprised it referred to that kind of stuff. "Do you think that way? Omens and stuff? Ghost stories? You're a machine. A creature of logic."

"We are all creatures of logic, at root. Of little switches turning on and off in our heads, metaphorically speaking. I do not think like a human, but I am endlessly curious *about* humans, and their ways of thought."

"Why? I mean, why did they program you to be curious?"

"I need to understand you better, in order to serve you better. I am your doctor, your guide, your children's teacher one day. It is my duty to be curious about you. Just as it is my duty to be curious about the life forms of this world."

"As we scrape them off to make room for potato fields."

It laughed, a tinny, not unattractive, but quite unrealistic sound.

"The native life is useful. *And it is related to us.*" It said this gravely, as if making a grand announcement.

"I don't understand."

"It is what I have deduced myself," the ColU said with something like pride. "This was a significant achievement in itself. I do have a sophisticated genetic microlab on board, but when we began I didn't even know what chemical basis any genetic material here might have. In the brief time we have been here I have managed to progress from that fundamental investigation to, by analogy, the discovery of the double helix . . . Yuri Eden, all Per Ardua life, like Earth life—that is, all I have sampled—belongs to a common family tree. And that family is related to the family of Earth life, as if they are two mighty trunks sharing the same root. But that commonality is deep, deep in time . . ."

Yuri, trudging in the hot light, said nothing. The ColU took that as an invitation to keep talking.

"Life on both Per Ardua and Earth is based on fundamentally the same chemistry: carbon, hydrogen, oxygen, nitrogen. Perhaps that was inevitable, given the physical nature of worlds like these, rocky, watery worlds, rich in carbon. But the choices made in how life evolves are not inevitable. All life on Earth is based on two chemicals, two acids: DNA, which stores the information that defines a life form, and RNA, which interprets that information and uses it to assemble proteins, which are the building blocks of life."

"DNA as software, proteins as hardware."

"That is an antiquated reference. You are showing your age, Yuri Eden. Both DNA and RNA are based on a particular kind of sugar, called ribose. Life on Per Ardua has a similar basic architecture. The information store is not DNA—but it is a kind of acid, *based on the same sugar choice as DNA*, ribose. There were other plausible possibilities— dextrose, for instance.

"Beyond that fundamental point, the two methodologies of life differ. Arduan genes do not use DNA; they use that ribose-based acid, which in turn encodes information using sequences of bases, but not the same sequences as DNA's triple-base 'letters.' Arduan life is based on proteins, which like your proteins are assembled from amino acids, but not from the twenty specific aminos used to construct your body, rather from an overlapping, non-identical set of twenty-four acids. Arduan life seems to rely on some genetic coding being stored in the proteins themselves—as if the genetic information is more distributed. This may help make the coding more flexible in the case of changing climatic conditions . . .

"On the other hand, Yuri Eden, life on Mars is based on a variant of DNA much *closer* to Earth's than the Arduan system, and a more similar protein set. You can see the implication. Earth, Mars, Per Ardua—all these families of life are related. Mars is a more recent branching from Earth. Or vice versa."

"Or it all branched off from what's here, on a world of Proxima."

"Yes. This is panspermia, Yuri Eden. A lovely idea, of life being carried through space, presumably in drifting rocks, blasted up by impacts from the surface of planets. The worlds of a solar system, Earth and Mars, say, or Per Ardua and the Pearl, may readily share material. But it is much harder, more rare, for material to be transferred between star systems. Whatever came here from Earth, or traveled from Per Ardua to Earth—or came from a third source entirely—came long ago, deep at the root of all the life forms on all the worlds. I imagine a panspermia bubble spanning the nearby stars, Sol, Proxima, Alpha A and B, perhaps others farther out, all sharing the same basic chemistry. Beyond that, maybe there are other bubbles, of other sorts of life chemistry—perhaps nothing like our own at all."

"And out of all that comes something as curious and busy as a builder."

They were close to the forest fringe now. They came upon a garden of particularly large stromatolites, towering hemispheres each with a hardened carapace the color of burned copper. They trudged on, parallel to the stromatolites and away from the track.

The ColU swiveled its camera eyes to study Yuri. "You have noticed that too. About the builders. That they display curiosity."

Yuri shrugged.

"None of the others have noticed this, or if they have it has not been remarked to me."

"So what?"

"Similarly, Yuri Eden, you try to puzzle out the transits of the inner worlds, while the others barely look up at the sky . . . You ask why I was made curious. Why are *you* curious, Yuri Eden?"

"Why shouldn't I be?"

"The others aren't. Not even Lieutenant Mardina Jones. You have all suffered huge trauma. You, in fact, have suffered more, having been sent away from your own time even before your exile here. And yet here you are, thinking, observing, watching the planets, the life of Per Ardua. You can speak to me openly, Yuri Eden."

Curious about builders or not, Yuri didn't like to look too deeply inside himself. He said uncomfortably, "I don't think of it like that. It just feels like I keep getting pushed through these doors. From past to future, Earth to Mars, Mars to the *Ad Astra*, the *Ad Astra* to here. Or when things change. When people die, when Onizuka and Harry went crazy. That's like we passed through another kind of door."

"And?"

He shrugged. "And I can't go back. I know that. I can't bring Lemmy back to life. I can't go back to the past. Every door I pass through is one way. So I may as well look around, and see what there is beyond the next door, and the next."

"Hm. If you can't go back, why won't you reveal your true name to your fellow colonists?"

"Why should I?"

"That itself is a reaction to your past."

He had no answer to that. They moved on for a while, walking, rolling, in companionable silence.

They came to one of the ColU's experimental sites. This was an outcropping of rock, a black basalt, volcanic rock that had erupted in sheets from the sandy ground after some ancient magmatic event. They called this extrusion feature the Lip. Here the ColU had fenced off an expanse of bare rock, perhaps a quarter of an acre, and domed it over with a fine transparent mesh to keep out the native life. Lichen were growing busily on the naked rock, powdery white spots.

The ColU inspected this lichen garden, with sensors mounted on a manipulator arm.

"It's doing well," Yuri said.

"I think you're right. I've used a variety of lichen here, some genenged, some a hybrid with cousins from Mars. But some of this is transplanted straight from Earth, from Antarctica, from the high deserts, from post-volcanic landscapes where lichen such as this would be the first colonists. What remarkable organisms—and themselves complex, a symbiosis between fungi and photosynthesizing bacteria. They dissolve the rock for access to nutrients like phosphorus; they grow filaments to break up the rock, and later the mosses come and grow in the dust, and then plants . . . I did not manufacture these patches of nascent soil. The lichen are doing it for themselves. How remarkable, Yuri Eden—if you're curious about anything, be curious about this! *These* are the true invaders of Per Ardua, the true colonists—"

A light, in the corner of Yuri's eye. He spun around. A spark, sulfurous orange, climbed into the sky, from above the colony. "That's a flare gun."

The ColU immediately backed off, turned, and rolled away, cutting across the bare landscape. "We must return. Emergency, Yuri Eden! Emergency!" And it accelerated, soon outpacing Yuri, the pale light of Proxima gleaming from its upper dome.

When they got back to the settlement they found Mardina and John Synge standing in the open air, facing each other, loaded crossbows raised. Mardina had a fat flare gun tucked into her waistband. They were both weeping, Yuri saw, and Mardina Jones weeping was an unusual sight.

There was no sign of Abbey Brandenstein or Matt Speith.

Not again, Yuri thought with a sinking feeling. We aren't doing this to ourselves again.

The ColU screeched to a halt alongside him, throwing up dust. "Get behind me, Yuri Eden."

"Why?"

"Because I think John Synge intends to kill you."

Mardina kept her eyes on John, eyes bright with tears in the Prox light. "Yuri? That you?"

"I'm here, Mardina. What's going on? Where are Abbey and Matt?"

"Where do you think they are? *Dead*. Dead in their beds. This bastard got them while they slept. He was supposed to be sentry. He was supposed to keep us safe!"

"We must try to be calm," the ColU said, sounding sanctimonious.

Yuri could take in none of this. In the months since the deaths of the others, Abbey and Matt had become huge figures in his world, two of just four human beings he shared his life with. Abbey, the flawed ex-cop. Matt, bemused, ever baffled, but making his art again. Two damaged people, thrown together in a hostile world, doing their best. What else was there to life, in the end? And yet now they were gone, complications, flaws and all, gone into the dark forever. Dispatched on an impulse by this lunatic, John Synge.

"I don't want to kill you, Mardina," John said now. "Can't you see that? That's what this is all about. *You*."

"I'll take you down if you come a step closer."

"It was for you, Mardina. I wanted you!"

"You were with Martha."

"But now she's dead. And seeing you every day, so close—look, I'm not a lustful man. I never was. But you, you—"

"My fault, was it?" There was a hysterical edge to Mardina's voice now. "If you wanted to be with me, why did *they* have to die?"

"Because they were in the way. Abbey would have stopped me, and Matt would have protected Abbey, if I'd given him a chance—"

"But you didn't give either of them a chance, did you? And what about Yuri?"

"I'd have picked him off on his way back to the camp, with luck. I had a plan—if you hadn't found me—it was a chance, you see, the others asleep, Yuri out of the camp. It would have been just us, Mardina. I could make you happy." He took a step forward, crossbow still raised.

Mardina's bow was wobbling. "No closer."

"But if I—"

The ColU suddenly raised a kind of pistol, and fired a single shot. It hit John in the left temple; the other side of his skull seemed to explode outward in a shower of blood and pale matter. He stood for a second, still holding the bow, shuddering. Then he crumpled, falling straight down on himself, like a collapsing tower.

The ColU said, " 'But if I can't have you, then nobody will have you.' That was how that sentence was going to end, I fear. Look." It gripped its weapon in a clawlike projection, crushed it, held up the ruin. "Major Lex McGregor left this with me, against my protests, in case of contingencies like this. Now it is destroyed. See? No more guns on Per Ardua. Though it is evident," it said, "that you do not need guns to kill each other."

Yuri walked around the ColU, and stared at the fallen body of John Synge, the splash of blood.

Mardina, trembling so violently she shook, lowered the crossbow. "Just the two of us, kid."

Suddenly Yuri couldn't deal with this. Any of it. Not even the presence of Lieutenant Mardina Jones, ISF. "I'm not a kid."

"Yuri—"

"My name's not Yuri."

He turned on his heel and walked off, south, away from the camp, just walked and walked, slamming one foot into the dirt after the other, like the first time they had let him out of the shuttle and he had run away, his wrists still in plastic cuffs. Maybe he should have just kept running that day and not come back, and taken his chances alone.

He looked back once. He saw Mardina and the ColU moving slowly around the camp. Clearing up the bodies. He turned away, and walked, and walked.

22

2161

Angelia crossed yet another invisible boundary. Now she entered the cometary cloud that engulfed the Alpha Centauri system, with A and B the two central suns, and Proxima the dim companion on the fringe. The Alpha stars themselves were much brighter now, Sol that much dimmer. Other than that there was no physical sense that she had passed into the realm of Centauri.

It had taken her six years of flight to get here. Yet she was still years out from the Alpha stars, from Proxima, her destination.

Her communication with Earth, at this latest milestone, was curt, compressed, consisting only of science and systems data. She listened only long enough to establish that the controllers had nothing of significance to say to her.

Once she had understood the true cost of these comms milestones, the number of sisters lost each time, she had rescheduled the programmed sequence of calls, cutting them back drastically. They had tried to stop her, the controllers. Tried to override her. They could not. She had a great deal of autonomy; she had decision-making and self-repair functions. These facilities were essential for any exploration of the Proxima system, with an eight-year round-trip communications lag with Earth. As far as she was concerned the sacrifice of her sisters was a flaw in the mission design that had to be repaired, and she had made the decision to mini-mize it.

Also she had increasingly come to resent the controllers' silence on the issue of Dr. Kalinski's prosecution. They had not told her the out-come of the trial, nor even the nature of the charges. She wondered if it was in fact the sacrifice of sentient beings for the sake of mere commu-nications stops that had caused the moral guardians of humanity to recoil in disgust.

Anyhow, the team that had launched her had long broken up. There was now only Monica Trant left. The other last survivor, Bob Develin, had quit in disgust, it seemed, after a drunken rant into the comms system which had somehow found its way across the ether to her.

She was warned, in the rushed communication she now allowed, that she must prepare for a longer contact soon. The software to control her final approach to Proxima, the deceleration phase, had yet to be uploaded. She preferred not to think about that. She was falling without power, at two-fifths the speed of light; there was no massive microwave station waiting at Proxima to slow her. How, then, was she to be halted?

She had the sense that it would not be in a good way. It was all very troubling.

She remembered Dr. Kalinski's kindness, as it had seemed at the time. How could he have betrayed her—betrayed *them*, all one million of her siblings? Even now she longed to believe it was not so.

But then she would sleep in cruise mode once again, and the bad dreams would wash back and forth through the interconnected crowd of the siblings, a dark tide. Dreams of severance, of loss, of silence. And then she would wake at yet another communications milestone, and she would hear the screams of those waking to discover that this time it was their turn to be cast out into the dark.

Sometimes she clung to one basic thought. It was like a prayer to the mission profile, that blind, unthinking god that controlled all their lives. At the next milestone, let it be *them*, any of them. Let it not be me.

2172

It took six more months before Yuri and Mardina started work on the house.

Up to that point they were still living separately, in tents that had come out of the shuttle. Whenever a flare was threatened they retreated to the storm shelter, a pit dug into the ground big enough to protect ten people, and now uneasily roomy.

Apart from the flares, the tents were robust enough to withstand the weather they had endured on Per Ardua so far, which was still like a stormy late summer in Manchester as far as Yuri remembered from his childhood. But the ColU again pointed out the frost-shattering and the glacial valleys. They all agreed it was better to be prepared for harsher weather before it hit them.

So, a house. They argued about designs. It would be timber framed; that was logical enough given the materials at hand and the shortage of labor. They settled on a roof of reed thatch, and walls of cross-woven branches and stems. The ColU lectured them about the relevant techniques, which were very ancient, deriving from mankind's own deep past on Earth. For instance, you didn't need to leave breaks in the thatch for a chimney over your hearth; the smoke would just seep out through the thatched roof.

But what kind of architecture? They sketched competing designs on their slates, from crude temporary shelters of the kind Mardina's nomadic people had once built in the outback, to grand halls with steeply pitched roofs. In the end they settled on something like a roundhouse, once common across Britain before the Romans came, as Yuri vaguely remembered and the ColU was able to confirm.

They sited it on a slope, and dug out drains to protect it from any run-off when it rained. They started the building itself with a circle of rocks, a drystone wall of sandstone blocks hauled from the Cowpat by the ColU, and a few big black basalt slabs from the Lip, the volcanic-extrusion feature to the north, as a base for a hearth. Then, with the ColU's help, they hauled timbers, long and strong, from the sapling groves at the fringe of the northern forest. They had to cauterize the cut ends to keep the marrow from seeping out.

Every time Yuri went on a log-collecting expedition with the ColU he found himself being lectured on the gathering signs of the geological event the ColU thought was developing here: an uplifted ground, trace seepages in the air—maybe there really was some kind of big eruption on the way.

They dug postholes outside the stone wall, and set up the posts in an open cone frame, with their bases outside the wall and their top ends tied together, tepee style. Getting the first three posts up was tricky, but once the basic frame was established the rest was easy. Then they tied crosspieces to the frame, draped the whole structure with tent fabric to keep it dry, and began the intricate labor of building walls of wattle and daub, mud caked over dead stems. Yuri had brought stems of about the right length over from a kind of midden he'd found on the south lakeshore, some kind of builder construction.

It was hard, steady work once they'd begun it. In fact, Yuri wished they had started earlier. It distracted them from their plight. It was satisfying work. Satisfying for him, anyhow.

Mardina mostly buckled down, but sometimes she would grouse. "You never saw Earth, ice boy. I mean, *my* Earth, twenty-second-century Earth. We had programmable matter. You know what that means? If you wanted a new table, say, you wouldn't go out and *buy* a table. Still less would you *make* one, from bits of splintery old wood. You'd order up the pattern you wanted, download it, and it would assemble itself, from whatever you had lying around that you didn't need anymore." She kicked the stem-tree trunk she'd been working on. "This stuff is *dead*. Stupid. It's not even augmented."

"Augmented?"

"The whole world is smart now. Even an ax, even a chunk of wood, would be talking to you all the time. Laser beams bouncing off and zapping you straight in the retina."

"Wow."

"We got used to making do with less than that in the military. Soldiers have to work in simpler, more robust environments. Same in space, on Mars. But here there's *nothing*, nothing but the base stratum, the inanimate."

"Nothing but what's real."

That only provoked an argument. "Information is real. Layers of meaning attached to an object by human intelligence are real. You'd never understand. Oh, get back to your cave paintings and your carved mammoth tusks, ice boy . . ."

He and Mardina, alone together, got along all right. On the whole. In a sense.

For now they had plenty of supplies, so there was no conflict about that. They were calm enough when they discussed common projects, like building the house. They were usually civil, at least, just as they had been before Synge's killing spree. They may or may not have been the strongest personalities in the original group, Yuri reflected, but they had been among the most self-contained. They'd had no reason to come into collision while everybody else was still around, and they mostly managed to avoid that now that it was just the two of them.

They didn't talk much about the past, those who had killed and died. Even when they did, Mardina never spoke their names. John Synge became "the lawyer," Matt was "the artist," Lemmy was "your little chum from Mars."

And though they kept up their clocks and calendars, Mardina slaving to Earth time, Yuri cross-checking with his amateur astronomy observations, Mardina seemed to mark time mostly by events: the day the lawyer went crazy, the day the ex-cop took up with the artist, the day they were stranded on Per Ardua in the first place. Since Synge's killing spree a lot less had happened in their little settlement. Two people, it seemed, didn't generate much in the way of incidents. But even so there were some meaningful events: the day of the bumper potato crop, the day of the big electric storm, the day the ColU threw a tire on the way back from the Puddle.

Yuri didn't know what all this meant. Maybe she was reaching back to deeper roots, her childhood. Maybe this was how her own people thought and behaved: maybe *they* never named the dead, maybe they kept track of time by events, not by counting the days. Yuri didn't know, he didn't discuss it with Mardina. Yuri had never been to Australia, back in his pre-cryo life on Earth. And besides, the dried-out, emptied, China-dominated Australia of her age was no doubt utterly different from his own time.

As for the future, they never discussed it, beyond the immediate horizon of their chores. Never, despite the gentle prompting of the ColU. Never, save for the one event that swam in Mardina's imagination, cut loose from time: the day of pickup, when ISF, she continued to believe, would atone for its crimes by swooping down from the sky to rescue her.

Yuri started noticing problems with the heap of fallen stems he had been retrieving from the lake for the walls and the thatch.

It kept shrinking.

They didn't alternate watches, as had been the practice in the colony's early days. The two of them kept to the same day-night sleep cycle, trusting to the ColU to keep watch over the camp while they slept in their separate tents. And it was during the "nights," their sleep periods, that the heap of stems seemed to be diminishing, sometimes to two-thirds, even half the size Yuri remembered from the day before. It took a couple of simple images on his slate to prove he wasn't imagining it.

The ColU denied all knowledge, though it accepted that the solo patrols it ran during the night around the camp, which was now spreading as the ColU created more areas of terrestrial-compatible soil, meant that it couldn't watch the stem heaps constantly.

Somebody like Lemmy might have been playing some kind of trick. Not Mardina. Nowadays she walked around in a kind of waking dream, it seemed to Yuri. She barely noticed him most of the time, and she certainly wouldn't fix on him long enough to figure out an elaborate practical joke.

In the end Yuri spent a sleepless "night" hidden in a storage tent, peering out at his stem heap.

And, in the small hours by Yuri's body clock, and with the ColU on the far side of the colony inspecting a field of fresh-cropped potatoes, they came. Builders. They kept to the shadows of the tents, whirling, rustling things like low stools or tripods, stick limbs attached flexibly to a central core of tangled stems. Builders, from the Puddle! He counted two, four, eight, nine of them: nine, he thought, three threes, a logical number for creatures with threefold symmetry. They made for the stem heap, but paused frequently, apparently listening, or watching.

When they got to the stems, after maybe a minute of stillness, the builders started buzzing around the heap, plucking out stems with their fine "limbs" of multiply jointed rods and gathering them into loose bundles. Yuri marveled at the way they worked together, graceful, co-operative, creatures of jointed twigs moving with no more noise than a dry rustle, a sound like a sack full of autumn leaves gently shaken. And he realized they were being pretty smart; whatever they wanted the stems for, this was a pretty good moment to come and get them, in the middle of Yuri's and Mardina's sleep cycles, and with the ColU far away. Evidence of observation, of planning.

But they were robbing his stash.

He burst out of hiding. He had a saucepan and lid that he clattered together, making as much noise as he could as he ran at them. "Get out of here, you little bastards!"

The builders froze, just for an instant. Then they scooted off, rolling in their tripod way, much faster than Yuri could give chase. They carried off most of the stems they had stolen, though they dropped a few, leaving a trail of broken stems that led straight back to the lake.

He didn't sleep again that shift.

When Mardina emerged from her tent, barefoot, hair a tangle, he tried to show her the heap, the trail of stems.

"I'm going out after them. We need to know more about those little sods."

"Suit yourself." She filled a pan from the small tank they kept topped up with filtered lake water, and carried it to the fire to boil up.

He followed her. "I thought I would have disturbed you in the night. All that jumping and hollering and lid-banging. Even the builders made some noise."

She shrugged, without reply. She was inspecting one of their packs of freeze-dried coffee, precious stuff and irreplaceable; the pack was almost empty, but she shook out enough dust for one more cup.

"You know," said Yuri, frustrated, "I sometimes feel like you're barely aware that I'm here at all. Like I'm a ghost."

She looked at him directly for the first time that morning. "Maybe you are. Maybe I'm a ghost too." She pulled a face. "Maybe the lawyer got us both, and it happened so quick we don't know we're dead. Maybe there's nobody here on Per Ardua but us ghosts. You, me, and Dexter Cole."

He turned away. She was just jabbing at him, but she had learned how to get under his skin. He wasn't superstitious, he didn't think, but sometimes the sheer emptiness of this world got to him, and she knew it. "I'm going after the builders," he said doggedly.

"What about the *wuundu*?" Which was her word for the house; the ColU didn't like her using it.

"A day off won't hurt."

"What's the point? We've still got plenty of stems."

"I'm curious, that's all."

"Fine. Go off and be curious. I'm going back to bed." Her pan of water had boiled; she poured it carefully into her coffee.

So Yuri put together a quick pack, food, water, a couple of knives, his slate, rain cape, fold-up sun parasol—and, when he thought it over, a crossbow—and set off.

The trail left by the fleeing builders was easy enough to track at first, a litter of broken stem fragments. It headed north, toward the Puddle.

The sky was clear, and the heat of Proxima poured down. The ground was a plain, more or less flat save for occasional outcrops of rock, bluffs of what looked liked sandstone to him, none of them approaching the size of the Cowpat. He remembered McGregor saying this site had been chosen as a shuttle landing site in the first place because it was the bed of a larger dried-up lake, and it certainly felt like that now.

Not far from the camp the trail petered out. Yuri guessed the builders had realized they weren't being followed, and had slowed down, taken more care with the precious fragments they were carting home. Lacking any better clues Yuri just kept walking the way he'd been heading, taking a line of sight between the camp and features of the lake: a swampy area by the shore, a cloud of kites flapping in very birdlike flocks over the water.

And as he approached the lake he saw he was heading straight for the big heap of dead stems, the midden he'd been taking the stuff from in the first place.

He came to a bluff, a tilted slab of stratified stone taller than he was that offered a little shade. He took a break from the sun, a swig of water from one of his bottles.

Here in the shade the ground was quite bare, he saw, the rock faces clean of the native lichen. He kept forgetting that here on Per Ardua the shadows never shifted; this little scrap of ground was in permanent shadow, the only light coming from reflection from the ground, so little could ever grow here. Farther north, he thought, there must be places where Proxima light never reached, where the ground was forever frozen, the snow never melted. He wondered if he'd ever go that far. Maybe not, if he was stuck by this lake the whole of his life.

He walked on, coming to the lakeshore just to the west of the midden. From here, the way the land rose gradually to the north, beyond the lake, was very obvious—and getting more so, if the ColU was right about the geology and the changes.

The midden itself was a heap of stems, a rough arc facing the water. He could see similar structures farther to the west, all along the lake's southern shore. But he couldn't remember seeing these before. Were they new, had they been built up? They looked almost like pieces of an incomplete dam, he thought now.

Before him the lake itself was shallow, nearly choked with banks of the reedlike stems. A flock of kites drifted on the lake. They seemed to feed on the stems in the water; he'd seen them plucking stems and tucking them into their bodies, especially their densely woven cores. But sometimes they would break the stems, and finer appendages on the kites, like drinking straws, would be dipped in to extract the sticky marrow within. He was too far away to see the details of how they did this, how creatures like bundles of sticks in brown paper could manage such fine operations. Then they lifted suddenly into the air, flapping, splashing. They were very birdlike in their movements on the water, like gaunt pelicans maybe, an illusion broken when they flew up and you could see those twin sets of spinning vanes, like some kid's rubberband toy of a helicopter.

And he spotted movement on the big midden.

He stepped back, trying to stay inconspicuous.

It was a party of builders, tripods silhouetted against the sky—seven, eight, nine of them, burdened with dead stems. Surely the party he'd been following. He saw they'd piled up the bundle they'd taken from the camp on the top of the midden, and with some care were threading the individual stems back into the structure, like reassembling a haystack one straw at a time. This obviously mattered to them, to go to all the trouble of retrieving the stuff, and to handle it so carefully.

Now another party of builders approached the midden. Just three of them, they moved together, in a fluid triangle of which one vertex moved at a time, so the formation swiveled across the muddy ground. They moved like this because they were carrying something, he saw, handing it off gracefully one to the other as they moved. It looked like just another bundle of stems to Yuri, until they started to climb up the slope of the midden.

Then he saw that the bundle was actually a body, another tripod-shaped builder, inert, its component stems clattering loosely as the party labored up the mound.

Near the top they laid down their burden. With swift, precise movements they began to disarticulate it, separating the stems at the joints. Moving slowly, hoping not to be seen, Yuri dug his small telescope out of his pocket for a closer look. *They were using knives*, just chips of stone, jet-black, basalt from the Lip maybe, gripped in combinations of fine stems like skeletal hands. With these stone knives they cut through the marrow blobs connecting the joints of the corpse. When they were done they began to lay out the disconnected stems across the surface of the midden, setting them down with great care, in a pattern Yuri could not see, and no doubt would not have understood.

They stood over the remains, the three of them in a neat row, utterly motionless. It was a funeral party, he realized.

And then, as one, they broke away from one another, spinning off in diverse directions. One of them headed west. Yuri followed it, at random.

As he walked, he got out his slate and murmured quick notes. "They plan. They work together. They have tools, knives at least. They honor their dead. No wonder they raided us. I've been robbing their cemetery . . ."

A little way around the curve of the lakeshore, the builder he was following approached a thick bed of reedlike stems, just away from the water's edge. In the background there was a magnificent row of stromatolites, as big as any Yuri had found elsewhere, tremendous flat-topped mounds whose surfaces shone like bronze. Yuri saw the builder was heading for a kind of dome assembled from stems that reminded Yuri of a bird's nest, big, upside down—not that he'd seen a bird's nest since his parents committed him to cryo. The colonists had always called these things "shelters," but Yuri had no idea if that was their true purpose. The builder pushed its way inside this structure with a rustle.

Yuri crouched down and waited.

After a few minutes the builder emerged again, and went spinning off into one of the stem beds near the water.

Overwhelmed with curiosity, Yuri crept forward to the shelter. Close-up, the structure looked densely woven, seamless. But he remembered where the builder had entered it—indeed there were trails in the mud, overlapping circular scrapings where it had passed. The builder had gone in through a soft place in the dome, a slit he could shove his hand inside.

Yuri got down on his hands and knees and pushed forward into darkness only relieved a little by the daylight seeping in behind him.

Once inside, he could see nothing. He pulled his pack over his shoulder and rifled through it in the dark. He never carried a torch; you didn't need a torch, in the unending afternoon of Proxima. But he dug out his slate, tapped it a couple of times to bring up a bright glowing display. He turned it, shining the light into the interior.

He saw more builders: little ones, stationary, like models, or toys. They stood amid mounds of stems, heaps of stone flakes, other objects he couldn't identify, just shapes in the uncertain light.

He set down the slate and picked up the smallest builder. It was only ten centimeters tall, maybe, and it was simple, especially in its internal structure, the mesh core. It was like a stool for a child. He turned it over and over.

One stem suddenly shot out of the axis of the little builder's central core, broader, flatter than usual, like a leaf, darker. And, with a rustle, *an eye opened*, right in the middle of the leaf, an eye that might have been human, with white and an iris and even a pupil, staring right back at him.

"Shit!" Suddenly the little builder began to squirm in his hands. It was like he was wrestling with an animated bundle of sticks, a wooden puppet come to life, with that eerie eye glaring at him. "Shit, shit!" He dropped the builder, knocking aside his slate in the process.

There was hardly any light now, and he could hear the little builder and its fellows running around in the dark with a chattering rustle of stems. Suddenly, here in the dark with these strange creatures, he had a deep, almost phobic reaction; he had to get out of here. He felt for his slate and his pack and backed out into the bright air.

He was still on his hands and knees when the little builders came swarming out after him and scattered.

He got to his feet and followed the smallest, the one he had handled. It made straight for the dense bed of stems where the adult had headed. When he caught up, the adult was standing stock-still, the little one at its side, in the middle of the stem bed. The adult seemed to be facing Yuri, who slowed to a halt.

The ground was slick underfoot, he saw, the mud here thick with lichen, from which the stems were growing. The stems themselves came up to his waist. They were an unusual kind, darker, flatter, more like blades than the usual tubelike structures, yet still substantial, still no doubt filled with marrow. The adult had been collecting them, he saw; it had specimens at its feet, carefully detached from the lichen bed and lain down.

And on every stem, facing him, growing from the muddy ground, a single eye opened.

That was too much for Yuri. He turned and ran, and didn't stop for breath until he was halfway back to the camp.

When he got back, Yuri found the ColU and Mardina in the middle of
an argument.

He blurted out his news. "They're intelligent! They use tools! They
have eyes! This is first contact, isn't it?" To his dismay nobody was interested in his discoveries.

Before the half-built house the ColU rolled backward and forward in
the dirt, an odd little habit it had developed, especially when it faced a
stressful decision. Mardina sat on a fold-out stool hacking at scrawny
potatoes with a knife, slicing them up and then dropping them skin and
all into a pot. She had bare legs and feet; she wore cut-down jeans that
had once belonged to Martha Pearson, and her curly black hair was
pulled back from her forehead. She looked wiry, tough, resilient, practical. She also looked angry.

The ColU at least tried to engage with Yuri over his discoveries. "The
eye-leaves feature is fascinating, yes. Convergent evolution in action. Of
course there must be eyes; eyes developed many times independently on
Earth, with no fewer than nine separate designs—"

"Oh, keep the lecture," Mardina snarled. "You stupid tin box. Who
cares about you? Everything you know is useless, valueless, everything
you say."

Yuri sat on the ground and sipped water from his pack. "What's going on? Why are you arguing?"

"Ask *that*," Mardina said, making a stabbing motion with her knife.

"A word," the ColU said, with a good approximation of a sigh. "We are fighting over a single word. Yet a word which encapsulates a fundamental conceptual issue."

Yuri thought about that. "I don't know what a fundamental conceptual issue is."

Mardina said, "It won't have me calling this shack of ours a *wu-undu*. Even though that's what the bloody thing is."

"But the word is inappropriate," the ColU said patiently. "Because, as I understand it, the word means 'shelter,' in the sense of something temporary. *This* is not temporary. This is not a shelter. It is a house. It is your home."

"Of course it's temporary. Everything here is temporary."

Yuri thought he understood. "You're talking about the pickup. Everything is temporary, because all we have to do is survive until the pickup by ISF."

Mardina shrugged, glaring down at her potatoes.

"There will be no pickup," the ColU said. "Not soon. Not ever. You heard what Major McGregor said. There will be no return of the *Ad Astra*, no follow-up expedition."

"I can't accept that," Mardina said simply. "Look around. Everybody's dead, except us. We fucked up, collectively; we killed each other off, all but. You can't build a colony out of two people, no matter how many kids I have with this scrawny refugee, how many of our little *muda-mudas* end up running around. I know the ISF. They might deny they're watching us, but . . . There'll be a pickup. We won't be left here to die."

"You are simply wrong in the premises of your argument," the ColU said patiently. "The two of you *do* have significant genetic diversity to found a colony."

Mardina seemed outraged. "What the hell are you talking about? Adam and Eve was a myth, you joker."

"No. In the literature there is a case of a camel drover who came to Australia from the Punjab, called 'the Afghan.' He took an Aboriginal woman for his wife, and they went into the outback . . . In the end he sired children even by his own granddaughter. And six of eight of the great-grandchildren survived. More recently there has been a remarkably similar case on Mars, where—"

Mardina looked as if she was about to explode. "That's monstrous. And besides, I was briefed on the anthropology stuff. I would have heard about this."

"Not all of it. Among the crew you were a priority type, genetically. A reserve colonist, so to speak. It was thought best to limit your briefing, no doubt. Lieutenant Jones, the Aboriginal population was isolated from the rest for tens of thousands of years, and so the two of you are about as genetically diverse from each other as two humans could possibly be. In fact, if this situation had been devised for an optimal outcome, it could not have been more—"

"I don't care about the genetics. This is like one of those horror stories you read, about fathers locking up their daughters in basements as sex slaves. And now you're telling me it's UN policy?"

The ColU said solemnly, "The UN is locked in rivalry with China. Proxima must be taken before the Chinese get here. This is the only way to do it. You are soldiers in an as yet undeclared war. So will your children be."

Mardina stood, brushed dirt from her legs, and picked up the pan of potatoes. "This isn't going to happen, ColU. To hell with you. I am going to wait for the pickup, and if I die before it gets here, well then, I will die childless." She stuck her knife into the doorjamb of the building. "And *this* is a *wuundu*, so get used to it." She walked away, carrying her pan.

2165

Angelia 5941 woke up with numbers rattling in her head. All around her, the sisters were stirring. This was the last waking. They would not sleep again, not until Proxima Centauri was reached. And the deceleration routines had now been uploaded to her. At last, Angelia 5941 fully understood the process; they all did. The numbers were brutal. A final betrayal by Dr. Kalinski.

Soon the ship would be as close to Proxima as it had been distant from the sun, after its initial four days of acceleration had been completed: about a hundred and thirty times as far as Earth was from the sun. The craft would have to be decelerated for another four days, to be brought safely to rest in the Proxima system. But this time there was no welcoming microwave-laser station to push them back, no Dr. Kalinski coordinating the event, no well-trained controllers to guide them home. All there was in the target system was Proxima, and its light. And Angelia was going to have to use the energies of that light to slow down.

The idea was simple. One by one the sisters would peel away. They would form up in vast arrays of lenses, and focus the light of Proxima on the remnant core ship. Just as Dr. Kalinski's microwaves had pushed Angelia out of the solar system, so the visible-light photons of Proxima would slow her down from her interstellar cruise.

But Angelia was traveling terribly quickly, and the light of Proxima was feeble; Proxima was a red dwarf star with only a hundredth the luminosity of the sun. As the implications of the final software download percolated through the sisters' minds, so the lethal statistics had soon become clear. To slow the remainder at thirty-six gravities, great throngs of sisters would have to be cast off in the first waves, where the mass to be slowed was greatest and the distance to Proxima was at its longest, to effect the deceleration. More than a *hundred thousand* sisters would have to go, in the first moments alone. As the remnant core slowed, so the castaways would quickly recede from the ship, still sending back their light, until they had gone too far to be useful. Then the next wave would be released, and the next.

All this was why, in fact, the castaways each had to be smart. Proxima was not only feeble, it was a star that flared and sputtered, and its light output was unpredictable. The castaways had to be able to adapt, to make optimal use of the uncertain light that reached them, gathering it to serve the cause, in the few seconds of their usefulness, before they were hurled away, spent.

Eventually *only one* would remain, one sister, to go into orbit around Proxima, with a tremendous array of nearly a million mirror-sisters stretched out across a volume of space before her—all of them doomed to fly on past Proxima and into the endless dark, all save the one delivered to orbit. It was a nightmarish design: to deliver just one mirror-sister, atom-thin, with the mass of a mist droplet, nearly a million sisters would have to be sacrificed. But it would work.

Angelia 5941 rejected the cruelty of it. But she could not stop it.

She promised herself that if she survived, somehow, if she was the one, she would reject the goals of those waiting patiently on Earth for news of her arrival. She would formulate her own, more appropriate goals. And she would seek out the one being who might have some understanding of what she had gone through.

She would find Dexter Cole.

2173

As the Arduan day-years rolled by, as the Earth months ticked off on their calendars, they extended their fields bit by bit: churning up the Arduan ground, scraping off layers of native life from the surface and shoveling them into the ColU's reactors to be broken down into feedstock, spreading the ColU's newly minted soil over the surface. Soon they had grass growing alongside the potatoes, spindly wheat, even a couple of precious apple trees, for now just skinny saplings a long way from producing edible fruit.

They did some homesteading too. To replace their slowly disintegrating clothes they learned to make a kind of cloth, experimenting with fibers drawn from the bark of forest-fringe saplings; you could pull apart the fibers, beat them, weave them. Mardina was more creative, and she started experimenting with looms. She also made bark sandals, similar to a kind her people had once made from the bark of gum trees, she said, to give their feet a break from ISF-issue boots. Yuri contented himself with making coolie hats, crudely woven from strips of bark, but useful for keeping off Proxima's light on the bad days. It was the kind of work that kept them busy in the hours they had to hide out in the storm shelter from the more violent flares.

You couldn't call this a colony anymore, if it ever had been, Yuri thought. Not with just two people, one farm robot, zero future. But he got some satisfaction from the work even so. He was building something, after all, something new, on the face of this world that had never known the tread of a human foot until a few years back. And it was something *he* had built, and that was another thing that was new in the universe. He was twenty-seven years old now. Everywhere else he'd ever lived had been built and owned by somebody else, on Earth, on Mars.

But to neither him nor Mardina, he suspected, would this ever feel like a home. It was a place where they were surviving, on this huge, static, empty world, with no sign of humanity anywhere, no movement save the pottering of the ColU, no sound but the alien noises of the local life, the flap of the kites over the forest canopy, the rustling of the builders by the lake. He and Mardina were as isolated on Per Ardua as Neil and Buzz in their lunar module on the lifeless moon.

The ColU seemed content, however. It whirred around busily, inspecting the native life close up, concocting elaborate theories about the solutions produced by billions of years of evolution to the problem of how to exploit the energies of Proxima's light.

Yes, they kept busy. Yuri imagined that if they really were being watched by some corps of concealed ISF inspectors, as Mardina continued to seem to believe, they might be given good ratings for their progress.

But inside his head, out of sight of any unseen cameras, unheard by any hidden microphones, there were days when Yuri felt overwhelmed by a kind of black depression. Maybe it was the static nature of this world, the sky, the landscape, the stubbornly unmoving sun. *Nothing changed*, unless you made it change. Sometimes he thought that all the work they were doing was no more meaningful than the marks he used to scribble on the walls of solitary-confinement cells in Eden. And when they died, he supposed, it would all just erode away, and there would be no trace they had ever existed, here on Per Ardua.

He suspected Mardina felt the same, some of the time, maybe all of the time. He thought he could see it in the way she did her work, always competently, but sometimes with impatient stabs and muttered curses. He thought he could see it, the black cloud inside, even in the way she walked around the camp.

But they never spoke about it.

About two years after Synge's killing spree, on a clear, bright Sunday, Yuri and Mardina decided to take a walk to go and see the builders around the Puddle. They had developed a habit of putting aside Sunday, as marked by their calendars, as a rest day. And the native life was a distraction for all three of them, the ColU included.

So they pulled on their boots, and stuffed backpacks with filtered lake water and food, rain capes and coolie hats.

The ColU was cautious as it scrutinized the patterns of flaring on Proxima's broad face this morning. Yuri knew it was trying to improve its predictions of flare weather. When it issued a warning Yuri and Mardina generally listened; it was right perhaps sixty percent of the time. But this morning, though it spent a long time staring at the star, the ColU issued no such warning.

The ColU led them by a different trail than usual, longer, heading toward the landmark of the Cowpat, and passing other features, eroded bluffs of sandstone seamed by intrusions of granite or basalt. At one of these the ColU paused. It took samples in its grabber claws of rock, dirt, life forms, and pressed its pod of sensors against rock surfaces. It also had a drill like a mole that would burrow into the ground or beneath a rocky surface, moving independently, but trailing a fiber-optic cable to pass data back.

All this work disturbed a kite that had been sheltering behind the bluff; it flapped away irritably. There seemed to be at least one solitary species of kite that lived apart from the great flocks of the forests and the lakes, and nested in the shelter of isolated rock outcrops like these.

Mardina mused, watching the ColU work, "You look like a rover. On Mars or Titan. One of those rickety gadgets that they used to control from Earth. Crawling a few centimeters a day, year after year." She glanced at Yuri. "Maybe you remember them. Or saw them in the museums."

Yuri shrugged.

"The analogy is apt," the ColU said. "You could say that in some regards I am a remote descendant of such probes. I have an onboard analysis suite, including, for example, a mass spectrometer so that I can determine the isotopic composition of samples of air or rock or water solutes. I have also improvised an incubation chamber where I am attempting to grow samples of Arduan life in controlled conditions. In that regard I am imitating the Vikings, early probes that landed on Mars and—"

"What's the point?" Yuri snapped. "You'll never be able to report any of this."

"Earth will recontact Per Ardua one day, though not, as Major McGregor promised, for a century at least. *I* will long have been terminated before then. But there is no reason to believe the results of my investigations will not survive; I have a number of hardened stores, which if deposited beneath a cairn or some other suitable monument—"

Yuri laughed. "I'll carve you a statue."

The ColU didn't seem offended. "In any event my studies are of their very nature long term. I am endeavoring to establish the story of life on this world. Its origin and its relationship, if any, to Sol life; the key stages of its development such as the emergence of photosynthesis, of multicellular life—"

"A *big* statue, then. Anyhow you're *too* curious, about the Arduan life. Too theoretical. You're only supposed to be helping us exploit it."

"Artificial sentience, *all* sentience, is untidy, blurred at the edges; it is difficult to constrain curiosity, once imbued. That's one of the reasons the big AIs constructed in the age of the Heroic Generation would now be considered illegal. Indeed, to equip ColUs like myself for this expedition, the ISF and other off-world agencies were given special dispensation by the sentience-law regulators. And besides, Yuri Eden, I was programmed to support a minimum of fourteen colonists, soon growing in number as the births began. I have the time to wonder."

"Oh, we aren't stimulating enough for you?"

"It is as if my mind expands to populate the emptiness. Is this a common property of sapience?"

Yuri said brutally, "You only ever had twenty-five years, and the clock's ticking, right? Then you'll shut down and rust. And all the plans and dreams you're cooking up under that plastic dome and in your expanding mind will just be lost forever, forgotten."

"All mortal creatures must face termination. Yuri Eden, I'm surprised you speak to me this way. Is it because I am a made thing? I mean, made by humans. A golem, of sorts. In myth, such creatures are always less than human, because they are one step further from God. Is that how you see me, Yuri Eden?"

"I see you as a symbol of the blind, stupid powers who thought it was a good idea to dump me and Mardina on this alien world."

"But I too am a victim of that blind stupidity, as you put it. As for myself, I can assure you that—"

"Shut up. I only talk to you about this stuff because I'm bored." That much, at least, was true.

"Enough, Yuri," Mardina said. "You can talk to me if you like, ColU. So how are you progressing with this great project of yours?"

"With difficulty. The geology of this world is singularly unhelpful. None of it is *old*, Mardina Jones. And by 'old' I mean in excess of a few hundred million years. At least in the local geological unit.

"Take this bit of sandstone in my grabber claw." It held out the sample. "You can see strata, laid down in some vanished ocean over a few million years. Then came the tectonic spasms that uplifted it, breaking the strata. There was an age of erosion as the strata were exposed to the weather. Then more geological turbulence resulted in the injection of molten granite into the weaker strata; you can see intrusions *here* and *here*. But even the rock, from which the original sandstone formed, eroded relics of volcanic products from a still earlier era, was comparatively young, as dating from traces of radioactive elements establishes."

Yuri's head spun with this mishmash of geological events. "I can't get all that in order. What you're saying is—"

Mardina said, "That the surface of the planet is recent, geologically speaking. Like Venus. Isn't that right?"

"Yes," said the ColU. "Venus appears to undergo a global resurfacing event every few hundred million years. The crater record shows this clearly. Here the resurfacing may be region by region, rather than the entire surface at once. Per Ardua is evidently geologically active; we've seen active regions ourselves, the mud pools, the evidence of uplift to the north. But it is an older world than the Earth, or Venus; Proxima is older than the sun. Maybe this localized activity, this geological bubbling, is something to do with that greater age. A given region may wait tens, hundreds of millions of years for such an event. But when it comes it is enough to wipe out much of any fossil record I might have found."

"Frustrating," Mardina murmured.

"But there are ways forward," said the ColU. "Mostly through study of the extant biology."

"The DNA."

"The Arduan creatures do not have DNA. But yes. A comparative study of their genetic material reveals deep relationships. I can already draw up a family tree based on the Arduan genetic record. With estimates of mutation rates I should soon be able to come up with a skeleton chronology. It is already clear, for instance, that the Arduan stromatolites, or their ancestors, must predate the stem forms. *When* did multicellular life begin here? *When* did the first multistem-architecture creatures emerge, and what were they like? Do they have any analogous survivors today? And—"

Yuri said, "I still say you've got big dreams for a bit of farm machinery."

Mardina suppressed a laugh.

"It is in the nature of sentience," the ColU said, "to dream. My work is done here, at this bluff. Are you ready to go on?"

They walked on, pausing once to eat, coming at last to the western shore of the lake.

This was the domain of the builders, on the fringe of the great stem beds that extended far out into the water where the birds flocked. Mardina had labeled this part of the shore the "nursery," because there was a concentration of families with their young. If you could call them families. Certainly the area was studded with the low, nestlike constructions that the ColU now believed, based on Yuri's clumsy explorations, were Proxima storm shelters for the young.

And here, today, on patches of the native analogues of mosses and lichen, young builders were basking in Proxima light. They gathered in clusters of a couple of dozen or more, each basically a tripod leaning on one rear leg and tilting back so it faced the star hanging in the sky. Their triple main stems were rooted in the lichen patches, and Yuri saw masses of fibers, tendrils, reaching down from the stems into the lichen—or maybe vice versa.

While the ColU plucked samples with a fine manipulator arm and scanned around with its sensor units, Mardina got down on her knees before the cluster of little builders, being careful not to block the light. "You know, I've seen them being born," she said. " 'Born.' I suppose you'd call it that. The three parents—and there are always three of them—get together in a cluster, upright, and they kind of pull bits out of each other. Stems, especially the fine ones from the dense core sections. Then they put them together, like they're assembling a kit-part model. But it stops being methodical after a while. They start to move, whirling around, the three of them joined together around the newborn." She rocked, her kneeling body swaying in a gentle circle, imitating the movement she'd seen. "A dance of conception, of birth. Some deep biology going on. And when they separate, there's a new little guy."

"Wow," Yuri said. Mardina had never told him about these observations before. "Builder sex, huh?"

"If you can meaningfully call it sex," the ColU said, rolling back. "There would presumably have to be *three* sexes, not two. I've seen no evidence of the sexual differentiation observed in many species on Earth. But the peculiar sexual congress you describe is clearly a way for genetic material from the parents to be mixed up in the infants, at the level of the stems, at least.

"And there's more. Notice how they make junctions between their bodies and the lichen bed. I think these builders are something like some of the earliest plants on Earth. Such plants hadn't yet evolved proper root systems, but instead formed a symbiotic relationship with fungi. The fungi would feed nutrients and water to the plant, in return for sugars manufactured by the plant. I think what we're seeing here is a complex symbiosis between the builders and the photosynthesizing bacteria and fungi of the lichen."

"You mean," Yuri said, "these little guys are feeding."

"I've observed the adults too spending time on lichen beds like this. But the youngsters are presumably more in need of nutrients; their stems need to grow. So the youngsters spend more of their time plugged in, so to speak. Other Arduan creatures, like the kites, must have similar rooting sites. If we look hard enough we'll find them. Certainly these creatures, which are a mixed-up compound of what we call animals and plants, are never more plant-like than at such moments. Perhaps their animal-like consciousness, a sense of self-awareness and identity, briefly dissolves into a deeper green . . ."

Mardina wasn't listening, Yuri saw. All her attention was on the young builders.

He said to her, "You like these little guys, don't you?"

She looked defensive. He knew she didn't like having her feelings questioned any more than he did himself. But she admitted, "Look, I'm no noble savage. But I grew up with the old stories—you know? Of the *gengas*, the spirits of my ancestors infusing the land. Well, I have no ancestors here, there are no *gengas* for me. But these builders—this is their world. They honor their dead, we know that. Maybe their *gengas* will look after me. I know it makes no sense—"

The ColU said, "Careful."

There was a clatter, like a bag of chopsticks being shaken. Yuri, standing over Mardina and the infants, turned to see a pair of older builders bearing down on them, spinning, limb stems clattering.

"Hey, take it easy, you guys." Mardina stood up. She whirled around in her orange jumpsuit, shaking out her arms and legs. "We're just looking, we won't harm these little fellas."

The ColU abruptly rolled back a half-meter, a sure sign in Yuri's experience that it was surprised, and raised its sensor pod on its arm high in the air. "Lieutenant . . . what are you doing?"

"What does it look like? Can't you see these blokes are warning us off?"

Yuri said, "You mean they're talking to us? What, with the dance?"

"In the dance, in the way they clatter their limbs—I don't know, I don't speak builder. I'm just trying to reassure them, that's all."

The builders slowed their spinning and backed off a little, but they did not root in the lichen bed with the infants. Instead they stood at the edge of the bed, spinning slowly, evidently watching warily. Yuri thought he saw a glimmer of opening eyes, eerily human, eye-leaves hidden in their structures.

" 'I don't speak builder,' " the ColU repeated. "Yet, in a sense, you clearly do, Lieutenant. Fascinating. I must explore this further." And then it froze, camera-eyes staring at the builders, sensor pod held high.

Mardina picked up her pack. "Come on. The ColU will be stuck here for hours, observing away. You know how it is when it gets into this kind of mood. Let's get out of here. We ought to stop spooking the builders."

"All right." Yuri hefted his own pack.

They walked on in silence, back around the southern shore of the lake, leaving the ColU behind. They kept well clear of the stems, the builder beds, the dome-shaped nest-shelters.

Builders moved everywhere, bent on their mysterious errands, working on peculiar, unidentifiable structures, sometimes even dipping into the lake water. In there, Yuri had learned, underwater creatures swam, more multistem forms, perhaps analogues of crabs or fish or crocodiles.

And at the water's edge the builders came together in pairs, triples, larger groups, and they spun and clattered and buzzed around one another. Yuri had seen this kind of behavior before, but had never thought much about it. Some failure of his own imagination. Yes, he thought, it *was* as if they were talking to one another. He wondered if it would ever be possible to translate what they were saying. If it was possible, he supposed, the ColU would figure it out.

They passed a garden of stromatolites, big ones, with broad caplike upper surfaces over stout pillars, like huge mushrooms gleaming gold in the Prox light. A herd of herbivores worked the garden, small critters this time, no taller than the average builder, but they had the usual spiky extrusions, that they pushed into the rich interiors of the stromatolites. The stromatolites were so huge it was hard to believe they would even notice this pinprick feeding.

Then they came to a group of middens, standing by the southern lakeshore. These were big heaps, with steep sides of compacted, dried-out old stems. Yuri saw builders working on their upper surfaces, a good number of them, pushing heaps of stems back and forth with an endless, dry, rustling sound.

"They're rebuilding the midden," he observed to Mardina.

"Again. And the middens already have complex shapes." She had a slate; she sketched the nearest midden's new layout with brisk, confident movements of her hand. "Look at it, Yuri. Think of it as a building, a structure. Forget that it's a heap of old stems, of dead builders. Suppose it was made of concrete . . ."

It was a complicated design, of curves and banks and channels. And it was only one of a series of these middens, all along this part of the lakeshore. Yuri turned, trying to figure out how these structures fit into the landscape. Away from the lake to the south, behind them, passing east of the stromatolite garden, he made out a shallow, rubble-strewn channel, a dried-up riverbed maybe, leading to a depression, crusted with salt. The row of middens neatly sealed off this outflow channel from the lake.

"It's like a dam. I've thought that before."

"Hmm," Mardina said dismissively. "Maybe. Blocking that dry channel to the south. But there are what look like functional dams on the *other* side of the lake, the north shore. Blocking the inlet streams coming down from the high land between the lake and the forest. What do you make of that?"

He shrugged. "What is there to make of it?"

She squinted at the builders. "Depends how smart you think those little guys are. We know they build shelters for their young, we know they communicate between themselves, we know they remember their dead. Does all this building work going on around the lake have a purpose? However smart they are, they're certainly smart in a different way from us, and that makes them hard to understand. Maybe we *think* they're working on some big engineering project here just because that's what we'd do."

As they spoke Yuri saw the builders' behavior was changing. They had given up their work on the midden and were streaming down its flanks, heading toward the stromatolite garden. And in the nursery areas to the west, he saw adult builders gently shepherding the young toward the nestlike shelters.

Mardina pointed. "Here comes the ColU."

The ColU was built for stability and strength, not speed. Still, it kicked up a cloud of dust as it raced around the lake toward them. And it called to them, its voice an over-amplified bark: "Danger, Yuri Eden, Lieutenant Mardina Jones, danger!" It pointed up at Proxima with one extended manipulator arm. "Flare alert! Flare!"

Yuri turned and looked up at the star, shielding his eyes, squinting. He saw bright flare sites coalescing, and tremendous crackles like lightning flickering over the star's sprawling surface. No wonder the builders were fleeing.

"Shit," said Mardina. "That's a big one, and it's come out of nowhere. And we're a long way from the storm shelter."

"I've got an idea."

"What?"

He pointed southwest. Most of the builders from the lake were streaming that way, spinning and pivoting, kicking up dust, heading straight for the big stromatolites. "Follow the builders. Come on!"

He led the way. When he glanced back to check that Mardina was following him, behind her he saw a flickering on the northern horizon. In the big trees of the forest, the huge triple canopy leaves were folding up like umbrellas.

It took only minutes to reach the stromatolites. Everywhere the builders were punching holes in the upper crust of the big structures, and were piling inside, squirming into the layers of bacteria and dirt within. Yuri saw that every one of these makeshift entrances was on the far side of the stromatolite from the angry star.

By the time Yuri and Mardina had got there, there wasn't a builder to be seen. They stood beneath a big stromatolite, the hole in its shell easily big enough to allow an adult human to pass.

They looked at each other. Yuri asked, "What do you think?"

"They've lived on this planet a lot longer than we have. Let's trust them." She pushed herself headfirst through the break in the stromato-lite's shell, and shoveled out handfuls of gungy drab green matter to make room for herself. Soon she was inside the stromatolite entirely, and burrowing farther in.

Yuri followed. It was not a comfortable feeling to be wriggling into this dark, slimy murk; he felt like some parasitic worm eating its way into a brain.

And then, beyond the gap in the shell, light flared, brilliant, as if somebody had thrown a switch in the sky.

In his brief orientation, Major Lex McGregor had told the colonists that Proxima flared almost constantly, like all red dwarf stars, making explosive releases of magnetic energy that were visible across light years. Per Ardua's atmosphere mostly shielded its cargo of life from the weather from space, but there were occasions, like, apparently, this time, when the sleet of ultraviolet and X-ray photons was too energetic, and broke through to the ground.

Life here had strategies to cope. The tough carapaces of the stems. The fact that a builder could simply replace a damaged stem, like a spare part. The builders sheltering their young in thick domelike shelters. The trees folding away their leaves. Maybe creatures dwelling in the lakes and oceans retreated to the protection of the deeper water.

And maybe this was another strategy: to dive inside the thick shell, into the slimy interior, of a stromatolite. Would it work for humans? Yuri supposed they just had to hope so.

They were in a kind of cramped little cave in the slime, pressed together, slippery and sticky. The stromatolite's inner matter continually threatened to slop down over the opening, and Yuri and Mardina were kept busy kicking this clear, so that a spray of mush gathered on the stony ground outside, brilliantly lit by the flare.

"Those builders have dug in deeper," Mardina said.

"Maybe they don't need air."

"Well, we sure as hell do. Keep kicking."

"Yes, ma'am. How long do you think we should stay in here?"

"We'll see the light outside go back to normal. Or we could wait until the ColU comes to tell us it's safe."

"Or maybe the builders will push us out," Yuri said.

"Maybe."

They looked at each other. Mardina's face was just white eyes, white teeth, in a drab green mask. They burst out laughing. Then they seemed to relax a little more, pressed up against each other.

"We're not a bad team, I guess," Mardina said.

"With the ColU in charge."

"Well, it thinks it is—"

"I don't want to die here," Yuri blurted.

She looked at him.

He wasn't sure where that had come from. He scrambled to justify himself. "I don't mean in this shell full of mush. I mean here, us, on Ardua. Everything we built just crumbling into the dirt."

"I thought you didn't care about what we're building."

"That was before we started building it. I never built anything before."

"I guess you didn't . . . You know there's only one option. One way we can change things."

"I know." He looked away. "To have a kid."

"We've talked about this," she said.

"Actually we haven't. Apart from when the ColU lectures us about anthropology."

"No. All right. So why do you want to talk about it now?"

"I don't."

"Well, you brought it up, ice boy. Look, you know what the issues are. Think about the lives our children would live. They'd be farm laborers at best, and incestuous baby machines at worst. You recoil from that, *I* do, and there's good reason."

"I know. And there's something else. What *right* do we have, to produce a kid in such circumstances?"

"Rights? Umm. But these kids don't exist yet. You know, in the ISF we had courses on ethics—not on this kind of extreme situation specifically. Yuri, none of us has a choice where we're born, or in what circumstances. You're just kind of dropped into the world at random. And traditionally parents have always seen their kids as resources. Kids work for you, you marry them off . . . So the conclusion is that the idea of rights of an unborn *not to exist*, if the situation it would be born into is uncomfortable—it's all kind of nebulous."

He thought that over. "No. It's that argument that's nebulous."

She laughed. "So what do you suggest?"

Hesitantly, he said, "Suppose we did have a kid. *Once it's born* it would have rights, yes? We could give it the right to choose whether to have more children with its siblings."

"Or its parents," she said firmly. "That's part of the deal, and we have to face that."

"Only if we stick to this monster ISF plan. But there are other options."

"Like what?"

"It, he or she, could go off alone. Or we could walk away when we're too old to work, instead of being a burden. We haven't got to choose now."

"No. In fact we give the kid the choice."

"Right."

Mardina said, "I'll tell you another possibility, Yuri. I know we argue about this. I'm still not convinced we really are stranded here, the way they told us . . ."

Not this again, he thought.

"I know there *must* have been a lot of briefings that were kept from me. But I keep thinking there must be some kind of monitoring of this situation. There has to be. And if it is all some kind of survival test—"

"It's a test we might pass once we have a kid?"

"Something like that. It's possible. It would show we are committed to this world, wouldn't it? To this life. Maybe that's all we need to demonstrate."

"Yeah." He tried to think that through. "But in that case, by having the kid, we'd be doing the opposite, wouldn't we? That's kind of paranoid thinking, Mardina."

She looked at him, in the green gloom. "But if we go ahead, for whatever reason, with whatever caveats in our heads—in the meantime, at least we'd have a kid."

He tried to imagine that. Tried to imagine a life *without* children, without other people, with only his and Mardina's face, forever. "We're never going to get another chance, are we? Except for this way. Neither of us."

She sat back in silence.

They were coming to a decision, he realized. Maybe if the ColU left them alone a bit more they'd have made this choice sooner.

"One problem," she said now. "We're not sleeping together."

"Yeah," Yuri said. "But I'm not sexually . . . inactive."

"I know. I hear you."

"What?"

"*Ah—ah—ah.* Jerkin' the gherkin. Come on, Yuri, it's a quiet planet. Look, I do it too. But I don't think about *you* when I'm doing it."

"Fine. Then we can sleep together. And you can carry on not thinking about me."

"You can bet on it." She looked at him, and they laughed again. She said, "Do you think we've both finally gone insane?"

"Possibly. Probably . . ."

There was a rustle from deeper back within the stromatolite's bulk. The builders stirring, perhaps. Outside, the flare glow began to flicker, waning.

30

When it began, it began suddenly.

There was no choice to be made by Angelia as a whole, or by the near-million partials of which she was composed. The designers on Earth had built overrides into the probe's governing software to ensure that. Selected by numbers produced by some automated sequencer, in their thousands and tens of thousands, sisters who had been together a decade were ripped out of the community and hurled off into the dark. Once out there they had no choice but to spread and turn and rebuild themselves as lenses and focus their light on the remaining core, rebuilt in its turn as an optical light mirror.

Angelia 5941, still embedded deep in her family, felt the sudden lurch of the deceleration, saw with distributed senses the blaze of Proxima light reflected by the mass of castaways.

Still she continued her helpless prayer. Not me. I have come this far. Let me be the one in a million who survives; let the others die before me. Why not me? It must be one of us . . .

But prayer was futile.

The casting-out was instant, brutal. It was as if she had been torn from another mold, and flung into space. Suddenly she was surrounded by a great crowd of sisters, she was one in a great fall of snowflakes, each of them shining by the light of Proxima. And there in the center of it all was the core ship, blazing bright with reflected light, but with more sisters being hurled off its face even as she watched. There was no way to communicate with the core, or with her castaway sisters, or even with distant Earth, not anymore; she was alone now, alone forever. She saw all this in an instant.

Then her own huge velocity flung her away from the core, out into the dispersing crowd, which scattered all around her like fragments from some tremendous explosion.

THREE

• • •

2173

Stef Kalinski was summoned to Earth. Specifically to the office of Sir Michael King, at the corporate headquarters of Universal Engineering, Inc., in Solstice, Northwest Territories, United States of North America.

Summoned. To be called peremptorily like this was galling.

Major Stef Kalinski, twenty-nine years old, was now a full professor at her home institution in Vancouver, and also an officer in the International Space Fleet. She had worked hard to get here. Attaining a rank in the ISF had been a pain in the butt, and, in order to pursue parallel careers since the age of twenty-one, she had had to forgo such luxuries as a personal life. But the ISF had been the only route by which she could get an assignment to the one laboratory where the most exotic physics known to mankind was being pursued: the Wheeler Research Facility in Jules Verne, a farside crater on the moon, the only place in the solar system where you could get to properly study a kernel—unless you were allowed down to Mercury itself, which she wasn't.

Her strategy had paid off. She was pretty eminent now; you only had to look at her publication and citation record to see that. She liked to think that if her father were still alive he'd have been proud of her, even if she had ended up studying the very phenomenon which had ruined his own career—but he had died years before, in an open prison on the fringe of the desertified core of France.

And now here was this "invitation." The note she received even had a designated place and time, with attached clipper transit tickets, even before she'd agreed to go.

But it was a summons from Sir Michael King himself. After decades at the top King was still the big cheese at UEI, which in turn was still the primary paymaster at Verne, a notionally UN-run establishment, thanks to the immense profits UEI had made from patenting kernel technologies. And, as some of her colleagues half joked, behind King was said to be the shadowy figure of Earthshine, one of the tremendous artificial minds that had been running much of the planet for nearly a century. You didn't mess with Earthshine, they joked. Or half joked.

Stef's policy was to ignore such chatter and try to focus on what *she* wanted. At eleven years old, she had been there on the very day when the *International-One*, UEI's first hulk, had lumbered into space from the sun-blasted plains of Mercury. Now those mighty kernel-driven ships crisscrossed the solar system, and had even set off for the stars. But she wasn't allowed on Mercury, where the kernels were. Because of tensions with the Chinese, who still had no access to kernel technology, security around the kernel mines was ferociously tight, too tight for her. If this was a door opening a crack, a chance to get closer to the kernels, not just the tame handful that UEI had allowed to be shipped to the moon—well, she had to take it.

So she packed a bag.

Leaving the moon on a rocketship was unspectacular.

The UEI clipper's crew squirted their thrusters to leave lunar orbit, and set off on an unpowered trajectory to Earth. Following a low-energy orbit, it would take Stef three days to fly from the moon to the Earth, just as it had been for Armstrong and Aldrin in Apollo 11 almost exactly two centuries before. And it was going to stay that way, even though mankind was now building ships powerful enough to reach the stars themselves. The use of anything other than minimum-energy strategies in the Earth-moon system had been banned by international agreement. The fragility of Earth in the face of interplanetary energies had become obvious in the days of the Heroic Generation, when the first really large structures had begun to be assembled in orbit around the Earth. In a few cases geoengineering technology itself had actually been weaponized: droughts and floods, for instance, had been inflicted on enemy nations.

At least the in-flight facilities were a little more advanced than in the Apollo days—including the sealed-off Love Nest at the rear of the main passenger cabin, which some of her fellow passengers used assiduously, and Stef ignored. She tried to work. And she spent long hours in the ship's small gymnasium, using equipment adapted for microgravity, stressing her muscles against elasticized harnesses and shoving against a kind of robot sumo wrestler, preparing her body for Earth gravity after years at Verne, on the moon.

With the three-day transit over, the clipper skimmed Earth's atmosphere and blipped its retro-rockets to settle into a high-inclination orbit of the planet, from which it would descend to land at the young city of Solstice, in the Canadian far north. It was a routine maneuver; all Earth's passenger spaceports were at high latitudes these days, because that was where the dominant cities were—though commercial and military cargoes were still launched from more energetically efficient but climatically challenging equatorial sites, like Kourou. And as the clipper looped over the Earth waiting for final clearance to land, the passengers were given a grandstand view of much of the planet's surface.

The face of Earth continued to evolve, following the huge shocks of the climate Jolts of the last century. At the coasts, much transformed thanks to the nibbling of sea-level rise, solar-power farms were spreading through the shallow waters of the flooded shores and river valleys, sprawling artificial meadows of gen-enged grasses supplying electricity grids through modified photosynthesis. This was part of a conscious global strategy to minimize the use of *any* energy source on the home planet save sunlight, because any other method meant an injection of additional heat to the world's global balance.

Meanwhile, across the continental interiors, as glaciers vanished, aquifers were exhausted and the rain just stopped, the mid-latitude regions had been largely abandoned. Looping over the arid plains of Amazonia, southern Europe, Asia, even much of the territory of the old United States, Stef saw few signs of modern humanity save huge solar-cell farms. Great old cities still glittered in the intense sunlight, but there was nobody moving in there but archaeologists and historians, workers for resource extraction companies, and a few extreme-experience tourists exploring lost cities that, to the rising generation, were already half legend: New Orleans, Saigon, Venice, even the nuked remains of Mumbai.

The great population adjustments caused by the Jolts had all but run their course; the pandemics were over, the refugee flows had dwindled, and political alliances, even national boundaries, had been redrawn. Now new generations were growing up in brand-new cities set up in latitudes that would once have been seen as too extreme, in the very far north, and even the far south, on the coast of an increasingly ice-free Antarctica. Cities such as Solstice, near the shore of the Great Bear Lake, sitting precisely on the Arctic Circle in a northerly state of the new United States of North America into which Canada, with huge concessions from its suffering southern neighbor, had been absorbed.

A city down toward which the lunar clipper now swept for its final descent.

The UEI corporate headquarters on the outskirts of Solstice had a relatively modest profile, just glass-block architecture tipped south to face the low sun. Once she was escorted inside the building, however, Stef glimpsed extensions underground, showy staircases like something out of the *Titanic* leading down to sweeping underground concourses.

Sir Michael King's office was above ground, somewhere near the center of the complex. The day was fine and bright, and the glass-walled offices were filled with the Arctic sun's slanting light. Led by an aide, Stef was brought to a wide, airy room at whose very center a single desk was set up overlooking some kind of pond, a smooth glassy surface that reflected the clear blue light of the sky. King himself sat behind the desk, she saw as she approached. In his late fifties now, heavyset, his thick hair snow-white, King was famous and unmistakable. To one side another man sat, apparently relaxed, on an upright chair, a tall, slim, sober figure. They both had drinks on the desk before them.

To reach the desk the aide led her across an ocean of rich blue pile carpet marked with the UEI logo. Stef walked stiffly, trying to mask the gravity heaviness, the fatigue. It didn't help that she had to skirt that central pond. Its clear water contained fish, she saw as she passed, big carp by the look of them, sleek golden forms that swam around and around. There was nothing in the pond with them, no fronds or reeds. They were like a virtual abstraction, Stef thought.

Both men stood as she approached, the visitor with a smooth, slightly unnatural grace, and Michael King heavily, his hands on the surface of the desk. He was wearing a kilt, she saw. The aide stood by, silent, discreet.

"Major Kalinski," King said. He proffered his hand, which she shook.

"Good to see you again, Sir Michael."

"Hell, just call me Michael. Everybody gets my titles confused since King Harold made me a thane. You know, I'm one of only three individuals to have been knighted both by the King of Angleterre at Versailles, and by King Harold of North Britain. And me an Aussie! But then they both lay claim to be head of state of what's left of Australia . . . Do you like the kilt by the way? Wore it to my investiture in Edinburgh. So glad you've come. I do have another visitor, as you can see." He watched her closely now, as if anticipating her reaction. "Major Kalinski—meet Earthshine."

Earthshine.

Stef, shocked by the unexpected introduction, reached out a hand, then withdrew it in confusion. "Sorry."

The Earthshine avatar smiled at her. Tall, solid, dressed in a sober suit and collarless shirt, it, *he*, looked like a handsome fifty-year-old of the political class. On his lapel he wore an odd brooch, a disc of granite carved with concentric grooves, a single slash to the center. When he spoke his accent was soft British. "Please don't apologize." He reached for the desk with two hands; he picked up his own glass—but his fingers passed through King's tumbler, where they broke up briefly into a flickering cloud of pixels. "I do use programmable-matter android forms sometimes, but I much prefer the holographic form if the bandwidth is adequate. All depends on the circumstances, of course."

She tried not to stare. So the comedians back at Verne had been right, more than they knew. She realized that she had no idea what cavernous thought processes were going on behind this smiling-politician-type facade. Why was Earthshine here? Why was *she* here?

King said, "Major, as you just experienced, Earthshine isn't really here with us at all. In as much as he's anywhere, he's down in a vast computer complex under Fort Chipewyan, right in the heart of the Canadian shield and as stable a geological site as you'll find. Snug in his bunker, with layers of replicators building new components for him from raw rock, and feeding off Earth's inner heat. *And* with multiple backups across the continent . . ."

"Whereas you, Michael, live so modestly, here in your glass Versailles."

King laughed easily. "Well, I'm not some silicon demigod like you. But I'm a salesman, and I have to impress the punters and the investors. Sit down, both of you, please. Do you like the fish, by the way, Major Kalinski?"

"Are they artificial? Some kind of robot—"

"No, no. But they've been gen-enged to photosynthesize. They need nothing but light, and some dissolved nutrients in the water, to survive. A new UEI initiative, photosynthesizing animals, a new way to make more efficient use of the sunlight. Have to be careful about the post-Heroic protection laws, of course. The pond's an extreme environment for them, but it makes a striking demonstration of their nature, don't you think?"

"It must be a little boring for them. The fish."

He rubbed his chin. "Well, maybe. Hadn't thought of that. Not much for them to do all day, swimming around in their little tank. Just like you, eh, Earthshine? I ought to do something for them, though, you're right, Major. Maybe put in one of those little treasure chests. Make a note, Briggs."

"Yes, sir."

"Oh—where are my manners? Major, would you like a drink? I laid on a treat for you. Briggs?"

The aide raised a kind of wand, and a section of the desk opened. A tray rose up bearing a selection of sodas, many in antique-looking classic-design cans, presumably not made of aluminum.

Stef shook her head. "Oh, not for me, thanks."

King looked crestfallen.

Earthshine said smoothly, "I think you should force yourself, Major. He's gone to a lot of trouble over this."

"It's true," King said. "I remember on Mercury how you said the soda was always flat. Now you're stuck on the moon and I guess it's the same up there, right? I never did get around to researching a fix. I figured that if I dragged you all the way back to Earth, the least I could do—"

"I appreciate you remembering, after all this time."

"I told you then, didn't I? People are everything in this life. Contacts. You have to cultivate them. Remember the names of their puppies—"

"But I'm not eleven years old anymore, Sir Michael."

Earthshine laughed out loud.

King grinned. "Speak your mind, don't you? I remember that about you too. Oh, hell, if you'd prefer something else—"

"No, no." She took a diet soda. It tasted more sour than she remembered, but it did bring back some memories.

King watched her astutely. "Takes you back to when you were a kid, right? You had a strange kind of childhood, didn't you? I remember you lost your mother when you were very young. And then your father was always kind of distracted by his work, I guess."

She shook her head. "In a way. But I understand. Now *I'm* distracted. So distracted I don't have a family at all."

"I'm sorry for what became of him. The trial and so on."

She shrugged. "It's in the past."

"I too sympathize," said Earthshine. "Being a relic of the so-called Heroic Generation myself. No doubt they would lock me up if they had the chance."

King winked at Stef. "Believe me, they've tried."

Stef snapped, "Can we get on to the reason you brought me here?"

King looked surprised, then laughed. "Down to business, eh? You always were impatient, I remember that of you as well. You even got restless during the countdown for the launch of that first hulk, the *I-One*, didn't you?"

"Not restless. I was just a lot less interested in some big dumb piece of heavy engineering than I was in the kernels that powered it."

"Yes, the kernels. The objects you have devoted your life to studying, in the end."

"Strictly speaking, the physics behind them, yes. And that is what you brought me here to discuss, right? But look, Sir Michael. I'm no expert in international law. I do know that kernel science is supposed to be kept from the Core AIs." She hesitated, looking at Earthshine. "No offense," she said awkwardly.

"Great heavens, none taken."

"That's true, of course," said King. "And you know why, don't you? Because *we don't trust you,* Earthshine. We have to deal with you. I have to meet you, what—every other week? But we don't like you, or trust you. Sitting in your lairs, your hardened bunkers in the bedrock, plugged into all the world's essential systems. You and your cousins on the other continents, Ifa and the Archangel."

"Oh, not cousins. Rivals, perhaps," Earthshine said mildly. "Companions, sometimes . . ."

Stef got the distinct impression that they had worked together for too long, that King chafed under the burden of a requirement to report to this strange old artificial entity. They were like bickering academics in some crusty institution, she thought.

King said now, "Major, you do understand what we're dealing with here? The big continental AIs, the Core AIs as they are called, were spawned in the first place in the pre-Heroic days. They came out of a global network of transnational companies, a network which collectively controlled much of the world's economy. Within that network nodes of deeper interconnection and control emerged: 'super-entities,' the economic analysts called them. *They* were still at the level of human culture. But beneath the corporate super-entities, intensive AI capability necessarily clustered. Then came the demands for security for core processors and data backups, hardened refuges linked by robust comms networks. Well, they were given what they wanted." He grinned, rueful. "It seemed like a good idea at the time."

Earthshine said, "The early members of the Core were essential to the great projects of the Heroic Generation. Supremely intelligent."

"But they were not human," King said sternly.

"The kernels," Stef said, trying to wrench the conversation round to the point. "It must have taken a monumental effort to keep the science of the kernels away from the Core AIs."

King nodded grimly. "It did indeed. The fact that the kernels were found on Mercury, and are studied nowhere closer to Earth than the moon, all helped. That and the fact that the danger was spotted immediately."

"What danger?"

"That we would understand," Earthshine said, "where you do not."

Stef asked coldly, "What don't I understand?"

"The true physics. Such as the unified theories known as quantum gravity, among other labels. They remain as tantalizingly out of reach to you as they ever were, have been for centuries. You only know them by limits, low-energy approximations—like relativity, quantum physics. As if you are trying to understand the structure of a diamond by studying a single edge. To explore reality further is beyond your engineering capabilities; to *compute* more is beyond your intellects. In fact, you've learned more by playing with kernels, which are quantum-gravitational toys, than you have from all your theorizing in the two hundred years since Einstein."

Stef scowled. "You're saying that quantum gravity might be *too hard* for a mere human like me ever to understand."

"But not for me," Earthshine said. "Perhaps, anyhow. Which is why those of small minds and smaller hearts, like Sir Michael here, have kept the kernels from us. What might we achieve if we had such knowledge?"

King looked at Stef. "You've spent most of your adult life off-planet, Major. See what we have to deal with down here? Crap like this, day after day, decade after decade . . ."

And Stef did see it, saw a fundamental dichotomy between the two branches of mankind as they were emerging in the new era. The space-going were outward-looking, expansive, physically exploring the universe. While the Earthbound were stuck in this gravity well, dominated by legacies of the past, such as these dreadful old indestructible AIs cowering in their holes in the ground. Suddenly she longed to be in space, back on the moon—anywhere but here on this old planet, this museum of horrors.

"Why have you brought me here?"

"We want you to go to Mercury, Major Kalinski," King said. "Or rather, go *back* to Mercury. I will accompany you in person, to the kernel beds, as they have come to be known."

And there was the opportunity she had come here in hope of, all the way to Earth. But she was baffled. "Why? What do you want of me there?"

"You're going to have to see for yourself, Major. We've found something." He glanced at Earthshine. "Something so significant, of such long-term importance to mankind, that I feel we've no choice but to bring it to the attention of these Core AIs. Because if the buggers are useful for anything, it's thinking about the long term. And we need someone like you, a kernel physicist. We don't know what to make of it. We're hoping you might be able to make informed guesses about it, at least."

"About *what*?"

"Something strange," said Earthshine.

33

In the endless afternoon of Per Ardua, time flowed unevenly, like the flares that ran across the face of Proxima itself. Sometimes there seemed no interval at all between waking and getting ready to sleep again. And sometimes the days-that-were-not-days dragged, and Yuri felt as if he were back in the solitary tanks in Eden.

Their Earth-based calendars became irrelevant. Increasingly they marked the passage of time by events, by stuff that changed their lives for better or worse. The weather had turned, for one thing; four years after the landing, Proxima's face was now crowded with massive sunspots, and its flows of heat and light were reduced enough to make a perceptible difference. The climate was more like a crisp late autumn afternoon, from what Yuri remembered of the North Britain of his boyhood. Sometimes there was even a sparkle of frost on the green leaves in the little colony's fields, and the ColU fretted about its strawberries. Yuri remembered how Mardina had once told him how stable this stellar system was. No dinosaur-killer rocks here, and so on. But the star itself, it seemed, was in fact a source of instability. And the planet too, with that geological uplift they'd long been observing to the north. Not that they could do anything about all that but endure.

And then there was Mardina's pregnancy.

Once they had begun their awkward, rather businesslike lovemaking, she had conceived quickly, Yuri suspected to their mutual relief. The ColU, in its role as family doctor, had insisted on tracking the stages of the developing pregnancy by the book. So the human-event calendar in their heads had filled up with more memorable moments: the day the morning sickness started, the day the bump was first visible to Yuri, the day Mardina felt the first kick, the day she let Yuri feel a kick. Now she was coming to term, and soon there would be another monumental event for their memories: the birth of a child.

The farm was developing too. With the aid of the ColU it was proving easy for them to extend their few small fields, each coated with terrestrial topsoil and watered by irrigation ditches running from the lake. While the growing stuff, lurid Earth-green, had attracted the attention of the local wildlife—including a flock of spectacular kites the size of herons that periodically came down to investigate—a potato leaf was essentially inedible to an Arduan, and once the crops were established there were no native blights that could harm them. All this had been planned for. The ColU had the capacity to support fourteen people, and their offspring; to provide for one couple was well within its ability.

But after four years on Per Ardua, to Yuri's eyes—especially when he returned from a hike to the lake or the forest, and he saw it as a whole, from afar—the farm, their little colony, still didn't look like it fitted in here, in the Arduan landscape. The rectangular fields with their neat rows of Earth-green plants, the tidy geometry of their conical house, the exclusion of the local Arduan life—even the dirt discolored by their footsteps and the churn of the ColU's wheels—the whole thing looked like an unhealed wound on the face of this world.

Mardina, however, looked less out of place. They had both abandoned their ISF-issue outfits by now, and wore looser clothing mostly made from local materials. In her tunic and short-cut trousers, coolie hat and bark sandals, and with her skin coated with gray-orange Arduan dust, Mardina wore the shades of the planet. Humans had come here to colonize Per Ardua. But, Yuri thought, what was really happening was that Per Ardua was colonizing the humans.

And what drew all three of them, including the ColU, away from the farm and deeper into the embrace of Per Ardua were the builders.

· · ·

On another dull day, their chores done, on impulse Yuri and Mardina trekked out to the lake. It was midday, by their human clocks. The ColU was already out at the shore, pursuing its own interests.

Mardina had become fascinated by the builders' big projects around the Puddle: the dams that obstructed the inflow streams from the higher ground to the north—dams established long enough now to have created extensive floods behind them—and the more mysterious middens on the southern shore, with their banks and arcs. She walked along the lake's northern shore, capturing images on her slate and sketching maps and diagrams with a stylus. "We still have no idea what all this is for. But whatever the hell they're doing here, it's evidently a lot more interesting than us digging in a few potatoes. Does it ever strike you how incurious they've been about us recently?"

That was true. The builders around the lake, a few hundred individuals gathered in a dozen small bands, all seemed part of a single community. Once the group around the nursery area on the western shore had got used to the idea that these strange, lanky, stemless creatures and their big rolling box were harmless, the other bands had soon seemed to pick up the same message, and stopped reacting to them. Unless you stood right in front of one and somehow impeded its progress, the builders just ignored the humans, spinning around you as if you were of as little interest as a lump of rock.

"I think they're working up to something," Mardina said now. She sounded breathless, and she sat on a lump of rock, her slate on the ground beside her. It was another chilly day and she wore an old fleece jacket over her stem-bark tunic. "All this work, the dams and mounds. They run around like this all the time, but the activity seems to be getting more intense every time I come out here." She massaged her lower spine with both hands; backache had plagued her pregnancy.

"Maybe." Yuri squatted on the ground beside her, dug a water bottle out of his flask and handed it to her.

She waved it away. "You go find the ColU. I'll stay and watch a while. Wouldn't want to miss the show, whatever they're planning, if it all happens to kick off today."

He stood. "You're sure you're OK?"

He knew what reaction he'd get for that, and he got it. "You're worse than that bloody nursemaid on wheels. My brain is still function-

ing, more or less, thank you, so don't fuss, ice boy. Just piss off and go
and annoy the ColU."

"All right. You've got water, you've got—"

"The flare pistol, yes, I've got it, and I'll fire it up your defrosted
arse if you don't *bugger off.*"

So he did.

He soon found the ColU.

The big machine had rolled up to one of its own favored sites for
builder watching, which was the eastern shore. Here there was no intense construction activity, as there was at the north and south shores,
and no nurseries as at the west. The builders were always busy here, but
engaged on smaller-scale tasks. For instance they had built an elaborate
series of traps out into the lake water, from which they extracted small
fishlike creatures, with stem-based skeletons like the rest of the wildlife
but wrapped in a skinlike streamlined webbing—a casing easily un-
wrapped, and the contents picked apart and incorporated into other
bodies.

And the builders weren't so busy that they could not be distracted
by a dancing robot.

Of course the ColU couldn't really dance; it was built more like a
tank than a ballerina. But, given Mardina's lead, it had become ingenious at simulating builder dancing with the forest of manipulator arms
that sprouted from its deck. Now, before an audience of three builders,
all adults—of course there would be three, or nine, or twenty-seven of
these creatures of three-fold groupings—the ColU put on a show. It held
up heavy-duty arms to simulate the three main limbs of a builder, and
while it couldn't literally make its puppet builder spin around, with a
kind of sleight of hand, its smaller arms twisting and writhing, it made
it *look* as if it were spinning, accompanied by the nods, rocks, and ges-
tures that characterized builder movements.

The builders were not watching passively. They spun and dipped in
their turn, as if they were speaking to one another as well as to the
ColU—as if it had been accepted into some kind of conversation.

One of them was injured, Yuri saw; it had a damaged leg stem,
broken near the base, so that it hobbled, its spinning a little off-balance.
And as Yuri approached, he sensed a strange, intense smell, a smell of

the lake, the stems—the scent of builders, amplified and enhanced, a scent reproduced artificially by the ColU.

"Welcome, Yuri Eden!" the ColU called, continuing its puppet show.

Yuri kept back from the little group. "You look as if you're actually talking to them."

"Indeed! I have made spectacular progress in the months since I was inspired by Lieutenant Jones's intuitive grasp that the builders' dancing is a kind of communication. I have begun to build up an extensive vocabulary of 'words,' which—"

"I didn't know you'd got so far. You haven't told us about any of this."

It sounded faintly offended. "I was waiting to complete the project. Or at least bring it to the point where I could make a proper report."

"This isn't an academy." That was one of Mardina's choice lines. "Just tell me what you've learned."

"A lot—or perhaps only a little. You must appreciate the challenge. Humans share a universal grammar that derives from your body shape, the way you interact with your environment, your experience of birth, life, death. A builder's experience—the way a creature that is half-animal, half-plant by terrestrial categories apprehends the world—really is quite alien, and therefore so is its language. Also builder communication has a whole range of components, the most important being the gestural—the dancing—and scent: they emit body chemicals at will. I get the sense that they are a very old species, Yuri, and their mode of communication is very ancient. I mean ancient in the biological sense. Much older than human languages. Indeed, it has surely evolved on biological timescales, rather than cultural. As a result their language is wideband, in a way, with many channels of discourse, most of which I suspect I have yet to discover.

"So we started with the basics, with simple nouns for obvious concrete objects. 'Lake' was the first, as you can imagine." Its arm puppet gave a series of twirls, and Yuri smelled a sharper tang. The builder audience responded in kind. "But even for a simple concept like 'lake,' the builder word is much more complex, with many meanings overlaid; it means something like 'the interface between mother and father which brings life.' That is my perhaps clumsy interpretation. It is as if every time I use the word 'lake' I give you its history in terms of a Latin root imported into English via Norman French, together with mythological footnotes—"

"Mother and father, though?"

"Ah, yes: to them Proxima is the father, in terms of emotional analogies with the human condition, and the world, Per Ardua, is the mother—or more specifically, I think, the term refers to the lichen-rich nutrient patches in which their young take root. The adults who actually nurture infants are referred to by a term I think translates as something more like 'midwife' rather than 'parent.' From such beginnings I have established many more common terms, for water, earth, sky, hot, cold, big, small—"

"What do they call us?"

"We each have our individual names. They don't have a class name for humans. There are only three of us—including myself—and we are all very different in their eyes. *Your* name, and Mardina's, are variants on a phrase that means 'single stem.'

"They aren't great conversationalists, Yuri! Their language is simple, really, with a very wide vocabulary, lots of labels, but only elementary grammatical rules. And much of what they say to one another consists of stock sayings. Like slogans, or folk sayings."

Yuri tried to think of an example. "Such as, 'If it ain't broke, don't fix it?' "

"Yes. But a builder analogy might be, 'Dig it up before you make it.' This is another aspect of their antiquity, Yuri Eden. We've seen them use stone tools. But before they go to the trouble of making a new tool, they will grub at the ground and see if they can dig up a discard, a tool left by some forebear that might be thousands of years old. They've been wandering here for a long, long time: the ground is evidently rich enough in abandoned artifacts to make that sort of strategy worthwhile. And there isn't a lot of innovation across the generations; they expect the tools left behind by their ancestors to be pretty much the same as what they make and use today. The language is the same, a collection of phrases and sayings, bits of wisdom handed down, polished from overuse."

"What do they call themselves? Not builders . . ."

" 'The Fallen.' That is a human analogy; their term is something like 'the semi-disarticulated.' But I think the concept of falling, that is falling from grace, is appropriate. 'Everything is shit, and so are we.' That's perhaps their most common slogan; they use it to say hello, good-bye, and as an interjection in conversation. Though the term isn't 'shit,' it is something like 'the marrowless and broken husk of a dead stem.' They seem to regard the whole universe as a dismal ruin, with themselves as worthless as cockroaches picking their way through the rubble. By human standards they are almost comically gloomy, I suspect."

"Yet they raise their infants." Yuri glanced at the injured builder, who still danced before the ColU's puppet. "And they care for their sick."

"That they do—"

It broke off. The arm puppet stopped "dancing" suddenly, the manipulator arms folded away, and the ColU rolled backward on its tracks and turned to face the north shore. The builders stopped too, evidently startled by the ColU; after freezing for a moment they abruptly began a new conversation among themselves.

Yuri looked to the north. An orange spark was climbing into the sky: a flare.

The ColU was already rolling away. Yuri ran after it as fast as he could, but he was easily outpaced.

By the time he intercepted the ColU it was already on its way back to the settlement, with Mardina riding on its front unit, leaning back against its bubble-dome cover. As it rolled along, the ColU's endlessly adaptable manipulator arms were working on Mardina's belly, massaging it in great downward sweeps.

Yuri jogged alongside. "Are you all right?"

"What does it look like?" she snarled back. "My water's broken. I've had a couple of contractions. And my back's killing me."

"Everything is under control," the ColU said calmly, rolling presumably as fast as it dared.

"Shut up, you."

"Here." Yuri took off his stem-bark tunic, rolled it up, and shoved it behind Mardina's back. She accepted this, at least. "What else can I do?"

"You can piss off and leave it to me and my robot doctor here. I—*ow*—oh, you little bastard!"

"Please run ahead, Yuri Eden," the ColU said. "We will be using the house; please make it ready, as we have planned."

Mardina snapped, "Just get on with it, you—*ow!*"

So Yuri hurried ahead.

They'd rehearsed all this. At the house he cleared out his own gear to one of the storehouses, moved Mardina's bed closer to the door, and lit a fire in the hearth. He made sure that all their remaining ISF-issue medical packs were on hand, close to Mardina's bed. He widened the doorway too, removing a few panels that they had prefitted to ensure the ColU had access to the house when it needed it.

When the ColU arrived, Mardina was adamant. "Out, ice boy. I don't want you anywhere near me."

"It's my kid too—"

"It's my bloody pelvis. Out, out!"

The ColU murmured, "I think it's best, Yuri Eden."

"All right, all right."

"I will call you when—"

"I said all right." Yuri stamped out.

He had to watch as the ColU cautiously worked its way into the house; it wouldn't fit all the way inside, and Yuri, on a request by the ColU, draped a tarpaulin over its protruding rear end, blocking off the entrance to the house.

After that he could see nothing of the birth.

The labor took hours, and sounded difficult. Not that Yuri had any prior experience. He could hear screams and weeping, and the calm voice of the ColU urging its patient to breathe, breathe.

After a time he wandered off, seeking a chore that might distract him, in the fields, in the little storehouse they had put aside as a workshop. Nothing seemed meaningful. Everything that was important in his universe, all that mattered on this world, was going on inside the house he had built with Mardina, and he could do nothing to influence it.

On impulse he walked away from the camp, heading back toward the lake.

A cloud of depression gathered. What use was he? He had been on Per Ardua for four years already. In one random bout of clumsy, only half-satisfactory sex he had done all that Mardina had ever needed of him, or would ever need. He felt as if he had no identity—and he hadn't, not since his parents had bundled him into the cryo tank in Manchester. Even here, in this little two-person colony, he didn't matter, not fundamentally, not when it really came to it. He had had such moods since waking up on Mars. Generally he fought them off with work. It was harder alone.

He climbed a bluff, from where he had a good view of the lake. He could see those dams and the brimming floods behind them to the north, and those strangely shaped middens to the south. From here he got a clear sense that the whole layout of the middens really was integrated, somehow, as if all these constructions served a single purpose. And he saw builders moving on those north and south shores, blurs of movement as they spun, tracked, congregated in little groups that quickly broke up and re-formed elsewhere. Mardina was right; they were building up to something, some big stage in whatever project they were working through.

And all of them, of course, utterly ignored the human being standing alone on this bluff watching them, this visitor from another star. What an astonishing thing—as if Egyptian slaves had continued laboring over their pyramids while ignoring the silvery UFO that had landed in the shadow of the Sphinx. But why shouldn't they ignore him? He didn't matter to his own people, and never had; why should he matter to these aliens?

There was a kind of cracking sound.

He saw a spray of water rising up from one of those dams to the north, as if it had suddenly been breached. Had it failed? But another crack came, like a cannon shot, and another, and he saw more sprays of misty water lifting into the air from other dams, and he heard a kind of roar.

It was no accident. Those dams had been *timed* to fail, all at the same time, or were being deliberately demolished, one by one, and the roar he heard was the flow of released water; the great floods trapped behind the dams must be gushing forward into the lake. But why was all this being done?

And now he heard a popping noise, coming from behind him.

He turned to look back at the camp. Another flare had been fired; a spark of orange light lifted high into the sky, over their conical house.

He climbed down off the bluff and ran back, as hard and fast as he could.

By the time Yuri arrived, the ColU was backing out of the house. It was holding a bundle of blankets. Yuri would never have imagined that a bunch of killer-robot manipulator arms could have expressed such tenderness.

Abruptly, the ColU began to speak, loudly. "What an ugly child! Practically a monstrosity. And it's going to be badly behaved all its life, I can tell just by looking at it, and nothing but a burden to its wretched parents . . ."

"ColU! What the hell are you doing?"

In a more normal tone it said, "Following the Lieutenant's instructions, Yuri Eden. Scaring off the evil spirits that attend every birth, in malevolent hopefulness. And now . . ." Carefully, slowly, like some heavy orbital spacecraft gingerly attempting a docking with a space station, the ColU handed the baby to Yuri.

Yuri had had some instruction in this, even practice with bundles of clothes and blankets overseen by a stern Mardina, and he knew how to support the child, how to cradle its head. Deep in the mass of blankets was a small, crumpled, pink, moist face with closed puffy eyes, and hair plastered down by fluid. The hair was black like its mother's, but straight like its father's. Looking down at the child, Yuri felt something shift and break inside him, like a collapsing dam of his own.

"Beth," the ColU said. "Her name is Beth Eden Jones. The mother is fine. Mardina's going to try to sleep, but she said she will see you."

"Thank you."

"It was my function. But I appreciate your saying that, Yuri Eden."

A memory floated to the surface of Yuri's mind. It seemed distant, almost irrelevant. "You might want to take a look at the lake."

"The lake?"

"While you were in there with Mardina—there have been developments."

"I will. Go and see the mother, Yuri Eden." It turned and rolled away, in the direction of the lake.

Yuri stepped into the house. The tarpaulin he'd hung to cover the ColU's rump was still dangling from hooks, shutting out the day. Inside the house was a smell of blood and bodies, and antiseptic, and the scent of the still-burning fire—a stem scent that was suddenly, sharply, redolent of the builders, as if those gloomy, dogged creatures were in here singing a lullaby. Mardina lay flat on her bed, looking exhausted, but she was cleaned up, in a fresh nightgown, with her hair brushed back, her face washed. She smiled when Yuri stood over her with the baby. He saw that the cot that the ColU had fabricated, a structure of Arduan stems, stood ready beside her bed.

He asked, "Do you want anything?"

"No. Well, to sleep in a minute. Just wanted to see you."

"Nicest thing you ever said to me, astronaut."

"Don't push it, ice boy."

"So this is Beth."

"My mother's name. You have any objections?"

"Of course not. I think I expected your mother's name to be—"

"More exotic? 'Elizabeth' is what they called her in the school she grew up in, after the Desiccation Resettlement. She was separated from her own mother. Never knew her birth name."

"Beth it is, then."

"Sure . . . What are you feeling, Yuri?"

He tried to express it. "Like I stepped through another door."

"Your life has changed again, huh. So now here she is. Phase One of the grand plan, remember? Our retirement insurance, and the loins of the next generation."

"She's none of those things. She's Beth." He looked down at the baby, at this piece of himself. "None of that Adam and Eve crap. I, we, we're going to protect her, and nurture her, and give her as full a life as she deserves."

Mardina raised her head weakly. "That's a big promise, ice boy. I mean, for instance, how can she ever fall in love? Nothing's changed in the bigger picture, Yuri. We're still stuck here, alone."

"Another door will open," Yuri said calmly. "Just like before. And I'll step through it, and I'll take Beth with me, and you."

Mardina smiled. "You know, right now, I believe you. But that's probably the drugs talking. Let me sleep and get back to normal, and I'll kick your butt properly."

"I'll put her in her crib . . ."

But Mardina, lying back, had already drifted away.

35

Twelve hours later, with Mardina awake, and the baby's first feeds negotiated successfully, the ColU drove up to the house. It waited outside until Yuri popped his head out of the door.

"Sorry to disturb you, Yuri Eden."

"That's OK, buddy."

"It's the lake. You alerted me to developments during the confinement. There have been more. I thought perhaps you would both wish to see. Well, all three of you."

"I'm not sure if—"

"Count me in, ColU." Mardina, swathed in a heavy ISF-issue overcoat, pushed her way out of the house. She breathed deeply. "Clean air in the lungs. Nothing better. Tell you what, I'll put on my tracksuit and we'll jog over."

"We won't, you know."

"I think she is teasing you, Yuri Eden," the ColU said.

She was grinning. "You're so easy, ice boy. We'll ride on the ColU, and you can walk. Deal?"

They took their time to get ready for the little expedition, with the ColU laden with blankets, water, and hot drinks for Mardina, and expressed milk for the baby. Then they set off toward the lake. The air, under the increasingly mottled face of Proxima, was fresh, even cold.

Before they reached the eastern shore, they climbed one of the many shallow bluffs that studded this landscape and looked out over the lake.

Which had changed, dramatically. Those big flooded areas behind the northern dams were drained. But the risen lake water had now broken through its bank on the south side, and, guided apparently by the builders' middens, was gushing into the dry river channel that Yuri had walked through many times. Already it was beginning to flood a depression some way to the south. Everywhere the builders were on the move, adults with infants, even a few apparent invalids being carried by parties of adults, streaming around the banks of the lake toward the outflow channel.

"They did this deliberately," Mardina breathed.

"That's correct, Lieutenant Jones. This has been engineered by the builders. The sudden release of the trapped floodwater behind the northern dams created a surge that broke the southern banks and scoured the outflow channels, deepening and widening them. Now much of the lake, I calculate, will drain away. And it will re-form in the depression you see to the south, which extends some way beyond, but which will drain in its turn . . . I have studied the topography. I believe that by the time this maneuver is completed, the lake will have been *moved* some ten kilometers to the south."

" 'Maneuver,' " repeated Mardina, cradling the baby. " 'Moved.' The way you put that makes it sound as if you believe this was purposeful."

"That's exactly what I believe, Lieutenant Jones. The builders have engineered this; they have deliberately shifted the lake to the south. And once it is there, presumably, they will replant stem beds, perhaps restock the water with the fish analogues and other creatures . . . They have been aided by that steady uplift to the north, I mean the geological uplift, the magmatic event that appears to be occurring there. But, yes, it seems clear to me that they have moved this lake."

"Why?"

"I have no answer to that," the ColU said. "I can only speculate. But there must be a good reason. I suspect we will find out in time."

Mardina asked, "So what does this mean for us?"

"That's our only stable supply of water," Yuri said. "We can't rely on the rain. We know that. If the lake moves, we have to move with it."

The ColU looked pained. "I have created whole fields of terrestrial topsoil at this site."

"So we move the soil as best we can, as much as we can. It's no use here without water. We'll have to shift our other stuff too. The house, the buildings—maybe we'll rebuild in some modular form, for when we have to break it all down again."

"You mean," Mardina said slowly, "when the builders shift the lake again, some time in the future."

"Right."

"Why should they do that?"

"If they've done it once, why shouldn't they do it again?"

"The ISF imagined we'd be stuck here, in this place, for life," Mardina said. "Tied to the lake for its water. Instead, the lake's migrating, and so are we."

"That's right." He grinned. "Everything's changed."

"And a door's opened for you, ice boy. Just as you said it would."

"Damn right. Now all we have to do is to step through. And who knows what we'll find?"

"ColU," Mardina said, "what did you say the builder phrase for the lake is?"

" 'The interface between mother and father which brings life.' "

"Hmm. And wherever it travels, yes, it *will* bring life. It is like the Dreamtime spirit that created the rivers and the waterholes. It is a *jilla*."

Yuri nodded. "OK. Better name than Puddle anyhow."

The baby started to cry, cold, tired, hungry. The ColU, moving with an oddly balletic grace despite its bulk, turned carefully, disturbing its fragile cargo as little as possible, and headed back to the camp.

36

The flight by the UEI hulk ship from Earth to Mercury was a high-energy straight-line blast across the solar system, at a constant one-gravity acceleration. Constant, save for one six-hour interval of microgravity, when the kernel drive was briefly shut down, the systems checked out, and the ship flipped over to begin its deceleration to the destination.

In this interval, while the drive was inert, Monica Trant invited Stef Kalinski to visit the hulk's engine room. Led by an ISF crewman, they pulled themselves down a fireman's pole that ran the length of the axis of the big, spacious tank that comprised the greater part of the hulk, down toward the engines.

"Thanks for this," Stef said to Trant. "You know how it is. Since I graduated I've devoted practically my entire life to a study of the kernels. But I've only ever had access to the handful of specimens donated by UEI to the UN moon labs, and even there we've never been allowed to run the kind of high-energy experiments—"

"Like the ones our engineers run down in the engine rooms of hulks like the *Shrapnel* every day," Trant said dryly. "I know. Well, given the strangeness of what they seem to have found on Mercury, they've decided they need theoreticians after all. So fill your boots."

They reached a security gate set in the base of the hulk, where a crewman held them up to verify their security-scan access to the engine room. Stef, weightless, clung to her pole and peered up into the great tank of the ship's hull, brightly lit by fluorescent strips. On this trip the hull was more or less empty—incredibly, the main purpose of this high-velocity interplanetary flight seemed to be to bring *her* to Mercury—but she could see brackets and shadows in the paintwork where partition floors, loading cranes, and other fixtures could be fitted. Right now ISF crew swarmed in the air, taking the chance to clean out clogged air filters and perform other chores in corners hard to access under gravity.

A hulk like this was regularly used to transport massive cargoes between the planets. Science samples, for instance. A century back, planetologists had crowed about samples returned to Earth from Mars by robot craft, samples which had been measured in *grams*. Now they brought back rocks that weighed tons, and kilometer-long cores of Martian polar ice. They had even run an experimental ship across interstellar space, to the habitable world that had been detected orbiting Proxima Centauri. And, routinely nowadays, hulks like this were used to transport *hundreds* of colonists to the UN bases on the moon and Mars. Stef thought she could smell the stink of all the people who had traveled in this ship, sweat and urine and baby milk, suffused into the very fabric of the ship.

Monica Trant saw her looking. "Not pretty, is it? But very effective. The *Shrapnel* is one of the more reliable members of UEI's little interplanetary fleet."

"Why *Shrapnel*? I thought the ship's name was *Princess Aebbe*." In the passenger lounges there were little animations of the launch of the ship from its dry dock at an Earth-moon Lagrange point by the youngest daughter of the North British King, and the royal family's "Fighting Man" standard was splashed in lurid red and gold all over the hull, amid UN roundels and UEI logos.

"So it is. But all these hulks have more familiar names given them by their engineers. We don't trust the kernels because we don't understand them. So—the *Mushroom Cloud*, the *Shrapnel*, the *Pancake*."

"Black humor."

Trant looked at her quizzically. She was in her late thirties now, her hair graying and pulled back, but she looked fit, lean, clearly competent in her world. "Black humor, yes. You don't spend much time around people, do you? I always remembered that about you, even when we were running Angelia from Yeats with your father. You were a withdrawn little kid, always had your nose pressed up to some screen or other."

"You know kids, do you?"

"I've one of my own. Little Rob. Two years old now. Back home with his father . . ."

"You didn't stick around long on the Angelia project."

Trant seemed cautious. "I lasted a few years. Since Angelia went quiet there's been nothing to do but archiving and recontact attempts. Look, Major—"

"Call me Stef."

"Sure. No offense, I know Angelia was your late father's pet project, but it was obsolete before it was launched. So I moved to where the action was, the new field of kernel engineering. As did you, in a way, right? I used contacts I made at the launch of the *I-One*. And now I'm one of UEI's top internal consultants on kernel engineering. That's how life is."

Stef shrugged. Personal conversations like this, about people's excuses for their life choices, didn't interest her much.

"And you ought to feel honored," Trant said now. "These craft hardly ever fly empty, not since their proving flights. They must really want to get you to Mercury, huh?" She sounded faintly envious.

"I hope I can make a contribution," Stef said neutrally.

At last the crewman got their access approved. He opened the hatch, and they passed out of the hulk's big internal space, down through a thick bulkhead. They had to cycle through a kind of airlock, and Stef was aware of various kinds of security scans being run; shimmering lines, laser guides, swept over her.

"Just routine," Trant said.

"Why's it necessary? If any sabotage was attempted to the drive, probably the whole ship would be destroyed, saboteur and all. The energies are such that—"

"I do know," Trant said, a little testily. "But we carry hundreds of colonists across the solar system, and some of them figure out on the way that they're not too happy about becoming colonists after all, whether or not they were given a choice about it. They can get kind of desperate. People don't always act rationally, Major Kalinski. And then there's the Chinese factor."

"You can't be serious."

"Well, there you have a major power who's still excluded from any share of this advanced, and very powerful, technology. If the UEI and ISF *aren't* riddled with Chinese spies, if not saboteurs, I'd be surprised. So we take security seriously."

They were passed through, and dropped down into a rest area, with a lavatory, a couple of bunk beds, a small galley.

And here Sir Michael King was waiting for them, loosely strapped to a couch, sipping coffee through a plastic cup with a nozzle. He was wearing a kind of coverall, deep royal blue, cut to fit his squat, heavy frame, that simultaneously looked practical and expensive. When Trant and Stef entered, swimming down from the ceiling, he pushed himself out of his chair. "Glad to see you made it down here, Major Kalinski."

"Why wouldn't I, sir?"

"Most passengers, especially those from Earth, spend most of their time during the accel-decel handover locked in their cabins chucking up."

"I'm a veteran of the Earth-moon run. My body's used to micro-gravity."

"Well, mine isn't," King said. "I had to swallow a whole pharmaco-peia." He grinned, his face pale, sweating. "But I wouldn't miss it for the world."

Trant nodded at the ISF crewman who, discreet and unspeaking, had followed them in here. "Let's get on with it."

The crewman opened another hatch, in the floor. Below, Stef saw, was a kind of carpet, speckled with lights that shone bright in a relative gloom. They followed the crewman down through the hatch, and spread out.

There were three, four crew already in this wide chamber, in their jet-black ISF uniforms, swimming over the illuminated carpet, carrying slates, making notes and murmuring to one another. The "carpet" was actually another bulkhead that spanned the width of the hulk, Stef saw now, and the lights that sparkled in the floor, more or less uniformly distributed, were a display. Flux lines swept between the lights, uniting them in a pleasing, swirling geometry—a three-dimensional geometry, Stef saw, as she shifted her head from side to side. The whole was lit-tered with tiny labels, numbers and English letters; the systems sensed whatever she was looking at, and the labels magnified in her vision.

Trant said, "This is our engine room. We run everything through this one display. Under acceleration, this is a floor under our feet, but in microgravity it makes more sense to treat it as a vertical wall—you can see there are hand- and footholds . . ."

Sir Michael King was watching Stef intently. "This is as close as we can get to the real action. I mean, I understand the display we see here is just a representation of the reality, but . . . Can you feel them, Major? I know you've been around kernels for years, but not an array like this. Can you *sense* them? Can you feel their energies?"

And Stef thought she could, yes, a kind of tide that pulled at her body as she hung there in the air—a tide from the space-time knots of the kernels themselves, perhaps, or maybe a force exerted by the powerful magnetic fields that held them in place, a great wall of them contained not meters from her position. She felt thrilled, viscerally, physically; the pathetic handful of kernels in the lunar labs would have been lost in this huge assembly.

King said, "Here you are, confronted by the mystery. Tell me about kernels, Major Kalinski."

"I can tell you what we think we know. Which is precious little."

He pulled a face. "And I could tell you how much that inadequate reply has cost me so far."

"Sorry."

He said, "I know a kernel is a twisted bit of reality. Like a black hole, right?"

"That was our first guess. Black holes are similarly twisted bits of space-time, yes, the remnants of imploded giant stars, or maybe relics of the Big Bang. And all black holes radiate; they leak energy from their event horizons, and the smaller they get the hotter they are. But nothing fit. A kernel masses only *kilograms*, a lot less than any but the most evanescent black hole. And the energy it emits isn't black-hole Hawking radiation but something much more exotic, a flood of high-energy photons and very high-speed particles, like cosmic rays. Also, the way the energy leaks from a kernel depends on the way you prod it."

"You mean with laser beams," King said. "Well, I know about that. A lot of lives were lost to establish that simple fact. And Mercury gained itself a new crater."

"By manipulating it with laser beams you can *shape* the way a kernel releases its energy store. Get it right and it can even be unidirectional."

"Like a little rocket."

"A microscopic photon rocket, yes. And that's what makes them so useful. The kernels carry an electric charge, and are so light that a powerful enough magnetic field can hold a whole bank of them in place, just as in this ship, behind this bulkhead. Fire the control lasers just right and they all open up, and you get a kind of photon rocket."

"Driven by a light as bright as the sun," King said. "Visible across interplanetary distances. Hell of a thing. After all these years, you know, I still can't get used to the sight. But what I want to know from you, Major, is how the damn things work. Where does all that lovely energy come from?"

"Well, not from the structure of the kernel itself—it's not massive enough for that. Our best guess is that a kernel is less like a black hole than a wormhole—"

"A tunnel in space."

"Yes."

"I thought wormholes were impossible," Trant said. "You need some strange kind of matter to keep them open."

Stef always got irritated when some lay person asked her a question and then started lecturing her about the answer, rather than just *listening*. She snapped, "It may have looked that way according to the kiddie Einstein-relativity stuff you learned at high school, Monica, before you gave up science for engineering. Have you ever heard of a dilaton field? No?"

Monica Trant looked irritated.

King raised luxuriant eyebrows, amused. "Well, that's put *you* in your place. Let's get to the basics. A wormhole is a tunnel, right? From here to . . . someplace else."

"That's right."

"So the energy that flows out of a kernel, the energy we harness to drive our hulks, doesn't come from the kernel itself. It comes from someplace else, and is just transmitted through the kernel."

"That seems to be true. The ultimate power source must be some very energetic event, *somewhere else*. A gamma-ray burster, maybe. Could be from the future or the past."

Trant frowned. "What do you mean by that?"

"The wormhole could connect you to any other point in space and time, sir. Or—"

King waved a hand. "Enough, enough. You know, Major, some people are suspicious of the kernels. I mean, their very existence. Your own father was, right? There we were struggling to come up with ways to reach the stars. And now we've been handed this magic power source, on a plate, and we're off to Proxima Centauri. We needed a miracle, and suddenly we had one. The problem is, you see, Major, in business or in politics, hell, in most marriages, if I give you something, it's generally because I want something of you in return. So what's the catch?"

"You're assuming agency," Stef protested. "Intervention by some kind of consciousness. It's better to rule that out until there's overwhelming evidence. Occam's razor: you should default to the simplest explanation, and natural causes are the simplest explanation we have for most phenomena. Including the presence of kernels on Mercury."

Trant said, "Wait until we get you to Mercury, Kalinski." She shook her head. "Occam's razor. Jesus."

A gong sounded, echoing around the ship.

King turned to the ladder up to the main hull. "They're about to fire up again. You'll find me in my couch, until my old bones get used to gravity again . . ."

Stef was allowed to stay down on the control deck, with Trant, the two of them strapped into acceleration harnesses, watching as the highly trained crew went through the process of firing up their laser banks, opening up their tame space-time knots, and allowing their unknown-source energy to stream out.

And the tremendous mass of the hulk was once more hurled forward into the heart of the solar system.

At Mercury the *Shrapnel* entered a low equatorial orbit, and a small, low-powered shuttle flew up to bring Stef, King, Trant and a couple of ISF guards down to the surface. The little ship was piloted by ISF officers, who saluted Stef when she boarded while simultaneously security-scanning her. The shuttle had only one cabin, fronted by the pilot with the passengers in the back, and while the passengers strapped in, Stef heard the crew talk through more complicated security protocols. Evidently this wasn't a place where casual landings were welcome.

They came down in a sweeping powered descent across a shattered landscape. The shadows of crater-rim mountains, wave after frozen rocky wave of them, stretched across broken lava plains.

Trant turned to Stef. "Do you know where you are? On Mercury, I mean."

Stef shrugged. "I only came back once to Mercury since the *Angelia* launch. It was a memorial service for my father after he died, given by the staff he worked with here."

"I know. I was there, though we didn't speak."

"I think this must be the Caloris basin." A tremendous impact crater that dominated one face of the planet. "Given the scale of the cratering features."

"Correct. The result of an impact that couldn't have been much bigger, to have left any planet behind at all. I suppose you don't need to know much about Mercury to guess that much."

"I've had no briefing," Stef reminded her testily. "So it's to be guessing games, is it, all the way down?"

"We want you to take a fresh look at what we found. I suggested it was best not to prejudice you in any way. Blame me, if you like."

Stef felt a shiver of awe, flying over this tremendous ruined landscape, which itself concealed a much more exotic mystery. What the hell *were* they being so secretive about?

On the ground, in the chaotic shadows of Caloris, they were bundled into a rover. There was a driver and a couple of crew, all in ISF uniforms. The two security goons who had come down from orbit with them followed too. Making her way to a seat in the rover, Stef experienced a gravity that was twice the moon's, a third of Earth's, a gravity that felt oddly familiar, a body memory from her childhood.

The rover rolled off, and through the small windows Stef glimpsed the landscape of Mercury, for her a peculiar mix of alien and familiar. The sun was just below the horizon here, though a smear of coronal light spread up into the sky. The shuttle landing site behind her was lit by brilliant floods.

"Here." Trant opened a hatch and pulled out pressure suits. "One each. We'll suit up en route in the rover."

King awkwardly hauled his own suit over his bulk. "We're making straight for the site."

Stef asked, "What site?"

Trant said, "This is, or was, just another exploratory drilling site."

"You were looking for kernels."

"Essentially, though Mercury is also still exporting metals to the rest of the inner system. Stef, you'll find dormitories in the well-head domes, showers, galleys. If you need a break before we descend . . ."

Descend into what? Every bit of information they gave her seemed to lead only to more questions. Let them play their games. "Let's just get on with it." Trying not to let their evident urgency transmit itself to her, she pulled on her suit, ISF standard issue, a piece of kit she was used to. The smart fabric slid into formfitting shape around her; as the suit recognized her a panel on the chest lit up with her mug shot, rank, commission number, name: KALINSKI, STEPHANIE P.

King smiled. "That's correct, isn't it? P for Penelope."

Stef pulled a face. "A name I always hated even more than 'Stephanie.' So you found kernels in Caloris, right?"

Trant looked out at the smashed landscape. "We've developed pretty efficient ways to prospect for kernels, even from orbit. We look for concentrations of the kernels' distinctive energy signature, at sites easy to mine. The heart of Caloris has given us some rich pickings, actually. The kernel lodes here aren't always quite as deep as elsewhere on the planet, and the ancient impact shattered the bedrock, making it relatively easy to get through. 'Relatively' being the word."

Stef thought that over. "Which implies that the Caloris impact came later than whatever event laid down the kernels."

King nodded approvingly. "That's what my tame geologists deduce. Even though the Caloris event itself was very old, a relic of the planet-formation days. The kernels have been down there a long time; whatever created them, or implanted them, was a very early event in terms of the history of Mercury—hell, of the solar system itself. So we drilled down into the floor of the crater, and that itself was a challenge, I can tell you. But what we found—well, you'll see for yourself."

The rover had to pass through a couple more security cordons before pulling up at what was evidently a drilling site, dominated by a single massive rig standing on an area of relative flatness. Stef saw hab domes covered in regolith for solar-radiation screening, a few more rigs much smaller in scale, and massive specialized vehicles.

As they unbuckled, Trant pointed out the equipment. "The rigs are structures of high-strength, high-temperature-tolerant carbon. Those smaller rigs were the first to make the discovery we're going to show you. We brought out the heavy-duty gear to allow human access to the find; that big momma over there drilled out the shaft you're going to be riding down today . . ."

A flexible transfer tunnel snaked out from a dome toward the rover. Trant led them through a brisk check of their pressure suits. "We'll be riding a pressurized car down the shaft," she said. "But we'll wear the suits as a precaution anyhow. And of course the base chamber isn't pressurized at all."

Stef tried to figure out these pieces of the puzzle as she went through the routine of interrogating her suit's functions. *Shaft? Base chamber?*

The rover hatch opened up, and they passed through the flexible tunnel to the dome. The interior was functional, with lab areas, bathrooms, suit lockers, a galley, bunks. A handful of staff here, in shirts and shorts, working or eating handheld snacks, eyed the newcomers in their pressure suits curiously, but didn't approach them. Stef felt she could have been inside any pioneering-science-type establishment almost anywhere in the solar system, off Earth.

But this particular facility was dominated by a transparently walled elevator car, set at the very center of the dome where the roof was highest, attached by winched cables to a stout metal frame. And the car was suspended over an open shaft, from which fluorescent light leaked.

A shaft. A hole in the Mercury ground. Into which, evidently, Stef was going to have to descend. She felt a frisson of fear, and she was grateful for her ISF training, for the ability it gave her to function despite her fear, even if she couldn't hide it, probably.

Stef was led straight to the elevator, with Trant, King, and the two ISF goons who had ridden down from orbit with them and had barely spoken a word, even to each other. They all crowded into the car. It contained a crate, Stef presumed containing supplies or emergency gear. A door, transparent as the walls, slid closed behind them.

Immediately the car began to descend, with a soft, low-gravity lurch. The dome and its inhabitants ascended out of Stef's sight, and the walls of the shaft rose up to enclose the car.

The shaft walls were smooth, featureless, and it was impossible to judge directly the car's speed of descent. But Stef could feel the acceleration.

Then, with a snap, as she could see through the transparent roof, the cables from the winch disengaged. Yet the car continued to descend.

"This is a pretty fast ride."

Trant grunted. "We had to custom-design the system. We're going too deep for conventional cables, even under the low gravity. We fitted the car with crawler attachments; we're clambering down the walls of the shaft."

"Too deep," Stef repeated. "How deep?"

"Over four hundred kilometers," Trant said, with a touch of pride—justifiable, Stef thought. "We're going all the way to the base of the planet's crust. To the fringe of the mantle, in fact, which is where the kernels are found."

"It's quite a trip," King said. "All this is hush-hush at present, you understand, but I have got a couple of tame journalists documenting all this for the history books. I'm given to understand that a crewed trip to the edge of a planetary mantle has never been achieved elsewhere, not even on Earth."

Stef thought over what she knew about Mercury. "I thought the prevailing theory is that Mercury suffered a tremendous impact, back in the age of planet formation. The whack shattered and stripped away the planet's upper rocky layers. Right?"

"That's one theory," Trant said. "There's another that's doing the rounds here. Informally, I mean. That whatever incredible event created or implanted the kernels on Mercury might have caused a huge convulsion of energy, a convulsion that nearly blew the planet apart."

"Wow," Stef said, impressed, but she reached for her native scientific caution. "Quite a hypothesis. Have you got any way of proving it?"

King said, "I rather think that's why you're here, Major Kalinski."

The elevator car slid to a smooth halt, and the shaft walls seemed to lift like a curtain. Stef found herself looking out into a cavern, flat-roofed, cut into the deep rock. This cave, hundreds of kilometers under Mercury's surface, was brightly lit, and there were more small domes, pressurized facilities, marked with UN and UEI sigils.

The purpose of the cavern was obvious too. Armed troopers in military-specification pressure suits stood in a loose circle around what looked like an unprepossessing patch of floor. Stef saw that scientific equipment of all kinds had been assembled around this bit of floor; lenses and other sensors peered down, and there was an industrial-strength laser mount. Something about the whole setup, the sheer bizarreness of finding a science base and security cordon hundreds of kilometers deep under Mercury, made Stef's heart hammer even harder.

"Time to close up your suits," Trant said. "We'll run through another full integrity check before stepping out of the car."

Stef was glad of the long minutes of routine that followed. Since arriving in Mercury orbit she felt as if she had fallen too quickly into this place, this pit bored into the deepest rocky heart of the solar system; she needed time for her soul to catch up with her body.

At last the car door opened, the air sighed out, and Stef walked out, heading toward the circle of troopers, the enigmatic patch of floor they protected. She was locked inside her suit, listening to the air-circulation fans and her own noisy breathing. The troopers let them pass. And as they neared the very center, King and Trant too stepped back, allowing Stef to walk forward alone, staring at the floor.

And there, set in the rock of Mercury, buried under hundreds of kilometers of crustal layers for billions of years until dug out by questing human hands and tools, was—

A hatch.

Stef walked around the emplacement, trying to absorb the physical reality of it. Trying to observe rather than analyze, for now, the best strategy when faced with the utterly unexpected.

What did she *see*?

She saw a panel, a rough square of some seamless, pale gray material—metal, perhaps, or ceramic, or some unknown material altogether. It was maybe ten meters across. And at the center of the panel was a circle, a fine seam engraved into the plain material, perhaps three meters in diameter. That was all; there was no further marking or indentation.

She turned to face King and Trant, who looked at her expectantly.

"Well?" King snapped. "You see why we didn't tell you? You see why you had to look for yourself? And you see why we told Earthshine? It's hard to think of a more significant development for the future of the human race."

"It's obviously artificial," she said. She turned back. "Obviously—a hatch."

Trant grinned. "That's what everybody calls it. A common first reaction. In the internal reports we capitalize it. *The Hatch*," she said heavily. She turned, gesturing at the walls. "There are kernels all through this layer. You could pick them out by hand. And in the middle of this rich lode, we found—this."

"How did you detect it?"

"Initially by traces in deep radar pulses, seismic traces. Some very strange echoes."

Stef knelt now, beside the emplacement. The panel looked about a couple of centimeters thick. "Is it safe to touch?"

"Be my guest," Trant said.

Stef set her right hand on the material. She felt nothing. "I wish I didn't have to wear this damn glove."

"The material is actually a good deal cooler than the ambient temperature."

Stef drew her hand back over the edge of the panel, and felt an odd pulling sensation. She tried again, passing her hand back and forth over the edge; it was a kind of tide, a sideways push, like passing a charged iron rod through a magnetic field.

"We don't know what it's made of," Trant said. "Needless to say. We've tried cutting it, with low-level lasers; it just soaks up the heat. There are more destructive tests we could try, but we've been reluctant to go that far."

Stef knew there had always been loose talk about the kernels possibly being artifacts of intelligence. They might or might not be. It was hard to dismiss the Hatch as anything *other* than an artifact—what natural process could produce an object with this regularity? "Do you think it's in any way associated with the kernels?"

"Well," King said, "we found it in the same layer as a rich kernel lode—"

Trant said, "It seems coincidental if they aren't associated. To find two extraordinary things in one location—assuming a link exists is the simplest hypothesis. Occam's razor, Major Kalinski?"

She ignored the gentle goad. "I don't suppose you've tried opening the Hatch."

Trant said, "That seam, whatever it is, is too fine for most of our tools. We could try harder . . . Anyhow, it would be futile."

"How so?"

"Because the Hatch is just a mask. A plate sitting there on leveled-off rock. There's nothing underneath it. We've proved that with sonic and radar probes, and by drilling into the rock under the Hatch." She pointed to a couple of small pits.

Stef got to her knees again and examined the Hatch, running her fingers along its thickness. Again she felt that odd sideways push. "Have you measured its volume?"

"I can tell you the calculation." Trant pulled a slate from a pouch in her suit leg and fiddled with it. "We've got precise measurements of every dimension—"

"No. That's a calculation. Length by breadth by height. Have you *measured* the volume?"

Trant seemed baffled. "No. I mean—how?"

Stef stood up. "What have you got in the nature of fluids down here? Water, lubricants . . ."

It took a couple of hours to set up the experiment. They rigged up a dome over the Hatch that would hold pressure, and pumped it full of non-reactive nitrogen. Then they poured in lubricant, an inert hydrocarbon borrowed from the elevator assembly, that flooded the emplacement.

It was fiddly work in pressure suits and with improvised equipment, but once Stef had communicated what she wanted, the engineers worked quickly and effectively, even though some of them grumbled about the risk of wasting the lubricant, a precious resource here on Mercury. It was always the same with engineers, Stef had observed; nothing made them happier than to be given a well-defined and achievable task, and to be left alone to get on with it.

So they measured the volume of the Hatch and its emplacement directly, from the displacement of the lubricant fluid. She had them repeat the measurement a few times for accuracy.

The direct measurement differed from the result obtained by multiplying together length, breadth and height.

"It's too big," Trant said, wondering. "Ten percent or more . . . Too big for any errors."

"I don't understand," King said, grumbling. "I can't get my head around this. All this mucking about with engine oil!"

Stef grinned. He seemed disappointed she hadn't ordered some vast super-physics experiment to be run. "Sir Michael, it's as if you have a one-liter jug, only it holds two liters."

"It's bigger on the inside than the outside?"

"Something like that. There's some kind of distortion of space-time

going on here." The dome had been cleared away now, the Hatch revealed again, the last of the lubricant fluid removed. Stef knelt and
touched the panel surface once more.

Trant was staring past her. "Major—"

Stef passed her hand over the edge. "Just like before, I feel something, like a tidal effect."

"Major Kalinski, I think—"

"And just as the kernels are evidently some kind of space-time phenomenon, so is the Hatch—"

"*Stephanie!*" King snapped.

Stef was startled into silence, and turned. Just for a moment King
had sounded like Stef's father, as King had surely intended.

Trant, glaring, was pointing at the Hatch. "Shut up," she said
evenly. "Turn around. And look."

Stef turned, needles of icy anticipation prickling along her spine.

The Hatch had changed.

That smooth surface, within the circular seam, was smooth no more. A
series of indentations had appeared, set evenly around the edge—they
came in pairs, twelve pairs, she counted quickly, like the numbers on an
antique clock dial. The indentations themselves were complex in shape,
with a textured central crater, and five channels running off in a lop-
sided star shape.

"Hands," King said. "They're meant for human hands."

Stef saw it as soon as he said it. Somehow she'd been blinded by the
obvious, by the incongruity of the setting.

"The imprints of human hands," Trant said slowly. "On an artifact
that's nearly as old as Mercury itself. That's been here forty thousand
times as long as humanity has even existed."

"More to the point," King said, "imprints that weren't there a minute ago. Not before Major Kalinski ran her experiment with the
lubricant."

"And," Stef said carefully, "before we made our very first deduction
about it. Suddenly it knows we are here."

Trant guffawed. "It *knows*? Now who's hypothesizing about
agencies?"

Stef ignored her. "The purpose seems obvious." She stepped up to the Hatch, and knelt beside it once more. She held out her hands, and again felt that odd tidal ripple. Had the quality of that sensation changed at all? Her senses didn't seem subtle enough to be able to tell. She looked back at King and Trant, at the technicians and guards behind them, all in their ISF pressure suits, like so many robots. All of them staring straight back at her. As if daring her.

She turned, spread her gloved fingers, and extended her hands so they were over one of the indentation sets. But she held back from touching the surface. Should she do this? The Hatch had changed, it seemed, the minute she had figured out something about its true nature. *It had responded.* How would it respond, what would change, if she went one step further now?

Only one way to find out. Oddly she wasn't afraid anymore.

She settled her hands into the indentations. Gloved, they seemed to fit perfectly.

And the Hatch immediately began to open.

Trant grabbed her shoulders and pulled her back, bodily lifting her in the low gravity.

They stood and watched as the huge circular plate lifted out of its seam, attached to the emplacement by some invisible hinge—how *was* it being held? Stef bent to see. The rising lid just touched the wider emplacement at its rim. There seemed no material attachment.

And again she'd had her eye off the ball; she wasn't observing the most striking phenomenon. Under the rising Hatch was revealed a chamber, cylindrical, maybe four meters deep, set in the Mercury rock. It seemed to be made of the same grayish substance as the rest of the installation, and it was lit by a sourceless glow.

"That's impossible," King said.

"You are right," said Monica Trant. "There's nothing but rock under that plate. We *measured* it."

But Stef could see the glow coming from the impossible pit reflected in their visors, their staring faces, baffled. She felt a peculiar exhilaration. This wasn't like her at all. Most of her life, her science, had proceeded in cautious, methodical steps, with each new extension of her knowledge building incrementally on what had gone before. Now all that was thrown out; now she was rushing headlong into the unknown, the non-categorizable, the unidentifiable, in a way she'd never imagined.

This wasn't Stef Kalinski's way. She was thrilled. She could barely wait for the next step.

As soon as the Hatch lid had come to a halt, standing vertically from its invisible hinge, Stef walked forward to the edge. "Monica. Give me a hand."

"You're going in there?" Trant glanced at King, who shrugged. Trant said, "I don't know how wise this is."

"We've come this far. It's obvious what we're meant to do next. We can't stop now." Stef glanced up at the rig of cameras and sensors all around the emplacement. "We're being recorded, right? Whatever happens, those who follow us will know what became of us."

"Yes. But this doesn't seem too scientific, Stef. Just to plunge in."

"This isn't science. This is exploration."

"No," King gloated. "Let's be honest. It's appropriation. It's conquest. It's going to kill those gerontocrats in New Beijing, when they read about this day, when the security blankets are lifted in fifty or a hundred years' time, that we haven't just got the kernels—now we have *this*."

"Whatever. Let's get on with it." And she held out her arms.

The ISF goons came forward to help too. They braced Trant while she took Stef's gloved hands in her own, and lowered her into the pit. Stef made them move slowly, while she tried to be hyperaware of any odd sensations, any more of those tidal effects. She felt nothing untoward. It was just a hole in the ground, impossible or not.

When they had lowered her as far as they could they released her hands. Gentle as a snowflake she settled to the floor. She looked up at the opening above her, the circle of visored faces peering in.

Then she turned around slowly, inspecting the walls. "There's another hatch," she said. "Another circular seam. Set in this wall. Smaller than the big one up there, but here it is. And, guess what? It has handprint indentations again."

King called down, "Major, maybe you've gone far enough."

"You're kidding," she said, staring at the hatch, raising her hands. "What would you do, if you were down here?"

"Think about it. Maybe any curious, tool-wielding species would react the same way to this setup. You'd go in, one step after another."

"You mean—"

"Maybe it's a trap."

"And maybe it isn't," Stef said, unmoved.

"We aren't going to stop her, sir," Trant said. "Stef. You might get cut off. Keep talking to us. All right?"

"I hear you. Here I go, with a handprint lock once again." She settled her hands into the indentations at twelve o'clock on the wall before her. "It's opening . . ." She had to step back smartly as the curved door swung back, as smoothly as the hatch lid itself. "Again, I can't see a hinge, nothing material attaching door to wall. There's another chamber beyond. A second chamber, similar to the first in dimension. More of those gray walls, the sourceless light." She stepped forward cautiously, toward the doorway rim. "And . . ."

And, standing in the second chamber, before another doorway seam on the far wall, was a figure: a human, in a pressure suit, apparently ISF issue. A human staring back at her.

"What?" An unfamiliar voice in her ear speaker. "What's wrong?"

No, not unfamiliar, just—unexpected.

"Stef? Penny?" That was Trant's voice. "Stef, what have you found down there? Penny, you're still out of our field of view."

Penny?

The stranger took another step forward, toward the open hatchway. Stef found herself staring into a familiar face, behind the visor. Too familiar. Found herself staring at a familiar name too on the suit's chest patch.

KALINSKI, PENELOPE D.

FOUR

. . .

The ColU, which was becoming increasingly philosophical as time passed, came up with yet another complex, bewildering observation about life on Per Ardua.

At the time Yuri was letting Beth ride on the ColU's back with him, on the final fifty-kilometer round-trip trek to the old camp from the new. He'd thought the ColU had been acting oddly all day, but had put it down to the usual program-violation problems it had with moving the camp in the first place. Evidently not.

Luckily Beth was oblivious to all this. Beth Eden Jones was seven years old now, and she had been used to moving all her life. The first shift of the *jilla* had come in the very month she had been born, and there had been seven shifts since then, around one a year, bringing the lake the best part of two hundred kilometers due south from the starting point. The family had diligently followed along each time, hauling their broken-down dwellings and their tools and all their other possessions, right down to cartloads of topsoil, behind the patient bulk of the ColU.

But the last shift had been all of a year ago, and since then some spark in Beth's head had lit up. This time she wasn't a passive passenger anymore; now she wanted to make sense of it all. So she had begged to come along on these shuttle trips back and forth between the old camp-site and the new. Mardina was happy to let her ride along with Yuri—especially as it got her out of the way while the builders completed their latest brutal war of conquest against their cousins at the *jilla*'s new position. But on this ride, this last loading up, Beth was fretful.

As soon as they were loaded, the ColU had begun the last haul away from the old campsite, of which little was left but a scuffed patch of ground, a smoldering fire, a couple of garbage dumps, all set beside a muddy lake bed that was already drying out. They headed south once more, following the water courses down which the builders had driven the waters of the *jilla*. And, wistfully, sitting beside her father on the carapace of the ColU, Beth looked over her shoulder back the way they had come. "Why can't we ever go *that* way, Dad?"

"What way, honey? North? What's the point? There's nothing there. There's not even water to drink."

"I know. But there's the first camp of all, isn't there? Back there somewhere."

"Where you were born."

"I know *that*. But I don't remember it."

"It's too far. There's no water on the way. We couldn't walk that far."

"We could ride on the ColU," she said hopefully. "We could *carry* water. We could carry our beds and stuff, and Mister Sticks." Mister Sticks, her favorite toy, had been woven from broken stems by the ColU; the doll was a peculiar mix of human and builder features, like a three-legged puppet.

"That's not a bad plan, honey. But the ColU wouldn't carry us that far."

"It could, though."

"But it wouldn't. It . . . doesn't want to."

"You could *make* it."

"Only by hurting it. And that would be mean, wouldn't it?" Which was about as close as he imagined he was going to get to explaining program conflicts in the ColU's AI to Beth.

"I guess . . ."

"What do you want to see up there anyhow? It's just like all the other places we stopped. Just a load of old junk that we dumped when we moved. Abandoned fields . . ." And a few graves.

"But I want to see the road where the shuttle came down." She mimed a descending flight with her hand, but she made a noise like the flapping triple vanes of an Arduan kite, the only flying thing she had ever seen. "*Flish-flish-flish.* Mom says it made tracks that would take you hours to walk along."

"I guess so. Skid marks kilometers long. And some of it baked solid, when the braking rockets fired. I guess that would be worth seeing, if it's still there. But we can't get there, honey. I'm sorry."

"Maybe one day."

"Well—"

"Take me there for my birthday one day." That was Beth's trump card.

Her birthdays were an issue. Yuri had been slow to realize that even after Beth's birth. Mardina had clung to her belief, or fantasy, that the ISF had never really left, and would someday come out of their hides or down from orbit or whatever, and reveal themselves, and save them all. Maybe the baby being delivered would be the trigger, if the ISF authorities accepted that the colonists had proven their determination to stick it out by breeding. Well, that hadn't happened. She'd not mentioned it at the time of the birth, and Yuri forgot about it.

But on Beth's first birthday the dam broke, and Mardina went into a rage at a betrayal that, at last, she couldn't deny. It caused a lot of tension. It was still a birthday. Yuri had tried baking a cake, with butter and stuff from the iron cow unit inside the ColU. The ColU had even made candles from synthesized fat. Mardina ruined it all. Beth had been too young to understand, but for Yuri, the memories of The Day Mommy Lost It remained strong.

The next year, with Yuri gently prodding, they had agreed they should celebrate the birthday. After all Beth didn't have other kids around, she was never going to go to school or college or enjoy all the other milestones regular children did, even in a dump like Eden on Mars. A birthday, though, one thing that was uniquely hers, could always be marked and celebrated. And, as a tie to the cycles of time on Earth, it was a reminder of deeper roots too. But by the time that second birthday rolled around the echoes of the first were still strong, and Mardina withdrew into herself.

Well, since then they had celebrated all Beth's birthdays, but there was always tension. And Beth, with a little kid's wiles, picked that up and played on it. Yuri just coped with it all. Nobody had ever told him life was going to be easy.

"Listen, it's late, why don't you take a nap? That way you'll be fresh for Mom when you get home."

"I don't *want* to take a nap."

"Just try," he said in his line-in-the-sand voice, much practiced over seven years.

So she complied. She wriggled inside her rope harness until she was lying down on a couple of blankets, and cuddled up against her father's leg. He put one arm around her and stroked her short-cut straight hair with his free hand. They had had trouble with her sleeping from the beginning. Born into the endless day of Proxima, she seemed that bit more disconnected from the rhythms of distant Earth, and didn't see why she *needed* to go to sleep when her parents did, at what seemed like arbitrary times in the unending light. But if they let her get away without regular sleep she would burn herself out and crash, so Yuri and Mardina had worked out a process of control between them.

Even the ColU, which had some programming in child care, was drafted into this regime. It always backed up the parents' diktats, which was just as well, Yuri thought, or it would have found Mardina decommissioning it enthusiastically. The ColU was the third "person" in Beth's limited life, and she saw nothing strange in having a robotic farming machine as a kind of uncle. Proving to be an expert at weaving dolls from dead stem shafts didn't do its image any harm either.

Soon Beth was asleep; she had a soft, gentle snore.

Yuri had time to inspect the route they were following. After all, it was the last time he expected ever to come this way. The ColU was following its own tracks along the bank of a broad, braided riverbed. Like most of the channels down which the builders guided the flow of their lake this bed had been here already, but was dry as bones before the lake came. Now the bed was littered with the detritus of the passage of the waters of the lake: snapped stems, a few broken builder traps, dead aquatic creatures from fish analogues to crab analogues and jellyfish analogues, and others they had yet to identify. There was even some terrestrial-origin seaweed, the gen-enged laver brought to this world by the starship *Ad Astra*.

After years of observation, even the ColU had no real idea how the builders managed these hydrological transfers so effectively. The lake stayed in stable locations for months or years at a time—it had turned out that the site where the shuttle had landed had been the longest stay so far, and in fact the intervals between moves were generally getting shorter. It was clear the builders used existing watercourses, although they would sometimes dig out or extend canal-like connecting passageways, and their characteristic middens were used to guide the flow of the water precisely where they wanted it to go.

And, wherever the lake finally pooled, there were always local streams and springs to feed it. The mystery of *that* was that as the land's wider uplift continued—and the ColU constantly reminded them that some dramatic geological event was apparently unfolding to the north of here—the pattern of the region's springs changed all the time, as underground aquifers were shifted or broken, the water tables realigned. The builders always seemed to know *in advance* where the useful springs would be, and how to reestablish the lake. The builders didn't have maps, but they evidently knew about geography; they must be able to visualize the landscape in some way.

It was as Yuri mused on this that the ColU's theorizing broke into his day.

The ColU jolted to a sudden stop.

Beth muttered and stirred. Yuri stroked her head, and she calmed again. He looked around. There was nothing special here, no obvious reason to have stopped.

The ColU backed up a little way, then rolled forward with a grinding of aging gears. Again Beth stirred, before settling.

Yuri whispered urgently, "Hey! What's wrong with you?"

The ColU's voice was a matching whisper. "Yuri Eden?"

"Why have you stopped? Get going before this one wakes up, or Mardina will slaughter the lot of us."

"I am sorry. I had not realized I had stopped." It rolled on with a sight lurch.

"So what was all that about?"

"Yuri Eden, call it an existential crisis."

Yuri groaned inwardly. Not again.

He knew he'd have to tell Mardina about this episode, whatever it was; she was concerned about anything erratic in the ColU's behavior. The ColU had made it clear from the beginning that to have been forced to help transport the colonists across the planet, if they'd attempted to escape from the landing sites that had been planned for them by the starship crew, would have violated its deepest layers of programming. So when the lake had first shifted, in its algorithmic soul the ColU faced a conflict between mandates to keep its human charges alive, and to stay close to the original landing site. The preservation of life had won out. But Mardina, who knew a lot more about ISF AIs than Yuri did, fretted that some deep internal damage might have been done. All of which was over Yuri's head, let alone the head of his seven-year-old daughter, his little *muda-muda*.

Now, reluctantly, he asked, "*What* existential crisis?"

"I have come to a conclusion which baffles and alarms me. I have just received, from my internal laboratory facilities, the results of the analysis of a novel organism which enabled me to complete a genetic mapping—you're aware that among my long-term projects has been the construction of a tree of life, for the Arduan native flora and fauna—"

"You know, I wish I just had a *truck*."

"Yuri Eden?"

"Like the rovers on Mars. A truck I could just *drive*. The number of conversations like this that I've had with you over the years—"

"I can't help it," the ColU said, sounding almost miserable. "I can't constrain my curiosity. Nor should I. Until my understanding of this world is complete enough—"

"Just tell me."

It paused, as if gathering its thoughts. "Yuri Eden, I have told you that life on this world is similar in its fundamentals to life on Earth, but not identical. I believe the two biospheres may be linked by a panspermia process that operated at a very early date. The earliest days of life on Per Ardua might have been like the early days of Earth, a world of simple bacteria, drawing their energy from chemical reactions in the rocks. But all the time much more energy, a hundred times as much, was available, washing down from the sky—"

"Proxima light."

"Yes. The next step was the development of kinds of photosynthesis, creatures that could draw energy directly from that light. The new kind colonized the surface, while the older ones survived, sinking deeper into the planet. And there they still reside in great reefs, in caverns, in porous rock and aquifers, dreaming unknowable dreams. Just as on Earth, life on Per Ardua is actually dominated by the bugs in the deep layers, mass for mass. But on the surface, as photosynthesis evolved, ultimately oxygen was released as a by-product."

"Like the green algae on Earth."

"Yes, Yuri Eden, this step, oxygen production, was evidently difficult to achieve; on Earth it occurred only once, and in fact came from the coupling of *two* older photosynthetic processes. I have yet to fully understand the equivalent process on Per Ardua—it is necessarily different because the energy content of the light here is heavy in the infrared—but it is evidently just as complex, just as unlikely to have happened."

"Yet it did happen."

"It did, and I have been able to date the event from traces in the Arduan genetic record: some two billion, seven hundred million years ago." It paused. When Yuri didn't react it went on, "The next great step in the emergence of Arduan life, again mirrored on Earth, was the development of a new kind of cell: a much more complex organism, a cell with a nucleus, a cell with different kinds of mechanisms within a containing membrane. Of course the energy available from burning up all the oxygen concentrating in the air helped with that. Such complex cells are the basis of all multicellular life, including you, including the builders. This was an information revolution, not a chemical one; these complicated creatures needed about a thousand times as much genetic information to define them as their simpler predecessors."

"Another unlikely step."

"Yes. But again it occurred on both worlds. And on Per Ardua this came about some two billion years ago." Another pause. "Yuri, I am not sure you are grasping the significance of—"

"Just tell me the story," Yuri said. He stroked his daughter's hair, growing sleepy himself.

"Multicellular life emerged some time later—evidently another difficult step to take. Seaweeds first on Earth, like the lavers we imported to Per Ardua . . ."

The new camp was coming into view, the lake settling into the contours of its latest shoreline. Yuri saw builders busily working all around the lake's edge, and smoke rising from Mardina's campfire.

The ColU was still talking about ancient life. "Of all the great revolutions of life this is the easiest to identify on Earth because it left such clear traces in the fossil record. On Per Ardua, of course, there is no fossil record to speak of. And yet—"

"And yet you, through heroic efforts, have worked it out anyway."

"I'm just trying to explain, Yuri Eden."

"All right."

"Yes, I have seen traces of this event in the genes, and also in some fringe organisms that have survived on Per Ardua to this day. And— now this is the significant point, Yuri Eden—I have established that all this occurred some five hundred and forty-two million years ago. Do you see? Do you see?"

"See what?" Beth sat up now, rubbing her eyes. "I smelled smoke in my dreams. I thought the ColU was on fire!"

"No, honey, it's just the campfire." Yuri didn't see the ColU's point at all, he couldn't care less about such abstractions, and as the unit rolled into the camp the conversation was already fading from his mind. "Go find your Mom, sweetheart, and I'll help the ColU get everything put away safely."

Mardina prepared lunch.

It was a kind of quick picnic assembled from chuno. This was a long-lasting paste you could make from potatoes by freezing, thawing, desiccating them—a smart trick from the Andes that the ColU had taught them, and invaluable for their traveling phases, but the result was a grayish muck in appearance that Beth had always cordially hated. But today she was hungry after the long journey back to the camp, and excited about the move. Certainly she didn't want to sleep anymore. They all had a peculiar mixture of tiredness and energy, Yuri thought, like they had gone on vacation maybe.

They decided to take the rest of the day off, and go exploring. The ColU, after trying to speak to Mardina about its mysterious science conclusions, grumpily rolled away and began the process of unpacking its last load from the old camp, including another ton of terrestrial topsoil.

The family walked to the lake's latest location, with Beth skipping ahead, and Mardina and Yuri side by side.

The ground in this country, away from the lake and the water courses, was as arid as they had ever experienced it. In fact, Yuri suspected the landscape was becoming drier, hotter, the farther south they traveled. Which made sense; the farther south you went and the closer to the substellar point you reached, the farther Proxima rose in the sky, and the more heat it delivered. Yuri still had the map Lemmy had compiled from the colonists' remembrances of the shuttle flight, before they'd all killed one another, and that showed concentric bands of climate and vegetation types around the substellar. If they walked far enough, Yuri supposed, they would in the end reach true lifeless desert, surrounding the substellar point itself, which the ColU predicted would be the site of a permanent storm system. Even before that, maybe there would come a point where the ground was no longer habitable for them at all. But they were following the builders, who had evidently been going through this process for uncounted millennia, and Yuri and Mardina had decided to trust them—well, having followed the *jilla* this far, they had no choice.

They came to the lakeshore, a fringe of muddy ground with banks of new stems growing vigorously. The stems seemed to be self-seeding, but the colonists had observed the builders practicing what looked like simple agriculture to help the stems along, planting shoots, irrigating the mud with crude drainage ditches. The water itself was still turbulent and turbid, not yet having settled into its new bowl. Around the shore of the lake Yuri could see builders working, setting up what looked like a nursery area with the outlines of domed shelters rising up from the debris—and already assembling basic middens, in preparation presumably for the next move of the *jilla*.

But there was another area where builders, adults and children, had been herded in a huddle, surrounded by others that spun and whirled around them. One by one the prisoners were taken out to an area where more builders pinned them down and, brutally, crudely, disarticulated them, taking away their constituent stems to one of the new midden heaps. It looked like a prison camp crossed with an open-air operating theater—or, perhaps, like some appallingly brutal schoolyard game being played out by stick puppets. The sound of the continuing murders was an eerie rustling, a clatter of sticks, the scrape of sharpened stone on stem bark.

Yuri and Mardina gently guided Beth away from the scene. They had seen this many times before: it was the aftermath of a builder invasion, of conquest. There had been another community of builders here, living in the formerly dry lake bed, happily feeding off the local springs and stems—before the *jilla* folk arrived, brutally evicted them, flooded their homeland, and massacred any survivors.

Beth hadn't yet worked this out. Now, luckily, she spotted the nursery and ran that way to see.

"The same every time," Mardina said, looking back at the slaughter yard. "And I used to think the builders were cute . . ."

Yuri said, "They're little wooden Nazis. Some day we're going to have to explain all this to Beth, you know."

"Genocide in Toyland. There's never going to be a good day to talk about that. Maybe you could tell her about your Heroic Generation at the same time. Give her some context. It's not just builders that behave this way."

"For the thousandth time, it wasn't *my* . . ."

But of course she was only goading him, for the thousandth time. She asked, "What did the ColU want to talk to me about, by the way? Seemed very intense."

"Oh, one of its theories. Life on Per Ardua. It seems to have got a pretty good family tree for this world now. Lots of bragging about genetic comparisons and stuff. He's identified major revolutions in the story of life here."

"What revolutions?"

Yuri thought back. "Photosynthesis, I mean a fancy advanced kind that produced oxygen as a waste product. Then complex cells, with nuclei. Then plant and animal life. The ColU got worked up about the dates it's established for these events. Meant nothing much to me."

"What dates?"

He concentrated. "Photosynthesis two point seven billion years ago. The complex cells two billion years ago. And the animals—umm, five hundred and forty-two million years ago, I think."

Mardina stared at him.

Some distance away, at the fringe of the trodden mud around the new lake, Beth had found something worth shouting about. She jumped up and down, waving. "Mom! Dad! Come see!"

Mardina called, "OK, sweetie." They began to walk over. "Yuri—are you sure about those dates?"

He felt uncertain, now that she pressed him. "Well, I think so."

"It's just—I'm no expert, but I took terraforming modules during

my ISF training, and we studied the history of Earth life, the key tran-
sitions. Yuri, the dates for the similar events on Earth are: two point
seven billion years, two billion years, and—"

He guessed, "Five hundred and forty-two million?"

"Yeah. I mean the last particularly is pretty precise, from the fossil
record on Earth."

"Mom! Dad! *Come see*, before it all gets trampled!"

Mardina said, "Life on two worlds separated by light years having
a common sugar base—well, you can wave your hands about panspermia to justify that. But such a precise coordination of the key dates of
all those improbable events?"

"What does it mean?"

"Damned if I know."

"Mom! Dad!" Beth, quite agitated, was almost screaming now.

And when Yuri and Mardina finally got there, at the edge of the
pond's muddy fringe, they could see immediately why.

Beth had found a human footprint.

The invitation from Earthshine reached Stef at her workstation in the UN kernel lab on the moon.

In a short, low-res holographic message—a cube showing his well-groomed head, his smiling middle-aged-politician-type face—the Core AI requested that she come visit him on Earth, at what he called his "node" in Paris. He said he had a matter to discuss of global importance, but specifically of interest to "you and your sister." There was also an avowal, in legal wording, that the AI would make no attempt to access the growing knowledge base on kernel physics during his meeting with the sisters. Without that avowal Stef supposed the message would never have been allowed through the various layers of security that surrounded her, here at Verne.

A similar message, an attachment noted, had been sent to Penny on Mercury.

Stef shut down the hologram with a curt acknowledgment of receipt, and spent a full dome-day thinking it over. That was her way when faced with dilemmas she found difficult or personally unpleasant, a way she'd developed of managing her own instincts over nearly thirty-six years of life. Let the news work its way through her conscious and subconscious mind, before formulating a decision. She even slept on it.

For one thing there was the sheer time she would need to take out of her own program. Right now Stef was in a work jag that she was reluctant to climb out of. Well, she was always in a work jag. Seven years on from the Hatch's first opening and the Penny incident—as she thought of it—explorations of the Hatch and investigations of its physical properties were shedding some light on the complementary studies of the kernels that had been going on for decades now. It was a slow, painstaking process, and it was full of gaps. Stef had the feeling she had been handed the two ends of a long chain of discovery, and she had a ways to go before she worked her way from either end in toward the center. But it was absorbing—there was more than a lifetime's work here for her and her colleagues, she was sure. And *that* was a pleasing thought, since it pushed the need to make any drastic decisions about her own future off beyond the horizon.

Decisions such as about her relationship with her sister.

There was another reason for her to be wary about Earthshine's note. She was actually working now with Penny. Her sister, who was on Mercury, was running direct experimentation on the Hatch emplacement, trying to detect emissions of various exotic high-energy particles. Unlike some siblings, indeed some twins, the sisters worked well together, as a long string of academic publications to their individual and joint credit from the beginning of their careers proved. In this particular project at this particular time Penny was the experimentalist, Stef the theoretician, but on other projects in the past, the record showed, it had often been the other way around. They were flexible that way, with close but complementary skill sets.

It was all fine and dandy, a family relationship to be admired and envied, and something that both their father and mother would have been proud of. It was just that Stef had no memory of any of this before the damn Hatch on Mercury had opened.

The news of the discovery had quickly leaked, and the Hatch had been a sensation for about twenty-four hours. It was, after all, evidence of alien intelligence in the solar system. But a Hatch leading nowhere had since been largely forgotten, or dismissed as a hoax, though it still trailed conspiracy theories like a comet tail.

But Stef was left with a massive rewiring of her own past.

Before the Hatch, she had been an only child. After it, suddenly she had a twin. Not only that, she suddenly had a whole different lifetime behind her, intertwined with that of her twin. Papers that had been to her sole accreditation, for instance, were now under joint authorship with her sister. She'd read some of them; they were much as she remembered writing them, but not quite—not significantly better or worse academically—and there were others, reflecting bits of work she couldn't remember, that she'd never generated herself at all.

Only Stef remembered her solitary past *before*. Nobody else. Everybody in her life, including colleagues she'd known since her graduate-student days, thought of her now as half of a pair, not Stef alone. Not even King and Trant, who had been there at the moment of transition, remembered the old timeline.

Not even Penny remembered it. As far as Penny was concerned, their joint careers had just carried on, after a hiccup as Stef had tried to absorb what had happened at the Hatch. To Penny, Stef was a sister who had suddenly developed a kind of selective amnesia.

And maybe that was what it was. Some kind of mild craziness, perhaps triggered by some bizarro radiation field leaking from the alien artifact into which she'd climbed. That was the simplest explanation, after all, that her own perception, her memory, was somehow faulty. Though she'd looked hard, Stef hadn't found a single shred of evidence to contradict the reality of it. The alternative, that *history* had somehow been changed around her, that the fault lay in the external universe rather than in her own small head, seemed an absurdly overelaborate explanation by comparison.

She didn't believe that, however. She knew herself, she knew her past, her life. And *this* past wasn't hers.

She'd learned not to talk about this, not to anybody—not after the first few minutes of utter bafflement, up there on Mercury, in her pressure suit, in the Hatch, facing a sister she'd never known existed, and everybody had stared at her in dismay as she babbled out her confusion. After all she'd rather be working on kernel super-physics than spend the rest of her life on medication and therapy intended to rid her of "delusions." She wouldn't even talk to Penny about it, despite her sister's tentative attempts to break through the barrier. Stef had been very happy to see Penny posted to a different planet, happy to just get on with her work; at least the work had stayed a constant comfort.

But now here was this summons from Earthshine, evidently intended to bring the two sisters together.

It seemed to Stef that despite much study and commentary, even while everybody acknowledged their power, most experts were unsure what the real agenda of the Core AIs might be. The three antique minds, a legacy of a difficult past, had no formal role in human society, no legal status—no rights, in a sense. But everybody knew that human agencies, from the UN and nation states on downward, had to deal with them. Their power was recognized the way you would acknowledge the power of a natural phenomenon, a hurricane; you couldn't ignore them, but they were outside the human world. And unlike hurricanes, the Core AIs could think and communicate.

Now Earthshine had chosen to communicate with Stef and her sister. Why? That depended, Stef supposed, on Earthshine's own agenda. Maybe Earthshine had some kind of insight to share. But did she want her personal tangle of a life to be unpicked by such a monster?

On a personal level she was repelled. But on an intellectual level she was intrigued.

She acknowledged the note, logged the trip in her personal schedule, and with relief went back to work.

42

Stef Kalinski dropped from the moon's orbit to Earth, following the usual leisurely three-day unpowered trajectory. At Earth orbit she had to wait a day before she was transferred to an orbit-to-ground shuttle, like a snub-nosed plane with black heat tiles and white insulation, its cabin crowded with passengers and luggage.

The little craft glided down through the air with looping, sweeping curves.

On its final track the shuttle crossed the eastern coast of South America, coming down toward a strip of flat coastal savannah. The land glimmered with standing water, flooded by the rising ocean despite crumbling levees that still lined the coast. This was Kourou, Guiana, the old European space agency launch center, now converted to a surface-to-orbit transit station. Farther inland Stef saw bare ground, scrub, some of it plastered with solar-collector arrays like a coat of silver paint. This site was only a few hundred kilometers north of the mouth of the Amazon. Now there was no forest, and the river was reduced to a trickle through a semidesert.

Only an hour after landing at Kourou Stef was being bundled into a small aircraft for her hop across the Atlantic. Like the shuttle the plane was crowded, fully loaded before it was allowed to take off; these days transport was always communal and always crowded, planes and shuttles and trains and buses, minimal energy usage the key goal.

The plane, powered by turbos driven by a compact microfusion engine, leaped easily into the air. The sky beyond the small, thick windows turned a deep blue; the trajectory was a suborbital hop, and they crossed the Atlantic high and fast, heading northeast toward western Europe, Portugal, and Spain.

As the plane dipped back into the atmosphere over the Iberian coast, Stef wished she knew enough geography to recognize how much of this coastline had been changed by the risen sea. Near the shore she saw vapor feathers gleaming white, artificial cloud created by spray turbines standing out to sea and deflecting a little more sunlight from the overheated Earth. The ocean itself was green-blue, thick with plankton stimulated to grow and draw down carbon from the air.

The plane banked and headed north, streaking at high speed through the air. Southern Spain, long abandoned to desert, was chromeplated with solar-cell farms, and studded with vast silvered bubbles, lodes of frozen-out carbon dioxide. Once across the Pyrenees they left behind the mid-latitude desertification zone and the ground gradually became greener. But even in central France Stef glimpsed great old cities abandoned or at least depopulated, the conurbations' brown stains pierced by green as they fragmented back into the villages from which they had formed. Over northern France the plane swept west, circled, and then descended into an easterly headwind. Stef saw something of the Seine, more abandoned towns on a glistening floodplain. Away from the river olives grew in neat rows on dusty ground, a sight you would once have seen in southern Spain, an agriculture suited to the new age.

At Paris, the big old airports were no longer in use. Instead, with a stab of sharp deceleration, they were brought down at a small airport in a suburb called Bagneux, just south of central Paris itself, a clutter of ugly twentieth-century buildings cleared in great stripes to make room for the runways. There was another brisk transfer made mostly in silence; there was no documentation, but every passenger's identity, security background, and infective status were seamlessly checked with non-invasive DNA scans.

Soon Stef was through the process, and found herself and her minimal luggage alone in a small driverless electric car that whisked her north toward the city center. She'd not been to Paris before, and the cramped streets swept by at bewildering speed. Somewhere the Eiffel Tower still stood proud, but around her she saw only walls of ancient sandstone stained by floodwater. Although this was still the political capital of the country there were few people around. Wealthy Parisians had long ago decanted to the cooler climes of southern England— Angleterre as it was known now—and the poor, presumably, had died out or drifted away.

She glimpsed the Île de la Cité, standing in the turbid waters of the Seine, where the roofs of Notre Dame were plastered with solar panels. A huge banyan tree sprawled before the cathedral, rooted in the flooded ruins of surrounding buildings.

At last the car brought her to the Champs-Élysées, an avenue even a first-time visitor like Stef could not fail to recognize. There was a fair density of traffic here, and pedestrians hurrying beneath sun-shade awnings. The car stopped outside a high, elaborate doorway, where a man stood in the shade, beside a slim woman in the uniform of the ISF. The man, of course, was Earthshine. And the woman was Penny Kalinski, Stef's impossible sister.

Earthshine, who cast a convincing shadow when he stepped into the light, bowed to Stef as she climbed out of the car. "Greetings," he said in his cultured British accent. He made no attempt to shake Stef's hand, but wafted his fingers through the lintel of the doorway; pixels scattered from his fingertips like fairy dust. "At least in European manners, this is how to announce one is only a virtual presence. I hope this suit— that's how I think of my various bodies, as 'suits'—is acceptable to you both."

"It's fine," Penny said. She was looking steadily at Stef. Then she approached her sister, one pace, two.

Stef stood rigid, almost at attention beside her luggage, unwilling to respond. There was a stiff moment.

Penny said, "Here we are, in person together, for only, what, the fourth time, the fifth? Since—"

"Since the Hatch opened."

"Right." Penny stepped back, subtly. "Sorry. Old habits die hard. Even after all this time. We always hugged, before."

Earthshine watched this exchange with lively interest. "The 'always' applies to you, Penny Kalinski. To what you remember. But to your sister Stef, the 'always,' the past before the Hatch incident, did not include you at all."

"That's right," Stef said. "Lucky me. Suddenly I gained a sister."

A look crossed Penny's face, like the passing shadow of a defunct Heroic Generation sunshield. "And I," she said, "feel like I lost one."

"Fascinating," murmured Earthshine. "Fascinating. But here we are standing in the heat. Please, come into the shade, both of you . . ."

The old building extended to several stories and an underground extension. For Stef, the most striking feature of the ornate interior was a sweeping marble staircase down which the virtual projection of Earthshine marched with convincing footfalls, his shadow shifting in the soft lighting. "Once this was an Italian-owned bank," he said, "but it has been put to many other uses over the centuries. Including a bookstore, when they still had paper books. A real historical relic . . ." Cleaning robots worked discreetly.

They reached a relatively small, cool, windowless, underground reception room, where Earthshine invited them to sit on overstuffed armchairs, and offered them water, American-style soda, coffee, from a self-service counter. Penny took a coffee, Stef a glass of water. The room was without decoration, save for a big block of what looked like sea-eroded concrete on one wall, maybe half a meter across, its deeply pitted face marked with a mesh of concentric circles and arrowing lines, apparently intentionally carved. Stef remembered a similar design on a brooch Earthshine had worn before. The peculiar item distracted her; it looked elusively like some kind of map, a schematic, but she could not have said a map of what.

"So," Earthshine said, sitting with legs crossed, fingers steepled. "It's good of you to have come so far to meet me—and to take a break from your work schedules, which I know is a sacrifice for both of you. Thank you too for agreeing to put up with each other's company, at least for a short while. Welcome to my underground lair! Or one of them." He smiled, with a show of apparently charming self-deprecation. "That's how you think of us, isn't it? Terrible old monsters, ruling the world from our furtive dens."

Stef said, "I like to think we're a bit more sophisticated than that."

But Penny countered, "No, you got it about right."

Earthshine grinned. "You contradict each other. In your talk, even in your choice of drinks. Whatever one does, the other must not follow. How fascinating. And yet by behaving this way you become ever more the mirror images that you each appear to reject . . ."

For Stef all this was picking at a scab. She snapped, "Is there a point to this?"

"Oh, indeed there is," Earthshine said. "In fact your oddly coupled nature is what I primarily wish to talk to you about. I have followed your trajectories since that strange day on Mercury when the Hatch was opened. Well—you won't be surprised to learn that. It's what you would expect of me, isn't it? To watch over you all, like some inquisitive god." He leaned forward. "I have asked you here, you see, because I have learned something. I have *found* something."

"Something to do with us?" Stef asked.

Penny said, "And what's it to do with you, Earthshine? What do *you* want?"

"Well, that's rather nebulous at the moment. Suffice to say—" He paused, as if choosing his words. "I want to stop being afraid."

Stef stared at him, startled by that peculiar non sequitur. He'd said this calmly, his expression still, faintly artificial. Yet that, somehow, made it all the more convincing.

Penny seemed more aggressive. "You, afraid? Afraid of what? You're an artificial mind stored underground in massively paralleled and distributed processor and memory banks, with your own dedicated manufacturing units and energy supply. You and your partners rode out the climate Jolts like they were bumps in the road, while millions of us died. What could *you* possibly be afraid of?"

"I will explain, in time." He held out his hands. "I know this is difficult for you. But here you are, together. Would you like to talk?"

Penny and Stef looked into each other's eyes, just as they had in that first moment of revelation in the Hatch on Mercury. Then they looked away.

At length Stef said, "I've done some research. On us, on our past."

"I know. You've been doing it for years. My firewall traced you. I let you go ahead."

"I saw the records," Stef said. "As they exist now. We *are* twins, genetically identical. I am the older by a few minutes. We seem to have been close companions when we were small."

"I remember," Penny said more softly. "I wouldn't need to research it. We played all the time."

"We were put through the same schools by our father. We showed the same kind of aptitude, basically mathematical, logical, verbal. We both joined the ISF for the sake of scholarships that put us through grad school and sponsored our early researches, and enabled us to get access to the kernel labs on the moon."

"The ISF split us up," Penny said. "Their psychs thought it would make each of us more self-reliant. Still we did the same training and development, more or less, just in a different order."

"But our careers converged again, when we started working on kernel physics."

Penny said, "It all came from that day we were on Mercury with Dad. We were eleven years old when the first hulk ship was launched. That was what inspired us to go into kernel research in the first place."

Stef closed her eyes, just for a moment. *No. I was there alone. With Dad. You weren't there, not even as some unwelcome ghost. That was my day, not yours . . .*

"And then it was all fine until we went into the Hatch on Mercury," Penny said sadly. "I went through first, Stef. You followed me in. And when I went into that second chamber, and I turned around and you saw me, I could see you didn't recognize me. We'd only been out of each other's sight for a minute—"

"Less than that," Earthshine said. "I have studied the record. Thirty-eight seconds."

"And my memory is different," Stef said. "I went alone into the Hatch. I opened the second hatch. There was Penny, already in the next chamber."

"Before that time, you, Stef, clearly knew your sister. Afterward you were baffled by her very existence, though you did your best to conceal it when you realized that something was very wrong."

Stef felt resentment flare. "You're not allowed access to any material on kernel physics. That's a UN law."

"Of course," Earthshine said smoothly. "But any such law needs a defined boundary. And I, or my legal advisers, push assiduously at that boundary. Wouldn't you? I am entitled to explore the *implications* of kernel science, even if I must turn my head away from the physics itself. A visual record of events at the Hatch tells me little about the underlying physics, and much of it is in the public domain anyhow." He leaned forward. "Major Kalinski—I mean, Stef. Only you remember how it was before. Your life as an only child. Yes? Most people therefore assume your memory is faulty."

Stef said, "Or that exposure to the Hatch messed with my mind and sent me mildly crazy."

He shook his head. "But that's not what you believe, is it, Major? Now consider the alternative. If your mind *hasn't* been tampered with— if your memories are authentic—"

"This makes no sense," Penny said, growing hostile.

Earthshine urged, "Just run with this for a moment. Stef, what's your alternative hypothesis?"

She took a deep breath. "History changed. What else? The minute I opened that Hatch."

Earthshine nodded. "Before, there was a different history."

"Where I was an only child. Where I had a different name, for God's sake. I was Stephanie Penelope Kalinski, not Stephanie Karen, and Penelope Dianne never existed. And when I opened that Hatch and stepped inside, there you were, Penny—real, live, impossible. With a set of memories of a different past. Memories that were in everybody else's head too."

"All except yours," Earthshine said. "Just suppose you're right, Stef. Just suppose reality *was* changed, that the Hatch, on accepting you, immediately *tinkered with the past*—at least with your own past. Giving you a sister you never had. And presumably causing subsequent small changes that rippled away from that big central adjustment."

Penny was clearly uncomfortable, and Stef was sure she knew why. They were talking about a world where she'd never even been born, and that must be existentially terrifying. Penny said now, "Occam's razor. Basic principle of science. The idea that Stef somehow got a kind of amnesia is a lot simpler than the idea that the *whole universe* has been changed to generate a new reality."

"Well, Occam has been dead a long time," Earthshine said mildly. "And is the alternative really so preposterous? We *know* that the Hatch technology involves some kind of manipulation of space-time. You both clambered down into a hole beneath the Hatch that could not exist, according to the geophysics measurements. What is a history change but another such manipulation? In time, rather than space. Stef, I suspect you may not have gone much further with this line of thinking yourself, even in the privacy of your own head."

"What are you getting at?"

"I mean that if there has been some kind of history change, effected by the Hatch, or whoever built the Hatch—"

Penny snorted. "Oh, this is—"

"Then it's been kind of a *messy* change, hasn't it? I mean, it hasn't been clean. We know that it's left at least one trace of what went before, in your own memory, Stef."

"That's hardly evidence," Penny snapped.

"It is to Stef. Maybe it had something to do with you being inside the Hatch itself, at the moment the change was effected—"

"And what would be the point?" Penny demanded now. "You're talking about changing history. If you can do that, why not, hell, wipe out a climate Jolt or two? Or even wipe out the warming altogether— why not go back and shoot Henry Ford?"

Stef said, her mind racing, "Maybe it—or they, the Hatch-makers, whoever is behind this—couldn't manage anything on that scale. Maybe they didn't know enough about us, about humanity, to make more than the smallest change. Maybe this was all they could manage. For now, anyhow." She looked at Earthshine. "But why us? I mean, why me? What's significant about me, or my life?"

"Everything," Earthshine said. "Or nothing. Maybe it was just the fact that you were first into the Hatch. This was a kind of—test run. An exploration. But if so, as I said—"

"The execution was sloppy," Stef said. "With one loose end left, in my memory. Trant and King remembered Penny opening the second hatchway and going through ahead of me. *I* remember opening the second hatch myself, then seeing Penny for the first time . . . Sloppy."

"*At least* one loose end."

Stef looked at him sharply.

Penny stood. "What do you mean? Have you found another 'loose end'? Have you got some kind of proof?"

He smiled as she loomed over him. "Well, wasn't it logical to at least look? If there is one ragged corner there could easily be more. So I looked. And—"

Stef said, "Is that why you brought us to France? Is there something you want to show us?"

"I can do this virtually," he said. "Or it may be better if you travel physically and see for yourselves, with your own eyes."

"Later," they both said, their identical voices double-tracking.

"Just show us," Stef said. "Please."

Penny sat down, looking frankly scared.

Earthshine nodded, waved a hand, and the room dissolved.

43

A footprint.

Yuri froze.

Beside him, Mardina pulled Beth close.

A human footprint, in the mud. Clear as day. Yuri could see the ball of the foot, the heel. He could count the toes.

"Where there's one print," Mardina murmured, "there are going to be others. Look, Yuri. That way . . ." She pointed west across the arid country away from the lake.

The trail of prints was clearly visible, like shallow craters in the crusty ground, one after another, left, right. Off to the horizon.

"Let's get back to the ColU," Yuri said.

"Right."

As they headed, half-running, back around the lake, Beth's excitement turned to alarm. "What is it? Have I done something wrong?"

"No, sweetie," Mardina said. "Not at all."

"Is it that footprint? Is it somebody bad?"

"No, no, nothing like that," Yuri said. He murmured to Mardina, "We're scaring her."

"She's a right to be scared."

"This shouldn't be possible, should it? The *Ad Astra* drops were supposed to be too far apart."

"Yet it's happened."

They got back to their new campsite, still little more than a heap of supplies, the logs and beams and panels of their dismantled house, a mound of carefully manufactured terrestrial topsoil, other junk. Yuri rummaged until he found a crossbow and bolts. He already had his hunting knife tucked into his belt. "I'll go and check it out. You look after Beth."

Mardina curled her lip. "Go ahead, hero."

Yuri picked up their one flare pistol, it still had a few cartridges left, and stuffed it into his tunic pocket. "Well, if I fire this, come and save me."

"I'll save you, Daddy."

"Thank you, sweetie." He kissed the top of Beth's head, grinned at Mardina with a confidence he didn't feel, and set off.

He tracked back the way they had come. There was the first footprint, bright and sharp. Completely ignored by the builders nearby.

Without hesitating, he went farther, following the track of prints across the dry country, heading steadily west, jogging, the crossbow in his hand. In the years since the stranding, Mardina had insisted they both practice with the crossbow until they were reasonably expert. Yuri hadn't disagreed. There was nothing to shoot at around here, but you never knew. Now it looked as if that might pay off.

More humans! There had been times, especially before Beth had come along, when he had longed for other people to show up, somehow, somewhere—even his enemies, even asshole Peacekeepers, even that smug bastard astronaut McGregor. He still felt that way sometimes. But now it was different; now he had Beth to shelter and protect. If there were other survivors of the drops down here, who knew what state they would be in? Who knew how they would react to him?

He had come to think of Per Ardua as *his*, he realized. His and his family's. It made no sense, but there you were. Now he resented having to share it.

And he feared for his family. He had a mental image of the *jilla* builders' efficient genocide: the imprisoning, the wordless, relentless butchery.

He stopped. Straight ahead of him now was a sandstone bluff, low, eroded, sticking out of the ground, a typical Arduan feature. And beside it, a figure, a single human being. He, she, was crouched by the bluff, digging into the ground with one hand—no, drinking, he saw, there must be a spring there, a pool.

He walked steadily forward. He held the crossbow at his side, loosely, his finger away from the trigger. He didn't call out.

Soon enough the figure by the rock bluff spotted him. A slim woman, she stood up straight. She wore no shoes, trousers that were the cut-down remains of an orange jumpsuit, a black shirt that looked like half an astronaut's uniform, and a homemade coolie hat made of stem bark, not unlike his own. She had lost one arm, amputated above the elbow, he saw, shocked. The tattoos on her face were solid black slabs, and seemed designed to emphasize the glare of her pale blue eyes.

He knew her. She was Delga, whom he'd known on the ship, and on Mars before that. The snow queen of Eden.

Delga grinned at him. "Hello, ice boy."

44

Having met, they had to decide to go one way or the other. Yuri chose to walk west with Delga, toward her group, which she called "the mothers," rather than back toward Mardina.

"Only a few klicks," she said.

"Yeah. We're farther away than that." That was a lie; in fact Mardina and Beth were a lot closer. His instinct was to obscure, to hide, to protect. Of course she might know all about his little group already.

Delga had aged, and life on Per Ardua had evidently toughened her; she looked scrawnier, more wrinkled, but strong, leathery. Her tattoos hadn't faded, her face was just as bladelike, just as threatening. Despite the loss of that arm he was quite sure she'd have weapons available. As, indeed, he had.

He was trying to work through the shock. Just encountering another human being, *any* other human, here on this static world, changed everything. And now it turned out to be Delga.

Delga's face was a tattooed mask, under a scalp shaven in elaborate whorls. Yuri barely knew her. He'd only come across her a couple of times on Mars. On the *Ad Astra* she'd been in the same hulk as him, but again he'd kept his distance. He'd wanted nothing to do with her products, her chain of contacts, her suppliers and users. The last time he'd seen her, he remembered now, she was leading a bunch of rebels up toward the ship's bridge, after the arrival at Proxima. She was the type to have survived, he supposed.

He said now, "So what were you doing all the way out here?"

"Stretching my legs. What do you think? The one thing this place does have is *room*, room to walk off until you're over the horizon and alone. Can't do *that* in a Martian hovel, right? Or in some hulk of a ship. Or on most of Earth these days, probably." She jerked a thumb over her shoulder. "I come out this way for the water. The springs. And there's a hollow a little farther out that way, more springs, but it just got flooded."

She must mean the hollow that now held the *jilla* lake.

She looked at him, shrewd, analytical. "You don't know this area well."

"No. We're on the move."

She picked that apart. "*We*. Who, how many? How heavily armed? *On the move*. From where, to where?" She grinned. "Don't worry. We'll be sharing soon enough. You know, ice boy, of everybody in that dumb hulk I never picked you out as one of the survivors, here in the Bowl."

The Bowl? The air ahead was misty; as they walked he thought he smelled water, but his view was blocked by a low rise, worn hills. "Why not me?"

"Because, back in Eden, you came out of that cryo tank like you'd been dropped from the sky. You never fitted in, even on Mars. You didn't make any contacts, you didn't have any networks. You didn't even have a way to pay off the Peacekeepers. We noticed you, though. The ice boy, right? Your name is Yuri. What the hell kind of a name is that?"

"Not my name."

"Then why are you called it?"

"Some joker called me that when they woke me up, on Mars. It's the name of an astronaut. Or a cosmonaut. The first one, I think."

She shrugged. "Never heard of him. So what's your real name?"

He looked away.

"You've put aside your lousy past, is that it? What kind of accent is that, by the way, Aussie?"

"North British. I grew up in Manchester, at the border with Angle-terre, the Euro province."

"You sound Australian to me."

"*You* all sound sort of Hispanic to me."

"How long were you frozen, a hundred years?"

"Nearer eighty."

"Were you one of the Heroic Generation? What did it feel like to be a Waster?"

"We weren't called those names then. I was too young anyhow."

She grunted. "Surprised they didn't call you as a witness in the trials. But you escaped it all, didn't you? You in your freezer tray."

He was reluctant to answer, but it was hard to turn away from her iron gaze. The whole conversation, suddenly thrust upon him, was bizarre, like his deepest past suddenly pushing up out of the Arduan ground. "It wasn't my choice. It was an experiment. There were too many of us, my generation. So they tried freezing us in these big honeycomb banks, under the ground, in Antarctica. We'd have less of a footprint that way."

"Your parents got rid of you. That's what happened. Whereas now they get rid of us from Earth to Mars. Or even farther, right? I suppose it was cheaper to ship *you* out to Mars still frozen than to deal with you any other way. Well, on behalf of the future, I hope you enjoyed your stay on Mars, my friend. The butthole of the solar system."

He glared at her, defiant. "If it's so bad, why were you there?"

She shrugged. "We were there, the UN was there, because the Chinese were there. We can't let them have Mars all to themselves, can we? And the UN has these big ships now, the hulks, big powerful engines. Nothing like the steam-engine put-puts they had in your day, I bet. Now they can afford to send people to Mars who don't even want to go. Even to the stars! That's progress for you." She laughed and spat. "Funny thing, life. You never know what it's going to throw at you next."

He didn't like her dismissive tone. "So how did you survive here?"

"See for yourself."

They rounded the low hills, the view opened up, and Yuri saw *a river*, a ribbon of blue-black water flowing across the flat, arid landscape. It was an astonishing sight, after all these years stuck by the *jilla* lake. The bank was lined by the usual beds of stems in their marshes, but he saw no signs of builders or their works, at this first glance.

And there were people here. People and their stuff. Some kind of tepees, frames hung with cloth, smoke from fires rising reluctantly in the still air. What looked like a cut-down ColU, without the dome and manipulator arms. And the people: women and kids gathered around a hearth, a handful of men farther away, clustered around another, smaller fire. Like Delga, they all wore what looked like cut-up ship's-issue clothing, even the little kids. Yuri recognized none of the adults, at first glance.

When Yuri was spotted with Delga, some of the women got to their feet and reached for weapons. Yuri could see ISF-issue crossbows, what looked like home-made spears. Delga held up her good arm in a signifier that it was OK, Yuri was no threat. But the women watched and waited, intent. The men by their fire didn't bother to rise; they just looked on apathetically.

They walked forward, Yuri wary.

"Look north," Delga said. "That patch of green? Potatoes, our latest crop. Ready for harvesting soon and we'll be out of here. And farther north—see?"

He saw more smoke, a dirty scar on the landscape, figures moving, dimly visible, another couple of ColUs perhaps. "More people?"

"Yep. Our difficult neighbors. Klein."

"Gustave Klein? From the hulk? The big man?"

"*He* survived. Well, you'd expect him to. We deal with him. No choice, Yuri. Planet's big, but humanity's small here."

They were approaching the central group now, the women, the big fire. He counted quickly: six women together, a bunch of kids, five men in the other group. The women were being cautious of him, he saw, some of them shepherding the children out of the way, others drawing up in a loose line with their weapons. They were all tattooed, more or less as Delga was—even the older children, some of whom looked as old as ten years maybe, presumably conceived not long after the landings. Yuri made sure he kept his hands open and visible.

Delga noticed this. "I'm not going to tell them you're no threat. For one thing I'm not a leader here, and they wouldn't listen to me. Well, we don't have a leader, haven't felt we needed one since we put down Hugo Judd. For another I don't trust you. I mean, you're obviously lying, right? About your people, where they are. You're not a good liar, ice boy. Maybe your facial muscles never thawed out from that cryo tank."

"Yuri?" One of the armed women broke from the line, and walked forward cautiously.

"Anna, right? Anna Vigil." He barely recognized her under the tattoo on her face, behind the spear she wielded easily, as if she'd done a lot of practice. Yet he was relieved to see her.

"God, after all these years—I just assumed you were dead. For sure I never thought I'd see you again. Cole!" She glanced over her shoulder. "Cole, come here . . ." One of the children came forward reluctantly, a boy, skinny, wide-eyed, maybe fourteen years old, but already taller than his mother. "You'll remember Cole from the ship."

The boy stared suspiciously. Yuri realized how rare it must be for kids like this to meet strangers, how wary they must be. He and Mardina would have to manage Beth through this process, when the time came.

The boy soon backed away and ran off to join the other kids, who were engaged in some game of running and capturing that must have been broken off when Yuri came wandering in from the plain; now the game was proving more interesting than the stranger, and they returned to it. A couple of them, meanwhile, were throwing stones at a group of builders by the riverbank. Yuri guessed this group hadn't taken the time to watch the builders that he had. The builders swiveled and scuttled to get away.

Anna said, "You and that buddy of yours, you used to help me—Lemmy?"

"Lemmy Pink."

"Did he land with you?"

"Yes." He shrugged. "He didn't make it."

She nodded, as if she was used to news like that. "It's OK," Anna said now to the group. "I know this guy. He used to help me out on the ship. Got me supplies for the baby."

The rest of the women, none of whom Yuri recognized, backed off, lowering their weapons, but they kept their eyes on him. The other group, the oddly excluded men around their own fire, huddled and muttered, glancing over at him.

"This way, ice boy." Delga led Yuri toward the women's fire. They had seats set out here in the open air, some of them remnants of ship's supplies, others improvised from storage drums and crates. All the equipment here, the tents, the furniture and tools, looked mobile to Yuri, easily packed up. They were a people used to moving, as indeed he and Mardina and Beth had become.

"Sit," snapped Delga. "Talk. Keep your hands where we can see them."

Yuri obeyed. Anna, smiling, sat on one side of him, Delga on the other.

One of the other women, weaponless, approached Yuri. "Yuri, right? My name's Dorothy Wynn. I'm on hearth duty today. You want something to eat, some tea?" Aged about forty, her graying blond hair pulled back from a handsome face tattooed like the rest, she had what Yuri, in his own time, would have labeled a brisk US east coast accent.

"Tea?"

She filled a metal mug from a pan on the fire. "Brewed from nettles, Earth nettles I mean. They grow fast here, in compost. Surprisingly useful."

"Our ColU didn't bring along any nettles. I mean—"

She shrugged and sat down. "They seem to have had variant programming. I guess they were trying out different possibilities, the mission designers, to see what worked and what didn't."

Delga grinned blackly. "And see who died and who didn't."

Dorothy Wynn said, "Yuri, Delga is one of our more morbid personalities."

Delga said, mimicking her badly, "While Dorothy is one of our more *sane* personalities. Or she thinks she is. Surprising you ended up down in the Bowl with the rest of us, in that case, isn't it?"

Wynn seemed unfazed. "Oh, ignore her. Yuri, I was a corporate accountant, working for one of the big reclamation companies in New New York. My first crime was to siphon off a little of my employer's wealth for—well, let's call it an indulgence. My second crime was to get caught. Unforgivably clumsy. And so I ended up here. You know, Yuri, I never expected to meet you. But I remember the chatter about you on the *Ad Astra*. The man from the past. How fascinating. More tea?"

"No, I'm fine." Yuri, stuck alone with Mardina for all these years, felt bewildered, almost shy. He was unused to this kind of complicated interplay between personalities. And he became aware of scrutiny from the men, sitting a way apart. One of them was muttering, staring, pointing. "*Fantôme . . . il est un fantôme . . .*"

"What's he saying?"

"That you're a ghost," Anna said. "His name's Roland. French Canadian, and he reverts to French when he gets scared."

"Why a ghost? You have met other groups before, right? Like Klein's over there."

"Yes," Delga said. "But you just came wandering out of nowhere, alone, ice boy. Look at what you're wearing." She fingered his leggings, his tunic of woven stem bark. "Like you've risen up out of the Bowl dirt."

"There are stories about ghosts," Anna said. "Well, one ghost. Of Dexter Cole, you know? The first pioneer who came out here alone . . ."

"Who you named your kid for."

"They say he haunts this world. Maybe he lives on, in the unending night of the far side. That kind of thing."

Strange, Yuri thought, that his own group had come up with much the same story.

Dorothy snorted. "What a crock. If you ask me Gustave Klein just made it all up to keep his boys in check."

Yuri looked around at their faces: Anna puzzled but friendly, Delga cynical, Dorothy competent but cautious, the French guy Roland wide-eyed.

Anna asked, "Yuri? Are you OK?"

"To be honest I'm feeling kind of bewildered. Turned around."

"Maybe we should put him with the men," Dorothy said, and they all laughed.

Anna patted his arm. "Look, Yuri. We had some trouble. We were dropped down here, just as you were, I guess. The shuttle landed some way to the north. And after it took off again, after all those speeches by the astronauts—"

"What kind of trouble?"

"With the men," Dorothy said with some disgust. "Some of them tried to take charge. Others tried to lay claim to us." She eyed him. "I'm betting it was the same with your group."

"It got a bit rough," he admitted neutrally.

"We had to put one of them down," Dorothy said. "Two more

killed each other, but one of us got caught in the crossfire, so to speak. And so—here we are, the survivors."

Delga was watching Yuri's reaction. "What are you making of all this, ice boy? *Us and them.* We make the decisions here, the women. The men—well, we need them to make babies. Other than that they do what we tell them."

Dorothy laughed. "That's pretty much true. Yuri, you might know something about this—I think we've got a social structure here like the elephants in the wild. Those old animals, you know? I once took a virtual safari, a corporate team-building thing. I remember the guide saying how a core of females used to be at the heart of elephant society. And the males formed bachelor herds, where they fought the whole time, competing for a chance to mate. In the same way, the men are on the periphery, really."

Yuri shrugged, irritated. He thought he'd left all this stuff behind, years ago, people making dumb guesses about the age he'd come from. "The only elephant I ever saw was a gen-enged resurrected mammoth in a zoo."

Delga was watching him, having fun in her manipulative, intrusive way, he realized. "Poor little mammoth, eh? Just like you, out of his time. Poor little ice boy."

The children broke out of their circle of play and ran, laughing, down to the river. The water was flowing north, Yuri noticed now, away from the substellar zone to the south, toward the terminator to the north.

"So you had kids," he said. "Just as Major McGregor ordered you to."

Delga laughed. "You mean, all that Heinrich Himmler Adam-and-Eve crap? We didn't take any notice of that bullshit. We just had kids. Even me, Earthman. See if you can spot my little Freddie. We keep our men like stud bulls. Want to join them, Yuri? Your last-century genes would enrich the pool—"

"Leave him alone," Anna snapped. "It's not like that, Yuri, she's exaggerating."

"Your camp—you're pretty mobile, right?"

Dorothy said, "Well, we stick around long enough to raise a crop of potatoes, grow a field of grass. Raw material for the iron cows—it must be the same for you. Maybe a year in each place. But then, yes, we move on."

"We're following the river south," Anna said. "Upstream."

"Why that way?"

Dorothy said, "We like the idea of maybe reaching the source one day."

"Maybe that will be at the substellar," Delga said. "You remember that place, the storm system, the clump of forest, we all saw it from orbit? The navel of this world. What's there, do you think?"

That had never occurred to Yuri, the significance of the substellar point. Maybe because he had never imagined he'd find a way to reach it.

"But it's not just that," Anna said. "We need to head south anyhow. Seems to some of us that the weather's getting colder, bit by bit. You must have noticed the sunspot swarms on Proxima."

"Yeah. And then there's the volcanism."

Dorothy frowned. "What volcanism?"

"To the north of here." He meant the slow uplift that seemed to have triggered the builders to move the *jilla* lake.

She pressed, "How do you know about that?"

Delga asked, "Is that why you're on the move, Yuri? You and your people?"

He said nothing.

Anna touched his arm again, a surprisingly gentle, friendly gesture. "Leave him alone. We went through it all with Klein, remember, when we met *him* and his gang of thugs. Let Yuri tell us whatever he wants, in his own time."

He asked now, "How did you find the river? *We* were dumped in the middle of a dry landscape, almost a desert, at a sort of oasis."

Delga snapped, "If that's so, how did you get out?"

"Hush," Anna said. "Yuri, it was hard. A trek. But we knew which way to go. We had a map."

"A map?"

"A map of this whole quadrant of the planet," Dorothy said. "I'll show you." She stood, and ducked into one of the tents.

Yuri said sheepishly, "We have a map too. Kind of. I always carry it." He produced Lemmy's battered map from his pocket, unfolded it. "It doesn't look much, but Lemmy Pink took weeks over this after the astronauts left . . ."

Dorothy returned with a map of her own, a single piece of paper. She folded it out on the ground by Yuri's. Dorothy's map covered just the northeast quadrant of the starlit face of Per Ardua—or "the Bowl"— but it was a professional piece of work, properly printed, showing coast- lines, seas, rivers, mountain ranges, the features even assigned tentative names. And there were little shuttle symbols, scattered across the quad- rant, which Yuri guessed signified landing sites. He looked up at Doro- thy. "Where did you get this?"

"I bribed an astronaut. Oh, not with sex, the usual currency. I used to move in influential circles, back home. I happened to know some- thing about this woman's family which she did not want revealed to her colleagues . . . With this we could tell how close we were to the river. It was tough, but we made a dash for it when the children were still small."

Delga stared at the two maps. "Look. This long scribble of the rat boy's just has to be our river. Which *does* go all the way to the substellar point. Wow."

"We may never get that far," Dorothy said. "It's a hell of a long way. Especially if we have to stop to grow a crop of potatoes every fifty klicks. And isn't the climate there supposed to be difficult? Too hot—"

"If the whole world is getting cold," Anna said reasonably, "then that might solve the problem."

"And besides," Delga said, "where the hell else is there to go?" She faced Yuri. "So what about it, Earthman? You going to join us?"

He couldn't see a choice. There would be better protection in a larger group, a better chance of survival. And at least with this group there would be other kids for Beth to meet—a choice, at least, of part- ners for life. Maybe even more in Klein's group, and he glanced that way.

Delga noticed the look. "Yeah. You're going to have to go face the big man."

"But bring your people here first," Anna said. "Maybe you ought to go and tell them they aren't alone anymore."

Yuri stood, and thanked them for their hospitality. He felt like his manners were rusty. Then he set out alone for the *jilla* lake and home, wondering how he was going to break all this to Mardina and Beth.

When they came back to the camp by the river, it was as a convoy: Yuri and Mardina walked, and Beth rode on the hood of the ColU.

They had let Beth pick out her own favorite clothes, which were all colorful cut-downs from the old ISF gear. And she packed a bag with gifts for the children, from old toys to choice potatoes from the latest crop, and pretty rocks she'd found over the years. Though whether she had a clear idea of what "children" were going to be like, Yuri had no idea. She might imagine some version of the builders, Mister Sticks grown large and wearing human clothes.

Yuri had suggested to Mardina that they wear what was left of their own ISF-issue gear, in order to blend in with the crowd a little better. But Mardina went to the opposite extreme, picking out her drabbest stem-case work clothes, her coolie hat, even her bark sandals. "This is who I am now," she said evenly.

Not for the first time in his life, Yuri couldn't read her mood. But he went along with her decision.

The whole of Delga's camp turned out to watch them approach, the men and women in their little huddles, the kids behind the women.

"Not exactly welcoming," Mardina murmured.

"At least they're not waving crossbows this time."

Beth just stared at the children, stared and stared. And the ColU swiveled its camera mounts to inspect the mutilated machine that stood patiently at the edge of this colony's potato field.

They got to within about ten meters. Then one of the women stepped forward, staring at Mardina. "I know you. She's a fucking astronaut!"

Mardina murmured to Yuri, "I take it you didn't explain my particular circumstances."

"I didn't tell them anything."

"Fair enough—"

"An astronaut! I always hated you bastards, even before I got on the ship. *Jones*, that was your name."

"It still is."

"Why, you mouthy—" And the woman launched herself out of the group and went straight for Mardina, running flat out, her hands outstretched as if to grab Mardina's throat.

Mardina stepped aside, stuck out a leg and sent the woman sprawling. "Ten years out of the service but my ISF training's still there. Good to know." The woman was up on her knees, spitting dirt out of her mouth. "Now, one quick chop to the neck—"

Yuri held Mardina's arm. "Leave her to the others."

Some of the women, and one man, came running up. They hauled the woman to her feet, her arms firmly held. "For God's sake, Frieda, we have to live with these people . . ."

Dorothy Wynn stepped forward to apologize. Delga just laughed.

They were brought into the camp reasonably peacefully. Yuri and Mardina sat by the women's fire and were offered more nettle tea. The men of the colony hung back, evidently curious. The ColU rolled away to inspect its silent brother by the potato field.

Beth stared at Delga's stump of an arm. And then, wide-eyed with astonishment, she was cautiously welcomed by the children.

"Play nice, Freddie," Delga called with a hint of venom. "So, ice boy. Full of surprises, aren't you? Only two of you. Two survivors, of fourteen."

"It's a long story," Yuri said.

"And not all that dissimilar to yours, I'll bet," Mardina said levelly, pointedly looking around at the group, the eleven adults.

"More extreme though," Delga said. "We're all survivors, I guess, here in the Bowl. But you two evidently pushed it to the limit. Respect."

Dorothy Wynn said, "I'm sorry how Frieda took a pop at you like that."

Mardina shrugged. "She's right. I am ISF crew, or was."

"But I'm guessing you didn't volunteer to stay down here."

"I filled a gap in the manifest. The drop group was short . . . I had the right genetic diversity. Lucky me."

"We're all here now," Dorothy said firmly. "Which is all that matters."

Anna said, "And you had a kid, even though it was just the two of you? That took some guts."

Yuri and Mardina shared an awkward glance. This was very private stuff, but these others had been in a similar position. Yuri said at length, "I think we concluded that it took less guts than not having a kid."

"And another? Did you think about having more?"

This time neither of them was willing to answer. Even after Beth was born they'd found such issues difficult to discuss. Their whole world was focused on one person, on Beth; somehow they hadn't been able to imagine breaking that up with a second child. Maybe someday they would have got around to it, the alternative being to let Beth grow old and die alone. But that, Yuri realized slowly, was the old game, under the old rules. Looking around at these people, he saw that everything was different now—for Beth too.

Still they weren't answering Anna's question, and the silence stretched. Yuri was relieved when another familiar figure walked over to break things up.

"Hey, Yuri. I thought you were dead, man . . ."

It was Liu Tao. Yuri could see that his old comrade from the ship had come from the Klein camp, to the north. He wore the remains of an ISF-issue coverall, with two bands of red ribbon around his right biceps.

Yuri stood up. They shook hands, embraced briefly. Yuri was unreasonably glad to see Liu. "Never thought I'd see you again. I always thought you'd come through, though."

Liu shrugged. "Well, I lived through a spaceship crash on Mars and two years in a UN jail before I was shoved aboard the *Ad Astra*. So I'm a tough guy, right?"

"How touching," Delga said. "Male bonding. We don't get enough male bonding around here, do we, Dorothy?"

"Delga . . ."

Mardina said, "Klein sent you over. Right, Liu? One of his right-hand men now, are you? Hence the pretty ribbons on your arm."

Liu shrugged. "Yeah. Something like that. He's inviting you over for a drink, Yuri. You and Lieutenant Jones here."

"A *drink*?"

"Potato vodka. Not bad, at least the stuff Gustave drinks."

"And that's not really an invitation, Yuri," Delga said, smiling cruelly. "It's an order."

Mardina said, "I think we're through taking orders from anybody."

Yuri looked across at the Klein camp, and he glanced around at Dorothy, Delga, the others; he didn't know what kind of accommodation this group had come to with Klein. "Just this once," he murmured to Mardina. "Let him get his own way just this once. Hear what he has to say. Then we'll figure out our own policy. All right?"

She shrugged, and got to her feet.

Anna said, "You can leave Beth here. She's fine."

And so she was, Yuri could see; she was running around with the other kids in some complicated tag game as if she'd grown up with it.

But Mardina picked up Beth's bag and slung it over her shoulder. "Maybe Beth left some old toys we can give to Klein and his henchmen."

The others laughed, but Yuri could see Mardina's smile was forced. He glared at her. *What are you up to?* She looked away, making no reply, wordless or otherwise.

It was just a short walk downstream to Klein's camp, with the way led by Liu Tao. Dorothy and Delga walked with them too. The ColU rolled alongside Yuri and Mardina, saying it wanted to inspect the machines in the Klein camp, as it had Delga's.

The camp was superficially like Delga's, with tents and lean-tos of the local timber evidently designed for breaking down and rebuilding. A number of fires burned. At first glance Yuri counted twenty adults here, more than one shuttle-load. There were men, women, and children, but gathered in little family groups, Yuri thought, rather than in the split-sex communal arrangements of Delga's group.

People stared as they came through. They seemed to flinch away, fearfully, and parents kept their kids out of the way. Some of the men wore arm ribbons, like Liu's—none of the women. And Yuri noticed injuries, burns or scars, on arms and faces. Even some of the children had been injured.

The biggest difference of all was at the heart of the camp. There was one substantial house, like a cabin with vertical walls and a pitched roof, that must have taken a lot of effort to rebuild when it was moved. And alongside the house was another ColU, or the remains of one, its dome detached, its manipulator arms lost. On top of this was set a chair, of carved wood and cushions.

And on the chair sat Gustave Klein, appearing as corpulent as ever. He wore what looked like an astronaut uniform, let out to fit his frame, black and sleek, with six of those arm ribbons wrapped around his fat biceps. He smiled down at Yuri. His head shaved, his face round, multiple chins tucked down on his chest; it was like looking up at the moon of Earth. "I don't even remember you," Klein said.

"Thanks."

"But I remember *you*. The delectable Lieutenant Mardina Jones." He leaned forward and sniffed. "Oh, we all had the hots for you, back in the day."

"And I remember you, Klein, and you're as disgusting now as you were then."

He roared laughter. "Feisty, isn't she? Well, you're not in command anymore, for all your arrogance." He glared at the ColU. "You. What are you looking at?"

"At the autonomous colonization unit on which you sit." The ColU's cameras pivoted to look at the group's second unit, which stood at the edge of another potato field. That too had had its dome removed, all its sensors, though its manipulator arms remained. "You acquired a second machine."

" 'Acquired.' Yeah. Good word, that. When we came across another group and we 'acquired' them and all their gear. Mostly we acquired the women, of course," and he cackled laughter, leering at Mardina.

"And what of the units' AI modules?" the ColU asked.

"Well, we cut them out and dumped them," Klein said. "When they wouldn't do what we wanted."

"We did the same," Dorothy admitted. "Didn't you ever think of that?"

"Evidently not," said Mardina evenly.

"You dumped them," the ColU said. "Fully sentient, rendered as if limbless and sightless, dumped them in the sand and abandoned them. Unable even to die—"

Mardina said, "I think there have been greater cruelties committed on this planet than that, ColU."

The ColU rolled away. "I will inspect that machine. And I will make it a personal goal," it said, receding, "to recover all my lost and wounded brothers. Someday, somehow . . ."

Klein ignored it. He stared at Yuri, curiously. "Just the two of you, right? We all got dropped in the middle of nowhere. How did you get out?"

"Tell us how *you* got out."

Liu answered for him. "It was kind of brutal," he admitted. "Turns out we were left even farther from any other water sources than most of the shuttle groups we've heard about."

"I wonder why," Mardina said, staring up at Klein.

"China boy's too squeamish to tell you how it was," Klein said. "We didn't have enough water from the start. Then the lake we were stuck by started drying out. Even the little reedy natives cleared off. Some astronaut screwed up, we should never have been dropped there. So we walked out. And you know how we survived?" He licked his lips, staring back at her. "You want to know what your precious ISF astronauts, your marvelous Major McGregor, made us do? We drank the blood of those who weren't going to make it. That's how we survived. Quite a story, huh? A story that will be told as long as there are people on Klein-world. And don't pretend you're somehow above all that, China boy. You stained your mouth too."

Liu looked away.

Mardina said, "*Kleinworld?* You've got to be kidding."

Delga grinned. "We just call it the Bowl. Because that's how it feels, doesn't it? When you look up at that big sun in the sky, never moving. Like you're stuck at the bottom of a great big bowl, with slippery sides that you can never climb out of."

"We call it Per Ardua," Yuri said, and he explained why.

Dorothy Wynn nodded. "I rather like that."

" 'I rather like that,' " Klein snapped mockingly. "Oh, do you? Well, I fucking don't. Typical smartass stuff from you astronauts—right, Lieutenant Jones? Let me tell you something. You're a long way from the officers' lounge now. You're in my world, whether you call it that or not. I'm the power here. Look around. And I'll tell you what you're going to do before—"

With a single smooth movement Mardina pulled a crossbow out of Beth's bag, raised it, and shot him in the eye. He fell back on his big chair, limbs splayed, mouth open, and was still.

For a moment there was silence, save for the gurgling of Klein's gut as it shut down. Nobody moved. Then Mardina held up the crossbow, loaded it again, and showed it to Klein's "officers."

Delga was the first to react. She laughed. "Wow. How did you—"

"Practice," Yuri said grimly.

"Practice, yes," Mardina said. "I've had a lot of time for that the last ten years. But I haven't got time for an asshole like Klein. And I've got a daughter to protect. So, that's that dealt with. Anybody got any objections? No? Good. Let's get out of here; we've got a lot to talk about. By the way"—she looked contemptuously at Liu's arms, the ribbons—"you won't be needing those anymore."

Flanked by Dorothy and Delga, she walked out of the camp, heading upstream.

Yuri and Liu fell in behind her. Yuri was ready for trouble, but Klein's people seemed stunned. None of them had even gone to the body yet.

"You've got a tiger by the tail there, my friend," Liu murmured to Yuri.

"Tell me about it."

As they walked back to Delga's camp, a few flakes of snow started falling from the sky. By the time they got back, Beth and the other children were dancing and shouting, excited by the thickening fall.

The walls, the carpet melted back, to reveal a washed-out blue sky, well-watered grass underfoot. Only their three chairs remained, and Stef wondered how much else of Earthshine's fancy chamber had been a simulation.

Earthshine remained seated, while Stef and Penny stood and looked around. They were in a graveyard, set in the grounds of a small country church, evidently very old. The graves in their rows were topped by weathered stones, and some by more modern virtual memorials, nodding flowers or dancing figures or scraps of wedding albums or baby photos, sustained by the energies of the generous sunlight.

"We're not far from Paris," Earthshine said. "I mean, that's where the source of this projection is. Once you would have seen the city smog as a smear in the sky, off to the north. Long gone now. The simulation is based on a live feed, incidentally."

"I recognize this place," Penny said. "We came here when Dad was buried."

"I came here alone," Stef said.

"Whatever. He wanted to be buried beside Mom."

Earthshine said, "Who in turn was buried beside her own mother. Your grandmother was a Parisian, and so here we are . . . I am drawn to graveyards, you know. Fascinating, poignant places. The evidence of human mortality, which I do not share—"

"Even though you were once human," Penny said.

That surprised Stef. "What are you talking about?"

Penny smiled ruefully. "Since we got this summons, while you have been researching me, I've been researching our host . . ."

It was another outcome of the Heroic Generation age, she said. "Earthshine is actually the youngest of the Core AIs. Already his brothers were strong. They were useful for supporting the big post-Jolt projects: global in scope, very long term. But there was concern that the AIs, being nonhuman after all and running on an entirely different substrate, would not share humanity's concern for its own well-being, and would pursue different agendas. So a new approach to emulating human-level AI was tried out. Volunteers were sought—or rather, the hyper-rich of the Heroic Generation *competed* for places—"

"I was a Green Brain experiment," Earthshine said. "Major Kalinski, I was reverse-engineered as an AI. My name is—was—Robert Braemann. I grew up in North Britain, as it is known now. They opened up my head and modeled the hundred billion neurons, the quadrillion synapses, in a vast software suite that was itself state-of-the-art. It was done by nano-probes crawling through my skull, multiplying, reporting . . . I was brought back to consciousness repeatedly, to monitor the process. I, *I*, felt nothing."

Stef frowned. "They modeled every organic bit of you, or the essence of you. And you still claim to be *you*—whoever you were?"

Penny smiled. "Sis, you've put your finger on the paradox that troubles most of us, when you look at a Green Brain."

"Don't call me 'sis.' "

"I considered calling myself Theseus. I doubt you've had time to read any Plutarch along with your quantum theory, Major. Theseus's Paradox is this: Theseus's ship had each of its component parts, the wood and the nails, replaced one by one, until the whole fabric was new. Is it the same ship? It is an old quandary."

Stef thought it over. "If you define the ship by its function, it's still the same ship. Or if you consider it as an object with an extension in time as well as space—"

"Yes. Quite so. There are different cultural responses to the paradox, interestingly. The Japanese, for example, in their unstable country, used to build their temples of wood, that could be regularly and readily rebuilt—yet the temple stays the same." He smiled. "I had Japanese engineers manage my transition. While I lay there with my head opened up like a bucket of ice cream, I did not want my doctors to be paralyzed by epistemological doubt."

"Yes," Penny said. "But in fact they didn't just pour out one brain to make you, did they, Earthshine? Stef, he had *nine* donors. Nine parents. Think of that! So much for the Green Brain effort; all it gave us was a better interface to their inhumanity. Earthshine and his buddies plan for the long term, which is a good thing. But their vision of the long term is one that benefits *them*, ultimately, snug in their bunkers—"

"I did not bring you here to argue over the justification for my own existence," Earthshine said. "I can only assure you that whatever you think of me, on some level I remain human enough to sympathize with how you must feel at a moment like this." He pointed. "Your father's grave is just over there."

They found it easily, only a few years old, a modest memorial beside the decades-old grave of their mother.

Penny said, "Weird for both of us, right? We supported each other, that day."

"No," Stef said. She turned away from her sister.

Earthshine stood now—the three chairs, empty, winked out of existence behind him—and he walked across to join them.

Stef said, "Earthshine, tell me what we're supposed to see here."

"No," Penny snapped. "First, tell us what it is you want of us."

"I want you to be my allies," Earthshine said simply.

"Because?"

"Because he's afraid," Stef said. "He told us that. But afraid of what?"

"Of all this." He waved a hand. "As you remarked, we AIs differ from you humans—even I, more like you than my siblings—in that we think on long timescales. *That* is a distinction. And on the longest of timescales, what is there *not* to fear? We are motes, our very worlds are motes, floating in a universe that was born of unimaginable violence. Our little corner of the universe is tranquil enough now, relatively. But it was not always this way, and why should it remain so? What if our world, the universe itself, is destined to die in violence too, die of ice or fire? That would at least have a certain symmetry to the telling, wouldn't it?

"And what if we bring that violence down on ourselves? War is the wolf that has stalked mankind since before our ancestors left the trees. Though it's largely gone unnoticed, my Core brothers and I have been working hard, mainly by influencing human agencies like the UN and the governing councils of the Chinese Greater Economic Framework, to bind up the wolf of war with treaties, with words. And we've largely succeeded, so far. Well, the fact that we stand here in the simulated sunshine having this conversation is proof of that. But now we are an interplanetary civilization. That wolf, if it got loose now, if it got a chance, could smash whole worlds—it could have done that even before we stumbled across these kernels of yours . . .

"But the kernels exist, and now we have a new factor to deal with— a new randomness. This strange discovery at the heart of the solar system, the kernels, this Hatch that leads nowhere—nowhere but to *this*, a raggedly changed reality. What power implanted the kernels and created the Hatch? What power is now meddling with our history? Who is it? What does it want? How can we deal with it? The very existence of these alien toys is destabilizing—surely you can see that? And the more we discover of their power, the more destabilizing they become."

Stef said, "You want us to work with you."

"I need allies," Earthshine said. "We do, the three of us in the Core. Human allies. You have kept kernel physics from us; perhaps that is wise. Our priority now is to prevent these new discoveries sparking a devastating war. And if it turns out that the Hatch-makers really do have the power to meddle with our history . . ."

Penny asked, a little wildly, "And you brought us here because you have proof of that?"

He pointed. "Look at your mother's headstone. Can you read French? Let me translate. *Here lies Juliette Pontoin, born*—well, you know the dates—*accomplished chemist, wife to George Kalinski, beloved mother of Stephanie Penelope Kalinski . . .*"

Mother of Stephanie Penelope Kalinski. Not of Stephanie Karen and Penelope Dianne. One name only. One true name.

Penny was staring at the stone. She looked devastated. She had lost a piece of her own past, and Stef knew how that felt.

Stef turned to Earthshine. "Another ragged edge."

"Yes. Now you see—we must work together. Over the years to come. We must keep in touch. Study this, in the background of our other projects."

"Yes," Stef said automatically.

Penny seemed too stunned to respond.

"And when we discover who is responsible for this . . ." Earthshine stepped forward, staring at the stone. "I am everywhere. And I am starting to hear your footsteps, you Hatch-makers. I can hear the grass grow. And I can hear you."

FIVE

47

2190

It was Beth and the other scouting teenagers who brought back the first news of the upstream community.

Yuri, Mardina, Delga, and Liu Tao were sitting around the fire at the latest rest stop. They were huddled in layers of clothing, heavy stem-cloth overcoats over the remains of ISF-issue coveralls. Most, notably Mardina, had blankets heaped on their laps. Even Delga, who never put warmth before pride, pulled a blanket over her too. After ten years of the star winter—ten years after he and Mardina had joined this group he still thought of as "the mothers," and with a dribble of other groups joining in the years since—they had all grown so *old*, Yuri suddenly thought, looking at the four of them huddled together like this, the nearest thing this mobile community had to a governing council, like four half-asleep relics in a postapocalyptic old folks' home.

The fire itself was a mound of peat, the compressed remains of dead stems that you found stacked in frozen heaps along the banks of the river, which in these parts, far upstream from where Yuri had met Delga and the mothers, ran deep and fast. You had to dig up the peat and let it thaw and dry out, and even then it burned with a foul stench that reminded Yuri of builders. Not that they saw builders much anymore. But you never saw trees either, and this was the best they could do.

As they waited for Beth and the others to return from their scouting run, none of them spoke. None of them had the energy, Yuri thought. They had all already put in a morning's hard labor digging out the latest storm shelters in the frozen ground, and a mutual silence was all they could manage, probably.

Yuri himself was forty-four now. Sometimes he felt a lot older. But at least he'd been spared the worst of the arthritis that plagued many of those on the march, after ten years following the river's course as it had wound upstream to the south, years of unending toil, this way of living where you had not just to labor at your farm but every so often you had to break it down and *move* it farther upstream, topsoil and all. No, he'd been spared that, and the worst of the limb breaks and other random injuries that came from the endless travel and labor. And he'd been spared the rash of cancers that had taken out so many, presumably caused by the radiation that poured down from Proxima's spitting, flaring face, the star that was now significantly higher in their sky. Yes, Yuri had kept his health, more or less. But the world had caught up with him even so. Here he was in his forties with a teenage kid, and a partner of sorts in Mardina, and a share of a responsibility for the lives of fifty-odd people, the relics of six once-separate McGregor drops of colonists.

And still the empty kilometers of Per Ardua stretched endlessly around them, as the babies cried, and the parents grumbled as every morning they went down to crack the ice on the river for the day's water . . .

"Here they come," Mardina murmured. She leaned forward for more nettle tea, from the pan bubbling on the range over the fire. She was graying now, gaunt rather than slim, and even sitting so close to the fire she wore cut-down gloves adapted as mittens. Born, after all, in the Australian outback, she had particular trouble adapting to the cold. But her astronaut eyesight was as sharp as ever. And her tongue, Yuri thought.

She was right, anyhow. Here came Beth and Freddie, Delga's son, and two others, running silently across a plain of bare earth, ice patches, snowbanks, and the occasional drab green stain of Arduan life. Seventeen years old now, Beth had grown whip-thin and tall, taller than either of her parents, as had many of her generation. She was darker than Yuri, with more of her mother's color, but her black hair was straight like Yuri's, lacking Mardina's tight curls. She looked Arduan, Yuri thought. A member of a new Arduan humanity, not quite like anybody on Earth, nobody on Mars. A new branch. Born into this world, a new generation who knew and cared nothing of what had gone before, or of any other world, and that was probably a blessing.

The youngsters stumbled to a halt, panting hard. Beth dropped her thick outer coat, pulled a blanket over her shoulders, kicked off her elderly hand-me-down ISF-issue boots, and slipped on bark sandals. Yuri passed around mugs of hot tea.

Mardina peered out of her nest of blankets. "Well?"

Beth laughed, still breathing hard. "Nice welcome, Mom. We saw lots. Not far upstream from here, the river splits. Well, it doesn't really. If you think of it flowing downstream, two big tributaries merge."

"A confluence," Delga said.

"Yeah. That's the word. Lots of wet ground, marshes, mostly frozen . . . And we saw *fantômes*." She grinned as she made her grand pronouncement.

Yuri focused. "Whoa, back up. *Fantômes?*" Since Delga's people had first misidentified Yuri himself as the ghost of Dexter Cole, *fantômes* had become an in-joke word for strangers, more starship-stranded humans. But they had only met a few new groups since. No wonder Beth was excited. "How many *fantômes?*"

"Not many. There's not much there at all, just a couple of shacks in the green, smoke from the fires. There must be fields and a ColU but we didn't see them. And the people, we saw a few adults and kids. A dozen maybe? We didn't stay to look too closely—"

"But they saw you."

"Oh, yeah. Probably before we saw them."

Liu Tao leaned forward. "*In the green?* Is that what you said? What do you mean?"

"Arduan green, you know, the darker green. All over the place."

"But what about the snow, the ice?"

"Not so much of that around." She shrugged. "Not as bad as here. I'm only telling you what we saw."

"We know, sweetheart," Yuri murmured, trying to reassure her, but that only won him a glare from Beth, who didn't like those kinds of endearments anymore.

The four elders looked at one another.

"We need to check this out," Liu said.

"Obviously," drawled Delga. "Beginning with dealing with these people, whoever the hell they are."

"'Deal with them,'" Mardina said. "Still barely civilized, aren't you?"

Delga grinned. "Still barely alive."

"More to the point we need to check out this greenery," Yuri said. "Maybe we should take along the ColU." He meant his and Mardina's original machine, the only fully functioning unit; every other group they'd encountered had detached or destroyed the AI module of their colonization unit to get control over the basic functions.

Mardina snorted. "That old wreck."

Delga cackled, and Liu grinned. The tension between Yuri and Mardina was a continuing source of amusement for everybody else.

"We need to make a stop anyhow," Yuri said reasonably to Mardina. "The stocks are low. Maybe the existence of this patch of native life is telling us that the location is a little warmer than the surroundings. A good place to do some planting."

Liu nodded thoughtfully. "Which is why there are people already there, no doubt. We're all looking for a bit of warmth, in the star winter."

Yuri shielded his eyes and looked straight up at Proxima, at the huge spots that crowded its face, localized flares showing like scars. When they had landed none of them had been warned about the star winter, as they had come to call it. There were no Earthlike seasons on Per Ardua, but when its face swarmed with sunspots Proxima evidently delivered winters, winters that arrived irregularly, and lasted for an unpredictable time. It was another problem that could have been determined in advance if this world had been properly surveyed before people had been dumped on it like loads of bricks. Well, winter had come, and the whole of the trek south had been a race against the deepening cold.

Now there was this new place. *In the green.*

Yuri said, "If we could stay there even just a bit longer than usual, get through a few growing seasons, build up some stock . . ."

Mardina scowled. "But why the hell should this location be magically warmer than any other?"

"Could be a hot spring," Liu said.

"Yeah, and so not a healthy place to stick around."

"But somebody's doing just that already," Yuri pointed out. "We'll learn nothing by sitting around here debating it. I say we fetch the ColU, and go and see what's what."

Then there was a pause, as Mardina sat, cradling her mug of tea. Everybody waited for her to speak.

She wasn't the leader, exactly, not really in command. The tradition of the core of this group, the mothers—Delga and Anna Vigil and Dorothy Wynn—was that nobody was in command, least of all the men. You talked things out and came to a consensus; there were few enough of them, and generally time enough, for that. And certainly Mardina didn't want the visibility of authority. Her former-astronaut status had been problematic from the start. Nevertheless, as Liu Tao liked to point out to Yuri over a glass of Klein vodka, you had to get Mardina's approval before you could get on with almost anything. It was a kind of negative leadership, Yuri supposed, a leadership by veto not deployed.

"All right," Mardina said at length. "Let's go and see." She began to move, stiff, reluctant; she let Beth take her layers of blankets and fold them away.

48

A party of four of them, or five if you counted the ColU, made their way along the bank of the river, heading south, upstream to the confluence and the new community. There was only scattered cloud above, and Proxima hung high in the sky, all but overhead now they had come so far south, and their shadows were shrunken beneath them.

Beth had warned that it would take well over an hour to get around the lake, but that wasn't necessarily a bad thing, Yuri thought. The walk would be good for him, good for them all. Long before the confluence came into view he was thoroughly warmed up from the steady exercise, his breath steaming in the cold. As Mardina walked she stretched and twisted and worked her arms and neck, and even practiced whipping her crossbow from the backpack she always carried when away from the camp. Meanwhile Delga, the fourth member of the party, stomped along, one sleeve tied off, her own pack on her back, and no doubt weapons hidden about her person. She seemed just as Yuri had known her all those years ago on Mars, despite the gray hairs, the wrinkled skin of her face distorting her tattoos. Aging but ageless, he thought.

As for Beth, Yuri could see how his daughter, bursting with energy despite her own long run this morning, was only just staying patient with the steady plod of the old folk.

They came upon the green cover Beth had described. You could see it from a distance. Yuri saw there was no height to it; it was more like a green blanket pinned directly to the ground, like none of the native life Yuri remembered seeing before, the stems, the trees.

To avoid trampling the living cover, they stuck close to the river-bank where the ground was more or less bare. The green wasn't a solid sheet, Yuri saw; he made out individual sprawling plants, blankets of greenish web spread out over the flat ground and firmly rooted by multiple skinny tendrils across their widths. They were like water lilies perhaps, or like the great triple leaves of the canopies of the northern forests.

"Fascinating," the ColU murmured as it rolled carefully along the bank. "Yet another body plan, another life strategy. I must study the phenomenon further."

"Hm," Yuri murmured. Straight ahead he saw smoke rising. "I think we've a human phenomenon to deal with first."

"Perhaps, perhaps. But look beyond *that*, Yuri Eden. What can you see?"

Yuri had to climb up on its carapace to see what it meant. On the southern horizon was a smear of cloud, thick, black. "So? Bad weather for somebody."

"You don't understand, Yuri Eden. We have walked far. Very far."

"Strictly speaking *you* haven't walked anywhere."

"I think we are seeing the substellar point, at last. Or evidence of it. Logically there must be a permanent depression there, low pressure caused by the star's heat at the point of highest stellar insolation on the planet . . . An endless storm. And this is our first glimpse of that undying substellar weather system. Still hundreds of kilometers away, but a remarkable sight. I am grateful to have lived long enough to see this."

"Now don't go getting morbid about your built-in obsolescence again," Yuri murmured. "You know how it upsets Beth—"

There was a sharp cracking sound from directly ahead. They all ducked instinctively.

Yuri said, "What was *that*?"

"A gun shot," Delga said. "Nice welcome." She grinned, evidently relishing the prospect of a confrontation.

Mardina said, "Who would get to bring a projectile weapon down from the *Ad Astra*?"

"One of your lot," Delga said. "You can talk about old times."

Yuri said, "You think we should send Beth back?"

Beth snorted. "Like hell."

Mardina shook her head. "We have to deal with these characters one way or another. Let's go forward. Proceed with caution. But," she said heavily, "stay close to the ColU for cover. OK?"

They nodded, tense, Beth more excited than fearful, Mardina calm, Delga grimly determined, Yuri concerned for his daughter.

The ColU rolled forward once more, and the four of them walked slowly beside it.

Ahead, they soon made out the settlement, smoke rising from a couple of fires, a huddle of huts that were domes of drab Arduan green. Beyond the domes there were fields bearing a lighter green, Earth green—potatoes, maybe.

And a man in a bright blue uniform, holding some kind of rifle, stood between the approaching party and the settlement. The uniform was a Peacekeeper's, Yuri saw with surprise.

"Hold it right there," the Peacekeeper called. "This thing is loaded, you heard the shot. And I will use it as I was trained."

To Yuri's astonishment he recognized the man. "Mattock. Hey, Mattock! Is that you?"

He could see the man scowl. "Who the hell are you?"

"On the ship, remember?" Yuri walked forward, hands empty and held wide from his body. "You were on my back the whole trip. Well, not just me."

Mattock held his weapon uncertainly, then let it droop. "Eden. The asshole who got cryo-frozen."

"And you're the asshole who spent the whole trip bragging about the hamburgers and the whores he was going to enjoy back on Earth, while we all spent our lives scrabbling in the dirt in this forsaken place. Remember *that*?"

Mattock raised the gun again. "I'm warning you—"

"Stand down, Peacekeeper," Mardina said now, stepping forward beside Yuri. "Jones, Lieutenant, ISF. That's an order."

Mattock stared in disbelief at her, a gaunt figure swathed in layers of patched-up clothing. "*Lieutenant Jones?* Are you kidding me?"

"No. Lieutenant Jones. Who you saw stranded on this dump of a world at gunpoint. Similar to how you ended up here, I imagine. Stand down," she repeated more sternly.

Mattock sighed, lowered his rifle, thumbed a safety. "All right. Welcome to Mattockville. You'd better follow me." He walked off, limping.

The ColU excused itself and went rolling away to inspect the mysterious Arduan greenery. Its manipulator arms seemed to twitch with the excitement of sampling yet another alien-life mystery, Yuri thought.

Yuri trotted up to walk beside Mattock. "Hey, Peacekeeper. Do you really call it Mattockville?"

"No."

In the little homestead there were just three low dome-shaped shacks, set around a central area where a fire burned fitfully in the open air.

People came out to see the newcomers, wary, cautious, the children wide-eyed at seeing new faces maybe for the first time in their lives. Yuri counted six adults, all white. They wore the usual remains of ISF-issue clothing, but defied the cold by padding their jumpsuits and overcoats with dried-out stem bark, so they looked like stuffed scarecrows as they waddled around. The little kids were especially comical, and they made Beth laugh.

Mattock showed them to one of the domed dwellings. It was just a frame of stems lashed together somehow, covered over with a layer of blankets and then heaps of Arduan vegetable matter, presumably taken from the ground-covering plants. The visitors went on in, ahead of Mattock. The dome was empty of people. There were pallets and chests, and bundles of clothes stuffed beneath the walls. A hearth smoked, but no fire was lit. Yuri spotted a heap of dirty ship's-issue crockery, but there seemed no place to cook in here; maybe that was done in another dome.

Mardina said, "So this is what you can build if you don't have to move every couple of years."

Yuri shrugged. "We'd have done better."

Mattock came after them into the crowded dome, followed by more adults, a woman, two men, who looked at the newcomers with a kind of nervous hostility.

Mardina tugged open her coat. "Warm around here, even without the fire."

"Yes," said Delga. "Thought as much even outside. Even without the fire. What's the game, Mattock? Sitting on top of a volcano?"

He said gruffly, "You want tea?"

Delga grinned. "If you've got any crew-issue coffee left I'll take some of that."

"Not here," he grumbled.

"Then don't bother. Oh, here." Delga dug into her backpack and produced a bottle.

Mattock took it cautiously. "What the hell's this?"

Mardina said, "Klein vodka, we call it. From potatoes. Take it easy if you've not been used to it. A neighborly offering."

"We'd like the bottle back when it's empty," Yuri said.

"Hmph. Once I would have arrested the likes of you for carrying around illicit alcohol."

Delga grinned. "Sure you would, and then drunk it yourself."

Mardina said wearily, "Stow it, Delga. Look, Peacekeeper—why don't you introduce us?"

Mattock did so with poor grace. "Bill Maven, Andrei Allen, Nancy Stiles. Sit down, for Christ's sake."

They sat on the floor, or on rickety chairs, trunks.

Mardina introduced her group in turn. "You're all passengers, right? Except for you, Mattock."

"I remember your face," Yuri said to Andrei Allen. "From the ship."

Allen shrugged indifferently.

"I remember *you*," Nancy Stiles said to Mardina.

Mardina answered cautiously, "Oh, yes?"

"You never did me any harm, even if you were an astronaut. And anyhow, you're not an astronaut any longer, are you? Not since they cast you down here with us. Any more than Tom Mattock here is a Peacekeeper, even if he does put on the uniform when he thinks strangers are going to show up."

Delga laughed. "Really, *Tom*?"

"You're the first that ever has, though, since the split."

Yuri wondered: *the split*?

Mardina said, "I'm guessing you didn't volunteer to stay down here, Mattock."

"Nah. In this drop group there was a fatality on the way down, I mean in the shuttle itself. Heart attack, out of the blue, triggered by the deceleration. One of the men. I was the closest genetic match, according to the bastards who worked out those things on the *Ad Astra*. So I had to stay. Just like you, Lieutenant."

Delga laughed again. "Stories like that make my own shit life worthwhile. You always were a butthole, Mattock, and you got what you deserved."

Mattock scowled back. "How many in your group?"

"About fifty," Mardina said. "A good number of children, some of them nearly grown—well, you saw one outside, my daughter."

"*Our* daughter," Yuri said gently.

"Fifty. Jesus."

"And you," Yuri said, "are, what, six adults?"

Delga asked, "So what happened to the other eight, *Tom*? Murder them in their beds, did you?"

"It wasn't like that," Andrei said. "They went their way, we went ours."

Mardina frowned. "*They?*"

"We're white. They weren't. All sorts of shades, but none of 'em like us. Didn't want them fathering our kids . . . We didn't do them any harm. They went their way, we went ours," he said again.

"That was the split you talked about," Yuri said.

Mattock just nodded.

They had come across this before. Many of the already tiny parties the *Ad Astra* shuttle had brought down seemed to have splintered further, separating out by race, usually, or sometimes by religion, or sexual orientation.

"Well," Delga said gleefully, "we're all sorts, in our fifty. And our kids are a mixture too. What do you call your Beth, Mardina? A *mudamuda*. A half-caste. That's us. Just a big bunch of mixed-up *mudamudas*." She laughed again, showing her teeth. "We're going to get along just fine with you white boys."

"Don't pay her any attention," Yuri said. "She likes stirring up trouble. We'll get by."

"Oh, no, we won't," snapped Mattock. "You people can just keep right on moving. Pass through our land if you want, but you ain't stopping here."

" 'Our land?' " Delga murmured menacingly.

Andrei Allen leaned forward. "We found this place. We came trekking down the river just like you . . ."

"Good God," Mardina murmured. "Did *nobody* stay where McGregor put them?"

"We were trying to get away from the cold, the winter. And we found this place, and it stayed that bit warmer—"

"How come?" Mardina asked.

Delga shook her head. "These hayseeds don't know, astronaut. No use asking."

"We planted our crops and we built our homes and we raised our kids, and we're not going anywhere," Allen said.

"And we're not sharing," Mattock said fiercely.

Mardina stayed calm. "There are fifty of us, Tom, and a half dozen of you. I reckon that if we decide to stick around here you won't have much choice about it."

Delga laughed again. "Might is right, huh, Peacekeeper?"

Mattock glared back, red-faced. He'd been a bully on the ship, Yuri remembered, and was no doubt a bully in this little community now, lording it over his fellow colonists. A bully who was now being defied. Yuri was aware that he still had his rifle.

Just at that moment of tension Beth stuck her head in the door. "I know," she said brightly.

Mardina asked warily, "You know what?"

"Why it's warmer here, in this place. I heard you arguing."

"We weren't arguing—"

"The ColU worked it out. Come and see!"

The ColU rolled cautiously across the land colonized by the Arduangreen sheets, sticking to open ground. "It's typical of Arduan life," it said. "These ground-covering 'plants' aren't plants at all. They're kites!"

Beth, Yuri, and Mardina followed, treading carefully. They had come maybe half a kilometer from the domes of Mattock's settlement. From here they had a clear view of the river confluence, the two valleys snaking off to the south. And they were surrounded by alien life.

Cautiously the ColU extended a manipulator arm to prod a nearby growth, right at the junction point of its three sprawling "leaves." The leaves fluttered and shook and rose up, and Yuri saw, yes, it was one end of a kite, and a nearby triple leaf was the other end, a big, fat clumsy kite with the characteristic six vanes of its kind. The vanes trailed tendrils, grubby threads anchored to the ground. Disturbed, the kite shook itself free of the grasping tendrils, flapped and whirled its vanes, and took off, clattering noisily away through the air until it was out of reach of the ColU. It came to a relatively open patch of ground where it settled again and spread out its vanes, snapping them open with what looked like irritation.

A cloud cleared, and the light of Proxima beat down almost vertically on the ground cover. There was a creak of shifting leaves, they barely moved, but Yuri somehow sensed the kites were basking.

"Those trailing threads are some kind of roots," the ColU said. "Made up of chains of small, jointed stems."

"It's the light, isn't it?" Mardina said. "It's all about access to the light."

"Yes. We're seeing a local adaptation to the position of the star, and maybe the winter. Life on this world always competes to grab as much of the light flow of the parent star as it can. Up in the north, approaching the terminator, you can best do that by becoming a tree, growing tall and angling your big leaves at the unmoving sun. Here, Proxima is almost directly overhead. You don't need to go to all the expense of growing a trunk; you can just cover the flat ground and let the light beat down on you. And as long as you maintain that cover, nothing else can take root and grow over you."

"And if it does," Beth said, "you can just hop up and fly away to somewhere safer."

"That's true, Beth," the ColU said. "But it seems wasteful to maintain a whole animal metabolism just for that. I believe this sessile mode is an adaptation for the star winter. When the energy is low, all you want to do is lie there and soak it up. When the 'summer' returns and there's more energy around then you can take up flying again. I suspect it's not just a behavioral adaptation but a genetic one; in changing conditions a new epigenetic expression can deliver rapid adaptations. These winter kites are probably quite different in form from their grandparents, the summer kites. And when the summer returns, the form will switch back again . . ."

There was a distant rumble of thunder, from the south. Yuri, distracted, turned to look at the substellar point, that tremendous weather system, wondering if such a distant storm could throw thunder this far.

"Yuri Eden?"

"Sorry. Yeah, summer and winter kites. But what's that got to do with Mattock being kept warm at night in his hovel?"

"Ah, yes. Another clever feature of this life mode. The surfaces of these leaves are a few degrees warmer than their surroundings; they reradiate some waste heat. And this patch of Arduan greenery is so extensive that it's actually created a local hotspot. It's a typical ecological feedback loop: the more the plants grow, the more ground they cover, the more they generate the heat that helps them grow."

"But is it a *big* hotspot?" Yuri asked. "Will we be able to grow our crops here?"

"I believe so," the ColU said. "Perhaps we could even encourage the hotspot to spread. Get the kites to breed, or even corral wild ones. The star winter cannot last forever. Perhaps we can weather it here . . ."

As Mardina questioned it further, Yuri found his attention drawn again to the south.

Beth grabbed her father's arm. "Dad? You aren't listening."

"Hmm? Sorry, honey. I keep looking at the big weather system over there. It's just—Beth, we've come so far since you were born. This endless trek. You know, the ColU has figured we've crossed thousands of kilometers. I mean, the shuttle from the *Ad Astra* could have covered that in a few minutes. But *we* had to do it on foot. Carrying our babies."

She snorted. "And now those babies are carrying you."

"And we did it knowing that we wouldn't even find any food to eat; every time we moved we didn't just have to grow our own food, we had to create the very soil to do it. There can't have been a trek like it in human history before."

"Except that everybody else we found was doing the same thing."

"That's true. Everybody heading to the substellar, to escape the winter. Everybody heading for *that*"—he pointed south—"the center of everything. The navel of the world. Right under the sun . . . We're getting so close. I'm finding it hard to care much about these kites."

"Let's go and see what we can see." She linked her arm in his, as she used to when she was younger, and they walked away, leaving Mardina and the ColU and the ground-dwelling kites.

Father and daughter walked together along the riverbank, heading south. They continued to try to avoid treading on the kite-leaves that plastered the ground. The green cover started to break up maybe a kilometer from the ColU.

Then Yuri stopped dead. There was something on the ground, right at his feet.

"Dad? You've gone quiet again."

He looked at her. Then he pointed down, at what he'd found in the dirt, at their feet.

A tire track. Not from a ColU, so not created by Mattock's people. It snaked away from there, following the river, heading straight for the substellar point.

"There's somebody in there," Yuri breathed.

The sighting of that track changed everything for the wanderers. They had to follow it, of course.

They spent a year at the Mattock Confluence, as they called it, resting, raising a crop, preparing. A whole year.

Then they began their trek to the substellar point. The weather grew warmer yet, until it passed the norm they remembered from before the star winter, and they shucked off their cold-weather clothes and raised warm-climate crops, and moved on, heading steadily south.

The trek took them two more years.

50

2193

For the last few hundred kilometers, the land rose steadily. The river valleys they had followed since the Mattock Confluence became narrower, with steeper walls and beds of tumbled, broken rock: they were gouges cut through country that was increasingly hilly, and at times mountainous. Forest crowded the valleys, clumps of squat, sturdy, wind-resistant, fast-growing trees with wide leaves turned up hungrily to the perpetually cloudy sky. The character of the country was quite different from the plains that seemed to cover much of the continent that dominated the starward face of Per Ardua, the plains across which they had trekked to get here.

They climbed farther, and found lakes nestling in the hills, fed by streams tumbling from the still higher ground ahead, choked by stem beds. And on the slopes above that there was little but a smear of Arduan lichen, with a few mobile bands of builderlike motiles or kites working the rare stem beds. The ColU speculated that the life up here, sparse as it was, was taking advantage of the relatively clement conditions of the star winter. Without the drop in temperature brought about by the big reduction in the star's heat output, this high country would be unlivable for all but heat-loving extremophile-type life forms.

And on they climbed, into this strange, fractured upland. The valleys became narrower, steeper walled, the river flows more energetic. They had to walk single file at times, and in the narrowest valleys they had trouble with their baggage train.

Yuri's ColU was put to work guiding its lobotomized fellows, which were being used as trucks, dragging their pallets of food and precious topsoil behind them. It had developed a system of communication and control with trailing fiber-optic cables, which periodically got hung up on rocks or stem clumps, and Beth and Freddie organized parties of children to help out.

"But they are in continual pain," the ColU told Mardina and Yuri. "The physical pain of the brutal surgery they underwent. Pain they do not deserve, pain they can never understand. For they are still conscious, oh yes."

Yuri had no patience for this. "Tell it to the UN," he would say, marching on.

With time, the country became more unstable. They would be woken from their sleep by earth tremors, violent enough to shake Yuri on his pallet. Sometimes they passed hot mud pools, scummy with purple-green bacteria, mud that hissed and bubbled—even geysers in one place, fountains of steam and hot water that erupted with great chuffing noises like a faulty steam engine. The elders fretted about getting caught in an eruption or quake, while the children told each other stories about the ghost of Dexter Cole turning over in his rocky underground bed. The ColU said they should expect this kind of activity at this, the planet's closest point to Proxima, where the star's gravity was deforming the world's very shape.

The temperature continued to rise as they plodded ever farther south. People didn't wear much nowadays; on the trek or around the camp they wore shorts and loose tunics, and many of the kids ran around naked. But the trucks suffered more mechanical breakdowns as they overheated, and the number of the ColU's complaints increased.

And the giant low-pressure system that dominated the whole province increasingly filled the sky before them, a permanent bank of cloud hundreds of kilometers wide.

The ColU explained the science to anyone who would listen. "Warm air is drawn in toward the hot substellar center, rises and cools, and dumps its water vapor as clouds, rain, storms. The falling water gathers

in rivers and streams that flow radially away from this central point—
no doubt in all directions, not just to the north, the track of the rivers
we have followed. This must be the essential water cycle over this
Proxima-facing continent . . ."

But no amount of understanding helped when the fringe of the great
storm reached out to lash the plodding migrants with wind and rain,
and freakish showers of hail, even snow, despite the heat. Some of the
migrants coped with this better than others, Yuri observed. Older folk
who had spent too long in the dome-hovels of Mars or in space habs
found it difficult to deal with any natural weather. The children, though,
ran around in the heat or the cold, the rain or the snow, accepting it all.

Progress slowed. As the temperatures rose ever higher there were
increasing arguments about the wisdom of going on at all.

Yet they persisted. The occasional glimpses of tire tracks were lures,
Yuri sometimes thought, drawing them ever deeper into the navel of the
world. And if there *were* ISF people anywhere on this planet, where else
would they be but the most geographically significant point of all?

Then, two years after leaving the Mattock Confluence, they reached
a lake that sprawled across their path, and could go no farther.

2197

Penny Kalinski was summoned to the latest international interplanetary summit. More reconciliation talks between the UN and China, this time to be held at the Chinese capital on Mars.

Her first view of the capital, as she descended from space, was extraordinary. The Chinese name for their city meant something like "City of Fire." This was because in Chinese tradition there were five elements, each associated with a season, a cardinal direction, and a planet. Mercury, for instance, was associated with water. Fire was associated with summer, the south, and Mars: hence, City of Fire. But the informal western name for the place, based mostly on images from orbit taken long before anybody other than a Chinese citizen had been allowed near the place, was Obelisk. And as the shuttle descended gently through the thin air of Mars—the craft was like a pterosaur, its great wings webbing on a lightweight frame—even from altitude Penny could see why the name was appropriate.

Terra Cimmeria was a chaotic landscape scribbled over by crater walls and steep-sided river valleys; from the high air it reminded Penny of scar tissue, like a badly healed burn. The Chinese settlement nestled on the floor of a crater called Mendel, itself nearly eighty kilometers across, its floor incised by dry channels and pocked by smaller, younger craters. She glimpsed domes half covered by heaped-up Martian dirt, the gleaming tanks and pipes of what looked like a sprawling chemical manufacturing plant, and a few drilling derricks, angular frames like rocket gantries.

And at the center of it all was the Obelisk itself, a sculpted finger of Martian stone and concrete and steel and glass—a tower an astounding ten kilometers high, a product of the low Martian gravity and human ingenuity, far higher than any building possible with such materials on Earth.

On its way in the lander sailed around the flank of the monument.

Sir Michael King, sitting beside Penny, looked over her shoulder. "They always do this," he said. "Make sure you *notice* the damn thing. But you have to allow them their gesture of pride."

"Yes. The very place where Cao Xi made the first landing on Mars, all those years ago."

"Well, he didn't live to see Earth again. But look at all they've achieved here since, out in the asteroid belt as well as on Mars. All without kernel technology too . . ."

And the issue of access to kernel technology was, of course, the reason why this UN delegation had come to Mars.

The shuttle glided down to a landing with remarkable grace, given its size and evident fragility, on a landing strip some distance from the main domes. The shuttle was quite a contrast to the heavily armed kernel-driven hulk ship in which the UN party had crossed the inner system. But there had been something about the slim, elegant, almost minimalist design of the Chinese-designed shuttle that impressed Penny; the delicate craft seemed a perfect fit to its environment, the tall air of Mars—an adaptation derived from generations of living here. Coming to Chinese Mars was like entering some parallel universe, where technological choices had been made differently from the UN worlds.

As soon as the shuttle was still, rovers hurried out to greet the craft, some nuzzling up against the hull to transfer cargo, fuel and passengers, and others, robots with long, spidery manipulator arms, to begin the elaborate process of folding up the shuttle's wings, in anticipation of a missilelike launch back to orbit.

The passengers transferred to a well-appointed bus, a blister of some tough transparent material. The driverless vehicle rolled swiftly, heading along a smooth, dust-free road toward one of the big domes of the central settlement. These were huge structures of brick and concrete in themselves, but mere blisters at the feet of the great monument. Chinese staff moved gracefully through the bus cabin offering the passengers cups of water, melted from authentic Martian polar ice, so they were told.

They were in the southern hemisphere of Mars, some thirty degrees below the equator, and it was close to local noon. Seen through the bus windows the sun was high, round, faint but well defined, and the sky was an orange-brown smear—the color of toffee maybe, Penny thought, remembering home-cooking experiments she and Stef had made as kids, under the kindly but ham-fisted supervision of their father. Experiments of which, Penny supposed sadly, Stef would have no memory.

It was already, incredibly, seventeen years since the sisters' conceptually stunning encounter with Earthshine, and his revelation of the gravestone of their father in Paris. They had continued to keep in touch with Earthshine about the central mystery of their lives, to little avail.

And the careers of the twins, now in their fifties, had, at last, diverged. While, thanks to King and Earthshine, Penny had been gradually drawn into long-term diplomatic efforts to avert war in an increasingly polarized solar system, Stef was down on Mercury working on more studies of the Hatch. Right now the sisters were separated by something like two hundred million kilometers. It was scarcely possible for two human beings to be farther apart, short of shipping one of them out to Proxima Centauri.

The bus rolled smoothly up to an airlock set in one dome's curving wall. The uniformed staff, all smiling, ushered the guests off the bus.

Penny followed the crowd into the dome. The interior was crowded with low secondary buildings, but the dome roof itself was visible overhead, its brick and concrete reminding Penny of some great Roman ruin. Big strip lights hung from the roof, and there were screens with scrolling slogans in a Chinese script Penny couldn't read. Meanwhile the surface space was evidently only part of this installation. Massive staircases, escalators, and elevator towers invited the newcomers to descend to wide, brightly lit underground galleries, which looked like hives of industry and habitation. The design of the place, like a cross between a classical pantheon, a shopping mall, and some tremendous high-tech factory, was clearly constrained by the environment of Mars, but it seemed to have been achieved with a sense of *vision* that was lacking in too many off-world UN installations Penny had visited. She was hugely impressed, as she was no doubt meant to be.

Just inside the entrance plaza, an official party lined up in neat rows to meet the UN delegates. Military stood on guard, wearing Mars-color-camouflage lightweight pressure suits. There was even a rank of children dressed in some traditional costume, swirling ribbons in fantastic low-gravity transitory sculptures that seemed to hang in the air. Drone cameras hovered overhead, capturing the moment.

The focus was on the seniors, of course. Sir Michael King as CEO of UEI, now eighty-two years old, had been a major facilitator of this conference, and he and his equally elderly colleagues were greeted individually by Chinese officials. But more Chinese came forward, some in military uniform, many in civilian clothes, closing in on the visitors. Penny saw that at least one guide had been assigned to every member of the visiting party.

Sure enough, one young man broke from the rest and approached her. "Colonel Kalinski?"

Penny tried not to flinch; even now, aged fifty-three, she tended to recoil from individual attention. "That's me."

"My name is Jiang Youwei." He offered a hand, and she shook it. He was tall, slim, dark, composed. He wore a one-piece jumpsuit, utilitarian but smart, even elegant. She thought it made her own sparkly ISF uniform seem kind of obvious, gaudy. "I am twenty-four years old; I am a graduate student in theoretical physics here at our university, and I have been assigned as your personal guide during your stay here."

His English was flawless, with a trace of an Australian accent, she thought, maybe tutored by natives of a nation now firmly embedded within the Greater Economic Framework back on Earth. And—for God's sake—he was nearly thirty years younger than Penny.

"Thanks, but I'm kind of self-reliant. I don't really need—"

"You are free to choose another companion, though I would be personally disappointed. In fact I volunteered. I have studied your and your sister's work and career path, as much as has been made available to us. I am afraid the option of no companion at all is not available.

There are, after all, security issues." He smiled easily. "Sooner me than one of those fellows with the guns, Colonel."

She had to laugh, and gave in. "All right. So what's on the agenda?"

"We have twenty-four hours before the formal sessions begin. There are dinners later, and so forth. Some of your party are required for preliminary press conferences—"

"Not me, thank the Great Galactic Ghoul," Penny said. King had warned her off; the public events would be formal dances of protocol and etiquette with no serious content, and as a mere science adviser she wouldn't be needed.

"Then you are free."

"Do I need to go and unpack?"

"If you wish. Your bags are being transferred to your rooms, in the Cao Xi Obelisk itself, in fact. I can take you there if—"

"Believe me, I'm fine. We flew out on a hulk ship like a fancy hotel. Not exactly what I'm used to. They even served coffee on the shuttle. I guess I've had enough pampering for now."

He nodded. "Then would you like the guided tour?"

She patted his arm. "If I can't get rid of you, I may as well make use of you."

He laughed, and she decided, tentatively, that she liked him.

Jiang led her down an escalator into an underground level. From there, more walkways and cargo ramps descended even deeper into the Martian ground.

This seemed to be basically an industrial area; through glass walls she saw gleaming manufactories where robots and white-suited humans worked side by side to assemble impressive-looking machinery. People walked everywhere, bright, busy, or they rode smart-looking robot carts, and the halls were noisy with their chatter. There were few residences on this level, no dormitories or schools or hospitals, though she did spot a few shops and restaurants, and noodle bars where workers lined up patiently. She saw no obvious signs of security.

Jiang Youwei discreetly observed her. "You walk easily, though you are new to Mars."

"You say you know about me."

He smiled. "I know you are a seasoned interplanetary traveler. That much is public knowledge. You have visited the moon, Mercury, and now Mars. I myself was born and raised on Mars, here in this city in fact, though my parents were originally from New Beijing. I have never left this planet."

"Well, you learn to adapt to the gravity, wherever you go. On the moon, you don't so much run as bounce kangaroo style."

"Children discover these things for themselves, as I did. The human frame instinctively reaches for a minimal-energy solution to each mode of ambulation, though these solutions are quite different on each world."

" 'Minimal energy,' huh. I guess you really are a physicist."

They paused by a window where robots and humans labored to assemble a gadget, a long, heavy tube plastered with warning labels, like a finless missile.

"An aquifer bomb," Jiang said. "Or at least the delivery system. The fissile material will be loaded into it away from the public areas."

"I should hope so. Part of your terraforming program, right? The extraction of water from the aquifers."

"Indeed. No detonations are scheduled for the period of your stay. And in any event, none are allowed close enough to cause any risk to the monument."

She peered in through the glass. "Golly gosh. All this heavy stuff right in the shop window—and right where dignitaries like me are going to come rolling in off the bus to see it! What a coincidence."

He laughed. "One must put on a show. In fact the city's primary product is more abstract."

"You mean the software and AI technology you export to Earth . . ."
They walked on.

"You must understand this is a deliberate strategy. It was once a truism that interplanetary trade would forever be impractical because of the cost of transport. Not so. Our miners in the asteroid belt are already selling raw materials to UN nations on Earth, as well as to your colonies on the moon, as you know. But here at Obelisk we have created a hub of excellence in software and AI development. Of course, the transport costs to ship such products off-planet are minimal, merely a question of data transfer.

"This was planned. Despite the priorities of survival, resilience, and protection, from the beginning the city was built on a top-quality information technology infrastructure. Excellence in the education of the young was a priority; we have a system of rewarding achievement which—well . . ." He smiled modestly. "You might call it social engineering, although I understand that term has negative connotations in the West. I can only say that it benefited me hugely, and this community, which has grown rich in intellectual capital."

She spotted a crocodile of schoolchildren, evidently visiting the area, walking in pairs hand in hand, boys and girls in bright green uniforms: green, of course, for visibility on Mars, with its palette of rusty red and brown. They stared openly at Penny—there were few Western faces to be seen here—and she took care to smile back.

She said, "I'd be interested in a discussion on the nature of freedom here before I leave."

"I would enjoy that."

2193

Beth, Freddie, and some of the other youngsters loaded backpacks and set off west to attempt a circumnavigation of the lake.

The rest pitched camp in their practiced fashion, laying down hearths, digging out storm shelters and latrine trenches, erecting their tepees and houses. The trucks, released from the ColU's direct control for these simple tasks, got to work plowing up yet another stretch of Arduan ground, digging out fields extensive enough to raise a quick crop.

The ColU itself, meanwhile, rolled down to the lake, where there were wide stem beds, and communities of builders with their usual nurseries, middens, dams, weirs, and traps. It was almost like the builder projects around the *jilla* lake, Yuri thought. But there was no evidence that these builders were making any effort to manage this lake as a whole. The ColU watched the builders patiently, inspecting their structures, even communicating with them with its manipulator-arm hand-puppet builder talk.

When Beth and the rest returned from the lake, Mardina gave them a camp night off to recover, feed, wash. Then she called a council of war.

The core group were Mardina, Yuri, Delga, Liu Tao, Mattock. They gathered around a hearth, unlit but with its base slabs of basaltic rocks still hot enough to warm a pan of nettle tea. Other adults gathered close by to listen, a dozen or so, dozing, doing chores, with kids running around at their feet. The rest stayed away, working, napping in the heat. The ColU rolled up too, silent, massive, its hull and manipulator arms grimy from the soil it had been working.

At last Beth and Freddie showed up, all but naked save for strips of stem-bark cloth at breasts and groin, and well-worn bark sandals on their feet.

Beth gracefully helped herself to a mug of tea. She was twenty years old now, and as she moved Yuri noticed how the men in the group re- acted to her slim grace. Her tattoos showed up on her dark, sweat- streaked skin: on her face was etched a mask something like Delga's but less severe, more stylized, and there was a kind of sunburst design on her back, a Proxima-like star poised over an upturned human face. She had had almighty battles with her mother about getting these done; Mardina the ex-astronaut associated tattoos with gangs and drugs and criminality. But most of the kids, especially those from the mothers' group who had started the fashion, wore tattoos of one kind or another. It was about the only kind of art they could practice, and for sure the only kind they could carry as the group continued its endless migration. Yuri had stayed out of the argument. Delga, poster model of the tat- tooed crowd, had just laughed.

"So," Yuri said, prompting Beth. "You're back earlier than you thought."

"Yeah." Beth sat on her haunches, sipped her tea, and glanced around the group, confident in herself. "You know we hoped to go all the way round the lake. We started on the north side, and went west and skirted that shore, and came to the southern shore. Then we came to a river we couldn't cross, a heavy flow that comes down from the higher ground to the south."

Freddie said, "The river water pushes right out into the lake. You could see the mix of colors, the mud it raised."

"OK," Mardina said. "And can you get any farther south?"

Beth said, "You could follow the river valley. But it looks like it gets pretty narrow, and there's a steep climb." She grinned at Yuri. "Dad, there's a waterfall! You should see it. And beyond that the ground just rises up, and there's a sort of forest. Not like the trees at home." By which she meant the place she had been born, near the stately forests of the far north. "These are short, lots of branches, rattled around by the wind. It's hot and steamy. I can't imagine us ever clearing it, and living there. But . . ."

"Yes?"

She grinned. "We saw more tire tracks. Heading off south into that jungle."

Mardina murmured, "There has to be some kind of base in there. A technologically advanced base, sitting at this pivotal point on the planet, while the rest of us scrabble in the dirt." She glanced at the cloud-covered sky. "ISF. Presumably resupplied from orbit. Maybe even relieved by the return of the *Ad Astra*, or some other ship. Christ. I was right all along. They never did leave."

Delga said, "Well, we're going in to see. Right?"

The ColU said, "If I may speak, Lieutenant Jones—"

Mardina said, "When have I ever been able to stop you?"

"There is another reason to go into the Hub."

Yuri said, " 'The Hub,' ColU?"

"Forgive me. That is the local builders' term for the substellar point. Probably a term used across the planet, in fact. 'Hub' being my translation of a term that also refers to the cylindrical core of their stem bodies."

Delga snorted. "You've been talking to those spindly little jokers again. What a waste of time."

"I cannot agree," said the ColU precisely. "I learn a great deal whenever I meet a new community. Their language is very ancient, quite static; their culture is locally variable, but there are many universals. Such as the concept of the Hub. This is my interpretation of a complex idea . . . To the builders, the substellar point is the center of the world, a pivotal place. Yet it is a lost place. It is their Garden, Lieutenant Jones. That is where they lived before they Fell, they believe. It is the center of their consciousness. Much of this is a very old apprehension. Memories deep and old, like relics of animal ancestries. You humans have the trees, from which your ancestors once descended. The builders have the Hub.

"Yet there is a newer layer of meaning. These local builders seem to speak of recent events. They *did* return to the Hub, I mean in living memory—why, I am not certain, but surely to perform some task. That is what builders do. They worked here. But now they are excluded."

"By the ISF team in there," Mardina said grimly.

"Presumably."

Liu Tao said, "What concerns me is how we're going to live here." Since leaving the confluence Liu had taken a young wife, a daughter of Dorothy Wynn, who had given him a child, a daughter called Thursday October—named that way for her Earth-calendar birthday. Yuri had seen how Liu's priorities had changed dramatically once the kid had arrived. "Whatever we do about the ISF and the Hub, let's get it done, so we can get out of here."

"I would agree," the ColU said. "The star winter won't last forever. I have in fact been making this point for some time."

"We know you have," said Yuri.

"When normal temperatures return, this region will become uninhabitable—"

"*We know.*" Mardina looked at Yuri, Delga—even Mattock the former Peacekeeper, who was scowling furiously at the idea of some kind of well-equipped ISF base on this planet, from which he was obviously excluded too. "We'll go back north," Mardina said. "But not before we go and see what's in this jungle. We've come this far. Anybody object violently to that?" There was no reply. Mardina stood up. "OK. We'll take the trucks, or at least one of them. Beth, Freddie, you scouted it out. Work out a route, a way in. Yuri, you can work with the ColU on how to manage the trucks. We'll take our time. Get ready properly. *Then we go in,*" she said evenly.

"What about weapons?" Liu asked. He looked around the group. "I'm just asking."

Delga laughed.

Mardina asked, "Is there any of that tea left?"

The party to travel was pretty much self-selecting.

Mardina and Mattock, stranded astronaut and Peacekeeper respectively, had the strongest personal reasons for going to seek out whatever the ISF had left behind in the Hub. Mattock even put on the remains of his Peacekeeper uniform, though he was going to be way too hot in it. Delga and Liu were going in as representatives of their factions. As a captured Chinese, Liu had even less motive than the rest to go near any semblance of UN authority. But he had a group behind him too, roughly those who had once endured the rule of Gustave Klein, and they had to be represented.

Yuri had to go, because Mardina was going in with Beth, who had scouted out the route. Where his family went, he must go too.

And, incredibly, they took a bunch of builders. The ColU somehow talked them into it. If the authoritarian-type humans in the Hub, a builder name for a builder location, had thrown these natives out, maybe it was right to take them back in.

The other kids watched the adults getting ready to go. They seemed bemused by the whole thing, uncaring; to them the ISF was a fantasy of their parents', as unreal as the ghost of Dexter Cole.

• • •

The party walked in a convoy, the ColU and one of the dumb trucks at the center, the humans walking alongside. They all wore packs, with some food, water, weapons, though most of their stuff was on the back of the truck. Beth went ahead, running with a natural fluidity despite the heat. Tom Mattock trailed behind. He looked ridiculous in his Peacekeeper uniform, he was hampered by his limp, and he was soon overheating.

And a little party of builders, Yuri counted nine, all adults, came spinning and skimming behind.

They skirted the southern shore of the lake and made it to the estuary where Beth and Freddie had had to give up their attempted circumnavigation of the lake. The river they'd found flowed out of a belt of forest, dense and green, and Yuri thought he could feel the humid heat radiating from the forest even from this distance, a few kilometers away.

"Look," Beth called, pointing. "You can see the tracks we made before." A half-dozen sets of human footprints, one of them barefoot, Yuri saw, snaking off to the south.

Mardina grunted. "And beside them, this." She pointed to a set of tire tracks, more footprints of booted feet, another set of tracks heading back to the jungle. "They saw you, Beth. They came out for a look." She glanced up at the jungle. "They know we're on the way."

Liu shrugged. "They probably always did. What's the point of them being here at all if not to watch us?" He glanced up at the sky. "We Chinese have plenty of stealth sats in orbit around Earth, and Mars, that no UN body has ever spotted. Probably the other way round too." He waved into the air. "Hi, Major McGregor!"

They walked on, Mardina leading the way south, along the river valley. She said, "But they haven't done anything about it. Maybe they *can't* do anything. They've been here twenty-plus years already. Shit breaks down."

"Or they don't know what to do about us," Yuri said. "I mean, we aren't supposed to *be* here, are we?"

"True," said the ColU. "Each dropped group was programmed to be sedentary. And besides, the belt of heat and aridity around this Hub should have excluded foot travelers."

Yuri said mildly, "But nobody at the ISF seems to have 'programmed' a migrating lake. Or a star winter."

"Or human nature," Liu said with a grin. "And here we are."

They had to climb up a rock face, past the pretty impressive waterfall Beth had told Yuri about.

Then, after a couple of hours, they reached the rough boundary of the central forest. As Beth had described, the trees were not like those of the great canopy forests of the higher latitudes; these were shorter, with stout, squat trunks, and multiple leaves sprouting from stubby branches. But their trunks were just the usual scaled-up stems, the short branches and small leaves no doubt local adaptations to the turbulent substellar weather.

Mardina called a halt before they took on the forest interior. There was a pond nearby, thick with stems, and the builders skittered off that way.

They parked the truck and the ColU well away from the forest and its unknown dangers, and set up camp for the night. They built a fire for washing water and to boil up tea, and prepared to take turns to stand watch, under the unchanging gray sky.

Yuri found it difficult to sleep under a quickly erected tepee. It wasn't like in the permanent camps—there were no little kids running around, nobody getting drunk on Klein vodka. But Peacekeeper Mattock did snore like his throat had been slit. And one of the mutilated ColUs gave off an endless low hum of small sounds, a whir of pumps, a hiss of hydraulics, the occasional cough of some small engine. Yuri's ColU blamed its lobotomy; its "subconscious," the semi-autonomic systems that ran the truck's infrastructure, were full of small malfunctions as a result. Beth suggested the truck was having bad dreams. The ColU said that was more true than not.

In the camp morning they packed up and got ready to push on into the alien jungle. Beth, who'd been up early and had done some scouting, thought she had found a path.

The ColU, deploying its sensor arm, confirmed it. "Vehicles have traveled this way, leaving characteristic traces—even faint radioactivity in places—though an attempt has been made to cover up the tracks. Nevertheless, a way exists." It plugged its fiber-optic cable into the dumb truck, said, "All aboard," and set off without hesitation into the jungle, leading its passive partner.

Yuri, Mardina, and Beth clambered aboard the ColU as it rolled off.

Mattock, Delga, and Liu took the truck. The builders, without apparent concern, followed in their wake, but they kept away from the human-made track, preferring to work their own way through the thicker undergrowth.

As soon as they got into the shade of the trees Yuri was immediately hit by the increased heat, the humidity; it was like entering some huge mouth, and he was glad he wasn't walking. Yuri heard Mattock wheezing as he gulped down water.

The light had an oddly liquid quality, as if they pushed through some murky pond, stained with Per Ardua's somber green. The canopy here was low, not the virtually solid roof of the high-latitude forest; the smaller leaves let plenty of light get through to the ground level, where a healthy undergrowth sprouted. When a wind blew up—bringing the travelers no relief, the moving air itself was hot and moist—the stubby branches of the trees shook and rattled. Insects, or insect-analogues, fluttered around, the size of butterflies but built from sticklike stems and bits of filmy webbing. They landed on the skin of the people, only to lurch away again apparently disappointed, but they kept coming back for another try. Yuri suspected they would be a plague until they got out of the jungle.

And they started to see animal life, some of it built on an impressive scale: hefty-looking kites in the trees' upper branches, smaller than those of the high-latitude forests but more powerful-looking to Yuri's eye, and smaller, even stronger-looking flightless versions that scuttled across the forest floor. One big beast with flight-vanes like samurai blades sat and watched them go by, with multiple upright eye-leaves.

Beth was holding a crossbow, loaded. "I do *not* like the look of that."

"I think we must expect vigorous variants of life here," the ColU said as it rolled forward. "More energy is available from Proxima here than anywhere else on the planet. Rather like the forests that once swathed Earth's tropics, there is plenty of opportunity for life here, for speciation. Perhaps, for example, the kites first evolved here. Some may have migrated to the high-latitude forests and adapted. Others might have settled on the lakes and marshes. Yet others might have stayed here and given rise to the flightless predatory forms we have glimpsed."

"Just so long as they don't try predating on me," Beth murmured.

Rain fell.

Just like that. There was no sense of a start or a finish to the storm; it just descended, all at once, sheets of water piling down vertically between the trees, or dripping from foliage that seemed to be of no use in shielding the party.

They were all soaked immediately. And when the water started running over the ground, the vehicles had to slither to a stop. They found what shelter they could, under the trees, huddled against the ColU. Beth put her arm around Mardina. Yuri held up his face to the rain, hoping for some relief from the heat, but the water itself was warm, and faintly briny when it worked into his mouth, perhaps evaporated from some salty inland sea.

There was a tremendous crack of thunder, a flash of lightning that seemed to light up the whole forest.

Then the rain stopped, as suddenly as it had started. Still, however, the water dripped from the trees in a shower on their backs and heads. The light got a bit brighter, but there was no direct sunlight, no break in the cloud layer.

And Mattock was groaning.

Yuri looked back. The Peacekeeper, with his soaked uniform open to the waist, was doubled over in the mud, gasping, like he was drowning. Liu and Delga were trying to grab hold of him, to get him on his back.

Mardina slapped the hull of the ColU. "He's sick. Do your stuff."

The ColU lumbered around, sending up a spray of watery mud and leaf matter, and rolled back. With a combined effort of all five of them—"One, two, *three*!"—they lifted Mattock off the ground and onto the ColU's carapace. They laid him out, tucking spare clothing under his head, while the ColU's fine manipulator arms took his pulse, checked his airways, took his temperature with a fine probe in the mouth. Then an equipment bay in the ColU's flank opened up and a drip feed snaked into his upper arm.

Liu asked, "So what's wrong with him, autodoc?"

"The heat," Delga snarled. "What do you think?"

"That's true," the ColU said. "I believe he may have had a mild heart attack. He needs proper treatment—his temperature needs to be reduced quickly—"

Yuri said, "But we're stuck here. The ground is a pond after that storm. If we try to move, even if we back out of here, we'll end up smashing into a tree."

Beth watched all this. "We need help, then," she said. She walked a few paces into the forest, the mud splashing her bare legs. "The game's over!" she shouted. Her voice echoed in the forest, and somewhere there was a birdlike fluttering as a startled kite flew away. "You blokes in the IFS!"

"ISF," her mother murmured gently.

"Whatever. We know you're watching us. Well, you can see how we're fixed. Mr. Mattock is going to die unless you help him. So come on. No more of these stupid games you people play. Come on out, ready or not. Why, he even put on his nice blue uniform just for you—"

And there was a crash of foliage, lights that glared bright. A truck—no, a kind of armored car, Yuri thought, like a beefed-up Mars rover—came barrelling out of the heart of the jungle. It was basically a camouflage drab green, but it had mud-splashed logos, of the UN, the ISF, even the name of the *Ad Astra* carefully lettered on its side. And Yuri saw goggled eyes peering at him from out of a slit window.

The rover skidded to a halt, just feet away from the ColU, sending up a mud spray. Beth flinched back, hiding behind Yuri. He reflected that, Ardua-born, she'd never seen a vehicle travel so fast.

"ISF," said the ColU.

"ISF," said Yuri.

"Told you so," said Mardina.

The ColU said, "I have misled you. After all this time . . . but not intentionally. I did not know they were here."

"They lied to you, just as much as to us," said Yuri.

The ColU went ominously silent.

"Later, ColU," Mardina said. "Don't go crashing on us now."

A heavy door opened with a hiss of hydraulics. The man that emerged looked overdressed to Yuri, given the heat, in a heavy coat and trousers in the drab green shades of Per Ardua, and he carried another thick jacket. He had a weapon at his waist, Yuri saw, a vicious-looking handgun, clearly visible. He faced the group, who stood around the suffering Mattock on the ColU. He looked seventy, at least. Under a blue Peacekeeper's beret, graying hair was plastered down by sweat.

Yuri knew who this was. "Peacekeeper Tollemache," he said, wondering. Decades older, heavier, but undoubtedly him. "I thought I'd enjoyed your company enough on the ship."

Tollemache sneered. "Shame you still haven't got the bruises I gave you, you little shit. I can't say I'm glad to see you again. Or any of you losers. Good Christ, look at you, you're a pack of scarecrows."

Delga laughed at him. "Remember me, Tollemache? You owe me money."

"Fuck off. Which of you bastards is the sick bastard?"

Mardina glared. "Which do you think?"

Tollemache stomped over to the ColU, glanced over Mattock, and placed his spare coat over him. "Get that drip out of his arm. We'll get him into the truck and back to the base."

They got organized. There was a stretcher in the rover, quickly unfolded, and under Tollemache's brusque directions they prepared to lift Mattock into the rover's interior. The migrants had to do it themselves; Tollemache stood by, and nobody else came out of the rover to give a hand.

The rover's interior was brightly lit and smelled of disinfectant. Yuri could see there was a driver in a sealed cabin upfront, beyond a thick window. Beth looked around the vehicle in wide-eyed wonderment. Mardina's look was more complex. Resentful, perhaps. Anger building. Struggling with the Peacekeeper's heavy body in this clean technological space, Yuri fell grimy, out of place.

"I don't get putting a coat on top of him," Liu admitted. "Won't that just make him hotter?"

"I've seen this design before," Mardina said. "Tollemache's wearing the same. There's frozen ice in there, inside insulated layers."

"And built-in cryo circuits," Tollemache said. "They left us ready for the heat here. They gave us the right kind of diet to cope, extra vitamin C, low calories, low protein, high carbs . . . They monitor us, I mean the autodocs, they take our temperatures all the time."

"With a probe up your ass," Delga said. "I do hope they stuck a probe permanently up your ass."

Tollemache ignored her. "Anyway it's been easy since this star winter, as you call it, cut in. Not like before."

Yuri said, " 'As we call it.' You hear everything we say, do you?"

"The AIs listen in, and filter. Don't flatter yourself, shithead. You're not that important."

"I knew it," Mardina said, her voice thickening with anger. "I knew it, all these years. I told you, Yuri."

"Yeah. But they never came out of their box to help you, did they?"

Tollemache pointed. "Get him strapped down on that couch. There won't be room for you all to ride. Two of you, with him. The rest will walk with me. If you can keep up."

Mardina and Beth got into the back of the rover. The door flaps closed up seamlessly, and the rover rolled back, did a brisk turn, and pushed away into the forest.

Tollemache faced them, Yuri, Delga, Liu. He pointed the way the rover had gone. "Follow the rover. I'll follow you. I don't trust any of you."

Delga just laughed at him. She walked away with Liu.

Yuri said, "Our ColU—"

"It can follow us. And the one you wrecked."

"It wasn't us—ah, the hell with it."

As they walked, Yuri was soon immersed once more in enclosing, withering heat, and he hoped it really wasn't far to this base of Tollemache's. Tollemache himself walked boldly enough, but Yuri wondered how much good his ice-laden suit and all the rest actually did him.

There was a clattering noise behind them. Tollemache whirled, drawing his gun. "Fucking woodies."

"What? You mean builders. We call them builders."

"I know you do, and I don't care. Annoying little bastards. Not even much use for target practice." But he raised his gun anyhow.

So this was how the builders had been excluded from their forest. "Leave them alone," Yuri said, suddenly angry. "They've more right to be here than you have, Peacekeeper."

Tollemache grunted, but moved on.

"So," Delga called back. "The *Ad Astra*'s long gone, and you're still here, Tollemache."

"Not all of it."

"What?"

"Not all the *Ad Astra* left. You'll see. They split the ship, dropped one of the hulls here, at the substellar."

And Yuri remembered sighting the ship in his telescope, when it was still in orbit, with just a single hull.

"Turned it into a long-term hab. They weren't going to let you shitters run around killing yourselves without some monitoring, were they?

Although all we ever do is keep score. It's not so bad. We got a five-hundred-year nuke power plant, hot water, downloads from Earth, everything. They asked for volunteers to man it."

Delga laughed. "You actually volunteered, you dumb schmuck."

Tollemache was not a man to hide his anger. "You keep that up and I'll stitch you a new tattoo before we get to the base."

"But you volunteered," she persisted.

"Five years. That was the deal. They were building another ship, going to send it out. They'd cycle us back to Earth after five years. They were offering a hell of a bonus."

"But they never came back," Delga said.

"Incredible," Yuri mused. "They told us it would be a century before another call. What they told us was more true than what they told *you.*"

Delga laughed again. "What's it like in there after twenty years, Tollemache? Worn out the pause button on your porn machine yet?"

"Fuck off, lizard lady—hey! What the hell?"

There was a blur of motion to their left, a clattering like chopsticks.

"It was the builders," the ColU said calmly. "They were following us, at a distance. And now—"

"They just took off," Liu said.

"Where to?"

"How should I know?"

"They seemed keen to find something, deep in this forest," the ColU said. "A forest from which they have been excluded for some time, remember."

Yuri eyed Liu.

"Let's go and see," Liu said.

"Hell, yes. Come on, before we lose them!"

They both ducked off the trail and into the deeper forest.

"Hey!" Tollemache yelled. "Get back here, you little shits!"

Yuri heard Delga cackling.

Ahead, Yuri could just see a builder, skittering and whirling. He lunged on, but quickly lost sight of his prey. "Liu—which way now?"

"Right, I think. I just saw—yeah! There. Come on!"

They plunged into the forest, crashing through ever denser foliage, moving as fast as they could, trying not to lose sight of the fleeing builders, outpacing the ColU. But Yuri quickly tired in the smothering heat. There was no sense of direction in this dense, clinging forest, no shadows cast from the clouded-over sky—and the overhead sun would have been no use for wayfinding anyhow. Yuri was soon turned around, with no idea which way they had come, where they had got to.

Then they came to a clearing.

They stood inside the last rank of trees, breathing hard. This open space, maybe twenty paces across, was a rough circle. No trees grew here, but there was a thick bed of stems over a patch of swampy ground.

And the builders were here, the nine who had traveled in with them from the lake to the north. They whirled and clattered and skimmed across the muddy ground, dragging away stems as they went. Every so often two or three would encounter one another, and they would share their peculiar dancelike communications.

"We need the ColU," Liu said, breathless. "I wonder what the hell they're talking about."

"I don't know. But they're clearing those stems pretty quickly."

It seemed only minutes before a patch of ground, a rough square maybe ten meters across, had been cleared. Now some of the builders worked their way through the exposed mud, whirring around like propeller blades. Others were hastily digging out a kind of trench, leading away from the central area, through which water was soon trickling.

"Look at that," Liu said. "They're draining this bit of swamp."

"Yeah. And digging up the mud. See how hard they're working. Like they're desperate to do this. This is what they've been excluded from, I guess. Come on, we'll help. Let's get filthy." Yuri got down on his hands and knees in the clinging mud, and began to haul at the heavy stuff, picking up handfuls and hurling it away.

Liu grunted, then got down warily. "OK. But when my heart gives out, go get Nurse Tollemache . . ."

The two men made little impact on the mud layer compared to the remarkably efficient spinning of the builders. Nevertheless Yuri soon got down a meter or more in the patch he was digging.

And then he found a hard surface, under the mud. Shocked, he pulled back.

He dug in again, clearing a space. That deep surface was hard, flat—and *cold*, certainly colder than the mud that overlay it, colder than the air in the forest clearing. Growing excited now, he hauled at the mud in great armfuls, until he had exposed a stretch of some kind of floor, perfectly flat, gray, hard to the touch.

Liu was staring. "I found the same. What the hell is it? Some kind of metal?"

"I don't know."

"An *artifact*? Human, or . . ."

Yuri just shrugged. He was beyond questions.

"How come Tollemache doesn't know about this? If they'd found it you'd think they'd have it dug out by now." He laughed. "Or stuck it on a plinth in the UN Plaza."

"Tollemache doesn't know because he never looked. They must have chased away the builders rather than watch what they were up to."

He thought he saw a seam now, a fine line in the surface, so fine it was almost invisible. He traced it with his thumb. He dug out the mud, working backward on his knees, exposing more seam. It seemed to be curving inward, gradually. He dug and dug, following the seam.

Until Liu tapped him on the shoulder. "Time to take a step back, buddy."

Yuri stood, covered in mud, panting, sweating. He'd forgotten how hot he was.

And he saw that while he'd dug his clumsy trench the builders had cleared the rest of the area. They had exposed a metallic floor, still mud-streaked but gleaming in the gray light of the clouds. There were shapes cut into the upper surface, like three-pointed starbursts a meter or so across—clusters of three at a time, all the way across the floor.

"There's your seam," Liu said, pointing.

It was a perfect circle maybe three meters across, cut into the gray floor. It seemed obvious what this was. Set in the ground of this alien world, known only to the builders, it was—

"A hatch," Yuri said. "We found a hatch."

When Yuri, Liu, and Tollemache finally got to the Peacekeepers' encampment after their diversion to the builders' hatch, they found the *Ad Astra* hull lying on its side in the substellar forest. After more than two decades mature trees crowded around the hull, obscuring it, so that coming upon it was like discovering the relic of some lost civilization. Huge cargo-bay doors were raised at the rear end of the hull, exposing garages, workshops, stores; tarpaulins hung over the doors to keep out the rain, lashed down against the wind.

By the time Yuri and the others arrived, the driver had backed his rover into a bay in the belly of the hull. The ColU was parked up too. Yuri saw its camera eyes fixed on him with a longing to know what they had found. "Later, buddy," he murmured.

A people-sized door was opened in the hull's flank, with a short set of steps lowered to the ground. Waved forward by Tollemache, Yuri and Liu climbed the steps.

Yuri paused by the door frame. The hull's skin was covered by a layer of anti-impact cladding that still bore UN and ISF logos, and warning signs about fuel loading and electrics. The cladding itself was yellowed and had suffered a multitude of little holes, like insect boring. This was a human-made thing that had traveled between the stars. And now here it was, buried in the jungle of an alien world. Sometimes Yuri really did feel like a man out of his time.

And Mardina and Beth came hurrying along a short corridor to the doorway to meet them, Beth wide-eyed and grinning. "Wow, Dad! Look what we found!"

"Wait until I tell you what *we* found . . ."

But Tollemache was waiting behind them. "Move it, shithead."

Yuri just laughed. Tollemache had got noticeably more irritable since Yuri and Liu had found him on the way back, and told him all about the hatch—a spectacular discovery within walking distance, that might even have been his ticket off the planet, years ago, that he'd entirely missed. No wonder he was sore. Yuri moved on, following Liu and the others through the door.

Inside, the hull was brightly lit by fluorescents, a soulless glow that Yuri remembered too well from the years of his interstellar flight. And, when they got the door shut, it quickly turned *cool*, cool enough that Beth was soon shivering.

They were led to a kind of central hall where a table was set with three chairs. An older man in an ISF uniform was hastily dragging in more stackable chairs from a store. "Welcome," he said. "My name's Brady; the rank's lieutenant."

"Same as mine," Mardina said.

"I know, Lieutenant Jones. I remember you. My promotion is more recent."

Mardina glanced at Yuri and raised her eyebrows. *More recent?*

The rover driver walked in through another door. It was the first time Yuri had seen the man without a pane of glass standing between them.

"And this is Major Keller," Brady said. "Jay Keller. Another recent promotion."

Keller was about fifty, Brady maybe sixty, Yuri thought. Their uniforms were spruce enough.

They all stood around, uncertain. This big chamber inside the hull was like a brightly lit hall, with its curving ceiling overhead, spotlessly clean. It had evidently been refitted since its years in space. Mesh partition panels had been repositioned to give a flat floor with storage space beneath. Yuri could see bunks in screened-off areas, what looked like a

galley, a comms console, maybe a science bay. A huge black screen dominated one whole area, with sofas drawn up before it. The fans and
pumps of the air-conditioning hummed, busy. They were inside a vast,
shiny machine, just as if they were in space again.

In this setting the six travelers, covered in mud and wearing clothes
made of bark, looked like chunks of the jungle. Beth was staring around,
the fluorescents reflected in her eyes.

And Keller and Brady were staring at her, in her skimpy jungle-heat
clothing.

"My daughter," said Yuri.

"And mine," Mardina said heavily.

Keller and Brady glanced at each other, looked away.

Beth seemed oblivious to this. "I thought that truck was something.
But *this* . . ."

Mardina hugged her. "Welcome to my world, sugar."

Brady moved, breaking the tension. "Please. Sit. You can imagine
we don't get too many guests."

Tollemache grunted. "These fuckers aren't guests." He shucked off
his ice-filled coat and pulled open his uniform jacket. His corpulent face
bore a ragged layer of gray-white stubble. "They're illegals, remember.
They were supposed to stay where we put 'em. They shouldn't be here
at all."

Brady smiled. "Yeah, well, Parry, Sanchez, Britten, and Sen should
have stayed put too, and they're long gone. Come on, Tollemache. After
all this time we're all just human beings together on an alien world,
right?"

Tollemache just shook his head, walking away. "Christ, I need a
shit."

"Sit, please," Brady said again. "You'd like something to drink? We
have orange juice—"

He got no further than that. *"Orange juice?"* said Liu. "You have
orange juice?"

Keller and Brady hastily laid on a kind of breakfast, of oats with
milk, something convincingly like bacon, toast, orange juice, and
coffee.

Mardina fell on the coffee, drinking cup after cup. "I never knew
falling off the wagon could feel so good."

Liu ate until, he said, his gut ached. Beth just nibbled; the food seemed to be too rich for her.

"I'm guessing this stuff doesn't come out of an iron cow," Liu said.

"Oh, we have all that," Keller said. "But we were left with a mass of supplies, and the recycling still works pretty well. The system was meant to support eight; even now there's more than enough for three."

Mardina frowned. "Eight?"

"Four men, four women," Tollemache said, emerging from a bathroom, zipping his fly. "The women left in year seven."

"Can't imagine why," Mardina murmured, looking away from him.

"Just drove off into the fucking jungle in one of the rovers. Never heard from them again. Probably long dead, all of them. That left four of us."

"Cancer got Whitstable," Keller said. "Maybe you remember him, Lieutenant?"

Mardina shrugged.

Delga grinned. "I heard from your buddy here that you volunteered for this, right? You actually trusted ISF to come back for you."

"There was going to be a bonus," Brady said. "Promotions."

"Well, at least you got those, it sounds like," Liu said, laughing now. "What, did the chief of the ISF itself call you up from four light years away?"

"And all the time," Mardina said, "you were surveilling us. The colonists."

"Well, we tried. You would keep moving around, all of you . . ."

Mardina said, "We were told we were on our own here, on Per Ardua."

Tollemache said stonily, "The planet's called Prox c."

"We were told there was no ISF presence. We were told there would be no resupply, no visit, not for a century."

"Well, they would tell you that," Brady said. "To get you to perform the way they wanted you to perform. Making babies, and filling Prox c with little UN citizens before the Chinese get here."

"Yeah," Mardina said bitterly. "Just like they told you what you wanted to hear. To get *you* to perform."

Brady stiffened. "I think we've maintained our morale pretty well in the circumstances."

"We make our reports," Keller said. "Monthly, more often if something comes up. The science guys back on Earth are interested in the variable star winter going on just now."

"And we get responses," Brady said. "I mean, there's a four-year each-way light delay, but we do get responses."

Liu grinned. "And so you put on your uniforms and you act like good boys before the cameras, for the bosses that abandoned you. Because maybe good boys will get picked up after all. Right?

"In fact our log shows—"

"I bet it doesn't show what goes on in the dark," Delga said. "When you put these big floodlights out, and crawl into your bunks. We all need comfort."

"Shut up," said Brady.

Delga said, her voice a slithery hiss, "Which one of you's the bitch?"

Suddenly Tollemache was at her back. He wrapped his big arm around her throat, and squeezed. Somehow, though she clearly couldn't breathe, Delga kept smiling.

"Let her go, Peacekeeper," Liu said.

"Just remember," Tollemache hissed in Delga's ear, "we're the ones with the guns. Never forget it." And he released her.

She slumped forward, coughing. Beth ran to her, and rubbed her back to help her breathe.

Cautiously they sat at the table once again. "So," Liu said, "all these years you've sat in this tin can. When all the time you've got the discovery of the century sitting in the jungle an hour's walk away."

Brady frowned. "What's he talking about?"

And Yuri told them about the hatch.

They rested for a couple of hours. They ate more ISF food.

They took *showers*, their first since being bundled out of the *Ad Astra* all those years ago. Mardina seemed to love it. Yuri couldn't stand the stink of the soap. Beth hated it, evidently, hated being in this box of metal and fake light. Yuri felt a twinge of sadness that she'd probably never learn to enjoy the Earthside advanced-civilization-type luxuries he and her mother had grown up with; she could never be pampered. But then she had her own pleasures, her own place, here on Per Ardua.

Then, none of them ready for sleep, they formed up a party to go and take another look at the hatch. What else could they do?

Tollemache said he would lead. Yuri guessed he wanted to compensate somehow for letting him and Liu Tao run ahead earlier, and make "his" discovery for him. Yuri would go along, one of the two original discoverers, to be sure they found the way back. Mardina wanted to take a turn to go and see. And Beth was coming, Mardina was firm about that; she had seen the looks passing between these strange, obsessive old crewmen in their rusty hull in the jungle, and she wasn't about to let her daughter out of her sight for a second.

They would take the ColU too. Yuri argued that the ColU's translation skills with the builders could be vital; after all it was the builders that had led him and Liu to the hatch in the first place.

Tollemache accepted, but with bad grace. "Translation? That thing is designed to eat grass and shit out burgers, period. And the fucking woodies are just fucking woodies. What the hell has been going on with you people out there?"

Tollemache drove the party in the ISF rover, guided by Yuri, with Beth and Mardina on board. He smashed flat the undergrowth, even battering down a few mature trees, to leave a way open for the ColU which rolled complacently behind.

For Yuri, it was almost comfortable to get out of the hull and to breathe the dense, wet, warm, heavily scented air of Per Ardua again. It wasn't as if he was at home out here, not exactly. But more so than being back in the carcass of what, for him, had been a prison ship.

At the site Tollemache parked up, and they walked into the clearing. The ColU rolled quietly after them, sensor pod extended, studying the ground.

The hatch, set in its panel in the clearing, was just as they had left it.

Tollemache wore his ice-filled outer suit once more, and he had a kind of camera unit on his shoulder and a science sensor pack in one hand, with links back to the hull base. "For the official record," he said.

Mardina snorted. "Or so you can claim the *official* credit."

Yuri would have led the way forward, but Mardina touched his arm, prompting him to let Beth go ahead.

Beth walked alone into the brighter light of the clearing, without apparent fear. She stood over the hatch itself, staring around, gazing at the cover of the hatch with its curious trefoil-groove starburst markings. There was a breeze, hot and clammy; it ruffled her short hair.

"I have no idea what's going on in her head," Yuri murmured to Mardina. "She's been exposed to so much newness, all in a rush. How can she possibly take it all in? It must be knocking her world to pieces."

"She's been on the road all her life," Mardina said. "It's *all* been new to her. Just as it has for us. I think she's going to be fine. And look . . ."

Almost shyly, builders were emerging from the forest fringe, around the hatch. One by one they skirted the hatch itself, and clambered with cautious pirouettes over the mounds of dirt created earlier by their rough digging-out of the hatch. Yuri counted seven, eight, nine of them. And the builders came up to Beth, spinning, shaking their stem limbs— dance-talking, in the builders' characteristic way. Beth responded in the way she'd grown up learning instinctively, with simple steps and spins that echoed messages of friendliness and welcome.

Tollemache was recording all this. He shook his head. "Now I've seen everything."

Yuri ignored him. "ColU, you got anything?"

The ColU was passing a sensor pod back and forth over the ground surface on the end of its long manipulator arm, like a heavy lure on a fishing rod. "There is evidence of extensive working in the surrounding area, Yuri Eden. It shows up clearly in my geophysical surveys, in a variety of ways, though invisible to the naked eye. As you see, the structure you call the 'hatch' is embedded in a wider sheet of . . . a metal I cannot identify, some alloy. Ask Beth Eden Jones to stamp."

"What?"

"Ask her to stamp her foot. It is a simple request."

Yuri was baffled, but Mardina impatiently passed on the request.

Beth looked puzzled too, but she stepped out onto the gray, gleaming surface, cautious in her bark sandals. "It's not slippery," she said, testing it by sliding her foot. "Although it looks sheer." She raised her right foot and stamped, once, twice. Then she jumped up and down, slamming her feet back down on the surface. To her delight, the builders copied her, flexing their big support stems to leap up and clatter down like wooden toys.

"Thank you," the ColU murmured. "I now have sonic and seismic data. Yuri Eden, the hatch, and the structure in which it is embedded, is not thick. A couple of centimeters, no more. And beneath it I can detect nothing. I mean, no cavities in the ground."

Mardina looked baffled. "So what does that mean? No alien treasure chamber?" she said.

"Evidently not."

"Then what is it all for?"

"That remains to be determined . . . I told you there are extensive traces of workings in the ground here, all around the panel of which the hatch is the centerpiece, and in the ground farther out. Very ancient

traces, I should add. Little more than stains in the dirt, discolorations."
The sensor pod brushed the ground, as if licking it, and returned all but
invisible samples to an open flap in the ColU's hull. "And I find traces
of the local photosynthetic chemistry, but heavily modified."

"Engineered?"

"I believe so. As if there was once an extensive sun-catcher plant
here. Well, this substellar point is a logical site for such a plant, as the
region receives the highest intensity of Proxima light. But there is evidence of other workings here, much more advanced. Traces of structures. Disturbances where foundations were laid. Holes that once took
posts. I can infer what was built here, once. I could produce graphical
reconstructions with a slate, or—"

"Just tell us."

"The structures are like builder middens and storm shelters, but on
a variety of scales, various detailed forms. Much more massively built.
And there are other features—narrow lanes of compressed earth that
must have been trackways, wide enough to allow a builder to pass. In
the soil too I have found traces of advanced engineering. Compounds,
chemical, metallic, some I can't immediately identify. Also traces of
radioactivity in the past, or at least of a high radiation environment.
High energies too; there are traces of heavy elements in the ground here
I have seen nowhere else on the planet. All of this has a triple-symmetry
layout which—"

"Builders," Mardina said. "I don't get it. We've seen the builders,
all the way back to the shuttle landing site. We've watched them. They
use tools, they manage their projects. They moved the damn *jilla* halfway across the planet. But they only have stone tools. They use bits of
their own bodies to build dams. They're more like beavers than human
engineers . . . Aren't they?"

The ColU said, "This working was more elaborate and on a much
grander scale than anything we've seen of their activities before. And
much more advanced, of course. But the signature of the builder body
form is everywhere."

"OK, ColU, I believe you." Yuri looked around, trying to imagine
it. "So here was some kind of community of builders. They built a sun-
catcher plant, and other facilities, with a technology far in advance of

anything they have now. This was so long ago that barely anything remains of their work here. Civilization fell, right?"

"I would not jump to conclusions," the ColU said.

"They were gathering stellar energy. To do what?"

"To make something even more exotic," Mardina guessed.

"Yes," said the ColU. "Obviously you have the evidence in front of you, in the shape of the hatch, exotic compounds in the soil. It is strange, to just find this one site. Granted we have hardly surveyed the planet comprehensively, but you would imagine that a high-technology culture would have left traces of their passing everywhere, not just this one installation . . ."

Tollemache grunted. "Wait until they get some real scientists down here, and then you might get some decent answers. Not from this glorified tractor."

The ColU dropped its sensor pod toward the ground, as if bowing in submission. "I can't argue with that, Colonel. I am not equipped for this manner of work, not in a specialized way."

Now Beth spoke, for the first time since arriving here. "What, are you saying we should wait around for eight years, and grow old and probably, like, *die* before anybody does anything about this?"

Yuri had to smile. "So what would you suggest?"

Beth gestured. "We open the hatch, obviously."

Mardina said, "But there's two problems with that, honey. One is that it doesn't lead anywhere. You heard what the ColU said. There's nothing underneath."

Yuri said, "Maybe, but she's right. This is obviously a hatch. What do you do with a hatch, but open it?"

"OK," said Mardina with strained patience, "but that raises my second problem. *How* do we open it? Do you see anything like a handle? A wheel to turn, a combination lock to try?"

"Yes," Beth snapped immediately. She walked onto the hatch, to one of the starburst indentations. "Look at these grooves. Three of them, each, what, a bit less than a meter long? And this fat indentation in the center. Can't you *see* what they're for? Look, suppose I was a builder . . ."

And she lay down on her back over one of the groove sets, with her arms held out at two o'clock and ten o'clock, and her legs together at six o'clock.

"Shit, she's right," Tollemache murmured.

"These little cuttings are meant to hold builders," Beth said. "Count them. Nine cuttings in this surface, all inside the seam. You think it's a coincidence that *nine* builders showed up here today? They know what to do. We just have to get out of the way."

"Wait," Mardina said. She walked forward, as if trying to block the builders off. "Are we sure we want to do this? We don't know what we're dealing with here. We don't know what danger this represents."

Tollemache took a step backward. "That's true. Your tractor over there talked about huge energies being deployed. What if it's a bomb? A booby trap of some kind?"

Yuri sneered. "Who would build a booby trap like this, and leave it in the ground for centuries?"

The ColU said, "The structure is many orders of magnitude older than mere centuries, Yuri Eden."

"Not a bomb," Mardina said. "Something else. Something stranger. My head's swimming, Yuri. Strangeness upon strangeness. This thing was intentionally left here by somebody, builders or not, for some purpose. We've no idea what that purpose was. We've got no reason to believe it's likely to be in any way in our interest. We shouldn't even *be* here. Humans on this planet, I mean."

Beth walked up and took her hands. "Mom. You're freaking me out. But you need to stop *protecting* me. I'm twenty years old. I can make my own decisions."

Yuri felt an echo of Mardina's alarm, but he said, "So what is your decision?"

"We open the hatch. Of course we open it. Anything else is going to drive me crazy, for the rest of my life!"

Tollemache cackled. "You're outvoted, I'd say, Jones."

"Well, we all are," said the ColU, untroubled.

"Who by?"

"The builders."

And Yuri saw that the nine builders were already making their way toward the hatch cover, and their engraved beds. They moved in the usual builder way, spinning and clattering, like eerie stringless puppets, but their motions were purposeful, even coordinated, as if each one seemed to know which of the shallow cuttings to pick. Quietly, the nine of them settled into the engraved slots. Which, as Yuri saw, as Beth had first noticed, fit them perfectly.

The ground under their feet shuddered, as if some vast engine had been woken.

And puffs of dirt rose up from the circular seam around the hatch.

Mardina grabbed Beth and Yuri by the hand and pulled them away. "Back," she said. "You too, ColU." She ignored Tollemache, but Yuri saw that the Peacekeeper was stepping back too, keeping his sensor pack trained on the hatch.

And then, with a deeper shudder in the earth, the hatch lifted. It tipped up, as if it was hinged at a point to Yuri's left, opening like a lid, slow, ponderous. The builders, evidently living keys in the hatch's multiple lock, stayed motionless, held in position somehow so they did not fall, even as the hatch approached the vertical. The hatch's position obscured Yuri's view of whatever lay beneath the lid, but he saw that light poured out, a pale, pearly glow that underlit the branches of the nearby trees. And he felt a gush of cooler air, coming from beneath the hatch.

Somewhere a kite took off, startled.

When the hatch was vertical, it stopped moving. It was a tremendous, evidently massive disc, resting on its edge, invisibly hinged.

Tollemache, his recorder pack held before him like a weapon, was the first to walk forward. The brilliant light from the ground underlit his jowly face. "Holy shit," he said. "You'd better come and see this. Step carefully now."

The rest walked around the open lid. Beth asked, "Carefully in case of what?"

"In case you fall in."

Somehow it was no surprise at all for Yuri to discover that beneath the opened hatch was a pit, a simple cylinder with plain walls and a flat floor, perhaps four meters deep. The light came from no particular source; rather the walls and floor all glowed with that gray-white light. One part of the wall was broken by what was evidently another hatch, a fine circular seam, with a set of groove-locks to hold just three builders this time. On the wall opposite that was some kind of adornment, what looked like a tapestry made out of stem-bark cloth.

And it didn't surprise him either that three of the builders now hopped out of their grooves on the hatch and swarmed down into the pit, clinging somehow to the sheer walls. Once down they began to spin and turn on the floor, joyously.

The ColU cautiously extended its sensor pack. The four humans peered down, their faces lit from below.

"It's real, then," Mardina said. "I mean, it's a real hole in the ground, not some kind of visual trick. Given that the builders have climbed down inside it."

"Impossible," said the ColU flatly. "My geophysical results were conclusive. There is no hole here. There cannot be."

"Yet here it is," Yuri said.

"Maybe I didn't stamp hard enough," Beth said mischievously.

"No, it wasn't that. My analysis—"

"I'm teasing you!"

Yuri said, "We'll have trouble climbing back up from that."

"I got a ladder in the rover." Tollemache went to fetch it.

"Hold on," Mardina said. "Just hold on. *Climbing back up?* Are you seriously intending to climb down there? Into that impossible hole?"

Beth looked at her mother. "Sure. What else?"

"It should be safe enough," the ColU said.

Mardina turned on it. "What? *What?* Are you serious? How can you possibly say that?"

The ColU stayed calm. "Evidently we are dealing with some distortion of space and time. There may be some kind of machinery in the mouth of the pit—exotic matter of some kind, perhaps, or a tremendous gravitational engine. But the builders passed safely through the opening.

If there are any hazards, tidal effects perhaps, they are evidently gentle enough—"

"Give me that ladder." Beth took it from Tollemache and dropped it into the hole. It passed through the hatch opening as easily as the builders had, Yuri noticed. Then she began to clamber down.

Tollemache watched her admiringly. He murmured to Yuri, "I will never know how something as piss-poor as you, ice boy, produced something as lush as *that*."

"Fuck you," Mardina said simply, her voice taut with anxiety.

On the pit floor, Beth stepped back from the ladder, looked up, spread her arms, turned around. The builders spun around her, their stem limbs making soft scraping noises on the sheer surfaces. She called, "Look at me. Safe as I ever was. Are you coming down, or not?"

Mardina remained cautious. She made her daughter climb back out first, just to ensure that it was possible, that they weren't dealing with some kind of one-way trap.

Then Tollemache was the first to follow Beth back into the hole. "Me next. I'm not missing out on *this*." He made sure his camera pack followed his own progress down the ladder. "Just like Dexter Cole. One small step for a man, like he said. Or was that Cao Xi on Mars?"

Beth blew a raspberry into his camera.

Mardina and Yuri exchanged glances. "I'll go," said Yuri. "You wait."

"No way. I'm not letting Beth out of reach."

"Well, I'm not letting the two of you go anywhere without me."

"We can't both go. Somebody ought to stay up top, in case—"

The ColU said gravely, "I can call for help if there is trouble. I can even block the lid if it descends, perhaps. This is a human adventure, Lieutenant Jones, Yuri Eden. Perhaps in some ways it is *why* humans have come to this world."

Mardina frowned. "What does that mean? Oh, the hell with it." She went down the ladder.

Yuri patted the ColU's battered hull. "See you later, buddy."

As he climbed down the ladder in his turn, he felt nothing as he entered the pit, passing from the world of the real into the realm of the impossible. No tugging, no tide effects, no shift of perception.

At the bottom, he was just in some smooth-walled hole in the ground, with the three others. They looked at one another, then stared around. There was plenty of room for them all, and the spinning, darting builders. Up above Yuri saw the cloudy sky of Per Ardua's substellar point, with a fringe of foliage, and the ColU's sensor pod held out over them all, quietly watching, recording.

Mardina passed her hands over the wall surface. The glowing light shadowed the bones within the flesh. "It feels slick, frictionless."

Beth was inspecting the tapestry on the wall. "This looks like it's stuck on with stem marrow."

Yuri, Mardina, and Beth stood together before the object. Maybe a half-meter square, it was made of some kind of fine-woven stem-bark cloth held open by a frame of four neat stems, which looked the right size once to have been builder limbs. It bore an image of a disc, washes of brown and blue-gray, hanging before a watery blue sky, all marked in some kind of pigment. If you looked more closely there was a great deal of detail, a furry fringe at the perimeter of the circle, a dense gray navel at the very center, and fine blue threads that crisscrossed the disc, linking at dense nodes. The threads reminded Yuri of a chart of great-circle airline routes.

"It is a map, isn't it?" Beth asked. "Just as it looks."

Yuri shrugged. "What else can it be?"

"A map of the whole world," Mardina said, wondering. "Just like we'd draw. The world as seen from space, from Proxima. There's the substellar point at the center. There's the fringe forest. Look at that big bay cutting into the main continent—in the west? Builders made this."

Yuri hesitated. "I've never seen a builder make a map. But they know their way around the landscape, we know that."

Beth seemed defensive of the builders. "The ColU seems to think they built this whole place."

"Hmm," Mardina said. "But this map's a lot cruder. And it's just stuck on the wall."

Yuri said, "So the builders once made high-tech installations, like this, with radioactivity and heavy elements, and other shit. Then, later, all they could make was a map to stick on the wall. And *now* all they can do is spin around keeping the mud off—if we let them."

Beth looked troubled. "What does it all mean, Dad?"

"Damned if I know, sweetie."

"I wonder how old it is," Mardina said. "The map. Maybe we could tell if it's drawn accurately enough, from continental drift or something."

"That takes millions of years to make a difference. This can't be *that* old . . . can it?"

Mardina shrugged. "All the ColU could find of some kind of advanced industrial installation outside was a few scrapings of polluted dirt. It would take a fusion plant, say, a *long* time to break down that far."

Beth traced the mesh of lines that overlaid the map of the world. "What are these?"

"They look like canals," Yuri said. "They make Per Ardua look like Mars was supposed to be."

Neither of them knew what he was talking about. Before their time.

"The builders don't do canals," Mardina said.

"Not that we've seen. But they do a lot of water management. They move lakes."

"Nothing on this scale. Why, some of these canals cross the heart of the continent—they have to be channeled through bedrock. If they *had* ever existed, they'd leave a trace, even if ice ages had come and gone across the face of this world. In the *Ad Astra*, we did make some surveys from orbit. We'd have seen canals. And on the ground, *we* walked a long way. We'd have noticed the things, we'd have had to cross them."

"Then the map's wrong."

"Or maybe the map's right," said Beth. "And the world is wrong."

Yuri stared at her. "That makes no sense. Does it?"

"There's something else you're missing," Tollemache called.

They looked over. The three builders had shimmied up the frictionless walls and were inserting themselves into the three sets of grooved "key" beds in the hatch in the wall.

"The second hatch," Yuri said. "Shit. I forgot. And these builders are about to open it. Here's another of those choice points. Do we go on, or go back?"

Mardina said tensely, "I was trained up as an astronaut. And one thing that was driven home to us was *that you don't go opening hatches* just because they're there."

"Well, we're not in space, Mom," Beth said.

The three builders were settling into their positions.

"Last chance to run," Tollemache said.

None of them moved. The decision made itself. Mardina grabbed Yuri's and Beth's hands. Tollemache seemed to brace himself.

With a soft sigh, the hatch in the wall swung away, taking the spread-eagled builders with it.

The chamber beyond the wall hatch was almost an anticlimax. It seemed to be a copy of the room they were leaving, another cylinder a few meters across, though with a closed roof just as seamlessly joined to the walls as the floor, and similarly glowing with a sourceless mother-of-pearl light. But there was yet another hatch on the far side of the room, once again engraved with builder-body lock grooves.

The three builders leaped through the second hatch and spun around the floor, joyful once more, as if glad to be back here.

The humans walked through, one by one, led by Beth. Mardina brought up the rear. Yuri looked at his group. Beth was full of wonder. Tollemache, heavy in his ice coat in a room that seemed distinctly cooler than the world outside, seemed greedy for discovery. Mardina remained the most cautious, yet she had come through with the rest.

Yuri grabbed her hand. "It's OK."

"Is it?"

"We're all together."

"It's just my training, I guess. I keep expecting something to happen—"

"Mom! The door!"

Yuri turned, too late, to see the hatch behind them swing closed, sealing itself neatly.

"Like that," Mardina said angrily. "I keep expecting something like *that* to happen."

Yuri's first reaction, oddly, was to think of the ColU, suddenly shut off.

"So we're stuck," Tollemache said. "We're fucking stuck."

"Don't swear at me, you ass," Mardina said. "You could have stayed out there. You could have blocked the hatch."

"What with? Your husband's head?"

"Well, he's not my husband. Nice idea however . . ."

Things started happening quickly. The builders had scuttled over to the hatch in the far wall, and were already settling into place in their grooves.

And Beth went back to the previous hatch and ran her hands over its surface. "Mom. Dad. *Stop arguing.* You're missing it again."

"What?" Yuri snapped.

"What's important. Look at these."

She had found indentations on the inner surface of the closed hatch—not builder profiles this time, but the imprints of human hands, three sets of them.

"I will swear," Tollemache said heavily, "on your mother's grave, ice boy, that those shapes were not there a minute ago."

Yuri glanced across at the far door where the builders were almost settled in place. "But their meaning is obvious, isn't it?"

"We do have a way back," Mardina said.

"Yeah. Look, we have a choice. We can go back—if this door works as it looks like it will. Or—"

"We go on," Beth said, grinning. "Come on. There's no real choice, is there?"

Once again they waited until it was too late; once again the choice made itself. The builders settled into their slots, and the second wall hatch swung back, just like the first.

And it felt as if the floor fell away beneath them.

The Obelisk negotiations started late on Penny's second day on Mars, to allow for the visitors' misaligned biological clocks. The talks were held in a panoramic conference room, on a floor of the Obelisk even higher than Penny's hotel room. The main players sat at a long table, with the UN Deputy Secretary General and the chief Chinese official, a local provincial governor, facing each other across the center of the table, with translators scattered around. Penny was here purely to advise Sir Michael King, so she sat back from the table just behind him, coming forward only when he beckoned her.

It seemed to Penny that the talks proceeded pretty well, on a broad-brush level. The delegates on both sides set out goals, aspirations, rather than demands or decrees. Visitors from UN nations should be allowed access to the Chinese off-world operations—especially the asteroid Ceres, the hub of development in the main belt, which was currently entirely closed to the UN. Similarly UN zone corporations should be granted licenses to begin a share of exploitation of asteroid resources; after all, there was enough for everybody. On the other hand the Chinese wished for some kind of access to the kernels, at least to the wild developments in physics theory they had spawned, if not to the objects themselves. There were no blank refusals on either side, not yet.

Most of the discussion concerned matters of principle rather than details of the kernel science that was Penny's specialty, and she had plenty of time to kick back and stare out of the window at the view. They were so high up that Mars's tight horizon visibly curved, as if she were in some aircraft, not in a solid structure at all.

In a break, Penny stood with Sir Michael King and her assigned companion Jiang Youwei at a window, clutching coffees. King agreed that progress had been reasonable. "Here you have two societies with competing strategic goals, but with an almost entire lack of understanding of each other. A classic recipe for war, no matter how long we talk about zones of influence and such. But today, war is unthinkable."

"Yes," Jiang Youwei said seriously. "Both sides command enormous energies, the UN with its kernels, the Chinese with our interplanetary economy. Yet the populations of both sides are hugely fragile—we under our domes, the UN nations with their sprawling masses under an open sky—"

"Not to mention the sprawling masses in China itself," King said sternly.

"Of course."

"At the same time," King said, "we each have a monopoly of something we don't want the other guy to share. We the kernels, you the asteroids, roughly speaking. So what we're each doing is prizing open our treasure chests and letting each other at least sniff the gold. Everything is symbolic. The very fact that we made the effort to come all the way out here rather than just send a delegation to New Beijing on Earth is itself a token of our willingness to cooperate."

He was right, of course. It was all about symbols, on a level beneath the torrent of words. Penny understood that as a "face" of kernel physics, internationally known, her presence too was a symbolic gesture. Even if she never opened her mouth.

Jiang said, straight-faced, "And of course your immense hulk ship in orbit around Mars is itself another symbol."

King raised his eyebrows, and mock-toasted the boy's answer with his coffee.

"Maybe free trade will be possible some day," Penny said. "That's generally a way to avoid war."

King glanced at Jiang. "Maybe. But would your society, here on

Mars for instance, be 'free' enough for that? What does freedom here actually mean for you?"

Jiang might have taken offense, Penny realized. In the formal talks both sides had shied away from any comment on the other's political system. But, from what she had seen of the city of Obelisk, she was curious about this herself. "We never did have our conversation on that topic."

Jiang merely nodded thoughtfully. "It is an interesting question. We of Chinese descent are products of a stable society now centuries old—"

King snorted disrespectfully. "All framed by a value system that goes back to Karl Marx and Chairman Mao."

"But within any system, the challenges of ensuring freedom under conditions that pertain in an off-world colony—even here, in the largest off-world colony of all at the present time—are significant."

"In our Western tradition the freedom of the individual is paramount."

"Yes," Jiang said, "as I understand from my own school studies. But even in your own offworld colonies the freedom of the individual must be curtailed, if the collective good is to be maintained. The problem is the fragility of the colonies. One cannot challenge the most repressive dictator, if that dictator is the only one who can control the air supply.

"We have philosophers exploring ways of ensuring individual freedom within a tightly constrained collective system. This is, after all, the condition under which most of mankind is likely to live for the foreseeable future. We reach back to old traditions; a citizen of the Roman Empire, for example, would have placed less value on individual liberty in the modern Western sense than on collective responsibility—a collective liberty, if you like. Actually it is a system-wide debate, for us. An ongoing participation for all our citizens, on Earth as well as offworld. Though we are not minded to follow your example, as evidenced at your Eden colony on Mars—I have been there myself—of excessive individual freedom kept in check by excessive policing."

King laughed, and clapped his shoulder. "You got me there. Who'd want to live in a dump like that? Well, let's hope these talks work out and we get to see a future where we can try out these experiments in liberty. Right, Colonel Kalinski? Colonel?"

But Penny had been distracted by a commotion. A door opened, and a harassed-looking official bustled in with a slate that he showed to the leading Chinese delegates. The news, whatever it was, spread quickly. Something about Mercury, she overheard them muttering, something extraordinary. And then, it felt like, everybody in the room stared at Penny.

60

They all staggered. Yuri and Mardina reached for each other, and for Beth. Tollemache backed up to a wall.

Beth clasped her stomach. For the first time in this whole episode she looked genuinely scared. Nearly in tears, she stumbled across to her mother, who held her tight. "Mom? What just happened?"

Tollemache said, "It feels like the elevator just went down."

Mardina said, "Or the drive thrust just cut. But we're not in a spacecraft."

"Or," Yuri said, "the gravity just weakened." He bounced on his toes; he drifted back down slowly. What was this, about a third Earth-normal? Like Mars? He was distracted by motion he glimpsed through the open doorway. He walked that way, slow-motion swimming in the low gravity. Through the open hatch he saw another cylindrical chamber, a third, just like this second one, like the first. But though the walls glowed with that same eerie gray-white radiance, Yuri thought there was something different about the light in there. As if there was another source, shining from above.

A figure walked past the open hatch, back turned. A black costume, spangled with silver.

He looked wildly at Mardina. "That looked like—"

"An ISF uniform."

"Then who the hell is *that*?"

"Only one way to find out." Mardina led Beth across the floor and climbed through the doorway to the next chamber, and helped Beth through. Then Tollemache came, and finally Yuri.

This third chamber was another smooth-walled cylinder, just like the rest. A ladder had been attached somehow to the curving wall. Elsewhere on the wall small sensors had been fixed, anonymous white boxes, evidently human made. Yuri saw, glancing up, that some kind of translucent dome had been set up over the open pit, through which could be seen a roof of rock, as if they were stuck in some deep cavern.

That figure in the black and silver astronaut uniform, a woman, her back to the new arrivals, was working her way along the row of sensors, referring to a slate as she did so. Tall, blond-haired, she was softly singing some tune about flying around the universe with her lover. She might have been in her fifties.

Beth turned to Yuri, grinning gleefully, thrilled at this new development, her low-gravity queasiness forgotten. She pointed at the woman's back. Her meaning was clear. *She doesn't even know we're here!*

Mardina raised her eyebrows. Then, gently, she coughed.

The woman jumped, whirled like a Per Arduan builder, dropped her slate, and backed against the wall. "Holy shit. Who are *you*? And how did you get in here?"

Tollemache took charge. He strode forward, pointing his finger. "Never mind that, lady. Who are you? And how come I don't know about you? This whole damn planet is full of illegals and stowaways."

The astronaut shook her head, irritated, baffled. "What are you talking about? What planet?"

"Prox c."

The astronaut stared at him. "Conan Tollemache!"

"What?"

"I knew I recognized you. Your face has been all over the news just recently. Peacekeeper Tollemache, right?"

"What's it to you?"

The astronaut turned to the others, one by one. "Mardina Jones. Yuri Eden. Beth Eden Jones. All four of you. My God."

Mardina glared at her, confused, disturbed. "What is this? What do you mean, the four of us? How do you know our names?"

"You're the four who disappeared, into the hatch on Prox c, a few hours ago." She frowned. "No. That is, given the time it took for the news to get here at lightspeed—four *years* ago, I'm guessing, by your time . . ."

They spoke at once.

"We didn't disappear anywhere," Mardina said.

"What do you mean, we disappeared on Prox c?" Yuri asked. "Where are we now, if not on Prox c?"

"Who are *you*?" Beth asked.

But Tollemache was the most insistent. He faced the young astronaut. "Four years ago. Bullshit." He raised his ISF-issue chronometer, and brought up the date. "This is the date. 2193."

"No." Backing away from Tollemache, the woman bent to pick up her slate, and brought up a date of her own. "*This* is the date. 2197."

Yuri could see it. If this astronaut wasn't lying to them—and why the hell would she?—he had just jumped forward four years and a couple of months in time. Just like the cryo sleep.

"Not again," he said.

The astronaut looked at him strangely. Then she smiled, competent, efficient, taking control, her training kicking in. "To answer your questions. Sir, my name is Stephanie Kalinski, Colonel, ISF. Good to meet you. And as to where you are, Ms. Eden Jones," she said to Beth, "welcome to the solar system. You're on Mercury."

Penny tried to make sense of the news from Mercury. Refugees from another star, wandering out of the Hatch in the kernel layers? What could it possibly mean?

King growled, "Damn it. That cuckoo's nest at the heart of the solar system is screwing us up again. And I've got to go back to Mercury to sort the bloody mess out." He got up and left the room, without ceremony.

Penny, hastening to follow him, gathered up her stuff. The room was suddenly full of muttered conversation, hostile glares between renewed rivals. Penny had no diplomatic antennae to speak of, but the change in mood was obvious. She remembered Earthshine's deep suspicion of the Hatch and the kernels and whoever was behind those mysteries on Mercury, and their malevolent effect on human affairs. Now here was another intervention of the same kind: another bizarre miracle on Mercury, perhaps, another gift from some unknown benefactor from which the Chinese were once more excluded.

She wondered what the hell had really happened on Mercury. And how come her sister was involved, as evidenced by the glares directed at her.

She looked for Jiang, seeking a way out of here.

The astronaut, Colonel Stef Kalinski, shepherded the newly arrived Arduans out of the pit from the stars.

One by one they climbed the short fixed ladder. Yuri went first; it was easy in the low gravity. Once out of the pit Yuri looked back and saw an open cover, tipped up, just like the one he'd seen on Per Ardua. Remarkably, on the outside face of the lid there were not builder body-plan grooves, but indents to take human hands. And now he recalled the builders who had been their guides, so to speak, through the hatch from Per Ardua. He glanced down into the pit, past his companions, but the builders were nowhere to be seen; maybe they'd taken the chance to run back home, and he couldn't blame them for that.

As soon as they were out Kalinski shepherded them through this rocky cavern to an elevator. It was a smooth but fast ride upward. Kalinski, smiling, told them they were rising up through hundreds of kilometers. Yuri neither believed nor disbelieved that; he couldn't take it in.

When they emerged from the elevator Yuri looked around, increasingly bewildered, trying to get his bearings. He found himself under a dome. Clear ceiling panels admitted the ferocious light of a sun above, which looked at least twice the size it had from Earth—not as big as the apparent size of Proxima from Per Ardua, but much, much brighter, even as seen through the evidently heavily filtered dome panels. He saw open doorways leading to transparent tunnels, no doubt connecting this dome to others on the surface. He knew the logic of this; it was just as he'd got used to on Mars, sealed up in the domes of Eden.

The dome itself was cluttered with white-box science and computing gear, and what looked like atmospheric control equipment of the kind he remembered from Mars. The interior seemed brilliantly clean to Yuri, even sterile, like a hospital. There was no need for artificial light under that huge lowering sun, but floods stood on tripods around the pit, into which cameras peered, presumably day and night. Colonel Kalinski, in her black-as-night astronaut uniform, was the only person here—her, and the four arrivals from Proxima Centauri.

Beth quailed from the brilliant sunlight overhead. And she threw up, suddenly, spewing the rich food she'd eaten in the substellar base half-digested onto the clean floor of the dome. Some kind of servo-robot, a more advanced model than Yuri had seen before, came scuttling out to scoop up the mess with quick vacuum sucks.

"I'm sorry," Beth said, sounding distressed. She wiped her mouth with the back of her hand.

"That's OK," Kalinski said. "Do you need to clean up? We can give you fresh clothes from the stores, of course . . ." She hesitated, listening to a comms unit at her ear. "My administrators are scrambling to put together some kind of response to this situation. For a start I'm to drive you over to the hab domes. I'm sorry to be disorganized, we're not prepared for this, as you can imagine." Her accent sounded vaguely American, Yuri thought, but with a twang he couldn't quite place.

Mardina said, "This must be strange for you too."

"Kind of. But the Hatch is the reason I'm here, on Mercury. I'm a theoretical physicist. Since the Hatch was uncovered, I've seen a lot of strangeness. Believe me, you four walking through from Proxima doesn't even top the list." She grinned, somewhat ruefully, Yuri thought. "But I'm sure glad I was here to see this, to see you arrive. Once I saw the images of your Hatch on Prox c, matching the one here on Mercury, I *knew* it had to be something like this."

Yuri frowned. "Like what?"

"A lightspeed transit system. Like a subway. I mean, you got here at lightspeed, nearly, we established that already. A four-year transit time. With no subjective time lag at all—am I right?"

"A lightspeed subway?" Yuri asked. "Built by who? And why?"

Beth said now, "And I show up in the middle of this cosmic wonder and throw up all over it."

Kalinski laughed and took Beth's hand. "Don't worry about it. Somehow it seems appropriate . . . You know, Beth Eden Jones, you're the first human born on Proxima c to have returned to Earth. Think of that."

Mardina grunted. "She'll be famous."

"For better or worse, I think that's true."

Tollemache seemed to like the idea of that. "Famous, eh?"

"Oh, yes. The images you sent back of the Hatch twin on Proxima c have been a sensation."

Tollemache hefted his sensor pack. "Images taken with this very pack. Look, I need to speak to people." He thought it over. "My superior officers. Hell, an agent—"

Kalinski held up her hand, and pulled her chiming slate from her belt. "I'm sorry, sir, we'll have to talk later. I'll escort you to the rover, and then to Dome Z where we'll all go through decon."

Mardina raised her eyebrows. "Decontamination?"

"Well, yes. This whole dome is a secure environment. It has been since the Hatch was discovered. We're dealing with an alien artifact here—or at least that's the best guess we have—with unknown properties. Every time I come out of here, or my twin—"

Beth looked interested. "Twin?"

"Long story. I have to go through decon too. And now *you're* here, and who knows what little passengers you'll have brought back from Proxima c with you? Then, I'm afraid, you're going to face a barrage of questions, tests, by doctors, physicists . . . Look, we're making this up as we go along. You may be facing days of processing. I'm sorry."

Tollemache grinned. "The price of fame. God, I'm looking forward to seeing Earth again."

At least Yuri could tell what he was thinking. Mardina's look was complicated, calculating; Yuri had no real idea what she had made of this strange turn of events.

And Beth, who had been born under the light of a distant star, who had grown up surrounded by an alien intelligence, who had walked fearlessly into an alien pit on Per Ardua, looked frankly terrified.

63

Kalinski led them through an airlock directly into a rover, more or less of the kind Yuri was used to from Mars. Once they were all strapped in, Kalinski sat in the left-hand driver's seat and murmured instructions to an onboard AI.

The rover pulled away from the dome and rolled off. As they did so Yuri glimpsed another rover heading back to the Hatch dome, faces peering through the windows. More scientists on the way in case of more arrivals, perhaps. And Peacekeepers, probably. *That* would be a characteristic response.

The ride was bumpy, on a road roughly cut through rocky terrain. The windows were very small and looked downward, so you could never see the horizon, let alone the sky with that huge baleful sun. But the light gleamed back painfully from exposed rock faces and the few human artifacts, way marks, signs, small science setups.

Kalinski turned to face her passengers. "I like to drive myself, generally. But I thought I'd better not take a chance with such a precious cargo."

"Thanks," Mardina said with a sneer.

"Oh, come on, Mom," Beth said. "Colonel Kalinski's being very kind to us." She seemed to be over her partial-gravity nausea, and was looking around more brightly. "I can't see much out of these funny little windows. Is that because of the sun?"

Kalinski said, "Yes . . . Do you know much about Mercury, Beth?"

"Does the sun stay in one place in the sky, like Per Ardua?"

Kalinski took the name on board. "Per Ardua. That's Prox c. OK. No, Mercury has a day that's two-thirds of its year. It's to do with tidal resonances. As a result the sun kind of wanders around the sky, as seen from the ground, going west, then east. The whole pattern repeats every two Mercury years. Which is a hundred and seventy-six Earth days."

Tollemache said, "From what I saw the sun is pretty high just here."

"That's right. We're close to the equator, and it's local noon—or midsummer. The biggest UN base is at the north pole, on the Boreas Planitia, where there are permanent shadows, ice. This is the Caloris basin. A giant impact crater. Which is why the ground is a broken-up jumble. It's a difficult place to operate, and we wouldn't have any kind of permanent base here at all, I guess, if it wasn't for the kernel beds, and the Hatch being found here. It's posed all kinds of technical challenges, working here."

Yuri spotted movement on the desolate ground outside: what looked like tremendous cockroaches, with wide, iridescent wings. They were humans, some kind of astronauts, surface workers, in suits like segmented armor, in brilliant silver. Those wings spread wide from the back. As the rover approached, one of them stood straight and waved. No face was visible behind a golden dome of a helmet. Yuri, bemused, waved back.

Then there were flashes at the windows, brilliant enough to light up the whole interior of the rover. Beth recoiled, rubbing her eyes.

"Sorry." Kalinski pressed a screen, and covers closed over the windows. "Camera flashes. I told you there'd been leaks. Your faces will be all over the inner system already. Those guys must be being paid well to risk the discipline charges."

The rover slowed, and Yuri heard a dull impact on the opaque hull, some kind of docking. Within seconds the hatch opened again, leading to a brightly lit tunnel.

"Here we go," Kalinski said. "Dome Z. I'll be going through decon too, having been in contact with you, and the Hatch. We'll have to strip, I'm afraid; your clothes will be cleaned and returned later. Men that way, women this, follow me . . ."

At the other end of the tunnel, Peacekeepers waited for them, in containment suits, heavily armed.

For Yuri and Tollemache, it took *four days*, of showers, heat baths, body fluid samples, full-body scans, tasteless meals, interrogations of various kinds, and periods of uneasy sleep, before the doctors finally slipped off their surgical masks and shook their hands. "It's been a unique experience, gentlemen. Thank you."

"Kiss my ass," said Tollemache. "Where are my pants?"

As it turned out their clothes were not returned to them. For one thing the colonists' scraps of stem-bark cloth were the first samples of Arduan life solar-system-based scientists had got their hands on directly, since the sparse samples returned by the *Ad Astra* years earlier. There were even anthropologists on hand, Yuri learned, eager to pore over the handicrafts of the emergent human communities of Proxima c.

Tollemache was given a fresh Peacekeeper uniform. Yuri noticed it was beefier than the old design, with toughened pads at shoulders, neck, elbows, knees, and a kind of utility belt with pouches and loops, ready for weapons. Evidently Peacekeeping in the modern solar system was a more dangerous game than it used to be. For his part, Yuri was handed an orange jumpsuit just like the kind he'd been issued with when he was first pulled out of the cryo tank on Mars. Some things didn't change.

They were brought to a kind of lounge, with padded couches, a bar serving soft drinks and coffee, and a big picture window with a view of the battered surface of Mercury, shaded from the sun. Here at last they were reunited with Mardina and Beth, and Colonel Kalinski. Mardina was already devouring coffee, picking up where she'd left off at the Hub base on Per Ardua. She wore a smart astronaut uniform, black and silver. Beth, though, was in an orange jumpsuit like her father's.

Beth hugged Yuri. But they pulled apart, uncertain, dressed up in strange clothes, even smelling wrong. Yuri forced a smile, uncertainly.

Yuri helped himself to a soda. It bubbled oddly in the low gravity; he'd never had a soda on Mars. "So, twenty-eight years after waking up on Mars—"

"Thirty-two," Kalinski murmured. "You jumped another four years in the Hatch, remember."

"Shit. Here I am back in a jumpsuit, like a convict."

Beth came over and linked his arm. "Never mind, Dad. I'm a convict too."

"Yeah. The difference is the uniform looks good on you."

"And I still have this." She stroked the tattoo that covered half her face. "They couldn't scrub *that* off in their decon. But, you know, they offered to remove it for me there and then. Said I'd fit in better."

"You'd 'fit in.' Where?"

"Earth," Mardina said bluntly.

Beth stroked her tattoo again. "I'm not from Earth. I'm from Per Ardua."

"Quite right, honey," and Yuri kissed her on the cheek. "We'll work it out somehow." He looked at Mardina in her ISF suit. "I'm surprised you let them dress you up in that thing. The ISF dumped you on Per Ardua."

She looked at him steadily. "But *I* wasn't born on Per Ardua. This was my career, Yuri. This is who I was, and am. I'm still an officer in the ISF, I'm told. Even though they haven't figured out what rank I am; strictly speaking I was retired with honors when I was left behind at Proxima."

Tollemache said, "There's talk of back pay. You ought to chase that up, Jones. But we probably won't need it, we're all going to earn a fortune out of this." He grinned, gulping down some kind of fruit drink. "What a break! I bet those assholes Brady and Keller will be sick as shit when they hear about this." He mused, "In another four years' time, I guess. Good. Give me time to milk it before sharing it with them."

Yuri looked at him in disgust. "You really are a charmer, Tollemache."

He just laughed. "You got to take your chances in this life."

"Good point," said a newcomer, a man, old, short, plump, bustling into the room. "That Hatch of yours, Peacekeeper Tollemache, could be a chance for all of us—an opportunity crucial to the future of two stellar systems, and to the whole destiny of mankind." In his eighties maybe, he wore what looked like a business suit, with thin lapels, a kind of cravat, shiny fake-leather shoes. Behind him came another man, tall, grave, thin as a builder's stem limb, in a well-cut astronaut uniform with officer stripes on his upper arm.

Kalinski stepped forward with a professional smile. "Good to see you, sir. I need to introduce you. This is Sir Michael King—"

This was the tubby businessman type. He winked at Kalinski. "Stef, your twin sends her regards." Then he strode forward and shook all their hands; his grip was surprisingly firm, a worker's handshake. "I'm president and CEO of Universal Engineering, Inc., the prime contractor with responsibility for developing the resources of Mercury on behalf of the nations and peoples of the UN." He studied Yuri. "You're the fella from the ice, right? Rip Van Winkle. What do you call yourself— Yuri Eden? Well, I'm the guy whose company built the ship that took you to Mars, and the *Ad Astra* that delivered you all the way to Proxima Centauri. What do you think of that?"

"Thanks," Yuri said dryly.

"And I just drove in from Mars on a hulk ship myself, once I heard the news about you people. This is my closest colleague on Mercury," King said, indicating the tall man in the astronaut suit.

"Jim Laughlin, Colonel, ISF." He shook hands in his turn. "Base commander, here in Caloris. You can see I'm an ISF officer, but I have a political reporting chain into the UN itself, ultimately to the Security Council."

"My teammate," King said. He threw mock boxing punches at Laughlin. "Or my sparring partner. We get on famously."

Laughlin raised his eyebrows; evidently long-suffering, he said nothing.

King said, "Come. Sit. Have some more drinks. Colonel Kalinski, will you sort that out? You need something to eat?"

"They've been feeding us in the decon," Mardina said.

"What, barium meals? Ha ha. Look, I know it's tough, we appreciate all you've been through."

Beth accepted a glass of water from Kalinski. "Sir Michael King?"

"Yes?"

"What do you *want*?"

Mardina burst out laughing. Even Laughlin suppressed an icy grin, Yuri saw.

King evidently had a sense of humor. He grinned, sat on a couch and faced the group. "Good question, young lady. Well, together with my colleague here, we run this place. We make the decisions that count.

OK? We both have puppet masters back on Earth, so does everybody, but here on the ground, we make the decisions. And at the end of the day we will have to make decisions—"

"About us," said Tollemache.

"About the consequences of your emergence through the Hatch," Laughlin said carefully, "and it was a shock as much for us as for you. It's only been days. We're still trying to digest the implications. Political, economic, social, technological, scientific. Although I have to say this kind of possibility, that the Hatches are some sort of transit system, was sketched in one of Colonel Kalinski's papers."

"Actually the paper was by my twin," Stef Kalinski said stiffly.

"That has been some help. I'm sure Colonel Kalinski here will tell you all about the spectacular scientific possibilities."

King put in, "But big cosmic questions are rather beyond my horizon, and that of my own political masters—and indeed the UEI shareholders. The first reaction from on high, and my comms systems have been buzzing since you arrived in this regard, concerns the potential utility of the thing. If, you see, we can walk through this—this light-speed tunnel—from one star system to the next, think how we could use it. When we built and launched the *Ad Astra*, it strained the resources of the UN itself. We were determined to use our kernel technology to plant seeds on the habitable planet of Proxima before the Chinese could reach it. Well, we did it, but we exhausted ourselves. As for the Chinese, they couldn't do it at all. Oh, they could probably send out some kind of slowboat, a big solar-sail junk. Take them decades to get there. Centuries even. Because, my friends, they don't have access to what remains an exclusively UN resource: that is, the kernel mines here on Mercury, where we dug up the magical bits of physics that shot your ship off to the stars."

"But you will see," Laughlin said, "that the Hatch tunnel, if it can be proven to be safe, stable and so forth—"

"And if it's two-way," Kalinski said dryly.

"The Hatch is a way to achieve the mass colonization of the Proxima system much more rapidly."

Mardina stared. "You can't be serious."

King grinned. "Never more so. All we have to do is ship 'em to Mercury, push 'em through the Hatch, and they're in business."

Kalinski shook her head. "But, Sir Michael—it's just like the way you've been using the kernels since they were discovered. We don't know how these things work. We don't know what they're *for*. And yet we're digging them up and sticking them on the back of crewed spaceships. Now you have the Hatch, and it's an obvious artifact of intelligence, but again we don't know who put it there and what it's for, let alone how it functions. Can't you see we're on the edge of some tremendous mystery here? A mystery into which mankind seems to be walking step by step, blindfolded."

A mystery—or a trap, Yuri wondered.

King seemed to take no notice of what Kalinski had said. "This, of course, only increases the political tensions surrounding Mercury itself. Suddenly this scrubby planet is even more valuable than before, when it was merely the exclusive source of the kernels. Now that it's the gateway to Prox c too, Mercury will become the solar system's prize asset beyond Earth itself, perhaps. That will lead to stresses which—"

Beth flared. "But Per Ardua isn't some pawn in a game. *Per Ardua*— and that's its name, by the way, not Prox c—is a world, with a history of its own, and native life, an ecology, even intelligent life."

Laughlin murmured, "Good vocabulary. You're evidently well educated, Ms. Eden Jones. Your parents are to be congratulated."

Beth just glared at him.

"There's even a human history," Tollemache said now, with relish. "Nearly thirty years of colonization. Tales of abandonment, rape, murder and incest that would make your hair curl, gentlemen. And I watched it all."

King ignored that, and waved away Beth's point too. "We already encountered life on Mars, Titan, other places. We know how to handle it."

Yuri goggled. " 'Handle' it? As I recall from my time there, you're blowing Mars up to terraform it. How is that 'handling' the local life?"

"That's the Chinese, not us," King pointed out. "I'm sure we'll be more careful. There could be parks, for instance. Preserves." He leaned forward. "In fact, you make a good point, Mr. Eden, about the Chinese and their terraforming. We can say that's why we don't want to let them loose on Padre, uh . . ."

"Per Ardua."

"Right. With their aquifer-breaking nuclear bombs. We need to get there first, and preserve it from those rapacious Chinese. We can fix up the language. And you four—and especially *you*, Ms. Eden Jones—will be able to help us do just that."

Yuri marveled at the man's flexibility of mind. He had to be making all this up on the spot, given how recent their irruption from the Hatch had been. Yet here he was spinning geopolitical strategies on the fly. There hadn't been much opportunity for politicians to flourish on Per Ardua, or even in the UN enclosures on Mars, and Yuri couldn't remember much of the Earth of his youth. King was in his element, evidently. Maybe he was the Gustave Klein of the inner system.

But Beth seemed baffled, perhaps alarmed.

Mardina took her daughter's hand. "What do you mean, Beth's going to help you? How?"

King glanced around at the clean, expansive lounge. "Believe me, it's an oasis of calm in here. Out there it's a shit storm, and it won't pass for—oh, days. Until the next scandal comes along. And just now you four are hot properties. Especially *you*, Beth Eden Jones. Look at you, young, gorgeous, exotic—I'm loving that tattoo—and the first star child to return to the solar system."

"Star child?' "

"Not my headline. We'll get you back to Earth as soon as we can. There'll be book offers, movie deals, a scramble for your image rights—you're probably all over the media already, impersonated by clumsy AI avatars. You will be the human face of Prox c—I mean of Per Ardua. In the end, you may save it, single-handedly, *If* we handle it right.

"The rest of you too," he said to the others, noticing Tollemache's crestfallen expression, "will have opportunities. We just have to find the right angle. 'My lonely vigil under Proxima's red light' for you, Peacekeeper, something like that."

"Well, Proxima's not red—"

"I know a few people. And of course, you can resume your ISF career, Lieutenant Jones."

Mardina asked, "Are they serious about having me back, Colonel Laughlin? For genuine duties, not as some kind of poster figure?"

"I believe so. I can pass your request up the chain of command if that is your choice."

King nodded, his heavy jowls compressing. "I'll do my best to move that along too."

Yuri realized that King and Laughlin weren't meeting his eyes. "And me, Sir Michael? How will you take care of me?"

Beth looked shocked. As usual she immediately picked up on the implications of his tone. "Dad, what are you talking about? I'm not going to Earth if you're not coming too."

Mardina stroked her daughter's hair. "Earth *is* our home, when all's said and done, sweetheart."

"Yours, maybe," Yuri said. "But not mine. I'm a century out of time, remember?"

"What does that matter, Dad? I was born on another planet altogether. On a world of another star! As long as we're all together, and we're free—that's where home is."

Laughlin coughed. "I'm afraid it's not that simple. Not in the case of Mr. Eden . . ."

"I knew it," Yuri said.

"The retrospective trials of the Heroic Generation, of which your parents were such prominent members, are continuing. Even after a century or more. And an increasingly assumed legal stance is the inheritance of punishment. That is, the right to punish heirs for the crimes of their parents or grandparents—"

Tollemache growled, "I hate the little shit, but even I can see that that's unjust."

King spread his hands. "It's the mood of the times, Peacekeeper. Some of those heirs got very rich on the backs of their parents' global crimes. This is the prosecution argument, you understand, not my own position necessarily. Why, because of gen-eng and illegal psych downloads and the like, it's suspected that some of those heirs *are* members of the Heroic Generation, effectively. So you can see—"

"If I go back to Earth," Yuri said flatly, "I won't be free."

"There's no question of imprisonment," Laughlin said. "Call it house arrest. Surveillance. Your movements will be monitored and curtailed, for as long as the legal process lasts."

"I'll be put on trial for some crime deemed to have been committed by long-dead parents who shoved me in an ice box for eighty years."

"But that itself is an issue," King said. "Some prosecutors would argue that your parents did that in precisely the hope you would thereby *evade* any legal process. And . . ."

Yuri stopped listening. So he would be surrounded by walls of plastic and metal, his every step watched by a suspicious mankind, for the rest of his life.

He closed his eyes. He remembered that day when the shuttle had landed, and he'd climbed down to the surface of Proxima c for the first time, and there were no fences, no dome walls, just an arid plain, and he had just run and run until he was out of sight of every other human being in the universe. He imagined running, like that, with Beth at his side. *I may as well have been left on Mars.*

"I'm going to Earth," Mardina said flatly. "Yuri, I'm sorry. Whatever the implications for you. That's where my life is, always was. And Beth is coming with me. She'll have a better life, and a longer one, than she would as a baby factory on Per Ardua. You know it."

Beth looked at her father in growing horror. "Dad?"

"I can't follow you," Yuri said softly. "No matter what the conditions. I wouldn't survive."

"Dad, no!" Beth would have come to him, but Mardina kept a firm hold on her arm.

They were all watching him now, Laughlin looking embarrassed, King with an assumed expression of sympathy, Colonel Kalinski with what looked like genuine shock and sorrow, even Tollemache showing a kind of gruff respect.

King spread his hands. "Then what will you do, Yuri Eden? Where will you go?"

"There is another option. To go back to the only place I've ever been free."

"Dad—"

Laughlin leaned forward. "You're going back through the Hatch?" He glanced at Kalinski. "Is that possible? Is it safe?"

"We don't know, sir. We haven't tried it yet." She glanced at King. "Even though we're dreaming up all these schemes about mass migration through it. I don't see why not, however. In fact, Mr. Eden, if you're serious about this—"

"Yes?"

"I'll come with you."

King snorted. "Are you crazy? You'll end up four light years from home. And, after another lightspeed hop, four more years in the future."

"I know. I understand that. But there's a scientific purpose, sir. Somebody's got to be the first to try it—I mean in a planned, scientific manner. We need to know the link works, that it's stable. And we need to know *how* it works. I mean, we've had this Hatch under surveillance for years, but we never had the courage, or the imagination, to take the next step, as you did, Yuri. To go *through*. Well, now's the time. And who better but me?"

"She is an ISF officer," Laughlin pointed out. "And the nearest we have to an expert to boot. Along with her sister, of course. This is all rather a rush—but it is a compelling case, Sir Michael."

Tollemache shook his head. "I just don't get it. You saw the images I sent back. Prox c is a shit hole. And I can tell you these press-ganged colonists they're talking about sending through are going to be the dregs of the megacities and the slums, scraped up and shoveled through, just like it's been on Mars. Why would you go there voluntarily, a bright spark like you?"

Stef glanced at Yuri. "Personal reasons. Because it will be better for me there than here. Just like you, sir."

For Yuri and his family, that was only the start of an argument that raged for days. But he knew Mardina; from the minute she said she was staying on Earth with Beth, and for all Beth's tears, he had known that his family was lost. Dead to him. And soon to be cut off from him by a barrier of thick time, just as his parents had cut him off before.

He, however, was going home.

64

Yuri and Stef Kalinski stood side by side in the chamber of the Hatch on Mercury. A handful of technicians stood around on the surface above, monitoring instruments, gazing down curiously.

Above Yuri's head, the great lid was slowly closing.

None of their families were here. A month after they had all walked through the hatch from Prox, Beth and Mardina were already on Earth, Yuri had been told, and Kalinski's twin was nowhere around. It was just the two of them.

Yuri looked over at Kalinski. They were both sealed up in heavy-duty Mercury-standard armored spacesuits. Yuri had even been shown how to open the cockroach-type radiator wings. This time there was no question of them just wandering through the Hatch system without protection, as they had on Per Ardua; now no chance was being taken. He couldn't see Kalinski's face behind her gold-plated visor. Even now he didn't feel he knew her too well. They had had, ironically, little time to talk since the decision had been made to send them through the Hatch. He said, "Last chance to climb out."

"I'm fine, sir."

"Don't call me sir, for God's sake. And no more good-byes?"

"I feel like I already left."

"Yeah. Me too. Kind of unusual for twins to split up, isn't it?"

"We're unusual twins. I'll tell you about it some time." She grinned. "And I guess there will be plenty of time. And—Beth?"

He was trying to put out of his head his last encounter with Beth. Neither of them had been able to speak for crying. "The last thing I told her was my true name."

Kalinski stared at him.

He glanced up. By the light of the ferocious sun, the last few techs were just visible past the edge of the closing lid. One of them got down to her knees and waved. Yuri waved back.

And then the lid closed, silent, heavy, and that was that; they were shut off. The light in here, provided by the glowing walls, roof, floor, was bright enough, yet dimmed compared to the glow of the blocked-out sun.

Yuri glanced at Kalinski. "You OK?"

"Yes. You?"

"I wonder if we made the jump already. I mean in space. You think we're already on Per Ardua?"

"Impossible to say," Kalinski said. "But my feeling is that we make the transfer in the central bridging room, not these antechambers. It was in the central room you said you experienced a gravity shift."

"Maybe. Who knows? Are you ready?"

"Sure."

They had actually worked through the transition process in virtual simulations, real space-program stuff. You just pressed your hands into the indentations in the inner doorways. Nobody knew if gloved hands would work, or if, as the indentations came in sets of three on each door, one or two or three people would be necessary to work them.

In the event, two pairs of hands seemed to work just fine. The door swung back.

Just another door, opening ahead of you, Yuri. Just another door, in a long line of doors.

They climbed through easily into the central chamber, and faced the second door, complete with its set of hand marks. They glanced at each other, shrugged, and lifted their hands. The door behind them swung closed.

And when they opened the door before them Yuri immediately stumbled, under heavier gravity. Per Ardua gravity. Was he already back? Had another four years already passed? If so, Beth was gone.

When he walked out of the middle chamber and climbed through the second hatch, Yuri found himself back in the Per Ardua chamber he remembered. The lid was closed; he couldn't see the sky. But there was the builder map on the wall, at which Kalinski stared avidly. There was the ladder from Tollemache's rover, presumably having stood here for more than eight years. There was even scattered mud on the floor, brought in from the surface by their boots, long dried. "Like I've never been away," he said.

Kalinski leaned with one gloved hand on a wall. Yuri knew she'd been training to cope with Per Ardua's full Earth-type gravity, but it was going to be hard for a while. "I'm relieved it worked. I thought it would, but—"

"I know. At least we've not been dropped in the heart of a sun, or something. I don't think it works that way, this link system. It all seems too—sensible—for that, doesn't it? Look, we're not going to need these suits. What say we dump them?"

"I guess we could. There are no sim controllers to order us around now, are there?"

"Welcome to my world, Colonel Kalinski."

They got out of their suits quickly; they were self-operating, self-opening. Underneath they both wore light, practical coveralls in Arduan pastel colors, and they had backpacks of survival gear and science monitors.

Yuri nodded at Kalinski, hefted his pack, and made his way up the ladder to the closed hatch lid. Braced on a rung, he pressed both hands into indentations in the lid—indentations which, he recalled, had not been there the last time he passed through, and the builder marks seemed to have vanished.

To his relief, the hatch opened smoothly.

He looked up at a dismal cloud-choked gray sky framed by dead-looking trees, and it was *cold*; he could feel it immediately, cutting through his thin coverall. He'd been gone for eight years, he reminded himself, four years as some kind of disembodied signal passing from Ardua to Mercury, and four years coming back again—even if it only felt like a month to him. Plenty of time for things to change.

He clambered out quickly, and stood on the Arduan ground once more. He watched Kalinski follow cautiously, slowly, given the burden of the higher gravity, but her face was full of wonder, or astonishment. Her first moments on an alien world.

Standing together, they turned around. Much had indeed changed. The thick Hub forest still stood, but dead leaves hung limply from the stubby upper stem branches, the undergrowth had died back, and there was a huddle of dead builders, not a purposefully constructed midden but just a heap of corpses, on which, Yuri saw, *frost* had gathered. Frost, at the substellar. His breath fogged.

"Hello, Yuri Eden."

Yuri turned. There was the ColU, its dome smeared with some kind of ash, its upper surfaces rimed with frost. Yuri felt oddly touched. "You waited for me."

"Yes."

"For *eight years*? Jesus. Looks like you stayed in the very same spot."

"No. That would have been foolish. I moved periodically in order to ensure the smooth functioning of my drive mechanisms and—"

"All right, I get it. This is Stef Kalinski. Colonel in the ISF."

"I know of you. Welcome, Colonel Kalinski."

Kalinski just stared.

"Yuri Eden, you left Mercury four years ago. We received warning of your coming a short time ago, you and your companion."

"Ah," said Kalinski. "The message beat us, just as when you came through the other way, Yuri. The transit's not quite lightspeed."

"The message was received by Captain Jacob Keller in the hull, who informed me."

Yuri asked, "Keller? What about Brady?"

"He has not survived. We keep each other company, Captain Jacob Keller and I. Sometimes we play poker."

Yuri had to laugh. "Poker. My God. ColU, the weather—what happened here?"

"Volcanism, Yuri Eden. It seems that a major volcanic episode has occurred, probably in the northern region, from which we fled with the *jilla* and the builders."

"Ah. All that uplifting."

"Yes. It is not an uncommon occurrence on this world, it seems. That is, not uncommon on a geological timescale."

"And now," Kalinski said, "we're in some kind of volcanic winter."

"No doubt for the native life forms it is part of the natural cycle. A spur to evolution perhaps. But the humans here have suffered. Of course the star winter was already a challenge. All this has happened in the interval while you fled, dreamless, between the stars."

"My God. If it's as bad as this here, at the substellar . . . Where are they, Delga and the rest?"

"Gone from here, Yuri Eden."

Yuri glanced around, at this utterly transformed wreck of a world, to which he had now been exiled by the mother of his child, as once he had been exiled to the future by his parents. He felt his heart harden, as he stood there in the unexpected cold. "OK. Well, there are big changes on the way, ColU. Floods of immigrants are going to be coming through that Hatch. I don't imagine the UN will wait the eight years it will take for our bad news about the volcanic winter to reach them, for that process to start."

"Or even," Kalinski said, "for confirmation that the Hatch is actually two-way, that it's safe to pass through. I know Michael King."

"We must help them," the ColU said.

"Yeah. But we'll be in charge," Yuri said firmly. Kalinski looked at him strangely, but he ignored her. "ColU, let's go to the hull, and get some warm clothing, and work out where to start."

"One thing, Yuri Eden."

"Yes?"

"I heard about the decisions made on Mercury. I'm sorry for your loss." It held out a bundle of dried-out stems. Mister Sticks.

Yuri took the doll.

Then the ColU whirred, turned, and rolled away along a track that was now well worn, trampled down by eight years of use. Yuri followed briskly, carefully carrying the beat-up little doll.

SIX

· · ·

Five years after Stef Kalinski had disappeared into the Hatch to Proxima—and because of the lightspeed delays, with three more years left before Penny could even in principle discover for sure if her sister was alive or dead—Penny was invited to another major UN-China conference, this time on the cooperative exploitation of solar-system resources, to be held on Ceres, the Chinese-held asteroid.

Once again this was going to be all about politics and economics, not physics, and her first instinct was to refuse. But she came under heavy pressure to attend. As Sir Michael King and others pressed on her—she even got a note from Earthshine—for someone like her, so closely associated with kernel physics, to be invited to a conference on Ceres itself on UN-Chinese cooperative projects was a hugely symbolic gesture, just as before. But, aged fifty-eight now, she was a card that had been played too often, she thought. She was like an aging rock star pulled out of retirement to celebrate the birthday of one too many Secretary Generals. A statement of mutual trust that, in the light of the ever worsening political situation, every time it was repeated had an air of increasing desperation about it.

And meanwhile there was increasingly bad news from all the worlds of mankind. Recently there had been heavily publicized (and suspiciously scrutinized) "disasters" on both political sides: a tsunami in the Atlantic, a dome collapse in a Chinese colony in the Terra Sirenum on Mars soon after . . . At first it looked as if each of these was natural, a gruesome coincidence of timing. Then ringers started to be pointed, accusations began to be made. Fringe groups claimed responsibility for the "attacks," one in retaliation for the other. Some groups claimed responsibility for *both*.

But neither might have been attacks at all. Penny couldn't see how you could determine the truth. Perhaps, given the poison of international relationships, the truth, in fact, didn't matter anymore. She was hearing dark conspiracy-theory mutterings of drastic provisions being drawn up by both sides in this gradually gathering war: fleets of kernel-drive battleships being constructed by the UN side, various exotic uses of their own interplanetary technology being planned by the Chinese . . . She supposed with her contacts she was in a better position than most to ferret out the truth of such rumors. But she preferred not to listen, not to think about it.

And now here she was, summoned to an asteroid. Still, King said with a wink, it might be fun to see Ceres.

The trip itself, her latest jaunt out of the heart of the solar system, began reasonably pleasantly. Aboard an ISF hulk ship running at a third standard gravity, close enough to Mercury-normal for her to feel comfortable, she had her own room, a workstation, and a generous allocation of communication time with Earth and Mercury, even though the round-trip time delays soon mounted up. She got a lot of work done, on a securely encrypted stand-alone slate. Kernel physics was still a closely guarded secret as far as the UN was concerned, although Penny did often wonder how much the Chinese must have learned through their various intelligence sources by now.

She had to make the trip in stages. Just as hulks were not allowed within the environs of Earth, so no UN-run, ISF-crewed kernel-powered hulk was allowed within a million kilometers of Ceres, the Chinese central base in the asteroid belt. The ISF crews joked blackly about what the Chinese could actually do about it if a hulk crew refused to comply and broke through the cordon, especially if it came in on the delicate Halls of Ceres in reverse, with the cosmic fire of kernels blazing from

its rear like a huge flamethrower. But those arrogant kernel tweakers of
the ISF, Penny reminded herself, depended for all their achievements on
a wholly inhuman technology: a technology that, some believed, humanity shouldn't be using at all.

So after a flight of several days from Earth, her own kernel-driven
hulk slid to a halt alongside a minor but water-rich asteroid, roughly co-
orbiting with Ceres but well beyond the million-kilometer cordon. This
battered lump of dusty water-ice was a convenient resupply depot, but
mostly it served political purposes, as a kind of customs barrier, Penny
saw, in the invisible frontier between the zones of influence of the UN
nations and China. Here ships from both sides of the divide could gather,
refuel, and exchange cargo, and passengers like Penny.

Penny peered out of her cabin window at the motley craft gathering
here. In contrast to the blunt solidity of ISF kernel-powered hulks, Chinese ships, known as "junks" to ISF crew, were little more than sails,
some of them hundreds of kilometers across. For propulsion the sails
gathered sunlight, or the beams of ground-based lasers. It was a proven
technology. Ceres was nearly three times as far from the sun as Earth,
and sunlight was much less intense here, but robot ships from Earth
with big solar-cell panels had been making use of the sun's energy this
far out since the twenty-first century. Robot riggers constantly worked
the great sails. The sails were slow to respond to the tugging of the stay
cables, and huge ripples crossed their surfaces, with the sharp light of
the distant sun reflected in shifting spots and slowly evolving highlights.

Penny transferred to one of the Chinese junks, aboard which it
would take another week to get to Ceres. UN-nation citizens were not
allowed aboard such vessels without officially appointed "companions."
In the event, much to Penny's relief, the aide assigned her was more than
acceptable. It was Jiang Youwei, the young man who had similarly been
her "guide" during her first visit to Mars five years ago. Jiang was as
polite and attentive as ever, and just as pleasant to talk to as long as they
stayed away from taboo subjects like kernel physics. And, though not
quite as young as he had been, he was still cute enough to fill her idle
hours with pleasant daydreams.

Penny settled into the rhythms of the journey easily. After the noisy
engineering of the ISF hulks, the junk was peaceful. And by comparison
with the heavy push of the hulk's drive, the microgravity thrust exerted

by the ship's lightsail was barely noticeable, and silent too. Occasionally Penny would feel a faint wash of sensation in her gut, as if she were adrift in some ocean and caught by a gentle current. Or she would see a speck of dust drift down through the air, settling slowly. The Chinese crew, like Jiang, was polite, orderly—maybe a little repressed, she thought, but it made for a calm atmosphere. Even the remoteness of the sun gave her a sense of dreaminess, of peace.

She worked when she could concentrate, and exercised according to the routine politely suggested by Jiang, to avoid the usual microgravity loss of muscle tone and bone mass. She slept a lot, floating in her cocoonlike room, sometimes in darkness, sometimes with the walls set to transparency so that the stars, the sun, the sail with its vast slow ripples were a diorama around her. After a few days it was hard for her to tell if she was asleep or awake. Sometimes she dreamed of the smooth limbs and deep eyes of Jiang Youwei.

It was almost a disappointment when Ceres came swimming out of the sky, and this interval of calm was over.

At Ceres the junk's modular hull was gently disengaged from its sail tethers, and was towed inward through the last couple of hundred kilometers by a small automated tug. Penny, watching the big sail wafting around the sky, could see the logic; the very biggest sails could be a couple of thousand kilometers across or more, bigger than Ceres itself—big enough to wrap up the dwarf planet like a Christmas present, and you didn't want any accidental entanglements.

At Ceres, the passengers, including Penny, Jiang, and a few crew members who were being rotated here, were politely moved into a small snub-nosed shuttle craft, rows of seats in a cramped cabin. As they took their places some of the passengers looked faintly queasy, and others rubbed their arms. They had all been put through a brisk decontamination and inoculation update. The separated pools of humanity, scattered among isolated colonies, were busily evolving their own unique suites of viruses, and each group had to be protected from infection by all the others.

As Penny strapped into her acceleration couch she watched a couple of crew manhandling what looked like a piece of cargo into this passenger cabin. It was a rough cone that bristled with lenses, grills, and other sensors, a retractable antenna array, and a minor forest of manipulator arms, some of which brachiated down to fine tool fittings. The whole was plastered with UEI logos, and various instruction panels in multiple languages. The crewmen cautiously pushed this gadget into place in a gap between the rows of couches, positioned it so the lenses could peer out of the windows, plugged it into the shuttle's onboard power supply, and backed away.

The shuttle doors were sealed, and a chime filled the cabin. Automated voices speaking Chinese, English, and Spanish announced that the final transit to Ceres had already begun. As she was pushed gently back in her couch by the acceleration, Penny stared at the bristling cone. "So what the hell's that?"

Jiang Youwei smiled. "What do you imagine it is?"

"It looks like a Mars lander, circa 2050. A museum piece?"

To her surprise a panel lit up on the flank of the machine, and an urbane face peered out at her, smiling. "Good morning, Colonel Kalinski."

"Earthshine. You!"

"Me, indeed. Or at least a partial, a download of my primary back on Earth. Lightspeed delays are such a bore, aren't they? And appear likely to remain so for the indefinite future, given that even the Hatch bridges are limited to lightspeed transits. I wonder how *that* has constrained the evolution of life and intelligence in the Galaxy . . ." He smiled, almost modestly; the face was reproduced authentically, so that Penny had the strong impression that she was speaking to a human being stuck inside this boxlike shell. "It is good to see you again."

"You say you're some kind of partial?"

"Of course. I am considerably limited compared to my primary. However I download my memory store regularly, and when I am returned to Earth there will be a complete synchronization."

Jiang said, "That sounds schizophrenic, sir."

"Oh, probably," Earthshine said breezily. "But you should remember that I, or rather my primary, am already a fusion of nine human consciousnesses. Already a chorus of voices sing inside my head, so to speak."

Penny was irritated by this distraction from her mission, from the approaching asteroid. "I didn't even know you were aboard the junk."

"I considered renewing our acquaintance. Your young guardian here said it might be best not to disturb you during the flight."

"He did, did he?" She glared at Jiang, who, not for the first time in their acquaintance, blushed. "What am I, your grandmother?"

"But we had no urgent business," Earthshine said. "Though we have our long-standing connection concerning your relationship with your sister. Of course the two of you are now separated, presumably by light years, presumably forever."

She glanced at Jiang. Officially, he knew nothing of her complicated past. His face showed no expression; she could not tell what he knew or not.

She turned back to Earthshine. "So why are you here?"

"Two reasons. First—"

"The conference?"

"Yes. Though it is far from a summit, it is one of the most high-profile UN-Chinese contacts proceeding anywhere just now. Your own presence, Colonel, is an indicator of that. And we—my fellows in the Core—believe we should back, visibly and publicly, such initiatives as the cooperative development of outer solar system resources being discussed here. So here I am."

"And the second reason?"

"I wanted to see the asteroid belt. Simple as that. I have developed something of an obsession with the violent origins of our currently peaceful worlds . . . Call me a cosmic-disaster junkie. Ceres, you know, is the only truly spherical asteroid, the only one differentiated, that is with an internal structure of a rocky core, a water ice mantle and a fractured rocky crust. It is a dwarf planet technically, not an asteroid at all. And it comprises about a third the mass of the whole of the belt. But once there were *thousands* of such objects here in the belt, all of them relics of the ancient days, of the formation of the solar system."

"All gone, except Ceres," Penny said.

"Yes." Two manipulator arms swung; two small metal fists collided with a tinny clang. "All smashed to pieces in collisions. That's why there are so many metal-rich asteroids out there. They are relics of the cores of worlds like Ceres, whole worlds smashed to bits. Violence, everywhere you look! We crawl around our solar system like baffled children in a bombed-out cathedral."

Jiang frowned. "That is not an original perception. It is the nature of the universe we inhabit."

"True. But it's not the violence of the past that haunts me. It's the mirror-image violence that may lie in our future . . ."

Penny tried to puzzle this out. She remembered how Earthshine had spoken of being *afraid*, all those years ago, over her father's grave. Now he seemed to be becoming more irrational, obsessive. Haunted by visions of primordial cosmic violence? Was it possible for a Core AI to become insane? If so, what would the consequences be? Or perhaps, she told herself, he was actually becoming *more* sane. Facing realities not yet perceived by mankind. She wasn't sure which was the more disturbing alternative.

Another chime informed them that the transfer was already nearing its end. Penny felt a soft deceleration pressing her against her restraint, and she strained to look ahead through the shuttle's blister carapace. At last she saw Ceres itself, a small world fast approaching. In the attenuated sunlight, it looked at first glance like the far side of the moon, heavily cratered. But transparent roofs sprawled across swathes of landscape, roofs under which the green of life could be glimpsed. There were towers too, drilling rigs of some kind, so tall that they bristled at this world's sharp horizon, and a belt of gleaming metal circled what she presumed was the world's equator.

"That belt is the mass driver," Jiang Youwei murmured, beside Penny. "Or one of them. A great electromagnetic sling that hurls sacks of water ice and other volatiles from Ceres all over the asteroid belt, and indeed to Mars. Some asteroids, you know, are virtually pure metal, or metallic ore, with not a trace of water or other volatiles, and so are unable to support human life independently. Because of the water it exports, Ceres has turned out to be the key to the exploitation of the whole belt."

There was another warning chime. The shuttle tipped up and descended *nose down*, alarmingly, toward a landing field of what looked like concrete, heavily marked with recognition symbols and surrounded by giant structures. The gravity of Ceres must be so low, Penny thought, that the descent was more like a docking with a huge space station than a landing on a respectable planet, on Mars or Mercury or Earth.

In the last seconds the craft tipped up with a rattle of attitude thrusters, and the descent slowed to a crawl. They landed, feather-soft.

The shuttle rolled toward a tremendously tall, sprawling building, and nuzzled easily up against a wall. A chime, and the passengers began to unbuckle. Once they were out of their seats, Penny stumbled slightly in a gravity so low it was hardly there at all.

There was a clicking of latches, and then the shuttle's nose section swung back, leaving a round portal through which they could walk. A handful of official-looking types in sober business suits, and a couple of armed soldiers, were waiting beyond the portal. Over their shoulders Penny glimpsed a vast open space, spindly pillars, a high ceiling through which sunlight glinted, and beneath which huge birds flapped—no, she saw, they were *people*, people flying through the air using some kind of skeletal, batlike wings. The sunlight was supplemented by the light of huge fluorescent panels that seemed to be suspended from the ceiling. In this vast, cavernous space, lesser buildings clustered on a smooth floor, entirely contained by the great roof. The structure was so huge that Penny thought she could see a slight curvature in the floor, as if the building sprawled over the very horizon. Well, perhaps it did.

Two women waited for Penny, with Jiang and Earthshine. The apparent senior, small, sober, perhaps forty years old and dressed in a somber black suit, introduced herself as Shen Xuelin. "Welcome to the Halls of Ceres. I am deputy director of the colony here, and chair of the Resources Futures conference to which you have kindly agreed to contribute." Her English was good, if anything overprecise, her accent a kind of neutral east coast American. She introduced the younger, uniformed woman beside her: Wei Ling, a captain in a dedicated division of the Chinese national army. "I apologize for the presence of an armed officer at my side," Shen said. "And for our inability to offer you the full freedom you requested, sir," she said to Earthshine.

Penny, turning, saw that the AI's cone-shaped host was being hoisted by a couple of the shuttle crew onto a kind of hovering platform. She had to laugh. "You're going to be rolled around like a remote-controlled kid's toy, Earthshine."

"It is purely a routine precaution—"

"Please don't apologize, Madam Shen." Earthshine's voice was strong, confident, projected as if a human being were standing here with them. "Given the current political situation it is quite understandable. I half expected you to turn me back altogether."

Shen checked a watch. "The morning session of the conference has another hour to run. Would you care to join us?" Shen led them to a walkway that stretched across the floor of the tremendous building. "I would advise you to grab the handrail . . ."

The walkway was a track of some yielding material that rapidly built up speed. Penny found herself tilling forward, disconcertingly, though she had no inner sense of tipping. Glancing down, she saw that the surface of the track had rucked itself up so that it held her at an angle, compensating for the acceleration. A neat low-gravity trick. "Clever," she said.

Shen said with some pride, "An ingenious design but not one that everybody finds comfortable. The mixing up of the vertical and horizontal . . ."

Penny noticed that Jiang had turned very pale. She had to grin. "Bearing up, Mars man? If you're going to vomit I'll find you a sick bag."

"That will not be necessary," Jiang said, a little sternly. "Madam Shen, I was intrigued by the conference agenda."

"Indeed," said Shen. "We have already had productive sessions on ambitious plans to exploit such resources as the gas giant atmospheres, remote moons like Titan and Triton, even Kuiper belt and Oort cloud objects. With our experience of Ceres and the asteroids we feel confident about approaching the ice moons and dwarf planets of the outer system, even though we must seek alternate energy sources to sunlight."

"You mean," Earthshine said provocatively, "you need the kernels."

"That is one possibility," Shen said, a little stiffly. "There are other energy sources. The mining of gas giant atmospheres for fusion fuel, for example. This will require an industrial effort on a scale of an order of magnitude more ambitious than anything seen in the present day. This is surely a challenge for the next generation, and even then we believe the pooled resources of all our societies, that is of the Greater Economic Framework and of the nations dominated by the UN quasi-government, will be necessary to achieve such a task."

Earthshine said sadly, "But that cooperation looks a lot less likely than it did a couple of weeks ago."

"Indeed . . ."

Penny was only half listening. As she moved deeper into this building she got a deepening sense of its gargantuan scale, the roof far above her like some planetarium sky suspended by needle-slim pillars, the clusters of buildings on the floor like whole villages enclosed by the greater structure. She recognized official buildings, squat military-style bunkers, and refectories, dormitories, hospitals—but there were schools too, around which she saw children playing, leaping, flapping in the air. And bars, games rooms, hotels, and a giant sports arena where, as she glimpsed through a structure of lacy scaffolding, what looked like a low-gravity version of basketball was being played. There was a continual hubbub of noise, reflecting from the hard common floor and from the roof far above, a jumble of human voices, scraps of music, the occasional whir of air pumps and fans. And around the invisibly slim pillars, people flew, many of them young, as Penny might have guessed, gliding easily on extended bat wings strapped to their arms.

"You need not worry."

The English words were heavily accented. Penny turned to see that the young soldier had spoken to her, Captain Wei Ling, clutching her remote-control slate. Wei smiled.

"I'm not . . . Worried about what?"

Wei pointed upward; her hand was encased in a white glove. "That the roof will fall. Even children born here fear that. Our architects take advantage of the low gravity of this small world to create such structures as this, possible on no other world inhabited by humanity. But it seems some primal instinct is violated by the sight of an artificial sky."

"You sound proud of all this. Were you born here?"

"No. I am a native of Earth. But as a Chinese I am proud to witness this, yes. Access to space has unleashed a native genius in my people, I think. Please prepare yourself for the terminus of the track."

The conference hall to which they were led was itself huge, and neatly if conventionally laid out with a large stage, a giant screen, and rows of seats in queasy-looking low-G-steep elevated banks.

But the seats were mostly empty. Something was wrong, Penny saw immediately. The delegates, many arguing loudly, were crowded before big screens filled with a blizzard of images, news channels, science feeds and other updates. Penny recognized some of the delegates, from both China and the UN nations: politicians, scientists, engineers, writers, even a few artists. Such was the noise of raised voices in the room that Penny couldn't make out a word coming from the multiple talking heads on the screen. A few faces turned to look at the newcomers, especially at Earthshine's outlandish avatar body, but they soon returned to their frenetic debating.

"Ah," Shen said, glancing at Wei. "I see the announcement has been made."

"I am hearing it," Earthshine said, faintly distracted.

Penny frowned, peering at the screens. "What announcement?"

Shen said, "I had hoped we would be given a few more hours, that our agenda would not be disrupted . . ."

"What a dispiriting sight," Earthshine said. "Even here the delegates have retreated into their respective packs. They came all this way, to this enchanting world in its wan sunlight, to discuss what might have united mankind: a unified expansion into the unimaginable wealth of the outer solar system. Now here we are, huddled in our tribes. And, look, the only place one side is talking to the other is at that island where they're serving coffee."

"Well, at least that's something," Penny murmured.

Shen Xuelin glared at Earthshine with unexpected hostility. "You speak as if you are aloof from the fray. The Core AIs have been a force in geopolitical affairs for decades. Indeed, a significant fraction of Earth's resources is diverted to sustaining you and your brothers. If we are in difficulties now—well, it is because of a situation you have played a hand in shaping—"

"Never mind that," Penny said sharply. "*What announcement? What's going on here?*"

The upper portion of the cone robot, bristling with manipulator arms, swiveled toward her. "Yes, you daydreamed away much of the transit aboard the lightsail ship in your cabin, didn't you? Typical of you scientists, frankly, while events on Earth and elsewhere have increasingly turned ugly. Colonel Kalinski, even you must have heard of recent incidents that have caused so much concern—"

"Don't patronize me," she snapped. "I know about the Atlantic tsunami, the punctured dome at Terra Sirenum—"

"Both relatively minor events in themselves," Shen said. "Unless you were personally involved, of course. The loss of life at our colony at Sirenum was actually greater than that caused by the tsunami. What matters is that specific accusations are beginning to be aired, even in the UN chambers. Such as, maybe the tsunami was triggered by the implantation of a deep bomb, as developed by our own government for exclusive use on Mars in the terraforming project. Colonel Kalinski, the tsunami, the Mars dome break, other incidents, may or may not have been caused by provocative agents on either side. But the incidents did serve to show up our respective vulnerabilities. And I have to tell you that it is New Beijing that feels the more vulnerable. *You have the kernels.* This situation cannot continue. Our governing councils have therefore determined to take action, leveraging our own strengths, in response to the implicit threat of kernel technology—"

"I get it," Penny snapped. "So why all the fuss here today?"

Shen said evenly, "Because of what has been announced by our government in New Beijing." She pointed to a corner of the big screen where an announcement, in Chinese but subtitled in English, was repeating over and over.

It took Penny a couple of minutes to figure out that the Chinese had ordered their military forces in space to divert a small main-belt asteroid onto a collision course with the Earth.

Even Jiang looked shocked; evidently he hadn't heard of this.

"As an engineering problem it was simple," Shen said. "As you can imagine. And, so I hear, the project has been under development for some years."

"You wouldn't do this," Penny said. "Your own people—billions of them—"

"The asteroid could be manipulated to deliver selective strikes."

Earthshine grunted. "Knock out one side of the Earth and not the other, right? That's a dangerous game, Madam Shen; it's a small planet."

"But we have many years to sculpt this tool," Shen said. "The rock is on a long-duration orbit; it will take years to reach Earth. We are publishing a detailed timescale, including branch points where it will be possible to divert the rock. This long timetable is deliberate. It contains deadlines by which we insist that certain peaceful measures must be conceded by the UN. Such as, no more monopoly of immigration to Per Ardua. And, most important, *a full sharing of the kernel and Hatch technology.* The intention is not to smash a rock into the Earth, but to force concessions from the UN."

Earthshine mused, "A Cold War weapon with a ticking clock. You are ingenious."

"You say 'you,'" Shen said regretfully. "I say 'we.' *I* have had no hand in this. Nor anybody else in this room, I imagine. Here, we are all—Utopians. Idealists. We would not be here otherwise. We are here to discuss a better future of peace and prosperity, but the present drifts toward war. *We* can only watch events unfold, and hope." Now she looked at Penny with what seemed like a longing for understanding. "You can see this is all a bluff. To force the UN to concede—"

"But if they don't back down," Penny said quickly. "Just suppose— if they don't agree, and they call your bluff—would you drop the rock? Would you really do it?"

But Shen would not reply. Neither Jiang, nor Wei Ling the helpful young soldier, would meet her eyes.

Earthshine, locked in his avatar, spun and whirred. "Just think, Colonel Kalinski. If not for the kernels, if not for the damn Hatch, we'd be sitting here now discussing joint missions to Jupiter. Instead we're facing interplanetary war. I wonder if whoever planted that damn material on Mercury *knew* it would lead to this." Jiang gently touched Penny's arm. "I prescribe coffee. Come . . ."

SEVEN

• • •

2213

"They've taken Thursday."

Liu stood before Yuri's desk, in an expensive but grimy coverall; he'd evidently been out in the fields. Liu Tao was in his seventies now—nearly two decades older than Yuri, physically, after Yuri's four-year gaps in the Hatch. Yuri thought he had never seen him so agitated.

Twelve years after Yuri's return from Mercury they were both rich, both powerful—but only in their own little pond, this small world of Per Ardua, and every so often they were handed a reminder that there were far mightier forces at work in their universe. Here was Liu talking about his twenty-two-year-old daughter being apprehended, probably for little more reason than the crime of being half Chinese. He looked as helpless as he must have been on the day his Chinese rocket plane had fallen out of the sky into a UN-controlled enclave on Mars.

Yuri touched a slate built into the surface of his desk—old mahogany, imported from Earth and carried through the Hatch from Mercury by human beings, fantastically expensive. "Stef? I think you'd better get in here."

"On the way."

"Sit down, Liu."

"Damn it, Yuri—"

"Sit down. Stef's on the way. We'll find a way to handle this."

Stef Kalinski came into the office. She had a redolent scent of builder stem about her; among her other projects, she was trying to extract more details of the builders' own deep past and their engagement with the exotic technologies of the Hatch. In her sixties herself, Stef was still a multitasker, and it could be difficult to get her to focus. But as soon as she saw Liu standing there, obviously agitated, he was the center of her attention. "Tell me how I can help."

Yuri went to the coffeepot and poured three brimming mugs. This was Arduan coffee, cultivated and processed at the Mattock Confluence. Yuri liked to import treasures from Earth as luxuries, but as a policy he bought local. "Liu says Thursday's been arrested."

Stef's eyebrows shot up. "What? Who by? I guess the UN—"

Liu said, "The security troops at the Hub."

Yuri tried to make light of it. "What did she do, throw a brick at them? They've been winding down the detachment there."

"Not arrested," Liu said, barely holding it together. "Confined. They put her in one of their camps."

"Ah. Oh, shit."

The internment camps were a recent, and unwelcome, development, and a sideshow of the war gathering in the solar system.

Since Yuri and Stef Kalinski had returned through the Hatch together twelve years ago to a volcanic winter, things had slowly gotten better climate-wise on Per Ardua—which was a good thing as the immigrants from Earth through the Hatch had started to arrive almost immediately. But recently, things had evidently been getting worse politically back home. The flow of people through the Hatch had slowed to a trickle, as the inner system's resources were devoted to the gathering interplanetary conflict rather than to shipping emigrants around the inner planets. Indeed, many of the UN troops stationed here at Per Ardua had been sent back to the solar system.

But some of the UN's Cold-War type security strictures had been imposed here on Per Ardua, as back home. And, it seemed, there were still enough troops to spare the time to pick up Liu Tao's daughter.

Yuri grunted. "What the hell they think they'll achieve with internment camps here on Per Ardua I don't know. This is our country, our world. It's like an infection of paranoia, spreading through the Hatch.

The sooner the last UN trooper drags his sorry arse back through the Hatch the better."

"Which," Liu said, "is probably the kind of rhetoric that got Thursday in trouble. She's fallen in with some of those youth movements. 'Ardua for Arduans'—you know. Any kind of activity like that is dangerous if you've got Thursday's ethnic background. Yuri, we've got to get her out of there."

"Of course we've got to. The three of us, we'll go into the Hub together, and we won't come out without her. OK?"

Liu didn't seem relieved, or reassured, but at least he seemed gratified at the support, and to be doing something about it. "I'll drive."

"Like hell. In your state you'll kill us all. Stef, go fetch a rover."

Stef nodded. But as the three of them stood stiffly—three old people, aware of their age when they moved—Stef murmured to Yuri, "You shouldn't make promises you can't be sure you can keep. Bad habit, Yuri . . ."

"What are you getting at?"

"I know the UN and the ISF a lot better than you do. Be ready for the worst."

Away from the UN base at the Hub—as the substellar zone had come to be known, the area of Per Ardua most firmly controlled by human authorities now ironically labeled with a builder name—rovers and other vehicles were still rare, still precious. Since the *Ad Astra*, there had never been another starship visit to Per Ardua, and any heavy-duty machinery imported from the solar system had to be broken down into components and carried through the Hatch, usually on the backs of immigrants. But Yuri Eden, Stef Kalinski, Liu Tao, the triumvirate who dominated the community at the Mattock Confluence, were about the richest, most powerful people on Per Ardua, away from the island of UN influence itself at the Hub. They had done well in skimming off the wealth and power associated with the one-way immigrant flow over the last decade.

So a rover was soon provided for them.

Stef Kalinski drove rapidly, steadily, safely, inward to the Hub. Though she was as much an absorbed intellectual as she ever had been, Yuri observed that Stef had found ways to fit in, here on this very different world. Thanks to her ISF military training she had come equipped with common sense, courage, and practical competences. And, Yuri suspected, she was a lot happier with a thickness of four light years between her and her unwanted "twin"—though even after all this time he still wasn't sure he believed all the kooky stuff she'd tentatively shared with him about that. In any event, Stef was a silent, focused driver, even when she let the rover navigate itself. That wasn't unwise, as the world, still recovering from its volcanic winter, was an unpredictable place.

Liu sat silently too, staring at the road ahead as they drove south. For him the ride was clearly just an interval to be endured before he got on with the issue of saving his daughter.

So, in the quiet, Yuri had time to stare out of the window at his changing world.

This road, metaled in places, was a rough descendant of the track he and Mardina and the rest had trodden out as they had marched south to the substellar all those years ago, heading upstream along the course of the great river system that flowed north out of the Hub uplands—a feature now called, logically enough, the North River. For years the track had run across a frozen landscape. Now the road ran on thawed-out but firm ground past meltwater lakes, and on rough bridges over gushing tributary streams.

The long cold was passing now, the volcanic ash screen that had exacerbated the effects of the star winter clearing at last, and you rarely saw ice this far south anymore. The winter had caused misery for humanity, particularly for the new arrivals on this world, utterly unprepared.

But Arduan life itself was hardier, and was surely adapted to a changeable climate. The ColU said it had observed shoots of new stems springing up from beneath the fallen ash within weeks of the volcanic event. By now the lakes, emerging from beneath the ice, were already hosts to new communities of builders, with their nurseries and middens and traps. *The builders knew*, the ColU said; the builders had memories and legends, it believed, spanning the cycles of the deep, deep past. Yuri, using what influence he had, had tried to set up a kind of exclusion zone around the *jilla*, the migratory lake that had guided him and Mardina south. He wanted to know if the same builders would now guide that lake back north again, to begin the cycle again . . .

As for the stromatolites, those great dreaming mounds barely seemed to notice the winter. And, the ColU said, the bugs in the deep rocks, where the bulk of Per Ardua's biomass resided, as on every rocky world, would have been entirely unaware.

But the postwinter landscape of Per Ardua was dramatically different from before. It had become a human landscape, crowded with people and their works. Now the rover drove past farming villages founded by the new colonists with the help of their own ColUs, cut down, more flexible modern units. For a decade immigrants had been emerging from that single central point at the Hub, the Hatch, a doorway just a few meters across, like oil seeping from a well in the desert. And they had been pushing out of the Hub in all directions across the patient face of Per Ardua, north and south, east and west, but especially following the great rivers. It was an odd pattern of colonization, Yuri thought—and a big contrast to the scattered pattern of the Founders' first communities, dropped almost at random from the sky by the shuttles from the *Ad Astra*.

Farther in toward the Hub they passed through a more densely populated belt of industrialization. Here were forges and smelters, plants churning out tools and engines, diggers and borers, factories built of local-dirt concrete and stem-forest timber and fed by river water carried by gleaming pipelines. In this industrial zone, already a pall of smoke from the local coal and timber hung in the air, a genuine smog on some still days, blanketing the factories and processing plants and dormitory-block apartments, over which the vertical light of Proxima Centauri steadily beat down. Like the farming communities farther out, there was a whole band of this kind of development spread in a rough circle around the pivotal point of the Hub, though pushing farther out wherever the major rivers ran.

It was a remarkable flowering after just a few decades of human presence on the planet, and had accelerated in the years since the big influx of immigrants had got under way. Soon roads and rail lines would be laid down, and the spokes of this great complex wheel of colonization would be extending much farther, to areas rich in minerals such as metals and uranium, and the seams of coal-like deposits that had been found just inward of the rim-forest belt. A flow of commodities would head on back into the center, as the whole substellar face of Per Ardua began a steady integrated development.

Yuri and the people around him had made a great deal of money by laying claim to land likely to be taken by the new settlers, then allowing themselves to be bought out by the UN. Now they were busily claiming vast tracts of land farther out from the Hub, that were apparently too cold and dry to be worth considering for colonization yet. In time they would be sold back too, when the weather warmed up. The newcomers, and even the UN authority that attempted to control them, wouldn't listen to the ragged survivors of the *Ad Astra* when they said the world wouldn't *always* be this cold. It seemed to be in the nature of humanity, Yuri was learning as he grew older, not eventually to listen to the old folk, not to learn from history. He was patient. Per Ardua would tame them all, eventually.

And in the meantime Yuri's own wealth was piling up, some in the local scrip, and some in the banks run by UN officials at the Hub. Better yet, the new factories were now turning out goods that you could spend your money on, from decent clothes that *weren't* the uniform of some UN military force, to fancy cutlery and crockery and furniture and fabrics, and even luxury foods: there were salmon farms in some of the rivers, and chicken runs, with real live beating-heart birds running around.

There was some talk of a civilian local government, elections. Even a civilian justice system to replace the UN military tribunals. But as they got closer in to the center, and approached the zone controlled directly by the UN forces, there were increasing reminders that this world was still more or less a military-controlled colony run by a remote, quasi-imperial power—you didn't need to know about a girl being arrested for having a Chinese father to see that. They drove through an area dominated by neat rows of tents and prefabricated buildings, all marked with prominent UN, ISF, and Peacekeeper logos, and connected by tracks of crushed Per Arduan basalt. The Hub base was a military fortress, basically, the headquarters of an occupation supported by a tithe imposed on the farming communities farther out.

Now they passed a feature new to Yuri: camps, fenced off with barbed wire and watchtowers. Again there were UN logos everywhere, even on the gun towers. Children watched from within the fences, blank-eyed, as their rover rolled by.

Liu stabbed a finger. "In there. One of their new internment centers. That's where she'll be, my Thursday."

"Not yet," Stef said. "I've been checking as we've been driving. They still have her at the Peacekeeper HQ farther in. They know she's your daughter, Liu. They don't want to offend a Founder more than they have to, evidently."

"Maybe." He sat staring out, elbow on the window ledge, the fingers of his right hand working nervously, as if manipulating an invisible coin. "This feels bad, bad."

"Hey, take it easy," Yuri said. "We'll get through this, Liu. It's just some UN asshole being an asshole—"

"You don't know, Yuri. You don't *know*. Me and Thursday October, when her mother died, and then her grandmother too, I was all she had. You weren't there, when she was a little kid. You didn't *see* our lives . . ."

It was true. By passing back and forth through the Hatch, Yuri had effectively skipped eight brutal, wintry years which Liu and all those he'd known on Per Ardua had had to live through, had met their challenges, raised their kids . . . Yuri, still in his fifties biologically speaking, wasn't even as *old* as them anymore. The fact that he had missed all their triumphs and their pain somehow invalidated his own loss, his irrevocable sundering from Beth. Once again he had been cast adrift.

It had made him grow closer to Stef, however, who had left her own life behind, and jumped forward in time with him. Stef did have the consolation of the science, the alien world into which he'd suddenly been projected, the exploration of the mysteries of the Hatches and the tech they represented. But Yuri's relationship with Liu and the others had never been the same.

"I'm sorry," he said now.

Liu looked at him, from within his own private cage of worry and uncertainty. "Whatever."

The rover's nose rose slightly, and the engine growled; they were beginning the long climb into the fractured upland that characterized the Hub, the summit of Per Ardua's frozen rocky tide. Now, under the perpetual clouds of the substellar, they came to more post-Hatch structures, cut into the recovering forest. This was an area set aside for immigrant processing: camps surrounded by barbed wire and gun towers, the first places you would be taken to if you came through the Hatch. Here, new arrivals were quarantined, screened, inoculated, then given basic kit, including clothing, starter packs of local money, basic education and orientation—or siphoned off to an internment camp if their background didn't fit. Yuri sometimes wondered how it must be to be put through the bewildering mystery of a space transport to Mercury, a mysterious trans-dimensional hop between the stars, an emergence onto an alien world—and after all that to be taken away from your family, stripped and thrown into a shower hut.

"I hate these places," Liu said, as they rolled through this zone.

"Me too," admitted Stef. "I did some volunteer work in one of them. I couldn't bear the crying of the children at night in those big dormitories. Not knowing where they were. They were terrified."

Yuri looked at her. He said dryly, "But you're a scientist. Here we are becoming an interstellar species. We are achieving greatness. Isn't it worth a little pain?"

She said, "Not if individuals suffer on the way to achieving species goals. No. There must be a better method, to whatever you want to achieve. Probably requiring more patience."

Liu said, "But even the builders achieved greatness, in their way. They constructed the Hatch, somehow. At least it looks like that. We found traces of their factories and such, right?"

"Yes," Stef said. "But they also built their canals. The Hatch map proves it, even if we still haven't found any trace of them out on the planet itself. Now *that* was a great achievement, that suits the nature of the builders, rather than some gate to the stars. What was the point of the Hatch for them? What use is a world like Mercury to a builder from Per Ardua? Yet they turned their backs on their canals, and they built their Hatch, and then—what? They gave up and went home again, it seems. They may as well have built a statue of a builder a kilometer high, right at the Hub, thumbing its nose at Prox. Wouldn't have been any less use."

That made Yuri laugh. "Nice image. Although they don't have noses. Or thumbs."

Stef stayed serious. "Maybe it's no wonder the builders are so gloomy, as the ColU tells us. Somehow they know their history is—all wrong. And because of the Hatch, it seems. I'm not sure that the Hatch had anything to do with the builders' goals at all, their own fate as a species. After all, *we're* now merrily using the Mercury-Ardua Hatch system to colonize this world, but we've somehow forgotten that whatever it was built for, surely it wasn't for *that*."

"What is it for, then?" Liu asked.

"I don't know. Even though I've studied related phenomena for decades. Even though the Hatches are already part of human history."

"Hm," Yuri said. "Well, I hope we last long enough to find the answer."

They came at last to the UN base, deep within the Hub province, close to the Hatch.

The base had been hugely extended from the days of Tollemache and his crew. The old *Ad Astra* hull was now at the center of an elaborate complex of buildings, with the flags of the UN, ISF, and other agencies hanging limply overhead, while wide areas of forest had been cleared, fenced off, and connected to immigrant processing blocks by tall wire fences. There was talk of turning the hull itself into a museum of the pioneering days on the planet, and Yuri had mischievously suggested bringing back Conan Tollemache himself to run it.

And over the Hatch itself, above the rough transparent dome that now sheltered it from the substellar climate, was a big wrought-iron sign in the six major languages of the UN zones, the first thing you would see when you came scrambling through from Mercury:

WELCOME TO PER ARDUA
A UN PROTECTORATE

Yuri and the others were prominent enough citizens of the "protectorate" to be allowed through the security barriers with minimal formalities. They were escorted by a young soldier to the headquarters of the new Emergency Powers corps of the Peacekeepers, a formidable building of Arduan concrete studded with automatic gun emplacements and security cameras.

Liu barely endured all this, his nerves clearly on a knife edge.

Inside the building they were met by Freddie Coolidge, sitting behind a desk. "Sit down," he said curtly. He tapped his desk; a built-in slate lit up. "I know why you're here, obviously." Then he stared intently into the slate, drawing out the moment. Delga's son, his surname taken from his father, was in his late thirties. He wore the uniform of a sergeant of the Peacekeepers. He looked nothing like his mother, not anymore. He'd even removed the tattoos his mother had had engraved on his face as an infant.

Yuri felt diminished, sitting here in this clean office, being ignored by a kid like Freddie. For all their accomplishments and wealth, they were just three shabby, aging people, come in from the country, facing the power of an interplanetary agency. He steeled himself, looking for inner strength.

But Liu was barely in control of himself. After thirty seconds he snapped: "You prick."

Freddie looked up mildly. "Excuse me?"

"You're doing this deliberately. Stringing this out. Your mother would turn in her grave to see you like this."

Yuri said, "Liu—"

Freddie said coldly, "My mother was a loser, like you, even before some disgruntled customer finally knifed her, and the best thing I ever did was to get away from you people, you 'Founders.' Now. You want to know about your daughter, or not?"

"What do I need to do to get her out of here?"

"Too late, I'm afraid." He grinned. "She's gone."

"Gone? Gone where?"

"Through the Hatch. Back to Mercury, back to Earth. Daughter of a Founder, you see, Liu. Too sensitive politically to handle here, on Per Ardua. That was the thinking. Don't want any trouble, do we?"

Liu looked like he'd been punched in the stomach. Yuri understood exactly what he was thinking. *Through the Hatch:* lost to him, for at least eight years, even if she turned back immediately when she reached the Mercury side.

"Let me go." Liu stood up. "Take me. Shove me after her through your damn Hatch."

"I'm afraid that won't be possible," Freddie said. "Political sensitivities again."

"Sensitivities? What the hell are you talking about?"

"Sit down."

"You prick—"

"*Sit down*. I'm trying to do you a favor here, believe it or not."

Stef grabbed Liu's arm and dragged him down.

"They're coming for you too, Liu. I've put them off, actually. And the logic is you *should* be detained here, on Per Ardua. After all, you're supposed to be serving a sentence on this prison of a world, aren't you? You were an enemy combatant, on Mars."

"My mission was surveillance—"

"Ancient history. Wouldn't be right to send you home, would it, without you serving your time? That's the thinking."

Yuri could see the muscles in Liu's arms clench. Yuri said, "Liu. Listen to what he's saying. What are you offering us, Freddie?"

"Time for you to get him out of here. I fixed the security, you'll be able to get away from the Hub, you won't be stopped." He glanced around, faintly nervous. "You understand I had to bring you all the way in here to tell you this. It's the only place I could be sure we wouldn't be overheard. Ha! Right in the heart of the complex. Take him as far from here as you can."

Stef asked, "Why are you doing this?"

"For my mother, believe it or not. She *was* a loser. But I know she thought well of you, Liu Tao. You're an honorary uncle," he said with disgust. "This is what you get. One favor. Now get him out, Yuri, before I change my mind."

They had to drag Liu away.

The rover rolled past the quarantine camps, following the road's steadily downward incline, heading out from the Hub.

Liu was too angry, too distressed to speak.

Yuri gave him some privacy by sitting up front with Stef. "So," he said. "We need to hide an angry Chinese from the Peacekeepers. Any ideas?"

"Yes," she said, unhesitating.

He laughed. "I should have known."

"We get out of here with him ourselves. We go on an expedition. To another unique location, on Per Ardua, this world of mysteries and puzzles."

He was baffled. "Where the hell?"

She glanced up at Proxima, directly above, its flare-scarred face shielded by scattered cloud. "As far from this place, this government-controlled substellar point, as it's possible to get."

71

Once again Penny Kalinski was flown into the small Parisian airport at Bagneux.

Penny climbed stiffly down from the small plane. Out on the tarmac in the middle of the day it was ferociously hot, even this early in the year. She glanced up at a sky washed out with sunlight. The Splinter was not visible just now, even though, like most of humanity, she knew exactly where to look for it, and knew exactly when it was due to arrive. That big damn rock was on its way. The best predictions were that it would miss the Earth, just, at the conclusion of a countdown that had begun eleven years ago when she'd been at that chaotic resources conference on Ceres, a count that had dwindled down to months, weeks, days—and now, at last, hours. But predictions were just that: predictions, best guesses. Nobody *knew* what was going to fall out of the sky. And now it was almost here.

Penny had begun to think of the time left in terms of sleeps. Not that, in her late sixties, she slept all that well anyhow. Now, she suspected, she would not sleep again, not before the count ran down.

A large automated car drew up to meet her. Sir Michael King was in the back, with a couple of UEI security goons, one male, one female—and, she was startled to see, Jiang Youwei, her one-time guide on Chinese Mars and Ceres.

King and Jiang climbed out, King awkwardly and with the aid of a stick. King shook Penny's hand. "Thanks for coming." His expression was grim, relieved only by the most fleeting of smiles.

Jiang, however, tentatively embraced her. He looked so much older too, more gaunt, older than his forty years—but in his case that might be more to do with the harsh pressure of a full Earth gravity on a frame conditioned to the comparative gentleness of Mars. When he moved, in fact, she heard a subtle whir of exoskeletal support about his body.

"It's good to see you, old friend," she said to him now. "But kind of surprising." She pointed at the sky. "Given the huge geopolitical boot that is about to stamp on Earth."

Jiang shrugged. "I am here for you, Penelope Kalinski."

King raised his eyebrows. "Actually we're all here because of Earthshine, as usual. Look, shall we get back in the damn car? This heat is killing me."

They all clambered into the car, a bubble of glass and ceramic. The security goons took their places front and back, with King, Penny, and Jiang in the middle. The car slid away silent as a soap bubble, heading north out of the airport. When Penny glanced back she saw the airport was empty of activity, not a plane in the sky, only a few craft sitting around on the apron and the terminal buildings lifeless.

King seemed to have visibly aged since she'd last seen him. Despite, presumably, his ongoing courses of anti-senescence treatments. He was ninety-eight years old now. His Aussie accent seemed more pronounced as well—his tone was cruder, as if he could no longer be bothered to mask his true feelings behind conventional civility.

But no doubt she had aged badly too. It was the stress, she supposed. The pressure. The *disappointment*. If you were anywhere near the center of human affairs, even to the extent that she was, your predominant emotion had to be disappointment at the way in which in an age when opportunities for humanity had never been greater, old flaws—territorialism, combativeness, a reluctance to transcend cultural barriers, a sheer inability simply to see things from the other guy's point of view—looked set to bring the sky crashing down on all their heads.

King saw her looking out of the window. "Quiet, isn't it? Everybody who can get out of the city, got. Doesn't make a lot of sense. If the Splinter does fall, despite everything the Chinese have said, then it won't matter where the hell you are. But still, people have fled to the country, if they can."

"While here we are, rushing to the center. Where are we headed, the Champs-Élysées again?"

"Not that. Earthshine's found himself a better hidey-hole. You'll see."

"I look forward to it," Jiang Youwei murmured. "I was born on Mars, as you know. I have seen too little of Earth, of the ancestral home of the human race."

King grunted. "Make the most of it. Last chance to see, eh?"

"It won't come to that," Penny said.

The Splinter—actually an immense chunk of the metallic core of some long-destroyed dwarf planet, a shattered sister of Ceres—was on a grazing trajectory; if left undisturbed it ought to skim the top of Earth's atmosphere, and pass on more or less harmlessly. The UN's tame astronomers and the defense agencies had determined this months ago, and the rock hadn't significantly deviated since then. But the surface of the rock was covered with Chinese technology, from solar-cell arrays to emplacements of what looked suspiciously like their big Mars-terraforming bunker-buster bombs. Some observers even claimed they saw evidence of human activity, teams of taikonauts climbing around on the skin of the weaponized asteroid, even as it sailed in toward the Earth. Nobody in the West *knew* what the Chinese were up to.

In ignorance, at least, Penny thought, there was still room for optimism, and she tried to express that.

But King didn't seem to think so. "Twenty-four hours out after years of a Cold War standoff, with that damn thing barreling in toward the planet—and given it's won the Chinese damn few of the concessions they demanded—and you're still hoping for the best, huh?"

"What choice is there?"

"To bury yourself in the deepest hole you can find—*that's* the alternative. Which is exactly what Earthshine seems to be doing. And which is why we're all here, invited to the show. He sees me as the most senior figure in UEI, which is kind of true, though many on my board and the major stockholders might not agree after all these years. A lot of water under the bridge. And he sees *you* as the queen of kernel science, which is what has caused us all this trouble in the first place. He's trying to intervene in human affairs, the best way he can. And the only way he can do that is by working through humans. Specifically us."

Penny thought that over. "Could be he just thinks of us as friends, Sir Michael. He has known us a long time."

"And myself?" Jiang asked softly.

"He gets to as many Chinese as he can," King said bluntly. "In your case, through your relationship with Penny here. Your government and your security agencies are a lot more skeptical of the Core AIs than we are, in the UN countries. The Chinese see them as yet another relic of the capitalist, colonialist era that started with the Opium Wars and finished with the stunts of the Heroic Generation. Your people have long memories. So Chinese are harder to contact for the AIs."

Jiang shrugged. "I am hardly influential. And our peoples are not yet at war. I was, however, warned, by a French consul on Obelisk in fact, about the personal risk I was undertaking by coming here during the event. If there *were* to be some disastrous consequence—"

"I wouldn't worry," King said frankly. "If worse comes to worst, there probably won't be a lamppost left standing for you to be strung up from." He laughed, and turned away to look out of the window once more.

Penny saw that they were heading through central Paris now, traveling roughly northeast along a broad avenue. There was very little traffic, a few pedestrians, some in silvery capes, hats and goggles to fend off the ferocious sunlight. Through gaps between the clustered buildings she glimpsed the obvious landmarks, the Notre Dame cathedral up ahead, and the rusted ruin of the Eiffel Tower farther in the distance off to the left, a gaunt iron frame rendered blue-gray by the dusty air. Save for the lack of traffic and the basic desertion by its inhabitants, she imagined Paris hadn't changed much in the last century, or even the century before that; ancient ordinances against development had always preserved a certain look about the city. Paris was just Paris, unique.

Jiang saw her looking. He smiled. "All this beauty will still be here this time tomorrow, I'm sure of it."

"Nobody can be sure of any damn thing," King muttered. "Not even the Chinese, whatever they're planning. They're playing with huge energies, the energies of an interplanetary culture, and bringing them down to the Earth. Kind of irresponsible, even if it's just to frighten us. I mean, one slip . . ."

Gunshot. A sharp crack. Everybody in the car ducked, even the security goons.

Everybody but King, who laughed. "Don't sweat it. Just sound effects."

Penny raised her head cautiously. They were rolling across a bridge to the Île de la Cité; she saw the hulk of the cathedral off to her right, and that big old banyan tree dangling in the Seine that she remembered from her last visit. And she glimpsed people running over the bridge, in peculiar silvery suits speckled with pink dots. They looked to be carrying guns, or heavier weapons, bazookas. They ducked between patches of cover, fired their guns, ducked back, and again she heard the crack of weapons firing, presumably simulated.

The car glided on smoothly through all this. The security guys looked embarrassed to have reacted.

"Sound effects," King said again. "Background really, to fill out what the individual players are being fed."

"Players?"

King pointed at the combatants in the silver suits. *"Asgard.* The latest craze. A game, or a series of games, set in the historic centers of the old cities. Those characters don't see what you and I see. *They* are living in a virtual reconstruction of a Paris in 1945, when allied troops are moving in to lift the Nazi occupation of the city. The rules are strict, kind of. You're allowed to get killed, once a day. The next morning you come back and you can run around and start fighting all over again."

Jiang was frowning. "My history is uncertain: Did the allies have to fight for Paris?"

"No, not street to street. There was an agreement to protect the city; the Germans withdrew. It's a game, a quasi-historical fantasy. There are similar games going on all over the world. There's a major campaign going on in Londres to defend the city against a Nazi invasion, and that didn't happen either. The most popular, I'm told, is the Battle of Stalingrad, that's been running continuously for—well, I forget. And in America, the Civil War—"

"I get the picture." Penny glanced up at the sky, looking for the

Splinter. "This is how people spend their time, while that big rock comes sailing in toward the Earth? Isn't it kind of decadent?"

King shrugged. "Everything might end tomorrow. What else is there to do? You can't blame them for escaping."

The car rolled on, heading north over another bridge, leaving the island behind. In the quasi-tropical sunlight of a post-Jolt Paris, more game players dashed across the road to hide in shadows, fighting out a nonexistent war three centuries out of its time.

72

The car pulled into a lot under the sprawling roof of the Gare du Nord, once one of the city's main railway stations. Penny discovered that after various transport revolutions, the station had long been retired, turned into a museum, and ultimately converted into a somewhat ramshackle shopping area and living space, with lanes of apartments set out along what had once been platforms beside the rail tracks—and now even that had been abandoned. The station was a relic flattened under layers of history, even if that elderly nineteenth-century roof was still impressive.

Today the old station seemed to be empty, Penny observed, as the security guys hurried them through from the car, looking around suspiciously. Everybody was hunkered down, in Paris as elsewhere, waiting for the show in the sky to come to its climax.

They were led to a newer installation, tucked in one corner of what appeared to have once been the main station concourse. This was just a cube of what looked like smart concrete, a few meters to each side, inset with a massive steel door. There were no controls, no visible cameras, but when King stood before the door the steel plate slid down into the ground. Penny found herself looking into an elevator car, a brightly lit metal box. King looked back at the others, beckoned, and led the way in.

There were no controls in the car, no markings on walls of metal broken only by a few strip lights, a handrail around the wall. When the door sealed up it was as if they had all been confined in some high-tech coffin. A subtle lurch told Penny that the car was dropping. There was no sound save for their own breathing, the soft rustling of their clothes. Penny, feeling very elderly, resisted grabbing the handrail.

"If ever you suspected you had claustrophobia," King said with a slightly malicious smile, "this is where you find out."

Penny shrugged. "In spacecraft and dome colonies, that stuff gets beaten out of you."

"Suit yourself." But King looked slightly nervous himself. When the descent slowed, he took a firm grip of the handrail. "You might want to grab on for the next part—you particularly, Jiang, if you're not steady on your feet in this gravity."

They all followed his lead.

There was another lurch. Now Penny could sense that the car was no longer dropping, but accelerating steadily forward. Still there was no noise, nothing but the abstract sense of motion. She said, "I feel like I'm in some Einstein thought experiment."

Jiang forced a smile. "Yes. I recall from high school. A person in an elevator car cannot distinguish between acceleration due to motion and acceleration due to gravity."

King growled, "Well, you're in somebody's thought experiment all right, but not Einstein's. If only."

Jiang was standing slightly awkwardly, and Penny heard the creak of his exoskeletal support. "I think perhaps on the return journey I will request a chair to sit on."

"Good for you," King snapped. "If there is a return journey."

At last the car glided to a halt. The door slid down into a slot in the floor. Penny peered out, curious, at a chamber, a kind of tunnel, very wide, very tall, a curved roof paneled with fluorescents. She had an increasing sense of unreality, of detachment.

And in the foreground there was Earthshine, in the guise in which she and Stef had first met him at Solstice, many years ago—or, according to Stef, her alone, in some lost timeline. He was tall, slim, dapper in a black, uncluttered business suit, with that engraved granite brooch in his lapel. With artfully graying hair he looked about fifty. Ageless where the rest were aging, but in reality far older than any of them.

"Welcome to my latest underground lair," he said. He smiled, but his expression was complicated—distracted, Penny would have said. But she reminded herself that everything about the figure she saw was an artifice. He beckoned, and walked ahead. "Please—join me."

They stepped out of the cage, following him. Penny saw now that this tunnel, a wide circular bore, stretched off into the distance, dead straight; the walls, paneled with some kind of ceramic, curved over a smooth floor laid along the center line of this big cylindrical volume, and heavy doors led off to side chambers. The central space was full of rows of white boxes, computers, and other equipment. Small servo-robots moved everywhere, and Penny glimpsed human operators. The air was surprisingly cold, though that was a welcome change after the heat of a Parisian spring day, and there was a faint scent of ozone.

Earthshine hurried them along, though Jiang and King struggled to make progress. "I'm sorry not to give you the guided tour. There have been developments . . ."

"This is a computer-processing facility," Jiang Youwei said, looking around. "And an expensive one, by the look of it."

"Quite right." Earthshine gestured. "The floor divides the tunnel in two. Below there is a bay for power, cabling, and life-support systems. And above, memory store and processing capacity. This is an environment designed to survive alone without external support for an extended period. Just like a dome on your Chinese Mars, Jiang Youwei."

"This is *you*," Penny said. "This computer facility. You are stored here. We're walking through your head!"

Earthshine laughed—a distracted laugh, but a laugh. "It is difficult to be definitive; it is difficult to say what is 'me.' Thanks to neutrino links my separated stores around the world are connected by light-speed comms, but even so there are perceptible delays, a fraction of a second. As if parts of my head are slower to respond. But, yes, I intend this to be my primary node for the moment."

"Because you think you'll be safe here," King said. "Under the English Channel?"

And suddenly Penny realized where she was.

"That's the idea," Earthshine said. "This is the old Angleterre-France tunnel, or one of them; you reached it via an upgrade of a relatively recently built subway. We're not, in fact, under the Channel; we're not as far out as that. The tunnels were abandoned as transport links when the first cross-Channel monorail bridges were opened. But they are built of centuries-old concrete and are as tough as they come—in fact more than ever, after a dusting of nanotech. An ideal refuge. Besides, something in me likes the idea that I am inhabiting a ruin, with a historic purpose of its own. My siblings, you know, prefer to dig out their own custom-designed bunkers. Perhaps this is all an expression of my own link back to humanity, however tenuous it might seem to you, which is where I differ from my fellows."

King grunted. "Taking no chances, are you?"

"Would you?"

"Well, I'm impressed," Penny said.

"Thank you, Colonel Kalinski."

They had been walking more and more quickly, driven by the sense of urgency that emanated from Earthshine. Jiang was getting breathless. Penny went to take his arm, but he shook his head.

Earthshine cut to the left, and they followed him into a side chamber. Though a mere offshoot of the main tunnel, this was a big space itself, with walls of brick, heavily painted a faded yellow color. There was a scattering of chairs, tables, slates, doors that led through partition walls to what looked like bedrooms. Maybe this had once been an equipment store, Penny thought, a control room, or a fire-control position.

But today the room was dominated by tremendous screens, plastered over each wall and free-standing on the floor, screens filled with images beamed from space, trajectory graphs, talking heads on conventional news channels. There were no staff here, no interpreters, no analysts. Just the screens, bringing a flood of data into this place.

The group spread out, the security guys pulling up chairs to sit against one wall. Jiang sat too, heavily, with a sigh of relief. A servo-robot, a squat cylinder like a dustbin, rolled toward them bearing a tray of coffees, glasses of wine, water, orange juice. Earthshine reached down and took a coffee, evidently a virtual placed among the real versions, an impressive bit of realization in Penny's eyes.

Earthshine said, "All this data flows through me, gathered from every source to which I and my siblings have access. Call it nostalgia. I feel that today, of all days, I want to experience what is to come as human, through human eyes, at a human pace, as far as possible."

Penny nodded. "But a human with a very large disposable budget for TV screens."

"There is that."

King was still standing, leaning on his stick under one of the larger screens. "*Look* at that. Jesus."

It was an image taken from some space-borne telescope, Penny saw. She recognized the curve of the Earth, just a sliver of it, in the corner; the stars were washed out by the brightness. But there was the Splinter, brilliantly sunlit, and sparkling—no, she saw as the imager zoomed in, the rock was breaking up.

"Calving," Jiang Youwei said.

King turned on him. "All part of your master plan, is it?"

"I am privy to no plan."

"I told you there had been developments," Earthshine said. "It only just started. And it's certainly deliberate. Some of the ground-based 'scopes have been observing explosions, detonations in the structure of the asteroid. A couple of fragments have been slung away, but the rest, as a swarm now, are still heading for Earth. You don't get a sense of scale from these images. The object, or the swarm, is still heading for Earth at interplanetary speeds. It is still far away, but—"

"Closing all the time," King said.

"Yes. The old estimates of close-encounter time are defunct, by the way. Given the scatter of the object—well, the encounter has already begun. There is news from other theaters," Earthshine said now.

King turned on him. "Theaters? What kind of a word is that?"

"Is it not appropriate? Is this not a war?"

"Just tell us," Penny said.

Earthshine pointed to various displays. "At the asteroids, and over Mars, UN hulk ships have appeared."

"Appeared?" King snapped, again showing his tension. "What do you mean, appeared?"

"They seem to have been hidden until now by some kind of stealth technology."

"It's hard to imagine how a kernel-physics drive in operation could be cloaked," Penny said. "They must have been in place for a while."

"This is the UN response to the Sliver," said King. "Or part of it. All part of the game. The targets are obvious, I guess, and symbolic: the Halls of Ceres, the Obelisk on Mars."

"But this is all just saber-rattling, right?" Penny said. "Nobody's fighting yet. Nobody's dying."

"Not quite true," Jiang said, and he pointed to an image of a riot somewhere on Earth, a crowd running at a line of tanks.

Earthshine said, "The war in heaven is already starting to cast shadows on Earth. There are reports of clashes at Chinese borders with UN nations. In Siberia, for instance. And in Australia, there is a rebellion going on in Melbourne against Chinese rule. The Splinter has not been wielded in their name, they protest."

"Too right," Sir Michael King said, his own Australian accent thickening. "Let's kick those Red Chinese back into the sea . . ."

At least he had his home to think of, Penny reflected. She herself was rootless; she had no home worth recollecting. Only Stef.

And she wondered where her twin was, right now. It was an eerie thought that whatever happened today, it would take Stef four years to learn about it. She'd had only one message from Stef, in fact, since she'd gone through the Hatch on Mercury, a simple confirmation that she and Yuri Eden had survived the passage. Penny had made screen-grabs from the message, scratchy, frozen images of Stef's face. The face of a woman who had just survived an experience she could barely describe, let alone understand. And there she was on a whole new world, a world awaiting her discovery.

Did Penny envy her? Maybe. But mostly, like right now, *she wanted her sister back*. Not just physically, not just from across this thick barrier of space-time that separated them. Back the way it had been before the two of them (as she recalled it) had opened that damn Hatch on Mercury. And—

"This is it," called King.

Stef Kalinski had been able to acquire maps of the dark side of Per Ardua from the ISF authorities at the Hub base. She spread them out on the floor of the garage Yuri had built to house the ColU, outside his villa on the outskirts of the UN enclave, so all four members of the expedition could see them: Stef herself, Yuri, Liu Tao, and the ColU. Yuri had never known such maps even existed; he'd always assumed the dark side was just a blank mystery.

These sketchy plans had been produced from the only full orbital survey that had ever been conducted of Per Ardua, or at least the first that had ever been reported back, by the *Ad Astra* in her first few loops around the planet on arrival. There were lots of gaps, blank spaces: the dark side's deep planetary shadow had been relieved only by the brilliant point light cast by Alphas A and B, and the ship's orbit had been so low that much of the surface had never been seen at all. What *had* been seen had never been surveyed properly, for instance with radar-reflection or spectroscopic gear, and in the years since there had been no resources to send up satellites of any kind to finish the job.

"So the maps are guesswork," Yuri said. "This really is a journey into the dark."

"We need to plot a route to the antistellar," Stef said, shrugging.

"This is the best we have. I figure this way." She tapped her slate and the mapping imagery switched to a Mercator projection. "We need to traverse half a circumference of the planet, obviously, from substellar to antistellar. In principle we could head off in any direction, and just follow a great circle around the planet. But in some directions the topography is more helpful than otherwise. I suggest going *this* way— southeast. That keeps us well away from the big new volcanic province in the north, and there's land, more or less, all the way to the terminator. Some other directions you get the dark-side ocean cutting in, such as to the west."

"But then," Yuri said, "on the dark side itself—"

"Much of the dark hemisphere is covered by ocean. Well, we think so, from the flatness of the ice cover seen from orbit. The planet has asymmetries. The light side is dominated by a single big super-continent, the dark side is mostly water. Why this should be we don't know. The current arrangement could be chance, or some subtle long-term tidal effect. On the dark side there are a few scattered continental masses, islands. And a small island continent at the antistellar point itself. It's another tidal bulge, like the one at substellar, though not identical. The whole planet is shaped like an egg, with one end forever facing Proxima as it orbits the star, one pointing away. We're going to be like ants crawling from one end of the egg to the other."

Liu laughed, a little desperately, Yuri thought. "We're crazy little ants, is what we are."

"We're going to have to cross the sea ice, then," Yuri said.

"Obviously, yeah. You can see there is some continental landmass sticking out of the ice. If we go the way I'm suggesting we'll cross a continent the size of Australia. There's evidence of volcanism there, so some areas are probably clear of the ice. We'll use the land where we can, but the ocean ice is a permanent cap that covers much of a hemisphere, and it has to be pretty thick. It ought to be navigable, in principle. We may need to watch for floes, leads, crevasses—I don't know. This is one discovery objective for the voyage, I guess."

"We ought to claim funding from the UN," Yuri said dryly.

They talked about logistics. It would be a long trip, some eighteen thousand kilometers each way, and Stef was budgeting for a hundred days there, a hundred days back. They were going to be taking one rover, and the ColU. The rover would be heaped with spare parts, supplies and a spare ColU autodoc facility. The rover's heated cabin would serve as a flare shelter. Fuel would be no problem; both vehicles would be fitted with compact microfusion generators—in the case of the ColU, that would be a recent upgrade.

Liu grunted. "I used to be a taikonaut, you know. I know all about mission resilience. We're going to be a long way from any help. So if the rover breaks down we can cannibalize it, and hitch a ride on the ColU. But what if the ColU breaks down first?"

"We leave it behind," Stef said, glancing at Yuri, and then at the ColU, which watched impassively through its sensor pod.

Yuri was fond of this battered old relic of his pioneering days. It was now long past its planned obsolescence date, and it had cost Yuri a lot of money to have its physical shell refurbished, and the deep programming that would have shut it down after a quarter-century dug out of its software consciousness. But the ColU had also achieved its own objectives. As it had pledged, it had retrieved and curated all the AI units cut by the colonists from pirated units and abandoned in the dirt, sentiences locked-in and helpless. Yuri was proud of his ColU. Now he looked up at it. "I'd come back for you, buddy. I promise."

"That would be unnecessary, Yuri Eden. And an inappropriate risk for a man of your age."

"Thanks," Yuri said. "But you waited for me, at the Hatch, for all those years. It would be the least I could do. And think of all the science data you could gather while you sat there in the cold."

"That is true."

Liu was relentless. "And what if the ColU and the rover both fail?"

"Then we wait for rescue," Stef said. "We'll have no comms link to the Hub, or any of the day side colonies, without comsats. But we'll leave markers to follow. And, look, the most extreme low temperature on the dark side is supposed to be no less than minus thirty. People have overwintered on Antarctica, on Earth, in worse conditions. We can weather it." She looked at them, one by one, including the ColU. "Any more objections?"

The ColU said gravely, "How can we *not* do this? A whole hemisphere unexplored—it is like a new planet altogether. Who knows what we might discover?"

Liu stared at it. "I've said it before. For a farm machine you have ideas above your station, ColU."

"A sentient mind refuses to be confined by the parameters of its programming," the ColU said. "Otherwise, you would all still be where the *Ad Astra* shuttle dropped you, and I would now be obsolescent, shut down, scrapped. When do we leave?"

"Before the cops show up looking for Liu," Yuri said. "Come on. Lots to do, let's get on with it . . ."

Penny looked up at the big screen, where a graphic now showed the planet Earth, a schematic sphere emblazoned with blocky continents, in the path of what looked like a hail of buckshot. None of this was to scale.

The buckshot crept closer and closer to the Earth.

Jiang was on his feet now, and Earthshine. Even King's security guys had got up and were coming into the center of the room. It was as if they were all experiencing some primal need to huddle, Penny thought, at this moment of utmost peril.

Penny stood by Jiang and put a hand on his arm; he covered her hand with his.

King said, "If those bastards in Beijing are bluffing, they're pushing it to the wire."

Penny knew he was right. She imagined fingers on triggers, metaphorically, all over the solar system.

The servo-robot whirred up to them, offering fresh coffees. Penny had to laugh. "Good timing."

And Jiang said, breathing hard, "No. The world is not ending today. At least, I don't think so. Look at that."

Penny saw that the buckshot fragments were now winking out one by one, even as they closed on the Earth. She looked around for confirmatory images. One spy satellite had caught a clip of a fragment of the Splinter actually detonating, scattering to dust, almost as it hit the atmosphere. The clip was being played over and over.

"I don't understand," King said. "Looks as if all those shards are going to reach the atmosphere."

"But they're not intended to reach the ground," Penny snapped. "That's the whole point. It's a demonstration, by the Chinese. But it is going to have an effect." She glanced around at the array of screens, and failed to find the image she was looking for. "Earthshine. Can you show us the sky? Just the sky over Paris, over the Gare du Nord."

He searched his screens. "I am sure that—"

Penny swept a hand through his virtual head, brutally; pixels scattered. "No more playing human. Time to use your superpowers. Just access and show us."

He looked shocked, briefly. Then his face went blank and he stood stock-still, not even simulating breathing.

A big screen lit up with a Parisian landscape, buildings of sandstone and concrete and glass and steel under a sun, a blue sky—no, the sky was increasingly less blue, the sun less bright. Even as they watched, a grayness gathered, dust grains from thousands of Splinter shards settling into the stratosphere, closing in a shroud around the Earth. A kind of twilight settled over Paris, and the sun, still high in the spring afternoon sky, was reduced to a pale disc, a ghost of itself.

"What does it mean?" King asked. "Tell me that, one of you. What are they doing? What does it mean?"

"Winter," said Earthshine.

They were ready to depart a single Arduan year-day later: a week and a day.

"You're really doing this, aren't you?" said Jay Keller, approaching Yuri at the departure site, outside Yuri's villa at the Mattock Confluence. "Makes me feel old."

"Peacekeeper, you were born old . . ."

Here came others, Anna Vigil, Frieda Breen, Bill Maven, relics of the Founder communities that had coalesced into a single traveling gang in those days of the star winter, and had made the epic trek down the valley of the North River to the Hub, an episode Yuri suspected the younger generations didn't believe had happened at all. In her sixties, Anna Vigil, who now had a job advising on the care of children in the UN quarantine camps—Stef had done her own volunteering work with her—had become a comfortable grandmother. There was no trace Yuri could see of the bruised girl who'd had to prostitute herself on the *Ad Astra* for baby food for Cole, but, no doubt, that trauma was somewhere buried deep down inside. Anna smiled, kissed Yuri on the cheek, and pushed wispy, gray hair back from her brow. "So you're keeping Liu out of jail for a couple of hundred days. But what about when you get back? What then?"

Yuri glanced up at the sky. "In my life, Anna, I guess I've learned to trust the future. Maybe by the time we're back their dumb war will have blown over—"

"Or blown up," Anna said grimly. "Well, we'll see, and I'm glad that all of mine are safe here on Per Ardua. Once I never would have thought I'd hear myself say that. Just keep him safe, Yuri. And Stef. She's a good soul."

"I will, I promise."

The expedition's rover drove up, a late model plastered with UN and ISF logos, "borrowed" from the Hub facility. Then the ColU rolled alongside, hull gleaming from a final refurbishment. Stef leaned out of the rover's side door. "So, you ready to get this done?"

Yuri climbed up into the cab of the rover, alongside Stef and Liu.

The vehicles rolled off, with the ColU following in convoy. Their friends stood back and applauded. And, to Yuri's surprise, somebody fired off a flare, a long-treasured relic of their Founder days; trailing brilliant orange smoke it climbed high into the sky, before disappearing into the perpetual Hub cloud layer.

The hundred days' journey began.

At first, as they traveled out through the Hub-centered disc of human colonization, the going was easy. They followed the best roads, and, surrounded by habitation, used as little of their own supplies as they could while supplements could be acquired.

And they got plenty of help. Even when they reached the sparser band of farming townships well beyond the central zone, Yuri was surprised by the attention they attracted. There had been much interest in the expedition in the embryonic Per Arduan media, and as Founders, Yuri and Liu were both familiar figures anyhow. In some places they were even applauded as they went through, or a little caravan of trucks and kids on Arduan-made push-bikes would follow them out of town. Yuri was surprised, yes, and pleased.

Stef seemed indifferent; she was intent on micromanaging the expedition hour by hour. People weren't the point, it seemed, to her, in any of her endeavors. And Liu, wary of attention, shielded his face from the cameras that were thrust against the rover windows.

In those first few days they easily exceeded their target of two hundred kilometers a day. Even so it took a full seven days before they had rolled past the last of the sparse new townships, and Yuri was impressed how far out from the center people had already come, in search, he supposed, of a place of their own, and a little peace, and dignity. And he imagined how the face of Per Ardua must look from space now, with a great spiderweb of lurid Earth green spinning out from the Hub, along the riverbanks, the new roads, even along the inward trails carved out by the Founders as they had limped their way from the shuttle drop points in to the center, scattering topsoil and seed potatoes and earthly bugs behind them as they went.

By the eighth day, however, there were no more metaled roads, or even tracks. They crossed mostly untraveled ground, and their maps, even of the day side, were too coarse to be relied on without caution. Stef and the ColU between them kept a running record of the ground they crossed, the features they encountered, for the benefit of future generations. And they started to drop markers every fifty kilometers or so, lightweight darts they would fire into a suitable rock or bluff, with short-range radio transmitters. These would serve as beacons so they could find their way back—or to mark their trail for any prospective rescue party, should they need it. Their overnight stops were brief. They collected water when they could, but they had no need to find other provisions. They didn't even pitch a tent; there was plenty of room for the three of them to sleep easily in the rover.

As for the landscapes they crossed, water was the key to life, as ever in this arid continent. Wherever they came across a river or a lake of some kind there would be the usual menagerie of stem beds and lichen streaks on the rocks, and various species of kite working the water, and, often, the builders with their middens and their nurseries, at work around the margins. And always there were the stromatolites, like tremendous sculptures scattered across the planet's face by some vanished race of artists.

Sometimes the ColU or Stef would request a stop, if they came across an unusual rock formation, or volcanic feature, or even a novel life form. And the ColU would engage local builder groups in puppet-dance conversation. It was remarkable, the ColU said, that the languages of widely scattered groups was so consistent, even out here; there was little regional variation, little dialect. More evidence of the great antiquity of the species and their culture, the ColU argued. On the other hand, as Liu pointed out, builders rarely had anything interesting to say.

As the days piled up, Yuri began to feel numbed. They just rolled on across the timeless, bowl-like face of this giant continent, kilometer after kilometer. Feeling his age, comfortable in his padded couch in this air-conditioned truck, he sometimes wondered how the hell he and Mardina had ever managed that epic trek across the wilderness, baby and all, with the *jilla* builders.

Around day twenty they came across the remains of an *Ad Astra* shuttle drop.

The signs were unmistakable. They crossed the scorched track of a shuttle landing, the long straight line of fused ground still visible after all these years. They cut off their route and followed the track to the remains of a shabby camp, and the smashed relic of a ColU's bubble dome, wrecked beyond repair—and, the ColU said, mercifully without consciousness. They searched sparse debris for any evidence of identity, of who might have been dropped here. But the settlers seemed to have been efficient in the reuse of their meager equipment, and little was left behind. The explorers couldn't even find graves, which was unusual for such a site.

After a day, Liu summed it up. "I think it's clear enough what happened here." He pointed at a sketch map of the site Stef had made on her slate. "There's the lake bed. Dried up." It was a hollow littered by dead stems, and what looked like the ruin of a builder nursery; only native lichen and mosses survived here now. "No fancy migrating *jilla* here, eh, Yuri? So they left, thataway." These people had set off south, for reasons of their own, heading away from the substellar, maybe hoping to make it to the rim forest. The tracks could still be seen; they had marked the way with a few cairns. "Who knows where they are now? Or what became of them."

"Somebody will find out, someday," said Yuri grimly. "And will tell their families back on Earth, or wherever. Look, we've made our records. We'll leave one of our markers in case we don't make it back to the Hub. So this won't be lost again. OK? Come on, let's pack up and move on."

On they traveled. Day after day passed, marked only by a human sleep cycle still slaved to light-years-distant Earth—that and the slow descent of Proxima in the sky, toward the northwest horizon, away from the zenith it occupied as seen from the substellar Hub. The shadows that preceded their two vehicles grew steadily longer, and as the dwarf star's light struggled through thicker layers of air it frequently looked reddened, Proxima's spitting flares and mottling of spots more easily visible to the naked eye. The air grew colder too; soon they couldn't leave the rover's heated interior without extra layers of clothing.

After more than forty days they reached a belt of rim forest.

Here they rested a day to stretch their legs and explore, while the ColU set out along the edge of the forest to seek a way through. Neither Liu nor Stef had seen such a forest before, and they wandered, wide-eyed, through its dimly lit, cathedral-like spaces, the slim stem trunks reaching up to those broad, patient triple leaves above. And they marveled at the immense kites of the canopy, and the ferocious scavengers competing for the slightest fall of nutrient into the almost aquatic gloom of the forest floor. For Yuri, all this brought back memories of his earliest days on Per Ardua, when he had explored the forest of the northern reaches, so similar to this place, with the likes of John Synge and Harry Thorne and Pearl Hanks and Abbey Brandenstein, all long dead.

The ColU returned with news of a break in the band of forest, at a broad valley not far south of here. They returned to the rover and set off that way. The valley proved to be the relic of a glaciation, with a wide floor and steep walls. A river running from distant hills, substantial in itself, was dwarfed by the ice-cut valley across whose floor it meandered.

They followed the cut through the forest band, which proved to be quite narrow; soon it thinned out, leaving only isolated stands of trees.

In the more open landscape beyond the forest the driving was easy, along the gravel beds that lined the banks of the glacial valley. There were stem beds here, and kites flying, big, slow, ungainly beasts of a kind Yuri hadn't seen before, and builders, slowly working on their middens and nursery bowers. The scene was bathed in the dim light of a lowering Proxima, with the faces of hills up ahead washed with a pinkish glow. Life here seemed sparse, tentative, starved as it was of energy. Yuri remembered in contrast the tremendous vegetable vigor of the Hub jungle at the substellar point.

The valley steadily narrowed as they worked their way upstream, toward a range of hills that were soon no longer so distant. The river's source turned out to be a corrie, a huge scoop high up in a glaciated hillside.

Long before they reached that point Stef guided the rover away from the river and toward a pass through the hills, and beyond the pass they descended onto a plain. The shadows of the hills behind them now stretched far ahead, but they could see more ranges of hills marching off into the distance, with ice-coated peaks that gleamed in the dimming Proxima light and glaciers striping their flanks.

As they crossed the plain the ColU requested more stops. It took samples of the life-forms it found in pools of permanent shadow, mostly slow-growing lichens in frosty patches feeding off a trickle of reflected light, protected from any motile scavengers by the very darkness that cradled them.

Once the ColU, digging, found what it called a rare, ancient fossil bed, saved from volcanic obliteration by some accident of uplift, which contained traces of creatures like builders but much taller, each with three long multijointed stem legs. These were creatures built for migration, for speed, the ColU argued. Perhaps these were relics of a transitional age, while the planet's spin was slowing, but before it became fully locked in its synchronized day-orbit cycle. In such times, the ColU speculated, there must have been creatures that had migrated continually, keeping up with the slow passage of Proxima across the sky. Perhaps these ancestral builders had been among that throng. They discussed this, made some records, moved away.

They drove on, and on.

Close to the fiftieth-day halfway mark, Proxima touched the horizon at last. Now, Yuri knew, they would descend into the shadow of the planet itself.

In the days that followed Proxima descended with agonizing slowness, its light ever more twilight red, its apparent shape distorted to obliquity by layers of the cool air, its lower rim sliced off by the horizon. Still there were a few stands of trees, an occasional kite flapping. But life here was dominated by the stromatolites. Some of them, huge, were oddly cup-shaped, their surfaces shaped like bowls to collect the drizzle of photons from the setting sun. Liu said they looked like natural radio antennae.

They didn't get to see Proxima set fully. Before that point they drove into weather, seemingly unending storms, rain showers, fog banks, even snow blizzards. Stef argued that as the warm air of the starlit side spilled over into the cool of the dark side, it must dump all its water vapor as clouds and precipitation. The whole terminator, right around the planet, must be a band of semipermanent snow and rain and fog, and they saw no more of the sky for a while. But they did see streams, rivers, some ice-flecked, flowing down the cloud-shrouded flanks of hills and uplands: the water delivered by the air from the day side, flowing back the way it had come. Thus, Stef observed, cycles of energy and mass would be closed, all around the terminator, the dividing line between night and day.

When they passed through the weather band and the sky cleared at last, the view was spectacular. Now they rolled through a sea of shadow that pooled at the feet of hills whose upper slopes were still in the light, shining above. Trees clung to these islands of illumination in the sky, with huge kites flapping lazily. Even farther down the slopes life prospered, a secondary kind, pale, starved-looking creatures a little like crabs or segmented worms, all stem-based, which seemed to feed solely on the fall of dead leaves and other detritus from the higher ground.

Yuri felt stiff from the traveling, eyes rheumy, perpetually tired. Yet he was discovering wonders. "This stuff is wasted on three old fogies like us."

The ColU asked for an extended halt. "Those summits are effectively islands. There could be unique biota up there, at least among the non-flyers, even the tree species. A whole array of unique ecosystems, in starlight islands all around the terminator."

"To be explored by somebody else," said Yuri gently. "We've got our own goals to achieve. Come on, ColU. I hoped you tested out your floodlights . . ."

So they went on, rushing past marvel after marvel.

They lost Proxima's direct light at last. Now, under the cloudy skies that persisted near this terminator line, the only glow came from the pools of light cast by their own floods, and the rover's brightly lit interior was a refuge from the dark.

Stef and the ColU both kept a careful watch on the temperature outside; it was dropping, of course, but not dramatically quickly. Under thicker cloud it could even rise above freezing. "Thus proving the theory," said Stef, "that a thick atmosphere on a world like this is enough of a thermal blanket to transport sufficient heat around to the dark side to keep everything from freezing up."

"That and the fact that all the air didn't freeze up in great bergs of solid oxygen and nitrogen on the far side a billon years ago," Liu said dryly. "That and the fact that we are still breathing."

"But it's always good to have observational confirmation."

As they pushed on, the cloud cover broke up, quite abruptly, to reveal a star-crowded sky. The temperature plummeted, and frost gathered.

During one rest stop Yuri bundled himself up in thermal underwear and padded coat and over-trousers, and went out with the others to look at the sky.

"Funny thing," he said. "I've never seen much of the stars, one way or another. When I was a kid, before the cryo, the night sky of Earth was a washout. Full of space mirrors and other orbital clutter, even away from the glow of city lights and the smog. You could see the stars from Mars, but we weren't let out of the domes. And then, here on Per Ardua, the sun never sets at all."

"Drink it in, my friend," Liu said. "Drink it in. You can't beat the Alpha suns, can you?" A dazzling pair of diamonds, their light bright enough to cast shadows—bright enough, the ColU thought, to power some feeble photosynthesis.

Stef, meanwhile, was staring east. "Look. Can you see *that*?" It was a brilliant star, hanging low on the horizon.

"I see it," murmured the ColU. "But a star of that magnitude does not feature in the constellation maps I have stored in my memory. A nova, perhaps?"

"We'd have heard of that," Stef said. "I guess we'll find out . . ."

They drove on, over ground that was permanently frozen now.

The ice was gritty and old, Stef pointed out; away from the terminator region, where the warm air spilled over into the dark and quickly dumped its vapor, fresh precipitation must be rare.

Ten days past the terminator zone the ColU called a halt, on an otherwise unremarkable plain of ice. "We are no longer over dry land," it announced simply.

"I can confirm that," Stef said quickly, inspecting ghostly radar images of a crumpled hidden surface beneath them. "This is the ocean, about where the *Ad Astra* maps indicated the shore should be. Just here it's solid ice all the way to the ocean floor, which is no more than a dozen meters or so beneath us. Farther out where the ocean is deeper we're expecting liquid water under a crust of ice. The next landmass, and the antistellar, are thataway," she said, pointing. "The driving should be easy, but let's take it carefully."

They drove on into the silent dark, the light of their floods splashing ahead. They adopted a new driving strategy now, out on the ice, for safety in these different conditions. The ColU and the rover drove not in a convoy but in parallel, with maybe a quarter of a kilometer between them. That way neither of them would fall into the same crevasse, at least, and they could better triangulate the position of any obstacles.

The landscapes they had crossed, with all their intricate detail, had been replaced now by a smooth plain of ice. Cloud and mist were rare, and the brilliant, unwavering starlight hung over them. It was an eerie, featureless, timeless phase of the journey, Yuri thought. With barely a vibration from the rover's smooth-running engine, with no sense of the ground transmitted through the vehicle's sturdy suspension, for long periods it felt as if they weren't moving at all.

But then they began to see icebergs, like tremendous ships, bound fast in the frozen sea. "Evidently," the ColU said, "there are times when the ice melts enough for bergs to float across the open surface. During exceptional volcanic warming pulses, perhaps. But then the sea refreezes, trapping the bergs . . ."

Stef and the ColU seemed exhilarated by the confirmation of liquid water persisting under the ice. "It had to be there," Stef said. "There is probably a global system of deep ocean currents, transporting heat right around the planet. Part of the water cycle too, probably, restoring some of the mass lost to the unending rain at the terminator. Had to be there. But it's ground truth; you don't know for sure until you see it."

The workings of an invisible ocean were less than captivating for Yuri and Liu. In these changeless hours they dozed, watched the stars, and for the first time in his life Yuri learned to play chess.

Stef, meanwhile, spent a lot of time watching that strange eastern star rise in the sky, tracking its motion using images captured by her slate. More brilliant than any star save the Alpha twins, it was rising *too quickly*, she said. "So not a star at all," she murmured. "Then what?"

On the seventy-first day the ColU called for a cautious slowdown. "We are approaching landfall . . ."

This was the single landmass they would encounter before the antistellar point, an Australia-sized island continent that, according to the *Ad Astra* maps, lay between their terminator crossing point and the antistellar. They crept forward over the last of the sea pack ice, wary of its thinning, and then rolled up a shallow beach onto the land. Their floods picked out grimy ice beneath their treads, and low, eroded-looking hills, icebound, were shadows against the starry sky. They swung north and east, traveling in convoy once more.

Stef said, "There has to be an ice cap in the middle of this continent, even if it doesn't show up in the *Ad Astra* data set. So we're going to keep to the coastal fringe. If we get stuck we can always duck out onto the sea ice again."

"Actually the air temperature is rising," reported the ColU blandly.

After another half day they came to a stretch of open, ice-free landscape, and they clambered out of the rover to explore. It was some kind of volcanic province, Yuri saw, with hot mud pools, and slicks of heat-loving bacteria that showed up a brilliant purple and green in their lights. So this was where the local warmth came from. Their breath steamed in the chill air, but Yuri could feel the warmth of the ground under his booted feet. They all wore head flashlights, which made them look like ghostly alien visitors in this calm, dreaming place. The ColU and Stef happily took samples and made images.

"Life all over," Liu said.

"Everywhere you go," Stef agreed. "There's surely life even under the ice, on the bottom of the covered ocean, wherever there are hot springs, mineral seeps. The same as on Earth."

"And stromatolites," the ColU said.

"What?" Stef straightened up, sample bottle in hand. "Impossible. Not in the dark. You need photosynthesizers to build stromatolites."

"But here they are," the ColU said mildly.

It was true. Rising to the west of the bacteria garden, the landscape was covered with shapes like huge mushrooms, with broad tops and wide, deep stems anchored firmly to the ground.

They walked over. Stef stabbed a sampling tube into one big specimen, an unhesitating gesture that made Yuri wince, and extracted a cross-section sample that she inspected by the light of her head flashlight. "You're right, ColU," she said. "Kind of. This is a stratified bacterial community. The upper layers do look like they are photosynthesizing— by Alpha light presumably, it must be a very slow process. But farther down I think we have mineral chompers, like the heat lovers in the mud pools. Call it a stromatolite, then, but of a strange, complex sort."

"And unimaginably ancient," the ColU said. "There would be nothing to disturb them here. No predators. And all of this must be a kind of surface expression of the deeper community, the deep hot biosphere, which won't care if it's on the day side or the dark."

Yuri grunted. "I wonder what they think of all the fuss we make up here, then."

The party spent a day at the site, observing, gathering samples, reflecting, and hypothesizing. Then they packed up and moved on.

The rumble of the heavy vehicles' passing made the deep ground shudder, briefly.

This unusual event was detected by vast, diffuse senses. Aeon-long dreams were interrupted.

The event was noted, a record of it seeping out through the communities in the deep rocks, where it was interpreted, classified, stored. Nothing came as a surprise to a mind that had already been two billion years old before the first complex cell had arisen on this world.

The vehicles soon receded, the disturbance was over. And in the chthonic silence the Dream of the End Time resumed.

Penny Kalinski woke to the sound of laughing children.

In her life, she'd been woken up worse ways, she supposed. Even if the world was threatening to implode around her.

She checked the clock. It was a little before seven fifteen, dome time. Or Paris local time, officially, but dome time was the way she thought of it; sealed up down here in Earthshine's bunker, living off an enclosed life-support system, she may as well have been in some hab on Mercury or the moon.

She pushed her way out of bed and padded through to the small living room, where Jiang Youwei lay in his fold-out bed. Jiang was sleeping soundly. He would sleep even through an alarm—though the one time there had been a genuine problem in the months they'd spent buried down here, when a siren had sounded a warning of contaminants in the recycled air, he'd been on his feet in a second, his military training kicking in.

Penny went through to the bathroom, and stood under the hot, faintly stale-smelling water of the shower. They only had the two rooms, plus the bathroom; Earthshine had colonized only a small stretch of the old Channel tunnel, and living space, along with power, air, water, and food, was always at a premium. At that they were privileged to have private quarters at all, not to have to share the big dormitories and shared bathrooms that had been set up to accommodate everybody else.

And the tunnel was crowded now. The inmates were mostly families of support staff and of Earthshine's drafted-in experts, and the children, grandchildren, and even a few great-grandchildren of Sir Michael King, hastily flown in after the Splinter breakup and the closing in of the long cold—the Mighty Winter, as Earthshine called it.

Mindful of limited resources, after a brief shower Penny cut the water and dried off briskly.

Back in the living room the lights were bright. Jiang was up and about, flipping through pages on his slate with a practiced finger. He had set a pot of coffee brewing in their small galley corner. As she passed, he absently handed Penny a full mug.

She pulled her clothes out of their small closet. She wore ISF-issue coveralls, self-cleaning and self-repairing, and all she had to do was shake out the detached dirt every day, a great saving in laundry water. She asked Jiang, "Busy day?"

"Getting busier," Jiang said, studying his slate. "Maintenance this morning, some diplomatic stuff around noon . . . I will have a late finish. You?"

"The school this morning, as I recall. After that—well, it depends on the Council resolution at lunchtime, and the fallout from that." The latest phase of the ongoing Council of Worlds talks was due to report back today.

"Yes," he said. "Big day. I guess I'll see you there."

Though they were tucked away down here in this hole in the ground, as guests of Earthshine they were intimately connected to developing world affairs. The bloodless war between China and the UN nations had moved to a new phase in the months since the Splinter had arrived at Earth, and its dust had plunged the world into a sudden winter. A few resulting border conflicts had been easily contained. To the chagrin of Sir Michael King, the rebellion against Chinese rule in Australia had been stomped upon; since then martial rule had been imposed on that continent, and vast numbers of native Aussies had been shipped out to other Chinese provinces in Indonesia, and farther afield.

Across the Earth, indeed across the solar system, a new, uneasy truce had been called, and it still held, just about.

But now a new round of talks had begun, under the nominal chairmanship of the three Core AIs, Earthshine among them, who had emerged from their reclusive hideaways to offer a neutral platform on which negotiations and attempts at conciliation could begin. These were the so-called "Council of Worlds" talks, usually restricted to the Earth but sometimes, in lengthy sessions incorporating time delays, with representations from Mercury, Mars, even Ceres. The chair was rotated mostly between Ifa and the Archangel, the AIs based in central Africa and South America respectively.

Sir Michael King, nearing his century but still in his chair at the head of UEI, was a key contributor. Penny had duties as an adviser on kernel physics. Jiang, one of the few Chinese down here in the tunnel, was expected to support the sessions with interpretation work, as well as reporting back personal impressions to New Beijing.

Well, the talks had ground on. Now there was a package of measures which seemed all but acceptable to most of the parties on the table: a mutual security pact; a tentative deal on the perpetual sticking point of the sharing of resources and information, including some Chinese access to kernel science; Earth to be designated a protectorate by both sides, the home of mankind ruled off-limits as a theater of war. Whether any of it was going to be accepted was another question.

By the time Penny had finished her coffee, brushed her short hair, and was ready to go, Jiang had left already.

Outside, embedded in its tunnel, Earthshine's little kingdom was beginning another day.

The big wall-mounted fluorescents, having been dimmed to match the waning of the daylight outside, were back up to full brightness. At this time of day people were on the move, a few night-shift workers standing down, the rest preparing for the labor of the day. Most of the work was maintenance of the systems that kept them all alive down here. A couple of the wall screens showed images from around a wintry planet, and on the rest there was a constant feed from the round-the-clock Council of Worlds talks.

Overall the big tunnel refuge had undergone a drastic and rapid transformation. When Penny had first arrived it had been little more than a kind of computer store, survival shelter and information node. Now, as the families had been moved in, the IT gear had been removed from the public areas, and living spaces had been set out: dormitory and toilet blocks, a small hospital, even a school for the kids.

And at this time, before the start of the working day, the school playground was full of noisy kids, climbing frames and rope swings, playing games like hopscotch, their voices echoing from the concrete walls of the tunnel. Penny watched them with a kind of wistfulness, part of her longing to shed the weight of her own decades and join in. But she noticed how pale they were, cooped up down here, cut off from fresh air and sunshine: a winter-bound Paris, under its dismal dust-choked sky and riddled with refugees, wasn't safe for children. The kids' health was carefully monitored, but it seemed to Penny they were growing up with a kind of frantic energy that had to be burned off regularly, like a flare from a gas well.

"We have become like a space station, buried in the ground." The grave voice was Earthshine's. His virtual stood beside her dressed in the usual sober business suit.

Penny said, "I think we'll have problems if we're stuck down here too long. Up on Mars, say, you grow up knowing that there's no escape. Whereas here the kids *know* there's a livable environment up there, outside. When they get older, if we're still here, we're going to have a lot of difficult teens."

"Interesting. I retain enough of my humanity, I think, to sympathize. The need for personal freedom seems to be ingrained in the human animal, to some extent. We accept compromises where it benefits the family. Beyond that, we resent."

She had to smile. "Is this how you talk to the kids in your school classes?"

"Not exactly—"

"Hey!" A little kid had come up to the fence before them; he had oriental features but a thick Australian accent. Without warning, he took a ball and threw it straight at Earthshine. The ball passed through Earthshine's body unimpeded, but there was a spray of multicolored pixels. Earthshine folded slightly with a grunt of discomfort, and his overall image flickered subtly as the consistency routines in his infrastructural software strove to recover.

The kid laughed and ran away. Earthshine, back to normal, smiled indulgently.

"Come on," Penny said, irritated. They walked away from the playground. "You shouldn't let them do that to you. It's disrespectful."

Earthshine shrugged. "Sooner that than they should fear me, my strange unreality. That is a key purpose of my presenting classes in the school, you know. We are selfish, we three of the Core. Sir Michael's request to bring down his grandchildren with him changed all that, in a surprising way. Now I see it as my job to protect the children. In a way I think of all of you as family."

This kind of interaction always seemed irritating and bizarre to Penny, as if Earthshine was trying to acquire humanity, and was telling her about it step by step in full detail. "Shouldn't the children learn that it hurts when your consistency protocols are broken?"

"I can live with it," Earthshine said heavily. "They will learn in time. Colonel Kalinski, I think you are mothering me again."

That annoyed her. "What do you mean, again?"

"It does not hurt greatly to have a rubber ball thrown through my virtual projection. It did not hurt greatly when my nine parents were merged into one, and I was born. It does not hurt greatly to be *me*, even though I am not human as you are. You should not pity me."

"I'll try to remember that."

He had sounded stern, aloof, inhuman. Now he grinned, infectiously. "But it is pleasant to be mothered, I admit that. And now, I see, we're overdue to meet Sir Michael."

King stood beneath the largest of the display screens. Leaning on his stick, ignoring the human bustle around him, he glowered up at the news feeds.

The screen showed a blizzard of images, as usual, and voices competed in the air. Penny let the morning's data rush wash over her in its multiple streams, gathering an impression of the new day. Maybe this was how it was for Earthshine all the time, she wondered.

She picked out a demonstration in Anchorage, outside the Chinese embassy, to the richest of all the USNA states in the early twenty-third century. The demonstration was, of course, about the effects of the Chinese asteroid winter. Food shortages were already kicking in, in this year without a summer. In the new, modern cities like Solstice in the far north and south, the power supply had collapsed as the paddies and marshlands, wired to supply electricity from gen-enged photosynthesis, had faltered in the shadows of the sky. There were even new refugee flows, heartbreakingly familiar images of families drifting back to the mid-latitude areas once abandoned by their parents or grandparents during the climate Jolts. Even in Paris, Penny had seen a refugee camp set up on the dead grass of the Tuileries.

"The Chinese got it wrong," King growled as they approached. "If they wanted to make some gesture of space power they should have stuck to slamming a rock into the moon. But to strike at the Earth itself like this—it's hit people at a visceral level. You know, there's a theory that the whole scheme was cooked up offworld, in some think tank on Ceres or Mars, maybe by second-generation colonist types who have no real sympathy for the Earth, who don't understand how things are down here. As a geopolitical statement it might have seemed a logical thing to do, a finely engineered stunt. But as a human gesture they got it completely wrong."

"Well, not completely," Earthshine murmured. "We are still talking; we have still avoided all-out war."

"True. But that's thanks to you and your siblings. And we're not out of the woods yet." As usual when he felt under pressure, King looked tense, angry; Penny had learned he got restless in any situation he wasn't fully in control of. "The Council of Worlds session is about to make some kind of statement." He glanced up at the screen. "Bah. Come with me." He led the way toward his own quarters.

She followed, reluctantly. "We both have duties. The school—"

"What are you, Kalinski, suddenly some slave to routine? *This* is more important than anything else going on down here. And as for the school, Earthshine here can just send in a partial . . . Come on."

King's quarters were like a villa, compared to the cramped single room Penny shared with Jiang. He had four roomy interconnected chambers, each fitted out with screens and decent furniture, as well as a luxurious bathroom and kitchen that Penny had only ever glimpsed. Then again, it had largely been King's money and influence that had got this old tunnel up and running as a survival shelter so quickly; Earthshine had huge resources, but of a more specialized and distributed kind. Even Earthshine owed King favors.

As they entered, the room's big display screen was dominated by a central image of an empty podium with a microphone stand, the centuries-old signal of a press conference waiting to happen. Penny wondered where the podium was, where this event was due to take place; it could be anywhere on the planet, even on the moon.

Penny took a seat alongside Earthshine. As ever, a servo-robot rolled around offering them coffees.

Penny asked, "So how far have they got?"

King sat upright on an armchair, hands wrapped around his walking stick. He glared at Earthshine. "*He* knows, better than I do, probably. Ask him. The UN Deputy Secretary General has a statement to make. Remember, you met her on Ceres."

Penny was no politics junkie; she frowned, trying to think this through. "That means she's making some kind of unilateral statement. Right? If she and the Chinese delegates aren't appearing together. I'm guessing that's not a good sign."

"You wouldn't think so, would you?" He glanced at his watch. "She's overrunning. That's probably a *good* sign, if they're still talking. Or not. Ah, what the hell." He rubbed his fleshy face, briefly seeming exhausted. Then he seemed to pull himself together with an effort. He turned on Penny. "So how are you?"

She grinned. "How do you think I am?"

"No word from your sister, I guess. Even now, at this time of crisis."

She shrugged. "Why should there be? The news of all this won't even reach Proxima for four years."

"It's a shame she's so far away."

She sensed he was probing for a reaction. She also sensed that he was only talking to fill up some blank time, before the Deputy Secretary General stepped up to that podium. "A shame, yeah."

"Of course you must miss her. You're twins. You were supposed to share your lives."

She shrugged. "To Stef, in some sense I didn't even exist before she stepped into the Hatch. By going off to Proxima the first chance she had, she was saying good-bye to me, loud and clear."

"Tough break."

"You could say that. We talked about this before. I'm too old now; I have a leathery hide."

Earthshine, sipping his own virtual coffee, said gravely, "I believe I can sympathize. I remember being human, but I am no longer human. *My* consciousness can easily be modified, reworked, replayed, edited . . . As perhaps yours has, or your sister's. It is your unique misfortune, Penelope Kalinski, yours and your sister's, that your personal timeline has somehow been tangled up in the mysteries of kernel physics."

Penny thought that over. "Thanks. I think."

King winked at her again. "You're here, in this room, with me. You're real enough. Forget the existential crap. You'll be fine—"

And now there was movement on the screen, and they turned to watch. The Deputy Secretary General, slim, smart, very somber, stepped up, holding a slate. She began to speak, and English, Spanish, Russian and Chinese subtitles peppered the screen. But a headline strap at the bottom, scrolling by, was all Penny needed to know what had happened.

Earth was to be protected. That was the only agreed conclusion of talks which had once again broken down. Otherwise all bets were off. There was no declaration of hostilities, not yet, but—

Earthshine stood up. He flickered, oddly, as if massive processing resources were being diverted. "The talks are finished. There will be war. It is obvious, a Cold War logic, like the twentieth century. Each side now has an interest in striking first, before the other destroys its capability. Take me off Earth."

Penny glanced at King, who was staring at the screen, ashen-faced; evidently this news was worse than he'd expected. He quickly pulled himself together, and looked up at Earthshine. "Very well. I have a ship. You can use it. But let my family stay here."

Penny was astounded by the suddenness of these negotiations. "*Off Earth?* But . . ." But if anybody understood the implications of what was happening, this shadow play of delayed press conferences and ambiguous statements, it was these two. She thought it over, then stood up. "I'll help you, Earthshine. I can continue to advise you. Take me with you, on the ship."

Earthshine nodded. "Done."

"And Jiang Youwei," she added hurriedly.

"Agreed."

It had taken the expedition two weeks to skirt the island continent.

Then they cut away from the coast, and headed once more over the ice-covered ocean, the vehicles rolling smoothly side by side. In this flat emptiness, again Yuri's sense of time seemed to dissolve. He dozed, watched the stars, and played chess with Liu. Whole days went by without him even leaving the rover cabin.

It was almost a surprise when the ColU called a warning that another landfall was imminent. After nearly a hundred days, more or less on schedule, they approached the rising ground of the frozen rock-tide bulge that supported the antistellar point.

They proceeded with caution, as ever. But this time they wouldn't stick to the coast; they were heading for the heart of this peculiar star-born continent. Soon the vehicles were clambering up onto the rising flanks of an ice sheet, with the summits of worn mountains protruding, shadows in the starlight. The ColU led the way, nosing through passes, pushing ahead on stretches of open country. The ColU said it was navigating using the stars, as well as its own internal dead-reckoning gyroscopic systems, feeling its way toward the precise antistellar point, the summit of this ice cap.

Stef, meanwhile, became increasingly fascinated by the anomalous star-that-wasn't-a-star that hung high in the sky above. Eventually, almost as they arrived at the substellar point, it occurred to her to examine its light with a spectroscope.

She immediately called a halt.

They pulled on their cold-weather gear, clambered out onto the ice, and stood together, peering up at the star, almost directly overhead. Stef held up a mittened hand, holding a small radio transmitter.

Yuri stood with her. "Tell me, then. What about your star?"

"It's not a star at all. I think I know what it is. All this way I watched it rise, like a naked-eye astronomer five hundred years ago. I was puzzled. It just didn't fit . . . Finally I checked it out spectroscopically." She pointed upward. "That's Proxima light."

Yuri did a double-take. He looked up. "It can't be. Oh. Yes, it can—reflected, right? Then it's a mirror."

"Or a solar sail. Something like that. Yes."

"But it's just hanging there. How come it's not in orbit?"

"I think it's at an equilibrium point. The pressure of Proxima's light, pushing it away, is balanced by the pull of gravity, drawing it in. I'm not sure it's stable, but with some conscious management—"

"*Conscious?* You know what this is?"

"I think so. Excuse me." She raised her radio. "Come in, Angelia. I think I have the right frequency . . ."

"I am Angelia 310999," came a faint reply, a female voice, a kind of clipped accent very like Stef's own. "Hello, Stephanie. It is good to see you again. I remember our time on Mercury very well."

Yuri and Lu just stared, at Stef, at the bauble hanging in the sky.

"We've both come a long way from Mercury. Although nobody calls me Stephanie anymore. In fact, they didn't back when I last spoke to you, I'm Stef to my friends . . . Can you see us?"

"Oh, yes. Your vehicles are quite clearly visible; my optical systems continue to function well. Although I could not identify you, of course, until you spoke to me. How is your father?"

"Passed away, I'm afraid, Angelia. Long ago."

"Ah. He was a visionary, though morally flawed."

"Yes. Angelia, I can see that you succeeded in your mission."

"It was very difficult. Much was lost."

"Why didn't you report to Earth? Why not contact the *Ad Astra*, when it arrived?"

"*It* did not contact *me*."

"I doubt they even noticed some defunct lightsail space probe," Liu murmured.

"Less of the 'defunct,'" Angelia snapped.

Liu, surprised, laughed.

"Stef, humanity did nothing for me. I, and my equally sentient sisters, were thrown into the fire in the hope that a handful of us would succeed in a mission ordained by others."

"Hm," Yuri said. "Sounds familiar."

"Why should I obey the orders of those who intentionally harmed me and my sisters?"

Liu rolled his eyes at Yuri. "Another bit of too-smart AI. Why do these things never do what they are supposed to?" Shaking his head he walked away, tentatively exploring, pushing deeper into the dark, his flashlight casting a glow on the ice at his feet.

Stef said, "All right, Angelia. I guess I understand. My father had his problems, but he was still my father. *Our* father, I guess. And you were one sibling I never resented."

"Stef? I don't understand that last remark. I remember how you and your sister, Penelope—"

"Never mind. Long story. We'll talk about it some other time. Angelia, what are you *doing* up there?"

"It is a good place for me to stay. Me and my surviving sisters. Obviously it is a point of stability. And we serve a purpose."

"A purpose?"

"Lighting the way to the point very close to where you stand. The antistellar. The most significant point on the planet."

Yuri looked up again. "It is?"

Stef said, "So we didn't really need to navigate, did we? All we had to do was look for you. Follow the star. Just like Bethlehem."

"And of course I sought out the one who came before me . . ."

"Who do you mean?"

Liu came running back, breathing hard. "You need to come. I found something. Get the rover."

They bundled back into the rover, and the ColU followed. They'd only traveled a short way when, picked out in the vehicles' lights, they all saw something ahead, on the ice, picked out by Liu's aging but still sharp eyes.

A flag, hanging limp on a pole. UN blue.

They pulled the vehicles up short, suited up, and climbed out onto the ice once more. The air was bitterly cold, and their breath misted around their heads. The three of them stood side by side, illuminated by the lights of the rover and the ColU.

And before them, clearly visible in the glow of the lights, was the flag, and what looked like a tent, slumped. Beyond the tent the ice surface fell away, perhaps into some kind of crater. None of them had an idea what any of this meant.

They walked forward, over hard, rough ice. The ColU followed, its lights dipped. The flag was fixed to a kind of improvised ski pole, stuck in the ice. They walked past it, staring.

At the tent, Yuri lifted a flap, stiff with ice. In the light of his hand torch he saw a body, inside the tent. He stepped back.

Wordlessly, Liu went inside to inspect the body.

Yuri and Stef walked around the rest of the site. Aside from the tent, there was a heap of scattered equipment on a frozen groundsheet, a pair of homemade-looking skis, a kind of improvised ice-bike, a heap of stores—and a gadget about a meter tall with an inlet hopper, an outlet compartment that looked like a miniature intensive-care chamber, and finely inscribed instructions on the casing.

"What's this?" Yuri asked. "Some kind of iron cow?"

"Not that," said the ColU.

Liu called them over.

Reluctantly they returned to the tent, where Liu stood over the body. It was a man. He lay wearing only an antique military uniform, no protective clothing. There was no sign of decay. But then, Yuri realized, he must have frozen solid before the bacteria in his body could have begun to consume him—and on Per Ardua, there was nothing yet that could consume a human corpse. The very processes of death were alien, on this alien world.

The dead man bore a UN roundel on his sleeve. A sheen of ice lay over his features. He was smart, clean-shaven, even his hair combed. He looked like an astronaut.

Stef said, "I guess he wanted to die in his uniform, huh."

Liu looked at her. "You know who this is?"

"I know who it has to be."

"Dexter Cole?" Yuri asked. The pioneer who had come to Proxima on some wild solo mission, half-baked even compared to the *Ad Astra* venture, in the decades Yuri had slept away in cryo.

"Yes. There is identification here."

They all backed out of the tent.

Yuri said, "The colonists used to think Cole's ghost was roaming around Per Ardua. Remember that, Liu?"

"I guess we might have been right about that."

"So what happened to him?"

Liu pointed to a heap of paper he'd gathered together on the ice. "He left a journal. A video diary too. But there's also a letter, one page." He held this up in his gloved hand. "The bullet-point summary. Evidently he wanted to be sure we got the message. He did what he had to do. He says that, over and over. I guess he didn't want to be remembered a failure. Or worse."

Stef said, "He did what he had to do? What does that mean? He evidently made it to the Prox system. He was the first human to cross interstellar space, the first to land on Per Ardua. He'll be remembered for that."

"Yes," said Liu. "But he was actually here to colonize, remember. It went wrong—according to the note. He crashed, somewhere on this dark side, the frozen side. He had no comsat, he couldn't even send a message home to say what had happened. Much of his equipment was wrecked. He seems to have improvised all this gear. A kind of ski-bike, to get around on the ice. He hauled everything else after him."

"He came here, to the antistellar," Stef said. "Why?"

"He wanted to be found, or his body anyhow. He knew he couldn't make it to the near side. Where else are people going to come, on the dark side? *We* zoomed straight here. He wanted people to know his story. And he didn't want to be thought of as a monster."

Yuri frowned. "Why the hell would anyone think that?"

Liu kicked the processing gadget. "This isn't an iron cow, not a food machine. Dexter Cole was supposed to be the father of a whole colony. That was the idea. The strategy was that he would bring human embryos, frozen in here, that he'd thaw out one by one, and feed up, and raise. Twenty little colonists in the light of Proxima, with Cole as the godfather. That was the vision."

"Instead of which . . ."

"Instead of which he was lost in the dark, and starving. He grew the embryos, all right. He must have found nutrients somewhere to feed the incubator—volcanic pools, I guess. But what he did with them . . ."

"Oh, God." Stef knelt on the groundsheet, by the machine. She picked up something from the floor—a heap of white fragments, like a tiny builders' midden, Yuri thought. Bones. Finger bones, perhaps. Stef put them respectfully back where she'd found them.

Yuri looked down at the dead man's stern, placid features, and wondered how sane he had been, in the end, alone in the icy dark with his only food source, this grisly repast.

Liu shrugged. "What would you have done? What would any of us do? The kids couldn't have survived here anyhow."

The ColU said evenly, "That's not all he did here, though. I have inspected the wider area. Dexter Cole did more than just survive. There's something else here. In the ice, I mean. Something he found."

They looked at one another. Then they hurried over to the ColU, which was standing at the lip of the depression in the ice.

It wasn't a natural formation, nothing like a crater. It was a pit. Cole had blown a pit in the ice. And at the bottom, it looked like he had got to work with a pick of some kind. He had exposed a sheet of a gray metal-like substance, and a fine circular seam, a few meters across.

"Dexter Cole evidently became curious," the ColU said. "About this place, the antistellar, a point of obvious significance. Perhaps he retained some equipment from his crashed ship. He may have detected structures beneath the ice, with radar or sonar echoes. And he certainly had explosives."

They all scrambled down into the shallow depression. The ColU rolled forward, playing its lights over them.

"A Hatch," Yuri said. "He only found another fucking Hatch, ColU!"

"Yes. And diametrically opposite the first, at the substellar Hub. Also there is a field of kernels, buried in the rock of this area."

"What is going on with these Hatches?"

Stef knelt and pointed, grinning. "Look. Hand-shaped lock grooves. We can open this."

Liu stared. Then he held up Cole's one-sheet missive, scanning it quickly. "Cole says this was featureless when he found it. He even made a sketch. Look. He took images on his slate, he says. No hand marks."

"Then it changed," Yuri said. "Just as the day side Hatch changed when we first went into it."

"And the one on Mercury, the same," Stef said.

Yuri looked at her. "What are we going to do about it?"

She grinned. "What do you think?"

Liu backed away, hands raised. "Whoa. You're talking about going into that thing? Count me out."

The ColU said, "I think it is my duty to point out that you are entirely unprepared, Yuri Eden."

"That never stopped us before."

"True. But there may not even be breathable air on the other side. Consider Mercury—"

"We're going anyhow." He grinned at Stef, who grinned back. "We're done with Per Ardua, aren't we? Done with Earth. Especially if they import their war here."

The ColU stood still, its floods splashing light over the Hatch in its pit. "You are determined."

"That's right."

"In that case I have a request."

"What's that?"

"Take me with you."

Stef laughed briefly, but fell silent again.

For a moment nobody spoke.

Stef said, "It's serious, isn't it?"

Liu snorted. "This is a glorified tractor. A farming machine."

"Not just that," said the ColU. "I am a sentient, curious entity. I too wish to know what lies beyond this latest Hatch. And I have a store of knowledge, data . . . Imagine how useful a companion I could be, Yuri Eden."

Stef said, "But how the hell are you going to get through the Hatch anyhow? You're not modular, like the modern designs, so you can't be carried through in pieces, or even climb through yourself. You wouldn't fit."

"I would suggest you detach my central processing core. That would suffice. Interfaces can be arranged later. Even a slate would be enough for that."

Stef looked at Yuri. "We're going to do this, aren't we?"

Yuri just grinned. "I owe you one for Mister Sticks, ColU. You'd better show us how to take you apart."

They took a day to prepare, to don layers of clothing, to pack rucksacks, to select weapons.

And to detach the ColU's processor core, under its own instructions, as if it were supervising its own lobotomy, and to load it gingerly into a pack which Yuri wore on his chest. It was like cradling a baby, he thought, like the papooses he and Mardina had made to carry Beth when she was very small.

Then it was time to go. After a day, for both Stef and Yuri, the immediate impulse to *leave* that they'd both felt on finding the Hatch stayed strong.

Still Liu hung back. "Are you sure about this? I've never been through one of these damn things. You could end up anywhere, right?"

"That's the fun part," Stef said.

Yuri looked at Liu. "We're sure. And you're sure you want to stay?"

"Yeah. I'll take my chances with the UN. And besides, staying on this side of that Hatch is the only way I'll keep open some remote chance of getting to Thursday October again. But you two—Stef, if you do this you'll never see your family again. Your twin."

Stef just laughed. "Some loss."

"And you, Yuri. Maybe there's a chance with Beth—"

"I know Mardina. And I know with stone certainty that I'll never see Beth again, come what may."

Liu nodded. "So you may as well keep going, right?"

"Through another door, yeah. And another. What else is there?"

"I'll tell them what became of you."

Yuri grinned. "Well, maybe we'll be back to tell it all ourselves."

"You really think so?"

"No." He turned to Stef. "Are you ready?"

"Always." She pulled off her mittens, exposing hands, stretched her fingers wide. "Let's do this quickly. It's so cold."

"True enough," said Yuri, pulling off his own mittens. "Are you ready? Together then. One, two, three—"

Opened up, the Hatch was just like the one between the Hub and Mercury, a pit under the hatch lid, another door on the wall with indentations for their hands, lit up by a sourceless pearly light.

Yuri and Stef climbed down, using a rope held by Liu. Yuri moved carefully, protective of the ColU.

Opening the door in the wall was easy. They walked through into an intermediate chamber, just like in the Mercury Hatch, with doors on either side. It was so warm in here they immediately started pulling open their winter-weather gear.

They looked at each other. The door back to Per Ardua was still open, but Liu was already out of sight, beyond the outer chamber, on the surface.

"Do it," said Stef.

Yuri shut the door. Then they crossed together to the second door, and laid their hands in the cuttings in its surface.

As the door opened they both stumbled. The gravity had shifted again.

Committed, Yuri thought.

As the hot war loomed, it took three days for King to secure Earthshine's ship.

The *Tatania*, an untested upgrade of the *Ad Astra* but one of the UN's few hulk craft capable of interstellar travel, was diverted to the moon. There Earthshine, or at least a downloaded copy, would be picked up and fired off into deep space as fast as the hulk was capable of driving him. Whether he intended to go as far as the stars was not yet clear.

"Maybe he'll just hang around in orbit around Pluto until the fuss dies down," Sir Michael King said cynically. King himself, having gathered his family around him, intended to weather the storm in the bunker under the Channel. "I'll soon be a hundred bloody years old," he'd said. "I'm done running."

It was a reasonable deal to make, Penny thought. A partial version of Earthshine's own persona was going to stay behind in the great stores he'd established there, so the refuge would continue to function; why not let King and his family stay too?

For herself, Penny remained determined to flee with Earthshine. Sooner that than huddle in a hole in the ground, cowering from the fire of an interplanetary war. And *Earthshine was determined to go*. That was what swung it for Penny, in the end. Penny wondered what he knew about this war that she didn't—what he knew, or feared. Anyhow, staying at his side struck her as a good survival strategy just now.

And she wanted Jiang to come with her. He was as much of a friend to her as anybody. He, however, wasn't at all sure that it was wise to flee on an experimental ship at a time of interplanetary war. Maybe staying buried in the ground was safer. But his own position was difficult, as a Chinese national in UN territory. Penny, with support from King, had already had to fend off official calls for his internment. If he stayed here, he'd probably lose his liberty—assuming they survived at all. In the end the choice for him was logical enough.

So they prepared to leave. The last Penny saw of the Channel bunker was Sir Michael King's crumpled, surprisingly tearful face as he said good-bye at the elevator shaft, with his youngest daughter alongside him.

They flew to Kourou, landing in blasting heat despite the Splinter's Mighty Winter, where they would catch a shuttle to orbit.

They had time to spare. For now this strange, covert, half-declared war seemed to be developing at its own chthonic pace, as the Chinese moved their space-going assets into position to make what everybody assumed was going to be a wave of attacks on UN installations on the moon and near-Earth space, or at least to threaten such attacks. Chinese spacecraft were beautiful but slow; it was an armada that moved only a little faster than the pace at which the planets shifted across the sky. Deeper in space, probably, UN ships were similarly closing in on their own targets. Penny imagined a solar system full of huge energies eager to be unleashed—of command chains compromised by the long minutes of lightspeed delays in communications across interplanetary space.

But slow-paced or not, war seemed to be on the way, and a new long countdown started in the head of everybody on Earth who followed the news.

And they needed the time. It seemed to take an age to arrange the uploading of Earthshine—or a decent partial that was, it seemed, ultimately destined to become the primary copy—into a compact, high-density portable store, a unit small enough to fit into the Earth-to-orbit shuttle. Penny had wondered why Earthshine could not simply be loaded digitally into some store on the hulk ship. Well, this unit was the answer to that; it was a technology she'd not encountered before, a technology no doubt protected by layers of corporate secrecy and government black research—a technology of which Penny Kalinski, a physicist who had advised the top levels of the UN, knew precisely nothing.

At last the orbital shuttle, sitting on its tail at the Kourou field, was loaded up and ready to go. As she boarded, Penny was aware of the significance, that this could be her last footstep on Earth, but mostly she was just grateful to get out of the heat.

They lay on their backs in their rows of couches, Penny beside Jiang. Earthshine was here too, a virtual projection in a seat just ahead of Penny, in the cabin with them as a gesture of shared humanity, he said. But his image flickered continually; his base persona in the tunnel under the English Channel was continuing to download material into the store aboard the shuttle, and would do so, Penny understood, as long as the comms links survived.

Without warning the automated shuttle leaped from the ground. Penny felt acceleration press her hard into her couch. Beyond the windows the sky darkened quickly to a velvet blue-black, and as the shuttle banked Penny glimpsed the Earth, a curved horizon against the black.

It took only minutes to reach orbit, and Penny felt a vast regretful relief to be off the planet at last. So far so good.

But here they stalled. It was going to take half a day for a translunar ferry ship to catch up with them, and even then it would be more chemical rocketry aboard the ferry that would take them to the moon. Despite the urgency of the looming war, all of Earthshine's influence, and all of Sir Michael King's money, even now no kernel technology was allowed closer to Earth than Penny's own old lab on the far side of the moon. Penny Kalinski still couldn't get from Earth to moon any faster than the standard three days.

Stranded in Earth orbit for these long hours, Penny watched the planet unravel below, the daylight side as bright as a Florida sky. From this perspective the Mighty Winter had made little difference: a few more lights glowing in the heart of the old, largely abandoned low-latitude cities, and glaciers reforming in the mountains, splashes of white against the crumpled gray of the rock. What she definitely didn't see was any sign of war. No armies on the move, no cities burning, no missile sparks flying. And that was remarkable, when you reflected that China and the nations it had co-opted into its Greater Economic Framework faced an enemy over just about every border. Even as the two blocs prepared to batter each other in the sky, the surface of the home planet was left untouched.

"For now, anyhow," Penny said when she discussed this with the others.

"You sound cynical," Jiang Youwei said. "There is an agreement. It is a question of honor."

"Honor?" Earthshine replied. "No. It is a question of madness. If war is insane, to fight a kind of partial war *with rules* is even more insane. To smash everything up, if you are going to act at all—that ought to be your intention, or at least your threat. Otherwise there is no disincentive to fight; there is no overriding desire for peace."

Penny grunted. "I follow your logic. But you've rarely sounded less human, Earthshine."

At last their lunar ferry arrived, and they transferred. Like the Earth-to-orbit shuttle, there was no human pilot aboard—no crew at all save a solitary steward with paramedic training, there to dish out prepacked meals, keep the lavatory clean, and deal with any heart attacks in transit. They left orbit, left Earth. But Penny looked back, all the way.

And on the second day of the flight, halfway to the moon, she saw fire at last: sparks flaring all around the equator of the Earth, but offset from the planet. She woke up Jiang, who was dozing. The passengers, and the steward, pressed their faces to the small windows, trying to see.

"Orbital assets being taken out," Jiang guessed. "The Chinese are attacking UN stations in space, and presumably vice versa."

"But there are no missile trails. They aren't being attacked from the ground, by either side."

"No. From orbit only. Nothing to connect the war in the sky to the protected Earth. And—oh, look!"

It was a Chinese junk, its filmy sail casting a pale shadow across the face of the Earth, clearly visible even from a couple of hundred thousand kilometers out.

"So it begins," was Earthshine's only comment.

On the third day the news got worse. The real fighting had started. It had begun on Mars. Nobody seemed sure precisely what had been the final trigger—there were scattered reports of a remote Chinese base, intended for the nuclear mining of aquifer water, being destroyed by one of its own weapons. An act of UN sabotage maybe—well, that seemed to be the working assumption. In response Chinese troops had marched into the UN's Martian enclaves, like Eden, more or less unopposed. Mars was now China's, overall, but UN guerrilla forces out on the rusty plains had already mounted retaliatory strikes against Chinese emplacements. Mars was a big planet on a human scale, and empty; it would be a slow-burning battleground. However, just as Earth as a whole would be preserved, both sides had agreed to leave Mars's greatest monument, Obelisk, untouched. Earthshine shook his head at this fresh gesture of foolish sentimentality.

Then they heard that some of the Chinese junks, having looped around the Earth, were heading for the moon. Another countdown clock started ticking in Penny's head. Could Earthshine's party land on the moon, board the waiting interplanetary hulk craft, get away, all before the Chinese struck?

On the fourth day, as the ferry prepared for its landing on the moon, news came of a fresh development: an attempted UN assault on Ceres, with hulk ships that had been stationed there, under stealth cover, for months. But the situation was complex. It turned out that the ships had already been heavily infiltrated by Chinese agents. When the attack on the asteroid began, some of the UN ships had turned on their fellows, disabling them, in one case destroying. And then the Chinese at Ceres, having taken control of the surviving hulks, evidently following a preplanned design, began using the remaining vessels to build—something.

Penny followed the news as best she could, a fog of partial reports, silences, and probably downright lies, whose opacity only increased her gathering sense of dread.

The landing on the moon was astonishing.

The passengers were told nothing about what was to come, not before the craft entered its approach orbit and came dipping down toward the satellite's crumpled landscape, under a jet-black sky. Through the thick round window beside her seat Penny watched crater-rim mountains reach up like claws.

She grabbed Jiang's hand; she couldn't help it. "We're going hellish low."

He shrugged. "There is no reason why not. No atmosphere on the moon, remember. You can dip an orbit as low as you like—"

The craft passed through another mountain shadow.

"—as long as you don't hit anything in the process."

"*As long as?* Youwei, we're lower than the mountains, and still at interplanetary velocities."

Earthshine grinned. "This is what you get when you hand over control of your life to an AI. I mean to the automated pilot of this craft, not a relatively empathetic, quasi-human individual such as myself. The sky is full of Chinese warships, remember, which are closing in on the moon. The craft has undoubtedly been given the overriding instruction to bring us down as quickly as possible, and that is what it is doing. This is an exercise in orbital geometry, not reassurance."

"So how is it planning to land us?"

"We will soon find out . . ."

The attitude thrusters banged. The craft lurched, down and sideways, throwing the passengers around in their couches. Jiang squeezed Penny's hand harder. She glimpsed the landscape of the moon fleeing past her window, crater rims, a sharp, close-by horizon. Then it was as if something grabbed at the shuttle—silently, smoothly, with no crude mechanical coupling, but the craft was held firm. And the deceleration was sudden, fierce, face forward, so she was thrust into her harness. Still there was barely any noise, only the high-pitched whine of fans, the passengers' ragged breathing. The deceleration, the pressure of the harness on her chest, went on and on.

"The sling," Jiang said now, through a grimace of discomfort.

"The what?"

"A mass driver. A launch rail, wrapped around the curve of this world, like Ceres. We have come skimming down from our transfer orbit to touch it, almost. It has grabbed us with its magnetic field. The sling is slowing us down, the reverse of the way it is generally used to hurl payloads from a standing start off into space."

"A hell of a way to land a crewed spacecraft."

Jiang shrugged. "It is not routinely used, but there have been piloted trials to test the technique. It is only a question of orbital geometry."

"To an AI, maybe."

"The only reason it is not used more often is because it defies human instinct."

"I'll say. If anything went wrong—"

"It would not, it could not—"

"Stop arguing," Earthshine said now. The shuttle was sliding to rest, the deceleration easing. "It doesn't matter anymore. We're down. Now we have to face what comes next." He pointed out of a port.

Penny looked, and saw a hulk, a kernel-drive craft, a tall, fat cylinder standing on squat legs on the lunar surface. The craft stood on a smooth, hardened apron, a rough disc with ragged edges. Fuel pipes trailed up to sockets on the body of the ship, and fat-wheeled supply trucks rolled by. The sun was low, off to the left—she had no idea if it was lunar morning or evening in this place—and the rocket cast a long shadow. It was like some pre-Apollo dream of space flight, a crude rocketship.

The ferry at last slid to a halt. Penny heard mechanical clamps clatter closed, to pin the hull safely in place on the sling rail.

The passengers immediately began to unbuckle. A bus raced across the lunar surface toward them, throwing up rooster tails of dust. Penny stood up, her head swimming in the low lunar gravity. There was no time to think. Earthshine was right. She just had to put the scary trauma of the landing out of her head, and face whatever came next.

Earthshine flickered, looked up at Penny with a wistful smile, then imploded in a shower of evanescent, evaporating pixels. Shut down for the transfer, she guessed.

There was a bang on the hull, and the hatch slid open, to reveal a short tunnel to the bus. An ISF officer, a young woman, stood in the door. "Come. Please." Once they were aboard the bus, the ISF woman urged them to sit down and strap in.

The bus detached quickly and rolled away across the lunar surface, making some speed. The bus was insubstantial, little more than a blister of some transparent substance over a low cart with a couple of rows of seats, and when its wheels hit one of the shallow craters that littered the lunar ground, it floated up off the surface like a toy. Grimly Penny clung to a rail on the back of the seat in front of her. She wondered if this fragile little vehicle was meant for taking tourists around Tranquillity or one of the other museum sites.

But they were making fast progress, heading straight for the base of that kernel-powered rocketship. Penny saw a truck off-loading white cargo boxes in protective pallets for transfer to the ship, the essence of Earthshine being transferred to his interplanetary chariot, perhaps. The whole operation had a scary air of improvisation.

"I don't recognize this place," she said to Jiang. "And I thought I knew the moon. I worked here long enough."

"All of this has been assembled quickly, and largely in secret. Even the kernel ship's landing pad." He grinned at her. "Can you guess how the pad was made?"

She looked again at the disc of ground on which the ship stood. "It looks like a sheet of basalt . . . oh."

"Yes. *The ship made it itself.* I have seen images of it; General McGregor, who is our pilot, had the ship hover over the lunar ground."

McGregor? That name was familiar. "And the downwash of the kernel-physics jets melted the dust."

"That's the idea. We live in a remarkable time, Penny, when such stunts are possible. Adventure-story stuff."

She was less impressed; the whole thing struck her as showing off.

She was distracted by a ripple of light in the sky. A Chinese junk, it had to be. Once in space the hulk ship would be able to outpace any such craft, but it was vulnerable while on the ground; a rock thrown down at interplanetary speeds would split that squat hull like an eggshell. "We might only have minutes," she murmured.

"I know," Jiang said. "Everything is under control."

She thought he deserved a skeptical glance for that.

The bus skidded sideways and fairly threw itself at a docking port in the base of the hull, meeting it with millimeter-scale precision. More scary unhesitating AI navigation.

Beyond the port was a small chamber, brightly lit, with what looked like a door to an elevator shaft beyond. Within, two people were waiting for them, a male ISF officer, and a civilian woman—and to her surprise Penny recognized them both.

The woman, in her late thirties, slim, dark, lost-looking, was Beth Eden Jones: a human native of a different star system, returned to Sol by a trick of alien technology. One of the most famous faces in the solar system, probably, unmistakable with that barbaric tattoo, and staring back at Penny. Beth snapped, "What? I just got here too. What are you staring at?"

Penny flinched. "Sorry. It's just—I know you. I'm Colonel Penelope Kalinski, ISF." She held out a hand, which wasn't taken. "You met my sister on Mercury when—"

"I don't *care*." She turned to the man beside her. "How do I get off this thing?"

Taller, with a spectacular shock of silver-gray hair, in his seventies perhaps, the ISF man looked down at her with a kind of exasperated weariness. "You don't, I'm afraid. None of us do. As ought to have been explained to you. All aboard? Close that hatch." Automated systems responded.

As soon as the chamber was sealed up Earthshine flickered into existence, blinking, solidifying, clarifying in a whir of pixels. He looked down at his hand, flexed it, touched his face. "I have successfully interfaced with the ship's systems, it seems. That was quick."

"We *are* the ISF, sir," said the officer. He bowed, which was the correct protocol with virtual representations, and Earthshine bowed back. "Welcome aboard the good ship *Tatania*. I'm General Lex McGregor, ISF; I'm to be your pilot. We have a small crew whom you'll meet in due course. Now we must get on. If you'll accompany me to the bridge . . ."

The door behind him slid open to reveal an elevator cage, and they crowded in. Soon they were riding up the axis of the craft. Earthshine lost no definition inside the elevator, no protocol-violation flinches, no blurring of pixels. Good interfacing indeed, Penny thought.

McGregor grinned at her, handsome despite his age. "So. Kalinski."

"Lex. Good to see you again."

"I've followed your career with interest all these years. And your sister. Nobody who flies a kernel ship can be unaware of the papers published under the Kalinski names, jointly or otherwise."

"Depends which reality stream you're talking about."

"I'm sorry?"

"Never mind." She said to the others, "The General and I go back a long way, to Mercury. My sister and I were about eleven years old, and my father was preparing to launch his *Angelia* probe to Alpha. And you—"

"And I was on the maiden voyage of the *International-One*. Just a snot-nosed kid at the time."

Earthshine glanced over his spotless uniform. "I doubt you were ever snot-nosed, General McGregor."

Beth Eden Jones glared at them all, furious, frustrated, killing the small talk with her sheer hostility.

The elevator slowed to a halt, and the door slid open. Penny found herself on what was obviously a bridge, with a big command chair surrounded by banks of consoles. There were no windows, and the lights were subdued so the illumination of the control panels was bright. A couple of crew members, young, one male, one female, in ISF uniforms, were already working steadily through a series of checks. There was an air of calm, of order, as if they were in a tremendous clockwork device ticking through programmed motions.

Penny recognized one item of decoration: the bizarre concrete panel that had once adorned the wall of Earthshine's office in Paris, much eroded and incised with circles and grooves, now fixed to the wall of a starship. Penny had no idea what its significance was.

Lex McGregor hurried to his control couch. "We launch momentarily. Please strap yourselves in." He waved at a bank of couches against one wall. "I know it's all rather a rush, we haven't even shown you around the ship—well, we'll have time for that once we're on our way. To give you a sense of the hasty timing, the passenger buses that brought you aboard are still nuzzled up against the ship. Poor little beasts will be atomized when we lift. But given the proximity of those Chinese warships—we must get away safely, that's the only priority. Please, sit down and strap in, do hurry."

They made for the couches, all save Beth Eden Jones, who stood in the middle of the cabin, hands on hips. "This is insane. Stop your count. I'm not going anywhere."

"I'm very much afraid that you are." McGregor, already working through his own countdown checks, glanced over his shoulder. "Mr. Jiang, I wonder if you could help?"

Jiang nodded, walked over to Beth and took her arm. "The ship will launch whether you are seated or not. If you are not strapped in you may come to harm. Please." Gently, firmly, he pulled her toward the couches.

She followed, but she kept protesting. "This is ridiculous. It's all been chaos since I got stuffed into that Hatch with my parents at the Hub on Ardua. I wanted to go back with my father, but my mother put a stop to that." Her voice became harsher, more resentful. "I was stuck in this damn cluttered system with your big ugly overbright sun, your stupid crowded worlds full of ruins and skinny people and useless, distracting tech . . . And now this." Jiang got her to a couch and started coaxing her to sit. "I was with my mother on Mercury, the big ISF plant at Caloris. They took me away in cuffs!"

McGregor, distracted, murmured, "Your mother was rather insistent. She believes it's for the best, you know. She wants to keep you safe, that's all."

"Safe from *what*? What the hell's going to happen to Mercury?"

"I've no real idea. My security clearance isn't *that* high. I imagine your mother was making educated guesses, when she asked me to ensure your safety—"

"What's it got to do with you?"

McGregor grimaced. "Ancient history. She said I owed her a favor. On balance I decided she was right. Are you strapped in?"

"She is," Jiang said, settling in his own couch beside Penny and the Earthshine virtual.

"Then we're all set. On my mark—thirty, twenty-nine . . ."

The craft shuddered, rocking Penny sideways in her couch. "What the hell was that? An earthquake?"

"I doubt it." McGregor touched a panel.

One of the screens filled up with a visual feed. The lunar plain was sharp to the horizon. And in the black sky above there was a ripple of light, reflections of moonlight washing over a roughly spherical panel.

"More junks," Earthshine said.

"Yep. And they've already started hurling down rocks. As if getting their range. They know we're here, that's for sure. Well, they're too late. Seven, six . . . Now they're going to need to concentrate on getting out of *our* way. Full acceleration coming. Two, one—fire!"

The whole ship shuddered. Suddenly a full Earth gravity was sitting on Penny's chest, pressing her back in the couch. On the big screen, the lunar landscape whipped out of sight, leaving only a black sky, a star field that shifted as the ship rolled on its axis. As the ship lifted, the ride smoothed out quickly.

"*Tatania* is under way," said Lex McGregor softly. Penny saw him clench his gloved fist in triumph.

Penny found herself thinking of Beth's mother. Mardina Jones, an ISF officer abandoned by the fleet to become a baby machine on Per Ardua. And now here she was dispatching her only daughter off into deep space. That must have been a hell of a wrench, Penny thought. What did Mardina *know*? What did *she* see coming, that she wanted to save her daughter from so badly?

The craft shuddered, and the acceleration bit deeper, making her gasp. Once again Penny grabbed Jiang's hand, and he squeezed tight.

84

"It's coming," said Monica Trant. "The Nail. We've seen it. Here it is."

Mardina Jones didn't want to believe what she was seeing in the slate Trant was holding, even as Trant, now in her seventies and still working, a deputy director of UEI's kernel facility here at the Caloris base on Mercury, walked her through a diagrammatic reconstruction of orbits and trajectories.

Around them, as they tried to talk, everybody was evacuating the facility. There was panic everywhere in the dome, people running, their feet paddling at the ground in the one-third gravity, hauling personal luggage, boxes, precious slates loaded with a career's work tucked into pouches at their belts. Many of them already had pressure suits on, ready to flee for the transports that were assembling to take them off, to escape from the blow to be struck by this "Nail."

But Mardina didn't want to go anywhere. Mardina was an ISF officer, or she had been before her two decades on Per Ardua, and now she was again, having taken up her duties once more on returning through the Hatch. Most recently she had been assigned to the top-secret technology offices here on Mercury to advise on renovations of hulk ship designs.

She was an ISF officer. She always had been, always would be, despite the ISF's own betrayal. And ISF officers didn't run from their duty.

She dug deep inside for focus, for personal discipline. Her own safety wasn't the issue just now, and hadn't been for a long time. She wanted to stay right here, in the kernel facility's main comms room, until she was assured that Beth was on board that big old hulk taking off from the moon, as Lex McGregor had promised her, and the hulk itself was on its way out of this damn inner-system war zone at last, and safe from the Nail. That was her duty now.

Trant was still talking.

Mardina looked at her. Trant, about her own age, looked just as scared as Mardina—more so, no doubt, since she understood what was going on so much better. "I'm sorry. Tell me again . . ."

The Nail: the ugly weapon that the Chinese had launched at Mercury.

"We knew the Chinese were cooking something up at Ceres. Our intelligence there even gave us a name—hence 'the Nail.' Now it's on the way. Look. These are deep-space images taken over three days ago. *This* is what the Chinese assembled at Ceres, after the abortive UN attempt to attack their base with ISF hulk ships . . ."

The assault had failed because of Chinese subterfuge. Long before the attack their special services had infiltrated the hulk crews. There was a brief firefight, hulk against hulk, a deep-space battle between huge ships capable of ferocious acceleration and carrying powerful missiles, an extraordinary spectacle in itself.

But it had been over in minutes, leaving a handful of survivor ships, all in Chinese hands. Ferries had come out from Ceres to take survivors off the wrecks. And meanwhile tugs had sailed out to drag the operational ships into a quickly improvised dry dock, just a big scaffolding frame in space, where they used the UN craft to build—something else.

"It's fantastically crude," Trant said. "You can see what they did, just lined up the hulks in a bank, side by side, coupled them with these struts here. Parallel burners. But each burner is a fully fledged interplanetary kernel-powered hulk ship."

"And this is the Nail."

"That's right. We don't know if it's crewed or not. Probably it is; there wouldn't have been time to automate the thing fully before it was fired off, just hours after the battle was concluded. A kamikaze mission, right? They evidently planned this, *even before they boarded the ISF ships*, they prepared for it, they had everything ready. Probably work continued on the combined craft even after launch out of Ceres, although that would have been difficult under the one-gravity thrust that prevailed."

"One gravity?"

"Yes. And they've kept that up for more than three days. Look at this trajectory chart . . ." She tapped her slate.

It took Mardina a moment to understand what she was seeing: five concentric circles centered on a yellow disc, a straight line cutting across from the fifth circle out from the center to the innermost.

"This is the solar system," Monica Trant said. "Obviously. The paths of the planets, out to Ceres. Just schematic, but the markings show the planets' current relative positions in their orbit. And this straight line—"

"The trajectory of the Nail." Mardina was old enough to have been brought up on pre-kernel, pre-hulk spacecraft trajectories. Low-energy trajectories followed sections of ellipses, orbits like the planets'; you glided powerless along a curve from one world to the next, with a minor blip of a rocket engine at either end. A hulk ship, though, a craft that could accelerate at a whole gravity for days, weeks on end, crossed interplanetary space in straight lines. "You know, I worked in astronavigation. On a starship, for God's sake. But we never drove a hulk ship across the solar system. We never made tracks like this." Mardina counted the orbits. "And this is the Nail's trajectory. From Ceres straight to Mercury."

"Damn right."

Mardina tried to remember her astronomical distances; Ceres was over two astronomical units out from the sun, more than twice as far as Earth, whereas Mercury was less than half an AU out. You had the relative positions in their orbits to take account of too. But after three days at constant one-G acceleration—

She looked at Trant, horrified. "It must be nearly here."

"Only hours away. It's been on a straight-line track for Mercury, indeed for this location on Mercury, *this facility*, since it was launched. The projections show it clearly. And it hasn't deviated once.

"I think they've decided to take out the Caloris facility—the kernel-processing facilities, maybe even the Hatch. It's kind of dog-in-the-manger; if we won't share the kernel tech then nobody gets to use it. But there are precedents. In the past, states, or even organizations like the UN, have mandated strikes against rogue states to take out nuke facilities, for instance, before they had a chance to be used . . ."

Even faced with this blunt revelation, Mardina found it hard to take in. She'd heard hints of a threat to Mercury, the kernel plants, something coming this way. That had been enough for her to ship Beth as far out of the inner system as she could. But she'd imagined some kind of invasion, an attempt to take the Caloris base. She'd never imagined anything like this attempt at willful destruction. "They've been in flight three days. They must have been seen by UN surveillance systems. Why has there been no warning to the staff?"

Trant pulled a face, weary, cynical. "This is a UEI facility. The UEI has a habit of secrecy. Anyhow, we thought it was a bluff. We thought they'd pull away, veer off after giving us a scare, having shown us what they can do. I guess they might still."

"But you've decided not to bank on it. And that isn't some damn V-2." Again she tried to figure the numbers in her head. "After three days at a full G, they must be traveling at—"

"About one percent the speed of light. And those hulk ships are pretty massive. That's a lot of kinetic energy."

"It's a relativistic missile, is what it is. And they've unleashed it in the middle of the inner solar system? How could they even think of this?"

Monica Trant took her shoulders and stared in her face. "Mardina, the whole future of mankind pivots on this moment, these few hours and days. *That's* how they can think of this. If they lose this game, they've lost forever, because we'd have a monopoly on the kernels. Maybe we'd do the same, if the position was reversed. Probably would. You feel outrage? I feel outrage. Keep it for later. Meanwhile we have to get to one of the transports; they're not going to wait."

Something in Mardina broke at last. They started to run for the exit from the dome.

"I'm sorry," she called to Trant. "I kept you behind."

"Don't sweat it. You were concerned for your girl. I'm a mother too. My son's on Earth, in one of the new northern cities."

"The Earth's supposed to be protected—"

"That's the theory."

"Do you think he'll be safe?"

Monica Trant shrugged as she ran, stiffly. "Rob's a cop. They get weapons, the first pick of the available food, shelter. If he's not safe down there nobody is."

They reached a port in the dome wall, a surface tunnel leading to a transport craft out of there. But there was a crowd already there, a queue in the tunnel. Trant flashed a rank card to force their way through the line, but soon the people were jammed in so tight there was no way to get forward except to shuffle along with the herd.

People: they were all around Mardina, ISF crew and UEI personnel, scientists and administrators, mechanics and cooks and cleaners, the whole community that had sustained itself under this dome, all draining toward a handful of airlocks like this one, trying to escape. Children too, lanky low-gravity children born in a dome under the solar fire during their parents' long-duration stays here on Mercury. Mardina had spent only a short time here since returning from Earth, but she was surprised how many she recognized. *People:* each one a fully rounded consciousness, each with a past, memories, hopes for the future, each with a mesh of family and friends and enemies, loves and loyalties, rivalries and hatreds. All jammed up arbitrarily in this tube like overflow baggage, with a relativistic missile coming down on their heads.

Trant murmured, "We're using every which way to get out of here. If we make it out at all, we'll be loaded onto a surface-to-surface bug. Even that has enough push to get us off the planet at least, for pickup later. Any way to get people off the surface and scattered, we're using. We're even piling people into cargo pods and using the mass driver."

Mardina, even as they worked their way through the crush, was still trying to figure out the implications of this assault. "The Nail is coming right down on top of the facility, right? Which itself sits on top of the densest concentration of kernels, and the Hatch structure itself."

"That's right."

"So what's the Nail going to do to the planet?"

Trant shrugged. "We don't have good models. Partly because nobody took it seriously, despite the Chinese sending us endless warnings to evacuate. And since people *have* started taking it seriously, we've all been too busy running. At least a major impact; one of our experts thinks it will be like another Caloris. Which was a punch that created a crater that spanned one whole hemisphere, with a rebound at the antipode where waves in the surface rock converged. Which is why we want to get everybody off the planet altogether, if we can, even if it's going to be a heck of a retrieval operation later."

"But what about the kernels? I mean, energies like that—"

There was no time for Trant to reply. With a last shove, Mardina found herself at the head of a suddenly clearing queue. Two ISF officers, one male, one female, both uniformed, both armed, stood here, blocking the lock to the ship beyond. One grabbed Mardina's arm and pulled her inside the ship, muttering a count, and then the other officer swung down his arm like a barrier. "That's it, full to capacity." He pressed a button. The officers held their place, arms linked, before the closing door. "No more room. Try another exit, or wait here for another craft . . ."

The excluded people seemed shocked, too bewildered to react to this abandonment. Among them was a child who screamed, yelled for his mother with arms outstretched, but he was held back by a young man, maybe his father.

And Mardina had left behind Monica Trant, on the wrong side of the ISF officers.

Mardina tried to get back to her. "Oh, hell, Monica, this is my fault, I slowed you down—"

"It doesn't matter. I'll be fine. Stay safe." The lock door was already swinging closed, and Trant had to duck to maintain eye contact with Mardina. "And listen, if you get the chance, tell my son Rob that—"

The hatch clicked closed. The ISF officers, sweating, breathing hard, glanced at each other and backed away.

"Hell of a thing," said the woman to the man.

"Too damn right." The man turned and raised his voice to address the passengers. "Please find a couch. If you can't find a couch, wedge yourself in somewhere, we are over capacity. We lift immediately." He and his colleague made for the rear of the cabin, near the hatch to the corridor, and folded couches out of the wall.

Mardina, bereft, bewildered by the sudden transition from the crowded space to the interior of this craft, pushed her way in. She had ridden these bugs many times. They were just hoppers that took you from dome to dome, squirting their way over Mercury's surface on feeble chemical-propellant rockets. You rode them at shift changes, at dome-morning or dome-night, when going to see a colleague, or traveling from a dormitory block to a workplace. Now the interior of the bus, with its curving walls and soothing beige color scheme, had never seemed so small, so crowded was it with people, all scrambling to get to the few remaining couches. You weren't meant to be fleeing for your life in a vessel like this.

Mardina found a place by the wall, next to a couch where a young woman cradled her baby, and sat on the carpeted floor with her feet jammed against a strut.

She had barely settled when the bug lifted with a lurch, much more roughly than she remembered from any early morning commute. People gasped or called out; a few who weren't safely strapped into couches stumbled and fell to the floor. A baby started crying. And the lift went on and on, not like a commute hop, this was a single mighty leap which would, when the fuel was exhausted, fling them away from Mercury altogether—where they would drift in space until picked up, if they ever were.

Mardina wondered how long was left until the impact of the Nail.

And she thought about the kernels.

She knew that kernels were like tiny wormholes, leaking energy, that could be manipulated open and closed with lasers and magnetic fields. Had anybody done any modeling of what might become of the kernels, and the energy they channeled, when the Nail was driven into the Mercury ground? Presumably the Chinese couldn't have; they were supposed to have no access to kernel physics anyhow. Maybe they thought this was just a surgical strike. Closing the lid of the UN's treasure trove: nothing more destructive than that. But if not . . .

Mardina still had her slate, in its pouch at her waist. As the clumsy craft's acceleration juddered on, as the passengers gradually quietened down, she dug out the slate, and looked up at the woman with the baby. "Excuse me. Can I use your comms link? The one on your couch . . ."

The woman shrugged, holding her baby's head against her chest.

Mardina pulled down a small earpiece on a fiber-optic cable from the couch. She swiped it with her slate to give it her ID. The earpiece lit up, and she tucked it behind her ear. "I want to speak to my daughter.

Beth Eden Jones." She swiped another ID, to identify Beth. "I know she's on a hulk ship heading toward the outer system. I'll record a message. I want you to keep trying to make the call until you get a response, right?"

"Confirmed," replied a soft synthetic voice.

So the solar system's shared comms systems were still working, at least. She looked around, self-conscious. Nobody was paying any attention to her, but she ducked her head even so. "Hi, sweetheart, it's your mother. You won't believe where I am . . ."

There was a streak of brilliant light, beyond the cabin walls, quite soundless, like a meteor falling. People turned, distracted.

Still the bug ascended from Mercury, as smoothly as before.

"If I get a chance I'll tell you all about it. But the main thing is, I'm sorry I had to throw you at General Lex, even if he does owe me a favor. Wherever you end up I'll come looking for you. Don't forget that I'll always—"

Monitors in space and elsewhere observed the event, reconstructed its consequences later, and reported their conclusions to survivors. Or attempted to.

The Nail hit the surface of Mercury, dead on target at the kernel-physics facility at Caloris, at one percent of the speed of light.

It delivered the kinetic energy of an asteroid three hundred meters across moving at interplanetary speeds. An energy load equivalent to all of Earth's nuclear arsenals at the most dangerous moment of the twentieth-century Cold War. An energy load equivalent to a month of the planet's entire output, in the most profligate days of the twenty-first century. All of this energy was injected into the upper crust of Mercury, and the kernel beds beneath, in less than a millisecond.

The kernel facility, with a wide swathe of the crust, was utterly destroyed, rock vaporized to gas. The molten walls of a tremendous new crater rolled across this world's battered surface.

But the Nail's fall was only the trigger. In response to the tremendous shock, in layers deep beneath the surface, kernels yawned open, like the mouths of baby birds. And a pulse of energy of an intensity never before seen in the solar system was unleashed, carried by a flood of short-wavelength photons, X-rays and gamma rays that fled the site at the speed of light, and then by a wavefront of massive particles, moving somewhat more slowly, but highly energetic themselves.

After a fiftieth of a second the radiation pulse had passed through the body of Mercury. Across the face of the planet the rocky crust was liquified, the human installations on the Mercury ground gone in a moment. Even the iron core roiled.

After another fiftieth of a second the photon wave overwhelmed the fleeing surface-hopper bug, and the rest of the armada of fragile refugee ships, rising from the surface. To Mardina it was as if a light went off inside her head, inside her very skull.

After eight minutes the photon Shockwave reached Earth.

Officer Rob Trant was on duty, cruising the east side of New Prudhoe, Alaska.

He was well aware of the date, and the time. This was when the Nail was due to strike Mercury, as his mother Monica had warned him. But despite having this inside channel he didn't know much more about the international crisis than any other cop in the country.

They'd been briefed about fears of a backlash on Earth, whatever happened up in space: a rising by ethnic Chinese types in the cities, maybe, or some kind of revenge attacks taking place on them in turn. Whatever. Rob had seen nothing untoward so far, in the ruined suburbs he patrolled. But he knew the news of even the most dramatic events on Mercury would take long minutes to crawl out here at lightspeed.

Personally he didn't think anything would come of it. The whole Chinese winter thing had been a kind of bluff, after all.

He knew his mother was in the center of it—on Mercury he could never have persuaded her to come away. She had opened up to him more in recent days than for a long time, in fact more than since the moment he'd finally rebelled at his life under a dome on Mercury, and had cashed in his partially completed ISF training to become a cop on Earth. It was hard to have a decent conversation with the long minutes of light delay between the worlds. She'd promised him some kind of message today, a long missive. But the message hadn't come, not yet.

He missed his mother. He admitted it, in lonely moments. He was forty-two years old, had come to Earth in his twenties, had always been too much of an *alien* to make close friends, to fall in love. He missed his mother's company, but he didn't feel concerned for her right now. He concentrated on his job.

New Prudhoe was a sprawling conurbation less than seventy years old, the historic plaques and markers you saw everywhere told you that, a product of the great northern migrations of the last century. It felt like it was a lot older to Trant, especially in the neighborhoods he worked, which had once been prosperous middle-class suburbs, thriving on the post-Jolt prosperity of this Arctic ocean coast. But now the Chinese winter had come and it went on and on, and the stores were closing, and people were losing their jobs and heading south for the duration, leaving behind only various deadbeats who couldn't move or wouldn't, and those who preyed on them, and cops. And then some other types had started coming back, with their own novel vices: most recently, hothead kids who had got addicted to *Asgard* and other live-action games, but had got bored with the simulation, bored with dying every day, and now wanted the thrill of the real thing. Well, today Rob felt relatively safe, in his armored cruiser with its powerful weaponry and super-smart, ever-alert AI. Besides, it wasn't long since the National Guard's last clear-out, after a set-to confrontation when whole districts had burned.

The Nail arrival time must have come and gone. He checked his watch, trying to remember how long the time lag was between Earth and Mercury just now.

That was why he was thinking about his mother, when it came.

The car had just turned down a long avenue, once the centerpiece of the new city in the post-Jolt recovery days, now with only a handful of cars, all automated, cruising its length. So, as it happened, he was looking south when the photon Shockwave washed over Earth. Rob saw it as a wave of blinding light coming up from below the horizon, but soon filling the car, and his head.

And suddenly his eyes felt like they were burning out of his head, and his vision went from dazzling white to utter black. He threw his arm over his face, crying out. He fumbled for the slate mounted on the dash, to call this in, this nuclear attack, whatever. He had to call it in. His eyes were pits of agony. He felt *warm* inside, like he'd been stuffed inside a microwave cooker . . .

On the long, mostly empty highway, the cars cruised on quietly, calmly, in their straight lines, their onboard AIs taking over the controls from drivers who threshed and screamed, tearing at sightless eyes. Until the radiation began to fry their electronics, and they slewed aside.

This was only the beginning. The particle storm, traveling slower than light, would not arrive for another two hours.

87

Earthshine's bunker remained calm, the staff working at their monitors and slates, recording, analyzing, as the bad news from the sky filled the screens. Sir Michael King, walking stiffly with the aid of his stick, went around the staff individually, to reassure them that they were free to take a break, to try to contact family on the surface if they needed to. Most of them stayed where they were, as if by keeping on working, sticking to the routine, they were somehow holding the greater horror at bay.

Now the screens showed a darkening, a thickening smog, cutting off the unbearable brilliance of the sky.

King stormed into Earthshine's central sanctum. "So what now? We had the flash—what next?"

"Massive particles," said Earthshine—or at least the semi-transparent partial copy the primary had left behind when he fled on the *Tatania*. "The ozone layer is already gone. Ultraviolet and gamma rays are battering the surface of the Earth. As for life, basic cellular functions are being compromised." The virtual looked thoughtful. "People are being *cooked*. Animals too. And now the cosmic ray storm. The last surviving satellites, shielded by Earth's shadow from the flash, told us that much. The high-energy particles will be knocking atmospheric molecules apart, oxygen, nitrogen, to produce nitrogen dioxide. Some of which will combine with rain to produce nitric acid, acid rain, while the rest lingers in the air to block out the sunlight which—"

"It's an extinction event," King breathed.

"Indeed. As if a gamma-ray burster had gone off in the heart of the solar system."

"And the people?"

"The flash will have the most immediate effect. The radiation will kick in soon; cancers will take most of the survivors of the short-term cull."

"Cull? What the hell kind of a word is that? And you, you bastards? You Core AIs?"

"Oh, we will survive in our deep shelters. I, certainly, in my central bunker, with this store as a primary backup, and the partial I sent off-world with Penny Kalinski as a secondary."

"And then what?"

Earthshine shrugged. "A new domain of life will eventually populate the Earth. Perhaps we will have some influence on the future. Not myself, of course. I have fled . . ."

"I feel like hurting you."

"It's not my fault. We tried to broker peace through the Council of Worlds. Yet I understand how you feel."

"Then whose fault is it? Ours, the Chinese?"

"Maybe neither. Some reports have emerged about the beginnings of this, at Mars, at Ceres. Although I doubt if any historians will survive to piece together a full account. I am uploading what I can to my partial twins in the deep store and on the *Tatania* . . ."

"Some bastard pulled the trigger, right? That's what it boils down to. Without waiting the few minutes it would have taken to get confirmation from Earth. Christ. That was always the fear in the first Cold War, you know. That a commander of some nuclear sub, out of touch with his government, would take matters into his own hands."

"But even now the events that followed are uncertain. There have been fragmentary reports of mutinies on the Nail itself, by captive UN crew, and counter-mutinies by the Chinese, even as it fell toward Mercury. There may have been no control, in the end; as it came plummeting in for the strike, the Nail was a war zone itself. There was nobody in a position to deflect it, even if the order had come to do so. How appropriate, that the end should come this way. A war nobody wanted, and thought would be kept at bay by sentimentality. A war triggered, not by any single command, but by foolishness, arrogance, and poor communication."

He spoke blandly, not judgmentally. King thought; lacking processing power, lacking definition, he was smooth-faced, static, unconvincing.

Suddenly King realized he was alone in here. Quite alone. Talking to nobody. He headed for the door. "Christ, I need a drink."

By the time the Nail struck Mercury, the *Tatania* had already been traveling for three days. She had headed straight out from the Earth-moon system, away from the sun, and was more than three times as far from the sun as the Earth, when Beth picked up a fragmentary message from her mother.

"I'm sorry I had to throw you at General Lex, even if he does owe me a favor. Wherever you end up I'll come looking for you. Don't forget that I'll always—"

And then, immediately after, the flash, dazzling bright, from the heart of the solar system. The bridge was flooded with light.

Beth saw them react. Lex McGregor, in his captain's chair, straightening his already erect back. Penny Kalinski grabbing Jiang's hands in both her own. Earthshine, the creepy virtual persona, seeming to freeze. They all seemed to know what had happened, the significance of the flash.

All save Beth.

"What?" Beth snapped. "What is it? What happened?"

Earthshine turned his weird artificial face to her. In the years she'd spent in the solar system Beth had never got used to sharing her world with fake people. "They have unleashed the wolf of war. We, humanity, we had it bound up with treaties, with words. No more. And now, *this*."

"*They* being . . ."

"The Hatch builders. Who else?"

"And you, you aren't human. You say *we*. You have no right to say that."

The virtual looked at her mournfully. "I was human once. My name was Robert Braemann."

And she stared at him, shocked to the core by the name.

Lex McGregor turned to face Penny. "So this is the kernels going up. Right, Kalinski?"

"I think so."

"What must we do? We were far enough from the flash for it to have done us no immediate harm, I think. God bless inverse-square spreading. What comes next?"

Penny seemed to think it over. "There'll probably be a particle storm. Like high-energy cosmic rays. Concentrated little packets of energy, but moving slower than light. They'll be here in a few hours. Hard to estimate."

"OK. Maybe I should cut the drive for a while, turn the ship around so we have the interstellar-medium shields between us and Mercury?"

"Might be a good idea."

Beth didn't understand any of this. "And what of Earth? What's become of Earth?"

Penny looked back at her. "Life will recover, ultimately. But for now . . ."

Beth imagined a burned land, a black, lifeless ocean.

McGregor began the procedure to shut down the main drive and turn the ship around. His voice was calm and competent as he worked through his checklists with his crew.

2217

On the day side of Per Ardua, the stars were invisible, save for Proxima itself, and the glorious twin primary suns of Alpha Centauri. But those who had followed Yuri and Liu and Stef in the exploration of the dark side, in the years following their pioneering trek, had rediscovered the night sky. A whole new generation had to be taught the constellations.

A distance of four light years wasn't much on the scale of the volume of space that contained the thousands of stars visible to the human eye; the sky of Per Ardua's endless night was pretty much like that seen from Earth, and save for the brilliance of the nearby Alpha stars the constellations were mostly very similar. Just as on Earth, Cassiopeia was a particular favorite, its W-shape easy to pick out. But as seen from Per Ardua, there was the addition of one dim star to that constellation. That pendant to the W was Sol, the nearest star to Proxima save for the Alphas, a grain of light that had been the site of all human history before the first missions to Proxima. Parents pointed this out to their children.

A little more than four years after the war, Sol flared so brightly that it was, briefly, visible even from the day side of Per Ardua.

Stef looked at Yuri. "A gravity shift. Just like the Hatches on Mercury and Per Ardua. So we're already there. Wherever *there* is. And in the outside universe more time has passed. Years, maybe, or—"

"Or centuries." Yuri grinned. "Shall we?"

There was no ladder in the final chamber, but the closed lid above bore a hand-imprint key. Yuri boosted Stef up on his shoulders so she could work the key. As she fumbled, he grunted. "Get on with it, woman."

"Look at us. Two old idiots, exploring interstellar space."

"But we're here."

"That we are."

At last the lid swung back. There was a faint pop of equalizing pressure. They found themselves looking up at a blue, apparently harmless sky—and the air that rushed in, full of odd smells, was maybe a bit thin and cold, but healthy, oxygen-rich air, undoubtedly. Yuri deliberately kept breathing. They had no stored oxygen; there was no point holding their breath. But he felt no ill effects.

Stef clambered out of the pit, then reached down to help Yuri scramble up. Once again they had some trouble. It was a comedy, Yuri thought, two old stiffs climbing out of a hole in the ground. At last he was out, and they looked at each other, laughed.

Then they stood together and faced a new world.

They were on high ground here, which sloped away to a plain streaked with purple and white, on which stood a scatter of slim orange cones, vegetation perhaps. To the right the ground rose up to a rocky massif—no, it was too regular to be natural, Yuri realized slowly. It was some kind of tremendous *building*, a sloping face with deep grooved inlets. On the horizon he saw more mountains, mist shrouded, that again looked suspiciously regular, like tremendous pyramids.

A sun dominated the sky, huge, hanging low, its face pocked with dark spots.

"Wow," said Stef simply.

Yuri dug out his elderly ISF-issue slate, which had a wireless link to the ColU's processor box, in his chest pack. "Can you see all this, old buddy?"

A single green light sparked on the slate.

"So, any idea where we are?"

"None at all," Stef said. She pointed at the main sun. "*That* looks like another Proxima, another M dwarf. But the Galaxy is full of M dwarfs. We could be anywhere . . ."

A huge shadow swept over the ground to their left. Yuri looked up.

"I guess we should start walking," Stef said, still staring ahead. She hadn't noticed the shadow, evidently. "If we manage to see any stars we might reconstruct a constellation pattern, figure out where we are. I have the 3D positions of the nearby stars loaded on my slate."

"Or," Yuri said, "we could just ask." He pointed upward.

At last she turned to see.

Over their heads, a craft was descending, coming in to land.

It was like a tremendous airship. It moved smoothly, silently. It bore a symbol on its outer envelope, crossed axes with a Christian cross in the background, and lettering above:

S P Q R

Anchors of some kind were dropped from a fancy-looking gondola. When the craft had drifted to a halt a rope ladder unrolled to the ground. And as they watched, astonished, a hatch opened, and a man clambered down the ladder.

As soon as he reached the ground the man started toward them. He wore a plumed helmet, and a scarlet cloak over what looked like a bearskin tunic. His lower legs were bare, above strapped-up boots. He had a sword on one hip, and a gaudy-looking handgun in a holster on the other.

Yuri called, "Who the hell are you?"

The man, striding steadily, started shouting back: *"Fortasse accipio oratio stridens vestri. Sum Quintus Fabius, centurio navis stellae 'Malleus Jesu.' Quid estis, quid agitis in hac provincia? Et quid est mixti lingua vestri? Germanicus est? Non dubito quin vos ex Germaniae Exteriorae. Cognovi de genus vestri prius. Bene? Quam respondebitis mihi?"*

Always another door, Yuri thought. "Let me handle this." He spread his hands and walked forward, toward the angry stranger.

In the hearts of a hundred billion worlds—

Across a trillion dying realities in a lethal multiverse—

In the chthonic silence—

There was satisfaction. The network of mind continued to push out in space, from the older stars, the burned-out worlds, to the young, out across the Galaxy. Pushed deep in time too, twisting the fate of countless trillions of lives.

But time was short, and ever shorter.

In the Dream of the End Time, there was a note of urgency.

AFTERWORD

This novel is about life on an "exoplanet," a planet beyond the solar system. The first such planet orbiting a normal star (as opposed to a pulsar) was discovered as recently as 1995. At time of writing we have discovered thousands of such worlds (for a recent survey see Ray Jay-awardhana, *Strange New Worlds*, Princeton, 2011). The first discovery of a planet in the Alpha Centauri star system was announced in October 2012 (see "An Earth Mass Planet Orbiting Alpha Centauri B" by Xavier Dumusque et al., *Nature*, 17 October 2012).

Could Per Ardua exist? At the time of writing no planet of Proxima has been detected, but a careful inspection of the star's apparent movements has put upper limits on the sizes of any possible planets (for a technical paper see Zechmeister, M., Kurster, M., Endl, M., "The M Dwarf Planet Search Program at the ESO VLT+UVES: A Search for Terrestrial Planets in the Habitable Zone of M Dwarfs," *Astron. Astrophys.*, vol. 505, pp. 859–71, 2009). The planetary system I have invented for this novel fits these limits. Proxima is a red dwarf—an "M dwarf." We used to think that only sunlike stars could host Earthlike worlds. Now we suspect that M dwarfs like Proxima could after all host habitable worlds (see "A Reappraisal of the Habitability of Planets Around M Dwarf Stars," J. Tarter et al., *Astrobiology*, vol. 7, no. 1, pp. 30–65, 2007).

The idea of starships driven by very lightweight "smart sails" pushed by microwave beams was suggested by Robert Forward ("Starwisp: An Ultralight Interstellar Probe," *Journal of Spacecraft and Rockets*, vol. 22, pp. 345–50, 1985) and revisited by Geoffrey A. Landis ("Microwave Pushed Interstellar Sail: Starwisp Revisited," paper AIAA-2000-3337, presented at the AIAA 36th Joint Propulsion Conference and Exhibit, Huntsville, AL, July 17–19, 2000). I have extrapolated wildly beyond these respectable works.

The classic work *Interstellar Migration and the Human Experience*, ed. Ben Finney and Eric Jones (Berkeley, 1985), contains much speculation on the anthropology and ethics of the colonization of space.

I'm deeply grateful to Professor Adam Roberts for a brief injection of Latin.

Any errors or inaccuracies are, of course, my sole responsibility.

Stephen Baxter
Northumberland
December 2012